"God save me! The devil is come!"

Wulfstan's voice cracked as he leaped from
his seat in the dining hall and pointed at
the insubstantial, glimmering shape of
Nilssen. His fellow ruffian, Leofric, clamped a
hand on his wrist and dragged him back
without saying a word.

Nilssen relished their terror. To these yokels
of the Dark Ages the misty shimmer given
him by the time-travel mechanism would be
horrifying enough.

But what made it unbearable for them—and
grimly satisfying for him—was the fact that
they knew with perfect certainty that they
had murdered him. . . .

Other Exciting Science Fiction from Dell:

THE
WALL OF YEARS

Andrew M. Stephenson

A DELL BOOK

Published by
Dell Publishing Co., Inc.
1 Dag Hammarskjold Plaza
New York, New York 10017

This work was first published in
Great Britain by Futura Publications Ltd.
in a slightly different form.

Dell ® TM 681510, Dell Publishing Co., Inc.

ISBN: 0-440-19431-8

Printed in the United States of America
First U.S.A. printing—December 1980

the second
is for Rob Holdstock
a fellow Chronicler of
the Anglo-Saxons
and other fabulous peoples

Acknowledgments

This book draws upon the accumulated efforts
of many scholars, whose contributions have
submerged themselves in the pool of knowledge
of the Anglo-Saxons under King Alfred the Great
and their antagonists, the so-called Danes under
King Guthrum. However, I feel obliged to give
special credit to A.H. Burne's *More Battlefields
of England* for the broad plan of events
immediately preceding and following the
Battle of Edington. Thanks are also due to the
unknown lady of the Devizes Public Library
who went to such pains in assisting the bearded
fellow in the blue quilted jacket that sunny
Friday in May of 1977.

ANDREW STEPHENSON
February 5, 1978

The past is a foreign country:
they do things differently there.

L. P. HARTLEY:
The Go-Between

PROLOGUE: *se weardgast of þæm hylle*

Again they were calling him out for a song. Reluctantly, for he was still very hungry, the bard put aside his scraps of salted pork and hard cheese, took a last mouthful of ale from his mug to sweeten his voice, lifted his harp from where it rested against the side of his stool and stood up. The packed hall cheered when he stumbled out of the shadows and halted in the flickering yellow light of the central fire. When there was silence and he could be heard, the bard bowed to the chieftain at the high table.

"What is your pleasure, High-Reeve Henglaf?"

Henglaf grinned a mouth full of yellowed teeth and half-chewed food. He gulped the food and paused to wash it down with a liberal draught from his silver-chased drinking horn. Then he chuckled.

"Nothing *you* could provide, minstrel."

All around his men burst into hoots of laughter. Half of them were reeling drunk and ready to laugh at anything. Henglaf waved them to silence and continued:

"But for the nonce I'll make do with a ballad."

"Any song, my lord?" The bard was a traveler, fresh in that same afternoon from the long and frosty road out of the settlements in the Vale of the White Horse miles to the southwest; though unfamiliar with local tastes he had heard stories of these wild hunter-farmers of the Thames Valley and was unwilling to risk boring them.

"*Any* damned song!" snapped Henglaf, taking another swig from his drinking horn. He belched. "And make it a lively one. None of your Wessex lullabies for my lads."

The bard considered his repertoire as he pushed his cloak back out of the way. Would they have heard the full account of King Alfred's humiliation at the hands of King Guthrum, whose Danes now lorded it over Saxon freemen, treating them no better than Britons if the rumors were true? It was scarce two years gone, a short enough time; if it did also chance to eulogize a man of old Wessex, what of it?—That man was dead; and all the world loves a dead hero. Besides, he could easily elaborate it to emphasize the rôles played by men from hereabouts. Yes, he would recite that one. He struck a chord from his harp: sharp and ringing, it cut through the surging murmur in the hall.

"*Hear me now!*" he said into sudden silence. Only the crackle of the fire at his back and the moan of the icy wind outside answered him. "You have heard it told how our fathers won this land from savage men—" Abruptly he was interrupted: a man at the high table shrieked and leaped to his feet, pointing, at him as it seemed.

Dumbfounded, the bard awaited the worst. But no one moved; and after some seconds he perceived that others were staring too, not at him but past him, toward the main doors that were shut upon the night. Slowly he turned to discover what had affected them so.

Between himself and the wide, solid, oaken doors was the fire, leaping, crackling, hissing in its trench. Its light spread out to embrace the entire hall. Beyond it, where the rushes were muddied by the boots of those who had entered from the dank night and its fretful weather, was an area of relative shadow, so that the paler timbers of the doors stood proud and clear. Against this background was the dim figure of a man through whose insubstantial form was easily discernible every detail of the hard wood through which he had just walked.

The bard retreated from the apparition, stiff-legged with terror, until the rough edge of the high table in the small of his back stopped him. The breathing of those behind him sounded loud, hoarse, ragged with fear. When at last it became painful to endure the waiting, the bard cried out:

"Who are you? What do you want with us?"

The ghostly figure turned, laboriously slowly, until it faced him. Its skin was black; it had no mouth; and its eyes were lidless orbs. There were tales from the heathen days, the bard recalled, that mentioned creatures which, man-like, walked but were not men: they were hollow, the servants of trolls and giants, shells of seeming. But such things had been banished by the coming of the True God, he knew. They could not exist, not amongst virtuous men. Even so—

Without a mouth to speak with, it spoke. A bass booming came from its black, lifeless face, but so faintly it might have been the creaking of a storm-wracked tree in the woods, a faraway sound like a voice of the grave.

"My property," it said. The words rolled out as if they would never be completed. "I want it back. Return it to me. Now."

CHAPTER ONE

Jerlan Nilssen's Sagu

Martial music echoed up the long, concave slope, from tower to tower of the City, until it reached the open window of Jerlan Nilssen's office, high up near the eastern rim of the Bowl. There a small part of it was intercepted by the slanting glass and deflected inwards, while the remainder lost itself against the overlying Dome. Down on the grassy arena of the sports stadium the Police Academy band was running through the last rehearsal before the morrow's passing-out ceremonies. Then it would be bright and cheerful; for the moment, however, the evening was tranquil and the music likewise. The rhythmic mutter of the brass and drums made a relaxing background to the thoughts the Commissar of Reestablishment presently wrestled with. Nilssen was aware that in his visitor's armchair Psychologist Yaer still sat awaiting some sort of an answer, yet he felt disinclined to break the spell of the moment simply to satisfy the man's professional impatience; so he listened to the music and made no attempt to grapple with the problem in hand.

Minutes slipped by. The band worked through "Light of Foot" and "Father Rhine"; they followed up with "Clan McRae" and paused. Regretfully Nilssen swung himself around in the window seat to attend to Yaer.

The psychologist sat as he had been: one leg crossed carefully over the other so as not to crease his trousers unnecessarily, his face calmly attentive, his noteblock ready.

He said quietly, "Any suggestions?"

"Yes," said Nilssen. "That fellow Crewkerne who joined us recently. I realize it's a bit of an imposition to ask the man to go through it all again so soon, but he will be graduating tomorrow and does know the target area."

"No good," Yaer said. He read from his noteblock, into which he had just entered the name, *"Crewkerne, Gwillem Yorg. Age, 32 subjective. Ortho-Caucasian BT-67 . . . Is estimated to be highly self-sufficient and adaptable, but until allowed an adequate period for normalization cannot be entrusted with field duties. Estimated time on home duty: until end of 2606."* Yaer glanced up at Nilssen. "Furthermore—and you won't find this in any written report, Jerlan—Crewkerne's case is a lot like an iceberg. He could wreck Yardstick. I nearly recommended him for a personality edition to save what's left after his traumatic experiences. I gather the project is urgent?"

"Without it we can't go a step further. We simply have to calibrate the new belts. Or so Rhys tells me. No, you're right, we can't wait even six months. Had you anyone in mind?"

"Well-l-l . . . ." said Yaer. "You'll laugh. But what we need is a lonely man."

Nilssen did not laugh; he stared. "You mean, needing a woman?"

"Shazol, *no!*" Yaer guffawed with uncharacteristic enthusiasm that Nilssen felt verged on crudity. "I said a *lonely* man, the proper meaning, not a . . . Never mind; no, he's got to be a natural loner, used to isolation although conscious of it at all times. And able to bear it. When he's out there, he's going to be more desperately alone than anyone has ever been because he won't even have the comfort of knowing he can walk back if all else fails. Between him and home will be a wall eighteen centuries high—and without the key to the only door through it he has no escape from the past. There's this crucial difference between him and the first experimenters: they were only guessing what they were into when they stepped from one world to another; our man has to be ready to do it in cold blood and live with his decision until the job is completed. He must be acutely aware of his differences from the society he's visiting, be sensitive to the moods of those he meets, and be strong enough both physically and mentally to stay alive by not succumbing to the strangeness of his new surroundings. As I said, we need a lonely man. Crewkerne would have been the one, if his head was in order. We have to find another like him: a very special man."

A lonely man, thought Nilssen, turning to look out of the window across to the west. There the setting sun was shattered into horizontal bars by the almost invisible Fregar dome that spanned the six-kilometer breadth of Frobisher Crater. Colors of warmth sank slowly from layer to layer, dripping like hot wax, sliding down the sky beyond the rainbow sheen of the force field. Flapping like tattered brown banners against that sunset, dust devils whirled through their never-ending dance across the dome.

The sunset had been as glorious on that last day he had spent in the Old World; only then it had been November, not July, and the air had been still, as it was no longer or so it seemed. And brown had not been the natural color of the Earth in those happier times. Now the only true greenery was protectively confined within the bounds of the City and its farm domes. The dust was a token reminder of the arid wastes that extended across the whole planet: Europe, Asia, Africa, the Americas . . . and in the polar regions. The land was a dry desert, the sea a wet one. Outside there was still life to be found; but it was no compensation for what The War had cost the Earth five hundred years earlier. *We're all lonely, now*, said an echo in his head. *Tomorrow we celebrate twenty-six years of loneliness.* And in three weeks he would have been celebrating Eva's birthday, had she been with him still.

He shook off the memory. It would not leave him; ragged fragments of the accusing past flew by as he watched the Dome. *Didn't you realize that, clever Doctor Yaer? This city, and a few dozen explorers out there where man no longer belongs: they add up to a scant two-and-a-half million survivors of a shattered world. You want a lonely man? Take your pick.*

Sighing, he suggested, "Varno Malchek?"

Yaer prodded his noteblock. His fingers thudded softly on the keyplate. He read to himself before saying, "He was one of my early selections but he won't do either. He's impulsive, hyperemotional in some circumstances—often the wrong ones—and too old. Besides, he has a blind spot in his right eye. Forget him."

Nilssen looked at Yaer dubiously. "Too old? He's not gone fifty—"

"Fifty-two, actually. Yes, Jerlan, I know you're only six years behind him and feel as if you've not reached thirty . . . but face it, Varno Malchek shows his years, while you don't. Your hair hasn't got a streak of gray in it, unlike most of us; it'll stay recognizably brown a while yet. And count the creases in your skin, if you can find them. No, don't make the mistake of judging by calendar time. The horrors of twenty-six years ago aged too many people too fast. Even our children feel something of it."

"All right," said Nilssen suddenly. "So who's your choice? Your 'lonely man'?"

"You," Yaer said, softly.

Dvorak, that's the tune, murmured the part of him still following the band. *From* **The New World**. A shiver made him stir and rub himself for warmth. His heart had stilled momentarily, only to race furiously immediately afterward; his hands and feet had become clammy. A dizziness made him close his eyes until he felt sufficiently recovered to say:

"I'm sorry, Doctor Yaer, it's quite impossible."

"It won't be easy, I'm sure—" began Yaer.

"*No!*" Nilssen breathed heavily for several seconds. "You understand how I feel about . . . what happened back then."

Yaer spread his hands in a helpless gesture, then placed them on his knees. Switching off his noteblock with a touch of a thumb, he asked, "Who else is there?" and thereby said it all, so that though Nilssen did not answer for a while, when he did he could only say:

"Nobody."

And that was that. Yaer toyed with his noteblock, biding his time until he judged the moment right for leavetaking while Nilssen listened to the last haunted notes drifting through the window, dreaming of other places, other times, and struggling to exorcise the torment the memories always brought with them.

In his imagination he sat again in the driving seat of his comfortable old Nash '99 Coupé as it droned along that country road in November. It could have been any November, with frost on the fields but the going dry and safe. The nightmare always began pleasantly. Trees and hedges blurred past, nearly bare of leaves. Now he would notice: those leaves that remained were black, crisped black by the ghost-bomb that had taken-out South Ellington the previous day. There was no stopping the memory this far into it. . . .

The engine missed as the back-pressure valve on the hydrogen gas tank tripped. Again. Then twice. It resumed its steady beat. There was, however, little point in continuing to ignore the warning of the fuel gauge;

soon the last of the gas would be gone. They knew from garages they had already tried that refugees were making off with all that was available.

He smiled at Eva, who sat curled in the passenger seat, hoping to reassure her. She hugged the hand case containing what few things they had been able to gather and smiled back. She was not deceived, he could tell. After only a year of marriage she could read him too well.

They swept around a bend and saw a minor crossroads ahead. A signpost and a phone booth stood next to each other on the curb, and Nilssen checked their route from the sign as he pulled up by the box. Left was to Laffingham, taken-out three days back; right led down to the River Thames; and straight ahead lay Bissam and its own crossroads. They would cross the Thames at Bissam, then take the Temly road that climbed high over Windhurst Hill to reach the Institute.

The phone box door opened with a juddering squeal from its hinges, for the same blast which had browned and bubbled its paint on the South Ellington side had warped the frame. Praying that the emergency phone system still worked, he raised the handset.

Dial tone. He breathed easier and dialed. The number would be compared with a special list of acceptable codes; then if it passed the test, his call would be routed into the private network of the Commissariat of National Integrity.

The earphone whistled loudly and went dead. He continued to wait. The system allowed for misdialed calls; at this point a computer at the Institute ought to be connecting itself to the line.

There was no challenge, however, only a short musical tone and a long silence. Then the phone at the far end was answered.

"Yes?"

It was a frightened voice, carefully controlled.

"This is Jerlan Nilssen of BRAF, Burcaster. Is that the Institute of Hypothetical Physics?"

"Just a moment." A hand muffled the other microphone. Nilssen could hear a discussion going on, picked up by the earphone. Then: "Nilssen?"

"I'm still here."

"Where's that? We expected you half an hour ago."

"I'm about . . ." He leaned out of the box and read the signpost. "Two klicks west of Bissam, at . . ." A glance at the center of the dial; the plastic window was brown and cracked by heat, but the number was legible. ". . . Bissam 88026, Laffingham-Burnden road."

"Near enough. You should make it in time. We're evacuating completely in an hour."

"The car's almost out of gas."

"Omigod . . ." The other man went away again but did not bother to muffle this time. . . . "*They're west of Bissam . . . hydrogen . . . I know, but . . . I'll tell him.* . . . Nilssen, listen to me: we're not waiting; we can't. But the Director can do this much: he'll set the demolition charge to blow in ninety minutes *and* tie it to the identity card reader on the outside door. You'll see some flashing blue lights. Follow them. Is your card up to date?"

"Yes, of course."

"Then don't forget to use it. Do what you can. Good luck."

There was a click with a brutally final sound about it. Nilssen left the phone box hurriedly and got back into the car.

"Bissam," he said as he started the engine.

It failed them two kilometers later just as they were running down the long slope into Bissam. Nilssen allowed the car to freewheel as far as it would, then they abandoned it and began walking.

Everywhere were marks of the ghost-war. It had

gained momentum in recent weeks and already the
small market town of Bissam was dissolving into the
no-man's-land between two versions of history. On the
one side lay the peaceful world Nilssen had thought
was all there had ever been; on the other, stark, ugly,
was the battlefield-world whose echoes were seen and
felt with increasing frequency throughout the Earth.
Side by side, merging smoothly, were empty lines of
houses in whose gardens were neatly cultivated flower
beds, the earth fresh-turned against the expectation of
another spring, and weed-choked ruins unvisited by
their owners for many seasons. This dichotomy was all
around, a bewildering insanity, an affront to logic, and
a deadly reality.

At the crossroads an overturned tank lay on its back
in a crater. Rust streaked its torn carcass, but the identification marks were readable; this tank, like several
Nilssen had seen lately, was from a regiment that had
long ago been disbanded in his world but had been
revived in whatever parallel but not quite congruent
version of history The War was leaking through from.
And both it and whatever had destroyed it were now
completely of Nilssen's world.

They hurried across the bridge, feeling the danger
signs of another Change. The crawling sensation on
Nilssen's skin attained a maximum, a burning itch
that he knew full well could not be alleviated by
scratching; from behind them there was a soft *plop*,
and when he looked back he saw that the old iron
bridge they had just crossed now lay in the river, its
back broken and creepers smothering it: no one could
have used it for years. It was but another example of
the noncausality that was at work in the world.

The road branched and they took the left fork up
the hill through what had been woods the day before
but were now hot ashes punctuated by the black
stumps of trees. Ankle-deep on the tacky tarmac of the
road, the ashes still steamed and smoked in some

places; they frequently had to be cleared away so that the travelers could stand awhile and cool off.

When at last they reached the gates of the Institute, they found that it too had caught fire in the blast from the South Ellington bomb. The newer, concrete-and-glass laboratory block, being constructed of largely refractory materials, had suffered only superficial burning. The top three stories of glass windows had been blown in, leaving naked bars in their frames. Soot smears darkened the southern end wall; in the abnormal silence Nilssen could hear one of the automatic sprinklers drizzling. The old house, however, had been gutted and had fallen in on itself. What King Henry the Eighth had begun in 1535, by demolishing the secular buildings of Windhurst Abbey, had been completed by the destruction of their successor, Windhurst House.

Through the rubble and the drifting smoke Nilssen could see the high tumulus. It had been built before all and would probably survive all, seeming to ride above troubles as it did above the smoke. Its shaggy head of rank grass was flecked with gray wood ash. The oak that had cast a cool cover over it and over much of the surrounding later-Christian cemetery was a charred skeleton. Yet the mound itself stood unaffected by wars or earth-changes or upheavals in Reality.

A man stood up on the tumulus. He moved swiftly; before Nilssen could draw breath or warn Eva, the stranger had raised the rifle he carried and had fired at them.

The bullet blasted a small crater in the gravel of the driveway at Nilssen's feet. The man's shout came to them clearly through the cold air:

"Stay exactly where you are! Both of you!"

He ran down the nearer slope of the tumulus, the rifle balanced in an easy right-handed grip. Skirting the ruins of the house, he momentarily disappeared behind the wreck of a van which was parked across the end of the drive. At once Nilssen pulled Eva with him and they made a dash for the double glass doors of the laboratory block.

"Wait!" said Nilssen. "My card!" Eva's hand had been on the doors. Groping for his identity card, he had it in the slot of the reader when the rifle fired again, twice. Glass splinters flew across the lobby. With a gasp Eva fell against the thick glass, which now was marred by a starburst pattern of cracks around a single hole. Her head turned. Nilssen saw her smile. She seemed puzzled. A dark spot on her back widened while he attempted to understand what had been done. He heard the stranger on the gravel drive, running, his footfalls crisply staccato in the hush following the shots. He saw Eva's left hand move in an incomplete gesture, before her legs buckled under her.

Gathering her up from the ashy ground, Nilssen carried her into the building, letting the doors swing shut automatically. His mind was darting about from anxiety over Eva's condition to fear of the man who had shot at them. Finding an empty office with a large comfortable chair free of debris, he laid Eva in it. Cradling her chin in one hand, he spoke her name, at first quietly, then louder.

Her eyes were shut. No breath stirred in her. When he took his hand away, her head lolled forwards.

A cramping hollowness had invaded his chest. In two minutes or less his world had ended. Two minutes ago, a mere one hundred and twenty seconds earlier, he could have said all those things he now wanted to tell her, but which now would fall on deaf, dead ears. Two minutes. He might have saved her. The second bullet might have struck elsewhere. If only he had known. If only he had not tried to run with her. The saddest words in the world: *if only* . . .

Time could bring down so many barriers, dividing the good and bad of existence into irreconcilable compartments, regardless of pain. He stood on one side now, gazing hopelessly back across the wall that had come between them.

Precious seconds passed as he tried to memorize her face. He kissed her on the lips once as if she were asleep. And ran.

Flashing blue lights guided him. He ran down narrow stairways, through thick steel doors emblazoned with prohibitions against unauthorized entry that stood ajar, through wrecked underground laboratories where reeking ashes piled in waste bins told of hasty attempts to destroy secret documents. He passed the garbage of a civilization whose tide had turned suddenly: an overturned chair, a stranded shoe without laces, a torn bank note, a child's stuffed toy. His own sounds came back to him from darkened corners everywhere, echoing and reechoing like his anguished thoughts.

And at last he came to the cellar containing the Gate.

A wall clock warned him he had only minutes left before five tonnes of high explosive tore the building apart and shut the door to safety forever. Even so, he took his time. With Eva gone his life had been changed. He needed to comprehend every detail of the transition from old to new so that he might recall it accurately later and lose nothing of it, or of her.

The Gate frame was much like a normal domestic doorway, save that it stood against a solid wall rather than in it. There was a metal jamb heavily bound with black plastic tape; it had been prefabricated from many smaller parts, some of which were adjustable. Colorful blocks of micro miniature circuitry could be glimpsed through ventilation holes. The surface enclosed by the jamb could have been a coat of mat black paint, though some people might have questioned whether any paint could have been so totally light-absorbent, or—when finally touched—so *fluid*.

Nilssen accepted the implementation of the miracle.

One took so much on faith. By experience he knew that on his side of that surface lay the twenty-first century of a world that had with one bullet become hateful to him. He trusted that on its further side there lay the twenty-sixth century of another world, like his—but unlike his in that it was as good as a place of exile. In recent months foolhardy exploitation of the new technology had set up stresses that had disrupted this world. Already much of it had been restructured as its matter flowed into new forms, copying the worlds it would have resembled had its people not interrupted time's natural progression.

There were worlds so similar to his own, Nilssen had been told, that they were populated by the virtual twins of everyone he knew, including himself. Those worlds too had their Institutes of Hypothetical Physics, though the names and locations varied, each engaged upon work distinguishable from that of "his" Institute only by the degree of success achieved so far. Given time, more worlds would discover the great secret of how to visit their neighbors. Given time, all the doors would open. Given time, chaos would ensue.

Furthermore, another discovery was made when the ability to move across time was augmented by that of moving into past and future times. The future, they learned, held war, devastating global war, after scarcely two more months of peace. All the nearer world would be involved, for there would be a common spark for all.

At once the Institute was at odds with the security services. The Commissariat of National Integrity, the cloak-and-dagger arm of the British Republics, hitherto had demanded that the secret remain exclusive to the home country and had been able to see that wish obeyed. Now it found itself obliged to inform all the governments of the home world. Two months was insufficient leeway for subtle countermeasures. This reverse rankled, and the CNI retaliated by investing the Institute with the strictest of supervisory regimes. Frobisher and Benyon, who had been the principal discoverers of the secret, were interviewed exhaustively. Eventually they were released unharmed, and the CNI began Operation Damocles, a plan which they saw as the means to prevent the spread of The War to the home world by the programmed elimination of all of Frobisher's and Benyon's analogues in other worlds. The home world alone would have the secret, they had decided, regardless of the theoreticians' anxious pleas for longer in which to assess the probable effects of such drastic action.

In the other worlds The War began as predicted, building rapidly from skirmishes to intercontinental bombardment, invasion, occupation, counterattack, devolving towards the cruelest forms of conflict possible to a technologically enlightened species. In the home world a tense period followed an earthquake that blocked the De Lesseps Canal and leveled all settlements in southern Egypt and western Saudarab. Forewarned, interested factions in that troubled area had taken precautions and none felt obliged to maintain its position by strong-arm tactics, so that the status quo was quickly reestablished. Indeed, there was so much international cooperation that at least two pairs of formerly hostile countries agreed to exchange ambassadors. The home world maintained the "small-arms-peace" that had prevailed for almost a decade.

Politics had won, for a while. Operation Damocles was pushed ahead mercilessly despite continuing opposition from the Institute. Overruled, the scientists were compelled to accede. Only later were they vindicated; and then it was in a manner no sane person would have wished for. Nilssen's world, a world that had become too different from its near neighbors, then had involved itself with them, began to collapse in on itself.

A distant refuge had been found. But that remote

world to which the few survivors had fled could not be thought of as a temporary home. This one was being pulled down. The universe was redeveloping this site.

The thickness of the Gate was more than space or time. It was a barrier separating two attitudes. Here, Nilssen knew himself as a man of one world, akin to a peasant who has spent his life within a day's walk of his birthplace, who owes nothing to people living beyond his horizon. In using the Gate he would admit the existence of those worlds resembling his, and though in one step he might overleap them, might outpace the war that was destroying them all, guilt by acquiescence would be his for life. The Gate symbolized the secret knowledge of time, and the power over it, needed by all those worlds if they were to save themselves.

Yet how real was that need?

He hesitated on the threshold. Had his people learned nothing, there was a chance The War might still have been averted within his time line, just as those others might never have learned the secret soon enough anyhow. Surely one implied the other. Unhappily there was nobody wise enough at hand to settle his doubts. Frobisher and Benyon were alive somewhere in that place of future refuge, but they knew about as little as anyone. Their formulae amounted to fragmentary representations of the universe, not the whole picture. And retrospective analysis of all that had happened was impossible, for the guilty parties in the CNI had vanished without trace. Suddenly no one had cared to admit membership of that organization. Only the minor officials and lowly enforcers had been caught by the lynch mobs.

It was, he decided, a question for stoics to answer. He spent a further moment of farewell in the small cellar room. One dim light hanging by a bare wire. A table. A half-eaten sandwich beside a cup of scummy coffee. And a clipboard with columns of names scratched through. Picking this up, he found his own name and Eva's, two names amongst many not checked off. He replaced the clipboard on the table by an overflowing ashtray and looked at the marks of feet on the dirty floor.

This is the way the world ends, he thought bitterly. And he stepped through the Gate into his future, and into that of another world. . . .

Yaer got to his feet, scraping his chair across the floor. "Shall I make the arrangements with Anthropology and Technical Sections?" he asked.

Nilssen studied him vacantly for a moment, then nodded. "Yes," he said, "do that." And he turned back to the window through which a setting crescent moon seemed to stare in at him from out of the night.

That moon shone down, apparently unaltered, on every world that had been discovered. Although the zone of serious exploration still lay within mankind's own backyard, it appeared probable that where they found the moon as they had known her in the Old World, they would find recognizably human beings also. But how close, Nilssen wondered, did that make the primitive peoples of each world? This world had been selected because of its extraordinary similarity to their own. Did that necessarily mean that the citizens of Wessex and the Danelaw had fought the same battles for the same reasons or kept to the same customs?

He hoped he would not get himself killed finding out.

CHAPTER TWO

Cupped warmly in its wide rocky cradle, the City dozed beneath the bright prenoon sunshine. The free weather outside in the open air seemed as calm as the controlled environment within the Fregar dome, so for the moment the dome had little work to do other than separate pure and poisonous atmospheres. Across the desert, southwards, a few dusty whirlwinds toyed with the dunes while down in the Bowl, where stagnant air tended to gather, artificial vortices whipped up by the atmospheric regulators wandered amongst the spires of high-rise buildings.

Nilssen adjusted his sunglasses and put them on, slowly, keeping his eyes on the screen of the flatplate television receiver hung from the balcony rail near his chair. Turned low, the receiver was babbling too quietly to be comprehensible but still too loudly for his taste. Because one had to, he tolerated the regulations which demanded that all entertainment equipment serve a second purpose as outlets for the public alarm system, so that one either had sound and picture or neither. Ordinarily he would have opted for neither; only the importance of the next scheduled program had caused him to leave the set switched on.

He, in common with most Citizens, preferred the predominantly natural sounds within the City. Few motorized vehicles disturbed the peace. Citizens traveled on foot, by bicycle, or aboard one of the numerous beltways that served every level and zone of the domed area. Industrial processes likely to be in any way offensive to the community were segregated from the City under subsidiary domes. Even background music was considered an abomination, an affront to the artists who had recorded it, and needlessly loud speech was one mark of a boor.

In the early years following the Exodus the silence outside the dome had been one more mental burden for the refugees. Coming from a noisy civilization, they had had to adjust to the aural void around them. The inanimate noisemakers, such as lightning, rain, hail, earthquakes, and streams, still sounded the same. But there were no longer birds to sing in the wastelands, nor animals to send their cries across the treeless plains. Citizens might shut out the air of Earth for their health's sake; they could not shut out the world itself; and in coming to terms with it they had learned to treasure some of its qualities.

The City had been and largely remained a beachhead emplacement. What few outposts that had been established gave some meaning to "north" and other directions. Otherwise the maps of the modern planet might as well have been blank, for there was nowhere worth visiting other than for the scientific interest it might hold. But access to the home world was gained by the back door; the front door opened on to an infinity of variegated worlds. Anyone who had ever stepped through that front door knew there were no absolutes when assessing lifestyles. Potentially, it was said, every man could be his own arbiter, king of his own realm. Yet no one left the City and those who went missing were accounted for, in one way or another. Once that had puzzled Nilssen, until he learned a few truths about the Gates and the people who used them. Now he understood why the good Citizen was taught self-restraint and modesty of ambition; why amid a feast of variety there was a strict diet of conformity.

THE WALL OF YEARS   31

The reason was their world was not as large as it
seemed. Theirs was a cramped and confined society
still recovering its confidence, bracing itself for the
effort of recapturing a planet. Conformity was a source
of comfort for many.

Nevertheless, they had not forgotten the pleasure of
a grand spectacle. These were staged regularly throughout the City's year, taking many forms and appealing
to many interest groups. The greatest show of all, the
one at which anyone with ambitions to be someone
made a point of being seen, was the Academy Finals.
Every year the City Lottery gave away a hundred stadium tickets to the passing-out ceremonies. For a few
hours the winners could feel important, special, privileged. Later they might brag to envious friends of how
their seat had chanced to be next to that of some civic
hero, or of how they had shared a joke with a real
commissar at the reception afterwards. At any rate, for
a short while conformity could be discarded. It was a
powerful lure; and the event itself invariably attracted
a large television audience.

That was why Nilssen fretted on the balcony outside
the private quarters of Chief Commissar Laheer. It
was rapidly approaching the afternoon of the ceremony, but instead of occupying his rightful place on
the reviewing stand in front of all the crowds and
cameras, he had been summoned peremptorily for an
interview with the old man.

Though a kindly autocrat, Laheer frequently demonstrated that his thoughtfulness and consideration
for others had strange limits. Nilssen had been ushered
on to the balcony, told to make free with the drinks
and television receiver, then abandoned for half an
hour. While Nilssen paced the hot tiles of the balcony,
Laheer sat beyond closed doors in his air-conditioned
office talking on the telephone, apparently ignorant of
his subordinate's discomforts.

Nilssen had a good idea why he had been called

for, but the choice of moment and the delay were presently beyond his comprehension. Laheer might be old, yet his wits were still sharp. He could only have timed the summons to take advantage of the inconvenience. Heat and frustration would help to soften Nilssen up.

Recognizing this possibility, Nilssen at once smiled. It was a ploy. It had meaning. So he would use the delay to unwind the knot of apprehensions he had so far entangled within himself. He would relax, and in relaxing he would defy Laheer. In a friendly way, of course.

The television was still showing the program preceding the ceremony, a three-hour documentary on the Emergency Police and their history since the Exodus. Down on the stadium grass the yellow-and-black uniforms were only just starting to fall into their starting formations. He raised the sound volume so he could hear the commentator.

So far Nilssen had resisted the temptation of alcoholic refreshment, though the array of bottles in the shaded coolbox beside his chair was most attractive. Alcohol would blur his reason during the coming interview but he had tried some orange juice, then had forbidden himself a second glass on the grounds that it, like alcohol and other naturally derived intoxicants, was a habit he could not afford. Laheer might be free to reorder supplies at whim; everyone else had to spend ration tokens wisely.

Seeking amusement, he fiddled with the television set.

In a column to the right of the screen were the usual three channel selector buttons. The day's fare was: the documentary, now full of the exploits of a certain Leader Preast who specialized in exploring topologically outré alternate universes, the sports program, whose current obsession was an edited but nevertheless prolonged review of a recent diving expedi-

tion to the Von Mörgan Islands with depressing vistas
of dead seabeds littered with broken corals and
conches, and the science program, in which a flustered
cyberneticist was outlining the features of a device
referred to cryptically as the "GK Plotter."

Growing bored, Nilssen investigated a numbered
keyboard that seemed to be a special feature of
Laheer's set.

He got what looked like a fourth channel, a view
across the stadium towards the assembling graduates,
but with the number he had tapped out inset in the
top lefthand corner of the screen.

Another number brought him another scene, an
open waste of sand where windblown dust veiled the
ground and a distant Fregar dome. A storm was rising.
As the camera panned left, a larger dome appeared,
which he recognized as the City itself by the elevated
flier platform and the tall radio masts. Glancing up
at the dome overhead, he saw tendrils of dusty brown
slipping past, hugging the ground as in the picture.

Another number: a dark tunnel somewhere in the
City's foundations. Seen by infrared light, a mainte-
nance robot snuffled along a wall, scouring away dirt
and renewing the moisture sealant.

It occurred to him that there must be thousands of
number combinations. Laheer had access to the City's
permanent monitoring cameras and theoretically could
spy on anyone. Everyone took the ubiquitous cameras
for granted, believing that only the main computer
ever looked through them. Laheer himself had ordered
that precautions be taken against clandestine tapping
of the network, and Nilssen had been the nominal
overseer of the installation. Were the truth to emerge,
the Citizens would allocate at least half the blame to
Nilssen.

Laheer had his head down, close to his telephone
screen. Momentarily Nilssen hoped his explorations
had gone unobserved. Then he laughed quietly. He

had been meant to discover the old man's secret. That too had been a ploy, an attempt to weaken his position in the confrontation.

Deliberately he called up the view of the stadium again.

Then on reflection he returned to the documentary. Voyeurism could be addictive too, he warned himself.

Seconds later the program ended and the outside broadcast began. With a crash of cymbals and a flourish of trumpets a band swung into "Under The Double Eagle." Bravely thrilling, paced by resonant drums, it was music to drive out doubt.

The same camera that Nilssen had used a minute earlier showed the stadium from high overhead without the inset number, then zoomed slowly in on the reviewing stand.

Police Commissar Kwambe stood at ease with one white-gloved hand resting on the green-painted rail before him. Not a crease of his tailored, black uniform was out of place; not the slightest stain blemished the silver-trimmed yellow stripes designating his rank.

Feeling quite the macaroni today, aren't we, Hector, thought Nilssen enviously. Theirs was an amicable rivalry, but just visible over Kwambe's shoulder was Nilssen's empty seat.

As the camera closed in on him, Kwambe turned, as though by chance, and gave it one of his easy dark smiles. The shiny brown plastic case of a cue receiver showed faintly against his right earlobe, suggesting that somewhere an aide of his had been assigned screen-watching duty.

Good one, Hector. Nilssen's mild pang of jealousy changed into grudging admiration. *You fox, you'll snatch a few votes with that trick.*

Not that Kwambe needed to maneuver for votes. As a First Generation colonist he commanded a political advantage of great power. Twice, by Nilssen's reckoning, it had kept him his job when his organizational ability had seemed on the wane before his good judgment had been proven. The rising generation had few superstitions, but at their root was a dread of the Collapse and an awe of those who had survived it. Kwambe had managed a large civil engineering company in Africa before the Exodus. Now he was in his sixties and in failing health. Perhaps, conscious that he had no need of cheap votes, he had arranged the timely smile purely for the sake of the gesture.

There followed a low-angle shot of the countermarching graduates. Nilssen watched them critically, trying to see in the ranks of men and women the merchants, explorers, and—sometimes—soldiers of a civilization on the brink of nonexistence. Most were too young to be other than Second Generation. Where would those who were sent foraging in other worlds and times continue to find the strength to resist the blandishments of an easier life elsewhere; what would bring them home voluntarily to the rigors of this world?

He remembered what it was he had to tell Laheer. That last problem would soon be no problem.

Still, was it fair to delegate their training to Kwambe? Was it right that someone as ill as he was should have to instill in them a dedication to a project that no one then alive could expect to see completed?

What did Kwambe think?

He had never complained.

Of course not. Kwambe had learned early what it was to be a good manager; he worked around problems and got the job done. That was why his road-leviathans had been the ones which laid the Pan-African Expressway, not those of, say, Congreco, Amway, or Pran Cheng. He set examples for others. Others, thought Nilssen, like himself, a childless widower who at fortysix had attained the second highest position of authority in a colony on a frontier planet. His qualifications were minimal, yet Kwambe had seemed to befriend him on occasion, had even seemed to have some say in his advancement. Kwambe had learned to lead from below as well as from above.

Did Laheer follow that lead? Nilssen thought not. Laheer was his own master; he would be aware of Kwambe's influence in the City and might sometimes find it inconvenient, but Laheer was the sort who wins wars, leaving lesser folk to win the battles.

But that interplay of power could not be relied upon to remain stable much longer. Laheer too was ill. Not as obviously as Kwambe, but ill with the terminal fatigue that ultimately saps the most vigorous leader. Expert as the City medical authorities were in curing formerly debilitating or crippling maladies, bent-backed, slowing from year to year, the old man was being overwhelmed by too many problems. People had taken to calling him The Chief, even to his face, as though he had forfeited his humanity and slid into being a puppet figurehead of the administrative system. That at least was an illusion; Laheer held the reins in the City. Nevertheless, though the strain had yet to make him slacken his hold on them, Nilssen was convinced a replacement driver would be required before long. Laheer twitched too often; and his recent absences from public events were indicative of a failing political will.

Impatiently, Nilssen switched off the receiver. If he could not be present at the real ceremony, he would rather not make do with the substitute sounds and pictures.

At once a hush seemed to flow up over the balcony railings, blended with the remote music.

Laheer's quarters were the highest of all, fully fifty meters above Nilssen's own, so high indeed that the balcony overlooked the desert outside the dome. Leaning on the rail, Nilssen admired the unique view of buildings spread out across the floor of the Bowl and curved up around its sides.

Six kilometers away and blurred by rising air, more apartments of the privileged were stacked against the opposite wall. In that segment were quasi-Moorish geometrical towers, capped by cupolas, mingled with lopsided, pseudo-Dogon rooftops. Farther right these yielded to late twentieth century flowform plinths, which evolved in their turn into clusters of turreted walls reminscent of Chinese Martial crossed with Arthurian Mythic. Style succeeded style, interpenetrating yet remaining distinct. Lower in the Bowl where the shallower slopes allowed buildings to sprawl, the contrasting neighborhoods assumed odd shapes. One walkway popular with evening strollers meandered for more than a kilometer between red brick walls dotted with over eight hundred species of flowering plant. Branching paths gave access to and from the varied zones through which the main way passed, as if the overhanging buildings were themselves growths cultivated by the Commissariat of Agriculture. An underground river that emerged from the north wall of the Bowl, destined to feed the urban water system, was trained into channels that brought it splashing down over roofs in dramatic sparkling falls, through formal Japanese gardens complete with pagodas and bonsai, to gather eventually in a chain of lakes that were also the principal reservoirs for the City. There was no simple plan. One could not point to any line of symmetry, whether of shape, color, or style. Even function was no constraint to form, for the largest structure, the Library, appeared to consist of more than a score of different buildings.

Viewed from a vantage point denied to the average Citizen, the City became a bewildering composition, like an Escher drawing. Only when one accepted that the interlocked precincts were not intended to be considered as a logical whole but were expressions of deliberately disparate aesthetic standards, did the City's geometry begin to make sense.

Mankind could not live unprotected on Earth, so mankind had withdrawn into shelters of its own devising. Physical safety was assured, for the feeblest manpack-dome could rebuff anything from foul air to a tornado, and the limitations of the larger units had yet to be ascertained. Power was plentiful. Food was controlled for nutritional reasons, not because of insufficiency. Raw materials, though recycled to extend the resources of the ruined Earth, could be imported from other worlds.

The commodity in shortest supply was intangible. Ambition, the City's planners had reasoned, might be exhausted quickly. The domes were not fortresses. The intention was to resettle the Earth, therefore people had to leave their shelters, albeit suitably dressed at first. Exposed to the sterile, blighted planet, human aspirations might become stunted. Its seemingly hopeless condition might cause people to forget the high standards the First Generation had set themselves and their descendants.

So the planners had incorporated a bold mosaic of intellectual challenges into the fabric of mankind's new home base. Daily the five senses would be stimulated by reminders of what human creativity had in the past summoned from the inchoate earth. Prejudice had certainly guided the planners; nevertheless, their eventual selection brought together the arts and sciences in an unrivaled display; what they thought to omit was undoubtedly present to some degree, owing to the cultural cross-fertilization that had gone on since mankind's earliest days. The purpose was not to offer perfect examples of each art form but to suggest possibilities. And this they had done.

Side by side stood primitive and advanced technologies: prestressed concrete beside locked force-fields; Corinthian columns of silica glass coexistent with Assyrian hybrid figures embossed on platinum friezes. An aluminum Chinese temple dog might guard a public telephone kiosk. The dodecagonal concourse of City Central, the station where the twelve radial belt-superways converged, had a floor of blue synthetic marble engraved with a peripheral band marked by the twelve signs of the zodiac which enclosed an accurately scaled diagram of the known planets' orbits and those of their moons. There were innumerable such deliberate contrasts.

Much of the City undoubtedly was a hotchpotch. Though aided by computers of great power, the early planners had been rushed in their work, and their successors were obliged to make the best of their mistakes. Rebuilding had improved the effect, and on the whole Nilssen approved. Elegance had not been the planners' objective, after all.

Emphasis was laid upon realism. No false standards were permitted. If fruit trees were to be planted beside walkways, they would be real trees, pollinated by real insects, and bearing fruit in the proper season. If a chair was to be carved from wood, it had to be real wood right through, no matter how rare or costly to obtain. If knowledge was to be stored in the Library for future dispensation to Citizens, no lies were allowed and errors were to be expurgated ruthlessly.

Though the ideal had not been attained, and though buildings remained incomplete, and though human fallibility had promulgated untruths aplenty, yet the City which had grown from those cardinal precepts already seemed to be succeeding.

It was a strange success. However strong an individual's dissatisfaction with present conditions might be, the majority of the new generation confidently anticipated the eventual achievement of their goal: gradually, most would assert with bland nonchalance, the atmosphere and oceans would be restored to their former health. Ah, but when? One day.

One day? reflected Nilssen wryly. *Come the Millennium, they mean. Most have no idea what a clean*

Earth is like. They're snug and happy as they are, when you get down to it.

Sometimes he wondered seriously whether the City nurtured its Citizens too tenderly, too reliably. In becoming their stable point of reference it had also constrained them with mounds of cotton wool. One could learn to rely overmuch on a system as an anodyne or as a source of mental stimulus. In the City the price paid for years of novelty was the shunning of earnest inquiry. "Do not seek too much too soon," could have been the watchword of those who prolonged their stays in assigned quarters until actually ordered by the rota-masters to move elsewhere. Everyone knew how wide the dome was; it was not hard to estimate how much variety such an enclosure could hold.

That, of course, might explain the perennially high recruitment rates the Emergency Police enjoyed. Not every officer won promotion to field agent, but the lure of unnumbered worlds of mysteries was far stronger than objective reason. If you made it, you were king of creation. You went on missions outside the confines of the world that everyone knew, into its unmapped alternates. And if you happened to be just an also-ran, you could still hope while basking in reflected glory.

The music blared and blatted on, ascending with the waste heat of the City. In the warm, turbulent air the small patch of green that was the stadium's image wavered like a mirage.

Two hundred and four trainees had graduated this year. Fifty of those could expect to be field agents within another three years if past experience was any guide. How strange, thought Nilssen, that not one of the nearly two thousand serving or retired agents had ever publicly discussed the hazards of their work. Losses were heavy. And how strange that even he, the Commissar of Reestablishment, had been kept ignorant of the implications for the welfare of the City. The scientist, Rhys, had warned that the remedy would be unpopular; could it be that Kwambe, Laheer, and the rest of their group were losing their nerve and preferred to conceal the dangers peculiar to time-traveling?

One of the sliding windows into Laheer's office opened, rumbling on its runners. He pretended not to have heard it.

"Not a bad show," Laheer said huskily, joining Nilssen at the rail. "Hector reports a forty per cent pass rate. Claims some are, hah, cracking good." Laheer allowed himself a smile. His left eyelid was fluttering fast. "A fine start to our second quarter century. Progress, Jerlan: *ohne Hast, aber ohne Rast.*"

Not a hint of an apology for the delay. That was typical of the old man.

"If you say so, sir. Only, with due respect to Wagner, haste and rest both have their uses."

"Goethe, blast it! Not Wagner!" snapped Laheer. "Well, come along. I can't spend all day on you."

Once they had entered the spacious office Laheer shut the window and switched on the acoustic dampers that rendered the walls, ceiling, and floor impervious to sound. As he helped himself to a glass of gin from his indoor bar, he remarked, "Security is an exercise in seeing all and telling nothing." He settled himself in a comfortable armchair by the window. There was a tabletop model of the City near his feet and he kept his eyes on it as he added, "And being certain of your associates."

Nilssen also sat, asking, "No action, sir?"

"Ah," said Laheer. "That's one of the things you don't tell."

"Of course." Nilssen could not relax, so found the old man's calmness doubly disquieting.

Suddenly Laheer came to the point:

"Yaer tells me you've volunteered for Project Yardstick."

"Yes, sir." The admission broke from him. Glad to be rid of it, he felt his apprehension leave. It was going to be a rough ride but a manageable one. "I elected for field duty."

Laheer radiated skepticism.

"Don't pretend, Jerlan. I know that man too well. Somehow he pressured you."

Nilssen adopted a thoughtful expression.

"I thought as much. Jerlan, you're to back out. You hear me?"

"Too late," said Nilssen. "I said I'd go. Technical Section have worked all night so I can start training this afternoon. Their efforts can't be wasted. Nor," he said slyly, "can we compromise security."

Checked for a second, Laheer counterattacked angrily, "And you imagine we can spare valuable personnel? Man, you're one of our best. I had hopes for you—"

"Chief." The old man chopped short his outburst. Nilssen went on, "Have you discussed it with Yaer? I mean, *really* talked it through: the problem, the alternatives, the sort of agent we need?"

"Haven't the time for that. All I know is, we're using you when one of Hector's rawest recruits would be adequate."

"Then, sir, you ought to spare the time before interfering in what is an extremely delicate matter." The old man's face stilled, save for a slight tic in his left cheek. Nilssen hurried to sweeten what he had said. "I'm sorry to be so blunt. We all respect your feelings, sir, and we vote for you each year because we believe you're the one to lead us. But lately we've been staggering from crisis to crisis in Hector's department. That business last summer when we had to mop up those time-travelers from this Line's past proved how precarious our hold is here. One accident could wipe us out." He took a breath. "We're at a breakpoint in the City's development. Day-to-day administration is relatively straightforward, but management of our time-travel projects is becoming damn near impossible; soon it'll break down unless we keep a tight hold on every movement made by our field agents. And in that, sir, you'll have to trust the experts. As I do."

Laheer tapped his lean fingers on the left armrest of his chair as he sipped his gin. He stared morosely out of the window at the brown-smeared blue of the sky beyond the dome. Then he clicked his tongue. "Very well," he said abruptly. "I consider myself advised." His eyes fixed themselves on Nilssen. "But I want some sort of an explanation. I deserve that, at least."

Relieved that the old man had taken the rebuke so well, Nilssen hastened to cooperate. "Of course, sir, I'll see to it that Technical—"

"Dammit, Jerlan, I'm too old to waste time listening to those wise fools. You say Yaer's convinced you; summarize his argument."

"It won't be easy. He has a way with words. Afterward you can't always remember them all. Besides, Rhys—"

"Turlough Rhys? Is he involved?"

"He started it."

"When?"

"Three months ago. Second week in April."

Laheer bared his teeth for a second, then pursed his lips over them.

"Go on," he said.

"Well, Rhys phoned me late at night. He sounded drunk. And scared. That alone made me listen; Rhys is teetotal. Then he said he didn't dare talk anywhere near the City, asked if I could join him in Area Five."

"That's a devil of a long journey for a social call."

"Exactly what I said. He wouldn't stop pleading though. So I went."

Rain streamed from packed banks of gray cloud, flattening the sea, as the flier skirted the western coast of Scotland. Nilssen, peering into the murky eastern sky, could just catch glimpses of mountains, distinguishable by their greater variety of grays.

Cutting across the Point of Stoer, the flier lost height above Eddrachilis Bay. The pilot pointed to port. "Down there," his voice rasped in Nilssen's headphones, "the ruins of Badcall. Big place once. The electricity company had a switching station there to handle the wave-powered generators of the Western Barrage. Only holes in the ground now. The metal was ripped out during The War."

Nilssen gave it a cursory examination. Ruins were no novelty to him.

They crossed the coast with high-flung spray from the breakers crackling in the flier's antigravity field and rose to clear the southern approaches to Ben Stack, a naked rock pile denuded of soil. Then they dropped sharply into the valley of Loch Stack itself. The rain was falling in drifting curtains as they landed and rolled into the dry refuge of the hangar attached to the laboratory complex known as Area Five.

Here all the most dangerous research into time travel was conducted. The mountains penned in the place, protecting it from much of the residual radioactivity of the Scottish Highlands; they also provided a barrier wall to contain any explosions that might occur. Not that explosions alone were likely; far worse was certain in the event of serious mishap. A handful of living people had seen a timestorm at work. Mere physical explosions were at least a comprehensible and therefore acceptable hazard to blame for the isolation, when it came to recruiting nontechnical staff.

Rhys met Nilssen personally. He seemed a man of repressed anger, willing his body to be polite, inwardly furious at the shortcomings of everyone with whom he had dealings. His short black hair clung to his pale scalp as if plastered there. His hands never relaxed, chopping and gesturing as an accompaniment to his staccato speech. His voice took on a jarring whine whenever he became excited but was never quite free of a plaintive note. No man, his manner suggested, had a right to stand in his way.

Nilssen made no protest when Rhys took charge of the reception, saw him equipped with overalls, dosimeter, and space stress detector, then hurried him to the darkened computer lab where he worked.

Rhys stood with his back to Nilssen for a moment, before saying:

"Shut the door, Commissar."

As the lock clicked and the air conditioning resumed its steady hum, he swung to face the light that shone through the frosted glass panels from the corridor. His fire was out, quenched by a pathetic helplessness. He sounded exhausted as he asked, "Can I get you anything?"

"No, thank you," said Nilssen. He wondered why Rhys did not turn on the overhead glow panels, until he understood that the ranked indicators on the equipment lining the walls were meant to impress him. "Pretty," he remarked, pointing to them. "Do they tell you anything?"

"Yes," said Rhys absently. "How was your flight?"

"Clear weather most of the way. Rain at the end."

Rhys would talk when he was ready.

"Oh, yes." The scientist laughed, like a clumsy actor reading through a strange script. "We get a lot of that up here at this time of year, I believe . . ." His eyes defocused momentarily and he shook his head. "No, what was I going to say?"

"Your message suggested something had gone wrong."

"What? Heavens, no, everything's perfect. Bloody marvelous, and that's gospel." Again he attempted a laugh, which sounded like a cough. "All like clockwork, as we used to say. Tick-tock. So smoothly I can't even remember if it's winter or summer—" He spun away suddenly, kicking aside a metal chair, which bounced across the floor and rebounded from a rack of memory planes. "Commissar, you're going to love this news. We've found a meaning for Frobisher's seventh equation."

Silhouetted though Rhys was against the status lamps, his teeth gleamed in the light from the door.

"That's—" Nilssen began. "No," he corrected himself, "I was going to congratulate you. But I don't think you'd want that. Why not?"

"Because the results prove how stupid we were a quarter century ago," Rhys answered. "Because . . . Commissar, suppose I told you we ought never to have bothered leaving the twenty-first century, that the twenty-sixth is shaping up as a death trap, that the harder we try to dig ourselves out of the hole we've put ourselves in, the deeper we'll sink? What would you say?"

"I'd ask you to explain yourself," said Nilssen quietly, though his heart was racing.

"And I, in turn, would reply that history is a fallacy. History, my dear Commissar, is indeed bunk, and Henry Ford should have been here to see himself vindicated. What we have so cleverly confirmed is that causality is active across time as well as along it. We can demonstrate—as if the Collapse were not enough—that the alternate forms of the Universe which coexist are not independent. They interlock like a stack of ball bearings: pull one out and . . . oh, such fun!"

He stepped sideways and laid a hand on some

switches, bringing up the ceiling panels so that their glow lit the banked faces of computers around the walls.

"You called these things pretty," he said. "They're not. They're deadly, glittering like the eye of a snake about to strike. Science for its own sake—accuracy that comes too late. Frobisher let himself be fooled, Commissar; he frittered away his life, mesmerized by the beauty of pure number, searching for perfection when the answers were already available.

"All this is heresy, of course. Dogma has canonized Frobisher along with Benyon. And I, as a pure scientist, am expected to kowtow at their tomb. Well, I damn well will not, Commissar! Eleven years ago I started here. I could have taken their lab notes and come to the same conclusions as now, if I hadn't been blinded by too much reverence.

"What was staring them in the face was that this world is walking a tightrope. If we make one bad move, the desert worlds which parallel this one will impress themselves on it, erasing us, as happened in the world from which we escaped. All these marvelous machines have added is the numbers. And *that*, Commissar, is what I have to tell you—to begin with."

"Excuse me," said Nilssen, righting the fallen chair.

"Oh, sit by all means," said Rhys. "Bit of a shaker, yes?"

Nilssen's head was buzzing, so he merely nodded.

Rhys rubbed at the fatigue marks below his eyes. "And there's no way out. We keep struggling, forever, or we disappear."

"Is there never to be stability?"

Rhys stayed quiet, so Nilssen repeated his question.

"Only at a price," answered Rhys. "We minimize timeshift operations."

Starting up, Nilssen exclaimed, "That's impossible! This world is ruined. We *have* to import materials!"

A sardonic smile lit half of Rhys's face. "Yes, Commissar, you need those metals, that oil, the food; and you can have them all, under certain conditions."

"You sound as if we haven't a choice."

"There is always a choice: extinction or . . ." He laughed. "Now, Mister Hobson, sir, will you hear the terms of the agreement?"

He takes too much pleasure in telling me, thought Nilssen. *Either the strain has broken his sanity, or he's witholding a simple answer. Or he really doesn't care.*

The last possibility was too awful to be taken seriously. Rhys was so far ahead of his colleagues as to be irreplaceable.

Rhys appeared to infer consent from Nilssen's silence. "Briefly: we must halt all exploration for three months while new timeshift units are introduced. Afterward a more restrictive code of practice must be applied to their use."

"I see nothing wrong with the present gates."

"Oh, what a commendation for them!" Rhys sneered. "My God, an angler fishing for minnows in a flash flood at midnight could do better! Have you never watched those fumble-fingered oafs probing for a new linkup, Commissar?"

"No," Nilssen replied stiffly. "I have not, Doctor Rhys. Do tell me about it."

Rhys promptly lowered a three-dimensional display sphere from the ceiling and activated it. "Then I'll draw you a picture," he said as the overhead lights dimmed. A cloud of red sparks bloomed at the sphere's center and began to swirl widdershins in a flat spiral.

"This selective relationship diagram is a sort of idiot's idea of space-time. We developed it to demonstrate some partial solutions to the seventh equation, so it only shows three of the infinite number of dimensions. Accurate simulation of the Universe would be a trifle taxing, so forgive the approximation.

"Each of those moving red points represents an entire evolving universe, a slice across a single time line. Its relationship to all others is shown by their relative positions: the closer they are, the more similar they are. As the configurations change, the universes drift around, occasionally becoming so similar to neighbors as to seem identical.

"However, no universe can have a true twin, for then they would be one and the same.

"Now, suppose we are *here*." One of the sparks turned white and pulsed steadily. "And we want to find another world with certain characteristics . . ." A green line extended itself from the white spark and probed about until it touched a red spark. "Ah, good, they've found something!" Rhys mimicked Kwambe's rolling intonation, "Send someone through the gate, chaps. See what we've caught, chaps." Woebegone, he pulled a face. "Too bad. Better luck on the next, chaps." The green line disengaged and found another red spark. "Oh, botheration, that's worse still, chaps."

"No need to continue," Nilssen said. "I'm sure Commissar Kwambe is making the best use of the equipment available to him. Had you some constructive suggestion?"

"What I am trying to say is that these hit-and-usually-miss tactics aren't good enough," replied Rhys in his normal voice. "Look at that diagram. Try to imagine how those points interact, how every transfer between them changes both starting and destination points, how delicate is the dynamic equilibrium of the whole system. Kwambe's out there, blundering around, moving matter to and fro, to places it doesn't belong, and upsetting the entropy budget. No wonder we had the Collapse. All it took was a few stupid moves by the CNI."

"The CNI doesn't exist any more," said Nilssen. "And your pictures are no help to me. Say what you have to, in words. Give me facts."

"Facts?" echoed Rhys. The red glow of the display

lent his face a demoniacal aspect during the silence which ensued. "Facts," he repeated at last. "Commissar, if by a fact you mean something that is true now and will always have been true, then I must tell you that there is no such thing as a fact." He tapped out a series of numbers on a keyboard, causing the display to scribe a vivid green zigzag radial on the whirlpool of sparks. "There you see a hypothetical world-line: the entire history of one single universe. I could draw you any amount of those through all the infinity of possible dimensions; each would be unique and independent.

"But watch this one. Observe how its shape alters as the whirlpool turns. . . . See, our past is changing, as is our future, as is our present, all pressing upon each other and upon the worlds about them, jostling for a place in Reality. There is no constancy in anything, Commissar, no point of absolute rest. Only change, the basis of existence.

"So if you ask me for facts, please excuse some evasiveness. All I can give you is a set of principles. If my contempt for Kwambe's clumsiness offends you, I can't help it. Neither can I pretend to love your politician's instinct that asks for the easy way out so you won't annoy the voters. If there must be one fact, let it be this: that this is a pragmatic continuum in which we happen to exist, wherein nothing happens because of divine law but only because it makes sense.

"We have been luckier than we deserve, Commissar. Sometimes I suspect that it made sense for us to survive. So far, that is. Now that we are aware of how Reality works, we have to behave responsibly.

"Our first option is to retain the grossly inefficient timeshifters and loot parallel worlds for their resources; our second is to rethink our strategy. Area Five's laboratories now have a new technology, but it is one whose implementation calls for political courage. Without it, we have an easy life, for a while. With it, although our agents will face more terrible dangers, the life of the City will be extended indefinitely."

His breathing had become heavier with his excitement. He paused to mop his brow with a handkerchief.

"I used to be a religious man, Commissar. Once. Then I lost my faith. How, I asked myself, could any real God treat His creatures so callously, first to give them knowledge, then to deny them a cure for the agonies it created? For years I believed there could be no salvation. Then, suddenly, there came the breakthrough. The answers came at us like a flood. But I still could not believe, not in Him at least. Because I saw that the answers came from the human mind, which is totally explicable as a chance effect springing from those moving dots. And I saw more: that we have here a human problem. That was the moment of my darkest despair, Commissar, when I realized that these answers would have to be handed over to people like you, people who cannot be expected to think objectively as I try to. Having discarded my own faith in an all-wise Being, how could I depend on you to have faith in me? That is why I didn't ask for your congratulations when you arrived. All I want is for you to believe in me."

The whirlpool of red sparks continued to rotate, dragging with it the flexing green world-line. On one of the computer facias a row of lights shimmered for a second; then they and the green line went dark.

"The end of a time line," said Rhys. "That universe has never existed, ever."

Overwhelmed by his own incompetence, Nilssen could only ask, "Why come to me if it's so clear-cut? Deal directly with Kwambe."

"Kwambe won't listen," Rhys said. "Whatever its pretensions, the Emergency Police is and always has been a political organization. Knowledge by itself can exert no leverage, Commissar. Give us your political will. Back us up!"

"I should have thought your little lecture would impress anyone."

"Not Kwambe. He dismissed it as a theoretician's fantasy. His imagination can only handle job sheets and heavy machinery—civil engineering. Abstruse probabilities don't worry a mind like his."

"Oh?" Nilssen looked sharply at Rhys. "And how do *you* sleep at night?"

"Because I know there will always be a tomorrow if there has been a today," he replied, looking straight back at Nilssen. "And because I know it will seem to follow logically from today."

"Even if you're not there to experience it?"

"Now we are deep in the verbal jungle, Commissar. Epistemology has never appealed to me as a game. *Dum cogito, sum,* as Descartes might have said had he known the truth about Reality. *While I think, I exist.* Beyond that consolation, what value is there in speculation?"

"Had it occurred to you that Kwambe might have perfectly good reasons of his own for rejecting your scheme?"

Rhys smiled weakly. "Are you sure he does anything for a reason?"

Frowning, Nilssen decided not to pursue the argument. Rhys, living in his mental box, would be ignorant of the pressures acting on Kwambe to keep the transtemporal gates open. Social pressures. Irrational pressures. "I'll talk to the right people," he said, standing. "More than that—"

"I know," said Rhys. "You can't promise a damn thing."

"Don't take it personally. I'm on your side, you know that."

"Sure," said Rhys without conviction. "Everyone comes to us for advice."

"It would be a damnsight easier if you could offer proof," Nilssen retorted.

"Proof?" asked Rhys. "So we're back to that . . . Let me show you something Kwambe didn't see."

He led Nilssen into an adjoining room. Equipped as a laboratory-cum-workshop, it had been lavishly outfitted. Every item of the specialized apparatus looked like a prototype, causing Nilssen to suppose that the collection might well be unique.

"My assistants are trying to package the new time-shifter as a man-portable unit like the Mark One belt," said Rhys. "Step over anything on the floor."

The far wall was bare but for a shelf on which was a toy railway track. A single rusty flatbed truck stood at one end and was linked to a small windlass at the other end by a fine braided metal cord. The shelf, the truck, and the cord were blackened, as though by intense heat.

"Everyone should have a hobby," Nilssen observed.

Rhys said coldly, "Commissar, this is probably the most expensive demonstration setup ever devised. . . . If you please, be ready to turn the handle of the windlass when I tell you. And don't stop, whatever happens."

From a cupboard he took an implement resembling a long-handled spoon with a mesh bowl covered by a mesh lid. A taped bundle of wires dangling from the handle ended in a multipin plug which Rhys inserted into a trolley-mounted box.

"Watch carefully," he advised. "We limit ourselves to one demonstration every three days."

"What if you did it more often?"

"Maybe nothing," said Rhys, rummaging through a scrap box. "We'd rather avoid provoking a time-storm." He selected a wedge of aluminum about three centimeters long. "Inserting this sample in the transmitter, so, we hold the basket above the truck, so . . . Prepare to wind . . . And we activate." His free hand dropped to the trolley, his slender index finger pushing hard on a recessed button. "Watch the sample, please."

Seconds passed without result. "Must be—" Rhys began.

The aluminum wedge flickered. Like a light being switched off, it winked out of existence.

"Wait," ordered Rhys, whipping the empty basket aside.

There came a smell of ozone with traces of nitrous oxide, so sharp that Nilssen's nose tingled. Then the wedge rematerialized in midair, exactly where it had been moments earlier, to fall with a clatter into the truck.

"Now!" shouted Rhys. "Wind that handle! Fast!"

As Nilssen cranked, Rhys bent to inspect the air ahead of the truck, talking all the while in a rapid monotone:

"The sample has been propelled ten seconds into its own future, a future in which it does not belong. Had we used a conventional transmitter, this would not be so; the dynamics of the old process are different from the new. As it is now, an object injected into a time unnatural to it reverts spontaneously by a temporal tunneling process. Thus the atoms of this sample will fall back at random through ten seonds, although they will remain at rest relative to the Earth's mass. What you will see, Commissar, in a few moments, are atoms lost by the sample as it progresses along the rails in that truck. Being finely divided, the aluminum will immediately burn in the surrounding atmospheric oxygen—there, the reversion is beginning! Or rather, ten seconds from now it will begin. . . . Look, but keep winding at a steady rate."

A few firefly-sized lights glowed in midair a few centimeters ahead of the truck. Floating above the rails, they proliferated into a cloud of fat sparks. The smell of ozone intensified. Gradually the fiery cloud extended itself along the track, but drew in its tail as though fleeing from the truck. Crackling audibly like a miniature thunderstorm, it shed a fine fog of white dust. Soon it was painfully bright and the acrid scent of charring wood was added to that of ozone as smoke curled up from the shelf.

Rhys muttered, "I think I chose too big a test piece. Be a splendid thing if we set the place on fire."

As the cloud burned, the metal wedge in the following truck could be seen corroding. A mild rash of pitting quickly deepened into cavities, and before long the bulk of it had been eaten away. For about twenty seconds the line of incandescent metal vapor lit up the workshop, casting sharp shadows of men and equipment on the walls. Then it faded away, leaving smoke drifting up from the shelf. Moments later the last crumbs of the wedge too vanished, just as the truck hit the buffers.

"That," Rhys announced, "is spontaneous entropic reversion. What do you think of it, Commissar?"

The horrific implications of the demonstration were still dawning on Nilssen, so he answered cautiously:

"I suppose this . . . reversion can be prevented?"

"Indeed," said Rhys. "The new belts will contain stabilizers. And?"

"It could happen to an agent?"

"Without question."

"No wonder you didn't tell Kwambe." Nilssen drew a fingertip through the powdery deposit of aluminum oxide and nitride on the track. "He'd have your head if he learned this was what you—. . . I presume this is the side-defect of the new timeshifter?"

"If a stabilizer fails, yes."

"And how can we stop this happening to our imports from other worlds?"

"We'll continue exchanging equal masses by a bilateral gate transfer once a solid link is established."

"But in the meantime an agent is exposed to this danger while on exploratory probes?"

"There's no other way around the entropy imbalance," Rhys sad stubbornly. "I've been honest with you, Commissar. Can you lean on Kwambe and make him see sense?"

"My superiority over him is largely nominal. It'll have to be done by argument. In a way I wish you hadn't shown me this party trick."

"Couldn't be hidden forever," answered Rhys. "By the same token, pretending we can carry on as we are won't rearrange the truth. The old equipment—the gates and Mark One belts—provided built-in stabilization by sheer inefficiency, at a cost we can't afford. The new calls for new attitudes. I told you, Commissar, it's Hobson's choice."

Even though at that moment Nilssen had no inkling of how Rhys's proposal was later to affect his life, he was acutely uncomfortable, knowing that he was at Rhys's mercy. If he agreed and Rhys had not told the truth, either mistakenly or deliberately, he could be ruined. If he disagreed and Rhys was right—

"Doctor Rhys, you can have your three months so far as I am concerned. And I'll fight any opposition. Three months of no traffic other than established trade links, yes?"

"That will do nicely."

"But if you've misled me . . ."

Rhys shook his head. "Commissar," he said, "you'll lose no votes because of me."

Laheer raised an eyebrow. "And did he come up with an answer?"

"Yes," said Nilssen. "Our Doctor Rhys has excelled himself. We have a new type of portable timeshifter and an entire operational procedure to go with it."

"So now they want a volunteer to test the blasted

thing? Jerland, I still don't see why it has to be *you*."

"The shifter was tested weeks ago. What remains unfinished is calibration and proving of the range predictors that interwork with it. Someone reliable has to take it to known space-time coordinates so we can be sure transfers are accurate."

Laheer shot Nilssen a caustic look. "Jerlan, one of these days your susceptibility to flattery will be the end of you."

"Flattery was no part of it," Nilssen answered hotly. "Yaer decided I was most suitable. It's not as if I have any great love for the past, you know that."

Laheer's face became still. "I'm sorry," he said. "Careless of me."

"Not your fault," said Nilssen quickly. "There's no cause for me to go near Windhurst Hill."

Laheer recovered his composure. "So they have a site picked?"

"I think so; but they're keeping it from me to make sure I don't learn up on one small area. Yaer's suggestion, of course. He also proposed the ninth century as the target date. It's early enough, yet well documented."

"I thought that man was on our books as a psychologist?"

"Maybe so. For all that, he's the nearest we have to a social dynamics expert. Rhys is happy; so is Maia Kim. Apparently there was a lull in the local politics for about a decade after Alfred trounced the Danes at Edington. Yaer said we should try for the Thames Valley, 880 AD, this time line."

"Dangerous?"

"I dare say," Nilssen replied guardedly. "But it'll be quick. My brief is to discover the exact date from someone like a priest, code it into a long-life clock, then bury the clock in a grave-mound. Dozens of them survived The War. Over the centuries the clock will count off lunar days by measuring changes in the

Earth's apparent gravity. Once I'm home it can be dug up again. Finally, its reading will be compared with other measurements made during the two-way transfer. Together they'll yield a solid set of corrective values. Rhys calls it redundancy."

Laheer did not respond to his wry grin.

"Far be it from me to imply that Rhys is unreliable, Jerlan," he said, "for had I anything but the highest regard for his expertise, he'd be out of Area Five in a flash. I simply . . ." He rose stiffly and stalked to the window, trailing his fingers over the clear domes of the City model. Without turning he clasped his hands together behind his back and said, "I think that man is dangerous. He reminds me of Cassius, in the play by Shakespeare. Right now his loyalties seem to lie with the City, because we give him shelter and the means to pursue his studies. But should he ever be balked, beware." He swiveled his head and looked sideways at Nilssen, who noticed how dry the old man's skin appeared and how taut were the tendons in his neck. The reddish light filtering through the Fregar dome put Nilssen in mind of Rhys when they had talked in the Area Five laboratory by the way it picked out the gaunt highlights of Laheer's cheeks and nose. "Will you remember that, Jerlan?"

Puzzled, Nilssen nodded halfheartedly. "If you want me to."

"You see," Laheer went on, facing the window again, "many people spend their lives repressing their true nature in the belief that some artificial ethic, essentially alien to them, matters more. The true self lies undeveloped and unmoderated. Greed. Laziness. Lust. Whatever popular morality says is wrong or whatever conflicts with the artificial ethic formulated by the individual. There are incentives to suppress it, so that it remains immature and supposedly harmless. The individual proceeds to construct a false persona, around which is gathered a way of life."

"We *are* discussing Turlough Rhys?"

"We are," Laheer said. "Unfortunately. Doctor Yaer uncovered quite a few interesting cases in his search through the personnel files. Addictions. Neuroses. Criminal tendencies. . . . And Doctor Rhys.

"What Yaer had to say is not the sort of news to be repeated verbatim. Furthermore, it's mostly theory." Laheer leaned forwards on the window sill to gaze down into the Bowl. "Yaer informs me that I have megalomaniac tendencies, which is comforting . . . And Rhys, he's an incipient case too. . . . Only, as you see, my urge has been satisfied, whereas his has barely been stimulated. Yaer suspects he was slapped down when young, so he took the only other remaining clear route to dominance: scientific research." Silent for a while, Laheer said, "How splendid it must be when thousands of your fiercest competitors are obliged to admit your superiority, if only in one small way. No wonder there used to be so much infighting over scientific papers and professional reputations. However—" and he pushed himself upright and dusted off his hands on the hem of his jacket "—Turlough Rhys is innocuous unless he gets the idea that he matters to us."

"How can we possibly prevent that?" asked Nilssen. "There's hardly another person who matters more just now."

"I'm amazed at you," Laheer replied evenly. "You, of all people, should have more respect for the workers who keep our civilization running. Rhys is no more important than anyone; he's on a straight par with them. And that's the message he must have hammered into him."

"All right. Fine. Good." Nilssen stood up and confronted Laheer across the City model. "Next time I see Rhys I'll order him not to get a swollen head."

"You'll tell him nothing! *Nothing*, you hear?" Laheer's outward calm was shattered; for almost ten seconds he seemed on the verge of saying more, before he waved angrily towards the inner door of the office. "Go and get ready for your charades," he said. "And shut it after you."

CHAPTER THREE

For two months Nilssen trained intensively. The Education & Data Resources Department imprinted him with fluent Old English and a grasp of ninth century Anglo-Saxon customs. Armaments taught him rudimentary swordplay and bare-handed combat. Geodetic Survey provided maps and scale models of the area he was to visit. Medical Services refreshed his knowledge of survival crafts.

Somewhere along the way they mentioned which hill they planned to use for the transfer point.

"Windhurst Hill?" he repeated slowly. Incredulously. "Where the Institute was?"

Coordinator Maia Kim was a woman he respected highly. This was an opinion also held by the large majority of the field agents who came under her aegis. Never had he felt inclined to question her advice. But in an instant he was totally at odds with her.

"I can't go there," he said emphatically.

Rhys, who was sitting in on the briefing, had no knowledge of Nilssen's personal history, so misunderstood. "Nothing wrong with that. It's the logical site. Dozens of people in the City used to work there. They've helped us enormously in mapping the terrain.

"I . . ." He tried to explain but shied away from putting his feelings into words. "No, it's private."

Kim tapped Rhys on the shoulder. She was tall and elderly, but she was also far from being a willowy granny. Solidly built, she could overawe Rhys without effort. When she pointed to the door and said, simply, "Out," the smaller man did not demur. "Five minutes," she called after him.

The door slid shut.

"Jerlan," Kim said, "hardly anyone knows what hit you at the Institute, because although it's in your file it's kept private, as you say. I was told because part of my job is to size up my charges before they even step into Dispatch. Some get attacks of nerves. I don't blame them—all that shiny hardware and those elaborate defense systems would scare anyone. They get reassurance with explanations of why we take precautions. Others look calm when they go through the gate but don't come back when they should. Then my professional opinion determines whether we send out a rescue team armed to the teeth, a counselor to jolly the agent into returning, or do nothing for a while longer.

"During the years I've been here I've seen all the types there are. Believe me, some have problems. You're above average; you've got the stamina to fight this block of yours. But the support staff in this experiment are living on their nerves: if it fails we'll be looking to them for another answer; and they don't think there is one. Don't make it harder for them by letting on what they've done to you. It was a coincidence. Rhys is right: it's the logical site."

Nilssen took her hand and squeezed it. "Thanks," he said. His throat felt tight. "A shock, that's all." Releasing her hand, he asked, "Do we call Rhys back?"

"Let him talk to my secretary," Kim said. "She fancies him." From a locker in one wall Kim removed a small plastic suitcase labeled with Nilssen's name and citizen number. "Your costume came this morning from the props department. I'd like you to try it on."

Nilssen accepted the suitcase but did not open it. "Is there somewhere . . ?"

Kim sighed. "Modesty? Okay, you can change in the toilet outside."

Feeling extremely peculiar in his strange clothes, Nilssen reentered the office, followed by Rhys. For a while Kim studied him.

"Not bad," she conceded. "The belt is worn over the tunic, though." As Nilssen was refastening the dummy timeshift belt provided for practice wear over his woolen tunic, Kim straightened the fall of the garment so that it hung level at midthigh. Suddenly she stopped and made a small sound of annoyance.

"Your cross-gartering is wrong on the left."

"Looks fine to me," said Nilssen, balancing on one leg and extending the other so he could examine it.

"Put your foot up on this chair." He complied and she skillfully untied the knot below his knee, unraveled the two thongs that ran down to become part of his shoe, and restrapped them. "There," she said. "A real Saxon would have wondered whether you weren't used to these clothes."

"And he'd be dead right," Nilssen said. "I can't be expected to learn all the idiocies of ninth century fashion."

"You can and you will!" she said with some vehemence. "This isn't a fancy-dress parade, Jerlan. This is real. Every stitch in these clothes is made the way they would have done it. The cloth is real wool from our own sheep. The leather is from real cows. You have to be able to withstand close scrutiny. . . . I'd better inspect the rest." Methodically she examined his clothing: shirt, breeches, hose . . .

"Scuff those shoes before you meet the public. They don't look travel-worn. It might be wise if you kept this outfit on until the experiment; get some body odor into it."

She ran a finger along the belt. "I'm not happy about this plastic. See it doesn't fall into the wrong hands."

Rhys grinned unpleasantly. "If it does, he's dead. Without his belt he comes home as a stream of disassociated particles."

"It'll do then. The sleeves of the tunic should be tied, so, and don't forget your cloak; it might rain."

"Yes, mum," Nilssen said.

Instead of a smile sadness settled briefly on her face. "Let me show you," she said, tugging the cloak around his shoulders with excessive force. "The corners meet at the front of your neck. The bronze brooch fastens them together. See?"

He nodded. Rhys chuckled.

"A proper man about town," he said.

The remark suggested to Nilssen that Rhys had failed to accept Kim's exhortation to take the reality of the Past seriously, as if in creating his invention he had done all that could reasonably be asked of him. All else was the folly of lesser minds. He had mastered what "time" was; what it *did* was beneath his notice.

The test site was ninety-five kilometers from the City, southeast across the level desolation of the Oxford Valley, so they took a flier. Clear of the Cotswold Hills and high in the sky Nilssen could see all the way to the vitrified waste that had once been London. Rhys was with him but moodily avoided conversation.

With the western scarp of the Chilterns behind them, they slowed. The ground was now a mixture of gravels, sandstone and chalk, severely eroded into a maze of meandering gullies that converged to feed the wide, slow Thames whose muddy waters slid past the foot of Windhurst Hill in a broad brown band.

Nothing moved but the water and the few insects that coexisted with lichens and mosses along the river banks. Colonies of algae had established themselves on mud flats, and from the air these appeared as green smears running parallel with the flow of the water.

Otherwise the landscape was a jumble of browns and yellows, daubed here and there with red ocher.

Windhurst Hill was the highest and most northerly point of a ridge that bordered the eastern banks of the river as it flowed north from Reading. At the foot of the hill the Thames turned east towards Temly, where it again turned, southwards, past South Ellington. Gathering silt, it ultimately merged with the broad, lifeless mudflats of the Thames Estuary, where the North Sea began.

Odd, thought Nilssen, *how we still use the old place-names.*

The summit of the hill had been covered with a temporary Fregar dome three hundred meters across. It looked as if a giant blowing soap bubbles had carelessly allowed one to envelop the people and aircraft that were gathered around the tumulus and the nearby ruins of the Institute.

They landed outside the dome, disembarked, and passed quickly through an air lock. There was too much carbon dioxide in the open air for comfortable, unhurried breathing, and far too much radioactive dust for safety. Once inside the dome Nilssen released the breath he had been holding and looked around.

A parked aircraft the size of a large bus seemed the best place to go. Police agents loitering by the hatch informed him that Kwambe was inside. The men were respectful, which worsened Nilssen's apprehensions about what was to come; it was a pleasure to discover Kwambe and some of his technicians in the forward compartment and begin positive preparation for the outward journey. Shaking hands, they sat down around a large model of the neighborhood. Casually Rhys placed the real, folded timeshift belt in front of Nilssen.

"The time now," said Kwambe, "is 1108 hours of Thursday, September the eleventh, 2606. By noon we want to be ready to go." He tapped the model. "You should be familiar with that area by now, Jerlan. It's what we believe the country was like around here at the target date of late August 880 A.D. More vegetation, hence more surface soil and a generally smoother conformation. Animals too. Beware of large predators, especially wolves, bears, and men. There will also be poisonous plants like nettles and one type of venomous snake, the adder. Mercifully the British Isles were relatively free of dangerous species, so your biggest concern should be to avoid accidents and brushes with the natives.

"Remember, by the standards of the times this was a law-abiding area. But by our standards anything could happen. Stay awake. Keep in mind what your instructors taught you. And get back to the tumulus sharpish."

"I have a question," Nilssen said. "The closest settlement that's likely to have anyone with an education is some miles north—I mean, kilometers . . ."

"Miles," said Kwambe. "Stay in character. Don't worry, your subliminal indoctrination is liable to supervene occasionally."

"Miles, then. Anyway, it's a long walk. To get there I'll have to cross the river. What if the belt and cuffs get wet?"

"They're waterproof," said a technician before Rhys could open his mouth; the scientist satisfied himself with a nod of agreement. "And," added the technician, "the metal parts are bronze on a welded platinum base. Don't mistreat them too badly and they'll survive."

The prospect of getting soaked through swimming the river, even in August, was not a pleasurable one. Nevertheless he nodded. It would have to be done.

"Fine," said Kwambe. "A last reminder: when you leave us, you'll stand near the base of the tumulus so you won't have far to fall if you pop out on the slope.

This allows for the spreading and settling of the earth in it: It will have become lower and wider by today. We don't want you materializing in solid ground."

"What if I did?"

"One of two things," cut in Rhys. "Either your atoms would merge with those of the ground, or you'd be pushed aside into open air. There's no saying which applies."

There ensued a lull. Everyone appeared to be trying to recall what if anything had been forgotten. Finally Nilssen got to his feet.

"As far as I'm concerned," he declared, "I'd like to get on with it."

Sometime during the fourth century A.D. the friends of a dead barbarian warrior had raised a mound over his grave, high on a hill above the Thames. Grass had covered it. History had allowed the man to vanish into nameless oblivion while his tomb remained, slowly subsiding but never quite becoming overgrown as so many others had. Modern times had hedged and hemmed it in. A war had cleared the land. The mound survived, its chalk rubble core exposed to wind and sun, and to the rain that fell unhindered by overhanging trees, diminishing by degrees yet seemingly everlasting for all that.

One day men came. The empty peace of desolation was filled by the roar of their machines, by their coarse voices, by the rattle of drills that rent the mound, by the clank of metal sections being set upright in its eastern flank where the hilltop was flat, by the asthmatic whine of bolt drivers tightening the nuts that held more sections in place. And then a night of peace again before a noisy dawn.

"On the platform, please, Commissar," said a technician.

Instruments were clamped to the metal parts of his

belt and to the engraved cuffs he wore on his wrists and ankles. Fine adjustments were made.

One of the operators asked for a clamp to be tightened. When this had been done he shook his head. "No good," he said. "Too much mass. We can't launch him."

Rhys swore and examined the instruments. His mouth set in disgust. "Commissar, you have to shed six hundred grams of mass."

"How much is that in practical terms?" asked Nilssen, his mind full of archaic units of measurement thanks to his training.

Rhys shrugged. "One shoe, maybe . . . No, that's well over. What's in your pockets?"

"I haven't any pockets. Just this pouch with the oxygen mask for when I return—and I'm not leaving that behind." Rhys had at once reached for the pouch strapped to Nilssen's belt. Nilssen tightened his grip on it; he might well return to a place or time outside the temporary dome, in which case the day's supply of oxygen the rebreather apparatus could provide might save his life. "Besides," he said, "it only weighs a couple of pounds."

"That's a couple too many," replied Rhys. "What's that knife at your belt for?"

"Personal defense."

"Blow that. Leave it behind; you can defend yourself with the sword."

. The clock which Nilssen was to bury had been disguised as a battered sword that any Saxon might mistake for a workaday weapon. The blade was not quite what it seemed, however, for the edge it carried was keener and more durable than any possible to the ninth century's metallurgists, skilled though some were. The handle was a still greater work of deception: much of its mass was layers of lead and boron screening the clock and the micropile power source at its center. Nonetheless, it *had* been designed to serve as a weapon, should the occasion warrant, so Nilssen felt unable to disagree with Rhys's suggestion.

Detaching the sheathed knife from his belt, he tossed it to Rhys. At once the operator raised a hand. "That's it," he said.

The clamps were removed from belt and cuffs. Cables and personnel were withdrawn to the perimeter of the dome. Rhys waved. "Proceed!" he shouted.

His heart was pounding. His mouth was dry. His fingers fumbled in their search along the lower rim of the belt buckle.

Everyone was watching.

He found the three shallow recesses and placed fingers in two of them. The metal was cold to the touch; its bulk weighed heavily in his hand as he took firm hold of it. An inch from his index finger was the third recess, but his finger was shaking so violently, he kept missing it. So he held his breath, put his hands down by his sides, then tried again.

Deliberately, blanking his mind to the consequences, he filled the recesses in the proper order.

He fell.

Impressions of many events smote him in rapid succession—

—he hit the ground, which was covered in long grass. Trees were all around, their shadows cool and deep, rustling with leaf-sound.

—he rolled a short distance with the grass thrusting sharp, dry spokes into his face. His right hand slapped a thorny weed and he recoiled, only to land squarely on top of the plant—

—something stabbed his left foot.

His world seemed to shrink, focusing down upon pain, unbelievable pain that paralyzed his entire left leg. Involuntarily he let out a cry that emptied his lungs. Gasping with the agony, he lay still, tears forming in his tightly closed eyes.

As he waited the pain dulled. After a while he opened his eyes.

High overhead, against a blue sky divided by a single streak of cloud, beech trees tossed their branches in the breeze. The air was comfortably warm. The grass which his hands had clutched in his throes was rough to the touch and crackled as he rubbed it experimentally between his fingers. The heartbeat hammer-blows of pain in his foot became bearable.

He sat up to learn what had happened. There was a small hole in the upper surface of his shoe about as large as might have been made by a stiletto or gimlet. Blood had oozed from it and trickled down past his ankle. Already it had reached his heel. The foot itself throbbed.

A trap might make such a wound, he thought; but there was no sign of a trap. Once sprung, it surely would not remain hidden. Then he saw higher up the slope at the head of a swath of flattened vegetation a single tall spear of ryegrass, red with blood and broken near the top. *There* was the stiletto.

Materializing, his foot had chanced to form around the blade of grass, which had not been pushed aside. It had remained in place. In falling he had pulled his foot clear of the blade. The wound had remained.

Exploring the underside of his shoe with his fingertips, he found a short length of grass protruding from the sole. Taking a deep breath, he tugged out the fragment. The renewed stab of pain convinced him he was in no condition to travel. He would have to wait, several hours perhaps, before digging a hole and burying the sword. Afterward he would climb the mound and return home without seeking local corroboration of the date; the clock's elapsed time reading alone would have to satisfy Rhys.

With an effort he crawled to the foot of a nearby tree in whose shade he composed himself for rest.

Lying back, he forgot his wound as he absorbed the

atmosphere of tranquility the place possessed. He had grown up in the country. His late teens had been spent with the air force, first as a student pilot, later as a flying officer, moving between stations around the world. Having seen nature in many guises, he had learned a profound respect for the intricate systems of life the Earth had developed. The War had cleaned the slate again. In renewing his acquaintance with the natural world he felt like one who finds a diary or a letter written by a stranger, full of secrets and strange attitudes to life, then recognizes the work as his own. Yaer had spoken of a wall eighteen centuries high; in reviewing his years in the City Nilssen discovered a barrier no less formidable. There were walls everywhere, he saw.

Someone was talking quietly amongst the trees not far away. He heard phrases of Old English, spoken with a nasal twang not unlike the twenty-first century Northeastern accent of Tyne-and-Tees. At first he had difficulty following what was being said, before his training asserted itself and the gabble became clear speech. "—up here somewhere. Must be."

"I say it was the other way." A wheedling voice.

"So go search if you're that sure."

—grumbling—

"Stop complaining and keep your eyes open."

A branch swished as two large bodies went by beyond Nilssen's tree. They sounded like ordinary Saxon commoners, but there was an eagerness about them that Nilssen found unsettling, although he made allowances for their strange language and accents.

"I'm sure it was a man," said the first voice.

"Fox, I tell you."

"Hear me, Wulfstan, bloody fox doesn't make noises like that! Wrong time of year and day anyhow."

"Fat lot you know about foxes. Who was it speared his own pig?"

"Shut your face."

Their footsteps receded. Quickly Nilssen glanced about for denser cover in which to hide himself. Wounded, he stood no chance against two healthy men. If their intentions were friendly, well and good; yet he would rather risk losing their help than risk an assault. He began crawling towards a thicket of brambles a few yards off, at the edge of the tree line.

The searchers returned, still arguing.

"Leofric, why don't we just get on with hunting? My wife will skin *me* if I come back without something to show for the day."

"Because I don't fancy explaining to Henglaf why we walked away from what could just as easily be one of the enemy. And don't depend on him never finding out. When you're drunk you'll say anything. Still want to go?"

Wulfstan sounded subdued. "I suppose not."

"So keep your sword handy and watch those bushes. There could be a dozen Danes lying in wait for us."

"I wish you wouldn't talk like that."

"It's common sense . . . *La!* Look!"

They had halted out in the open. No doubt they had seen the flattened grass; dry, it would not have recovered from the trampling it had received. Nilssen carefully slid backwards on his stomach, keeping the brambles between himself and the two men. A profusion of beech saplings grew only a few yards away; with luck they would hide him.

Soon he was descending a slope thinly covered with short grass. Rolling onto his back, he tried to stand and discovered that he could limp along at a fair speed if he could endure the sharp jabs of pain from his left foot. Within seconds the saplings were behind him. On the far side numerous clumps of holly formed a screen, so that between them and the saplings was a natural aisle in which he promptly took refuge. Hearing no more from the searchers, he sat on an earth bank to recover his breath.

The silence persisted. Surveying his surroundings, he saw he was on the fringes of open beech woods that ran down the slope into the valley. The ground was matted with the dead leaves of past years. Sunlight spilled through gaps in the roof of living leaves, spattering branches and trunks with yellow and gold. There was a warm scent of summer. Somewhere a blackbird sang.

"In your opinion, Wulfstan," said a voice over his left shoulder, "what could a stranger be doing skulking in these woods?"

Without bothering to ascertain how far away the speaker was, Nilssen flung himself forwards onto his hands and knees, rolled and drew his sword. His back was against a substantial tree before either Saxon had moved. Gritting his teeth because of the pain in his foot, he faced his hunters.

His first impression was that they were a tough, dirty pair of thugs. Leofric, the one who had spoken and whose mouth hung open to expose a row of discolored teeth, was about as tall as any man of the City. He overtopped Wulfstan by a whole head. Otherwise their build and attire were similar. Their clothes seemed to be of patched, dun-colored wool. Wulfstan wore a badly scarred leather jerkin over a homespun shirt. Their dark hair hung in matted hanks to their shoulders and partially obscured their eyes. Their beards and generous moustaches likewise were unkempt and filthy.

Leofric's eyes flashed white as he glanced at his friend. "What d'you think? An honest man? Eh, Wulfstan?"

Wulfstan's head shifted fractionally from side to side. "Can't be, not so far from the highway. Not so much as a halloo from him either. Must be up to no good."

"My feelings exactly. Well, fellow, care to explain yourself?"

An idiom from the past intruded itself into Nilssen's frantic thoughts: *a hanging jury*. These two were not interested in guilt; they merely planned to kill him quietly. Leofric's avaricious admiration of the clock-sword suggested a motive. The man's workmanlike grasp on his own sword suggested intent.

"I got lost," Nilssen extemporized while reposition-ing himself so as to contrive a clear arc of defense from the holly thicket on his left around to that on his right. He rested his sword arm on his right knee and looked directly at Leofric. "Are you men from around these parts? Can you show me the way to a village?"

Wulfstan thrust a stumpy finger into his right ear and scraped out some wax which he rubbed between thumb and forefinger. "Maybe," he said noncommit-tally. "Depends if it's worth our while."

"I can't offer much," said Nilssen. Their eyes grew intent. "I'm not rich. But your efforts won't go totally unrewarded."

The men hardly blinked an eyelid, yet Nilssen sensed their purpose hardening. Leofric smiled, say-ing, "Yes, I know, God will bless us for our charity to strangers. . . . Wulfstan, you take the righthand side. We move together."

"You're making a terrible mistake!" Nilssen shouted, hoping there might be other folk nearby who would come and investigate the noise. "I'm on the king's business!"

For that lie an ordinary citizen might expect to be put to death. *Small change,* he thought; he hoped it would buy him the opportunity of making an escape into the open, preferably to the summit of the tu-mulus, so he could risk using his timeshift belt. A shift where he was could well drop him into one of the erosion gulleys that rift the future hillside. The fall was a likely to be fatal as a sword in his belly.

Leofric's left hand went up sharply. Wulfstan halted.

"A king's messenger?" asked Leofric suspiciously. "You bear proof?"

Wulfstan's eyes flickered between his partner and Nilssen. "It's a trick," he said. "I say he's a foreigner. Listen to his accent. Come on, one dead Dane more or less won't be missed."

"I want to see his warrant," insisted Leofric. "Fellow, this is your last chance. Prove who you are. Or else."

"For a start, I'm no Dane," said Nilssen. Suddenly inspired, he asked, "Can you read?"

"Me?" said Leofric. "Don't be bloody funny." Seeing Nilssen turn to Wulfstan, he added, "Nor him. We're warriors, not canting priests."

"Too bad," said Nilssen. "My warrant is a written document."

"Let's see it."

"But you said you—"

"Hand it over." Leofric's mouth was set so that the lips were almost puckered; his words emerged without feeling.

With as much show of ceremony as he could muster, Nilssen slid his left hand into the inside pocket of his tunic, where he had a collection of maps and fact sheets relating to local politics and history. By touch he selected a false personal biography encoded as groups of numbers. It had been meant as a prompt sheet for his cover story in the event of capture; as he threw it to Leofric, Nilssen trusted that its appearance would be sufficiently impressive.

The hunter picked it up and shook off the leaf mold that adhered to it. Turning it over several times, he frowned, then gave it to Wulfstan who repeated the examination.

"Well?" said Leofric to his partner.

"I'm not sure," said the smaller man. "There's no seal. But that's good paper. Funny stuff, actually . . ."

And he scrutinized it. Nilssen watched him hold the sheet of thin material up to the light, then run a finger over the print. "Smooth. They say the Pope uses parchment like this."

Leofric expelled a hearty belly laugh. "You'll have him claiming he's a papal legate, next. . . . Let's stop this mucking about."

"That's queer," remarked Wufstan suddenly as if he had not heard. "It's falling to bits." He flicked the paper with a finger, which punched a clean-sided hole. With a small cry of revulsion he flung it from him. Horrified, Nilssen saw the paper flutter downwards, breaking into fragments that dwindled like snowflakes in a draft of hot air. None survived to reach the ground.

Both Wulfstan and Leofric stared at the brown mat of dead leaves into which the paper seemed to have passed like smoke. All at once Nilssen comprehended the full import of Rhys's warning about remaining within the field of influence of the timeshift belt and its associated cuffs: if he strayed outside it, he would vanish as the paper had . . . and arrive in the future, smeared across time like the wedge of aluminum scrap.

Wulfstan, on the other hand, appeared to have deduced a different explanation for the phenomenon. Grabbing Leofric by the arm, he tried to drag him away, saying urgently:

"I don't like this. Let's go—while we can."

Leofric shook him off roughly. "Go? Have you lost your wits? We've gone too far already."

Wulfstan's eyes were wide. His voice was shaky. "By God in heaven, Leofric, have you not yet realized what we're up against? This is witchcraft!"

Leofric regarded his partner contemptuously. Then he looked at Nilssen again. "All the more reason to kill it," he said. Slowly, placing one foot cautiously ahead of the other to avoid slipping on the leaves, he advanced down the bank.

Nilssen braced himself. *What a bloody, futile waste,* went a bitterly resentful thought in the back of his mind as he automatically hoisted his sword to block the first stroke.

Sparks showered from the clashing metal. His wrist turned numb from the blow. Leofric sprang aside. Light winked on his blade. Nilssen warded off the second vicious down-cut, but he missed the return. Leofric's arm seemed to twist and dart upwards past his guard. A sensation of coldness brushed his upper swordarm; his tunic twitched open, gaping like a greedy, bloody mouth around the wound which appeared in his flesh. Suddenly Nilssen found it difficult to keep his forearm up, for his biceps muscle no longer responded to his demands on it. He realized he was being slaughtered gracelessly and felt sickly ashamed to have failed so easily.

The Saxon took his time in returning. Wulfstan still dithered fearfully high up the bank, his own unbloodied sword hanging slackly by his side.

Nilssen noticed that his right arm was growing damp. When he examined it, he found a dark red stain below the cut in the tunic. The wound itself was choked with glistening gore. As a gesture in the face of certain extinction he reached across and took hold of the sword with his left hand, then waited for Leofric's attack. His foot hurt. He knew he could only wait, lying at the foot of the tree, for them to finish him.

"Make peace with your god," said Leofric suddenly.

This, then, is my end. He tried to pray; but he failed to find any sort of comfort in the God of his childhood. Their relationship had never been, for him, a rewarding one: conventional acts of worship, dutiful obeisance at the prescribed times before socially approved altars. Unlike Rhys, he had never even learned to believe. So instead he resorted to the hope that Maia Kim would sense when to write him off as lost and that the City would dare to send another venturer after him. Then, too, the aggressive fatalism of the Cult of Shazol which preached noble defiance of the inevitable and was espoused by people like Yaer, had never appealed to him either. Rather than resign himself to the workings of nature, he raised his eyes to meet those of Leofric and said quietly, "I am ready."

The muscles of his left hand felt weak. Angrily he gripped the hilt of the sword still tighter and tensed his whole body for the lunge he intended to make when Leofric came close enough.

However, the Saxon merely circled back and forth beyond his reach, studying him.

"No fighter, are you?" he jeered.

"I told you, I'm a king's messenger."

"Might have been, once. But where's your warrant now, hey?"

"Does writing on paper matter so much?"

"Not a lot. Never had time for it."

"So you'd have killed me anyhow?"

Leofric nodded. "A man has to live," he said, apparently without ironic intent.

"If you let me go, I'll see you're well rewarded."

This time Leofric shook his head. "I think not."

"My friends have gold."

"And rope."

There was a lull in the talking. The Saxon's shoes rustled the leaves as he prowled around. The wound in Nilssen's arm began to ache as it cooled and he realized that this was what the killer was waiting for. Once weakened by loss of blood and the effects of shock, Nilssen would be easy prey.

Wulfstan stirred. Sheathing his sword, he said, "Leofric, I'm going.'

"You'll stop where you are."

The smaller man bit his lower lip and looked unhappy. "Someone might come."

"Then they'll not find a living witness who'll swear against us." His face grew hard. "Fellow, put aside your sword and I'll make it clean for you."

"Go to hell," said Nilssen, meaning every word.

Leofric's cheeks creased in a gap-toothed grin. "Well —" he began. Abruptly he lunged. His sword arrowed for Nilssen's chest. With such short warning Nilssen had time only to begin his own counterstroke.

The Saxon's sword tip did not at first strike flesh, for Nilssen had jerked himself aside far enough for the other's aim to be spoiled. Instead the belt was hit: the hard blow to his midriff made Nilssen gasp. Simultaneously, Leofric's eyes widened. His hair seemed to move of its own accord, while his mouth opened and he grunted in surprise.

The few seconds respite this granted Nilssen allowed him to stand before he had to defend himself again. This time, through a thickening haze which rendered all about him darkly obscure, Nilssen felt the sword strike home.

It seemed the blade only touched his chest and rested there. But he knew this was not so, that it had cut through cloth and flesh, had scraped against bone as as it pressed home through ribs into his heart . . .

It seemed the blade only touched his chest and darted away again. He found himself falling backward through the bushes. There was a moment of darkness before he saw the trees above him again, dim in the gray-blue haze; then he fell on his back on the ground and rolled a short way. Sitting up, he searched for the sword but realized he had dropped it and was now defenseless.

So he got to his feet and began limping up the hillside towards the tumulus, hoping to reach it before the two Saxons traced his escape route through the holly bushes or made a detour around them.

Short of breath, he crested the hill. There were no sounds of pursuit. No sounds at all, in fact; not a bird, nor rustle of leaf, nor creak of branch. Even his own labored breathing was strangely attenuated.

The air had grown thinner. He had at most a couple of minutes in which to mount the tumulus and re-activate the belt before anoxia rendered him unconscious.

At the summit of the mound he nearly blacked out but managed to press his fingers into the belt slots in the correct code.

He waited.

Dimly he perceived that nothing had changed. The slaty light persisted. There was still the blurred suggestion of a wood around him.

Then he saw that the shadows of the trees were moving. Convinced that this must be an hallucination induced by oxygen starvation, he opened the pouch at his belt and fitted the breathing apparatus over his face.

At once he was able to think clearly. Shortly afterwards he noticed that he had no shadow.

The dead silence around him . . . the abnormal blueness of the daylight . . . the blur which fogged his perception of the world . . . these forced him to admit to himself that the impact of Leofric's sword on the belt had thrown it into a functional mode that even Rhys had not envisaged. And whereas Rhys might have guessed at a remedy, Nilssen was helpless. Again and again he tried to reactivate the belt, and failed.

With time to think he began to notice other changes in the world. The sky was now black, though the sun still shone brightly—too brightly. Furthermore, the sun was moving, slowly yet alarmingly fast. And his foot no longer hurt so severely when he put his weight on it, for his weight seemed less. Though he was convinced that the effect was illusory, he felt like an astronaut walking on the moon, possessing mass but robbed of weight.

Bewildered, he still retained his wits. There was no longer any advantage in remaining on the tumulus; to do so was to invite rediscovery by his attackers. So he reentered the shelter of the trees where the shadows now were like night to his obscured vision, and made his way back to where he had left the two Saxons. They had the sword; if he could scratch a message on its rustless blade and bury it, rescuers from the future would know of his predicament and how to find him.

He came upon the Saxons crouched over something in the aisle of trees. They were moving quickly, as if frantic to be gone. Nilssen wondered if some hapless passerby had investigated at the crucial moment and been killed for his curiosity. If so, he had much for which to thank the stranger.

He sidled around to a better vantage point. Wulfstan was wrestling with the man's belt while Leofric unfastened his shoes. Together they rolled the corpse onto its back. And Nilssen saw his own dead face.

Cold, weak, sweating, he tried to lean against a tree. It would not support him; like two shadows meeting, he and it passed through each other. There was no sensation of contact or coexistence, only an eyeblink of lightlessness while his head was inside the trunk, followed by a languid tumble down the slope beyond.

Coming to rest no more than half a dozen paces from the corpse robbers, he recovered the breath that had been knocked out of him by the fall. Hard at work, they had not heard him. Wulfstan had removed the belt and was fondling the plastic and false bronze of which it was made. Leofric spoke to him angrily; his lips fluttered, and Nilssen heard, very faintly, a high-pitched squeak: *"Leave that. Help me strip him."*

They pulled off the shoes and tunic and were starting to tug at the shirt when Wulfstan, who was holding the corpse up in a sitting position, let out a scream as shrill as a whistle and backed off.

Leofric's head jerked up. The corpse slumped against the tree and disintegrated. Pieces of pulpy meat peeled from crumbling bones. The head fell off and rolled away, deliquescing and leaving a slimy trail that quickly seemed to evaporate. Wulfstan's eyes bulged; his hands flapped before his face. He laughed hysterically until Leofric struck him so hard that he stumbled across to the earth bank, where he sat down with a bump.

The men were still for a second. Leofric said something in a falsetto chatter. Like marionettes jumping on strings, they picked up the belt and sword and, after the briefest of arguments over who should have what, scuttled away down the hill.

There was little left of the body—*his own body,* Nilssen thought with a shudder—by the time he reached it. The flesh had melted. The bones had the wispy appearance of spun sugar. The clothes were a few rotten swatches.

The cuffs, however, had survived. They, like the belt and sword, embodied their own stabilizers and would last as long as their circuits operated, which might give them a life of a thousand years or more. He tried to pick them up; but his ghostly fingers might as well have clutched at air.

Worse, while he stayed crouched over his own remains, the light shifted. Shadows glided whereas earlier they had crept along. Time was speeding up for him.

Was it possible, he wondered, that the belt in the "real" world still exerted an influence over his atoms? Or was there some tenuous relationship between that belt and the copy he wore, a freakish kinship that might still save him? Anything was possible, he decided: while he was near the real belt, time was normal for him, but when he and it were far apart, his body traveled forward into the future ever faster, like the atoms of the vanished body that had lain at his feet. The difference between the two bodies was that his, the live one, still wore a full set of stabilizers.

There was no logic but the logic of survival. If in this phantasmal world some fact seemed true, he would take advantage of it. If the other belt controlled him still, he would try to get it back in the hope that its intact mechanism would pull him into reality. Then he might put it on. Afterward . . . He would not plan beyond that time. It might take him home safely; it might scatter him throughout all of space-time. At least it gave him a purpose. The first goal was to track down his own murderers.

CHAPTER FOUR

Clouds boiled in the sky. Their fugitive shadows flickered across the open countryside before, gathering briefly against the sunset, they fell into darkness as the night came down. The sun, rushing headlong at the horizon, vanished. The moon sprang up and sailed through a sky resplendent with wheeling pinpoint lights.

Nilssen could accept that the lights were stars, yet their constellations were strange to him: with the acceleration of time dim red sparks blazed blue-white; while others, formerly brilliant, shaded into the invisible regions beyond the ultraviolet.

As he picked his way down the hill towards the Thames he found his insubstantial state both a help and a hazard. There was no fear of his blundering into trees or being savaged by the wild beasts he had been warned of. Instead he quickly learned that carelessness in choosing his footing could lead to serious falls.

The ephemeral life of the countryside could not touch him. The earth itself, more permanent and solid, could. Often it was difficult to tell which surfaces were safe and which were not, for his grip on them seemed dependent on their composition as well as their steepness. The usual rules hardly applied. Chalk beds and soil rich in humus were like slush, treacherous going, whereas the older sandstone outcrops were usually firm. Rhys, Nilssen reflected grimly, would

have been ecstatic at such an opportunity to test his
theories about entropic levels.

Night became day in an eyeblink-dawn that brought
shadows swirling from every tree and thicket. Not far
away the dark metallic gleam of water waited in the
bluish light of morning. Beyond its further bank the
wooded foothills of the Chilterns-proper were alive
with moving flecks—cloud shadow, rain, or sweep of
wind through the treetops; he could not say which.
Time was racing ever faster as he dallied. The night
returned; and swiftly after it came the dawn.

Tentatively he placed a foot on the surface of the
water. It bore his slight weight. Gaining courage, he
walked out from the bank a few paces and discovered
that if he kept moving he could treat the water as dry
land. Much heartened, he crossed quickly to the northern side and ascended the gentle slope in the direction
of the Saxon settlement he would one day, somewhen,
know as Laffingham.

His extraordinary crossing of the river had, he
realized, left him emotionally untouched. True, it had
conveniently proved that he was freer than he had
first imagined. However, he was not moved to wonder
at it. His entire world was out of joint. Walking on
water was no more astonishing than his fundamental
predicament.

The world grew older by several weeks before he
gained the level ground that topped off the first ridge.
Autumn was largely lost on him, for the time dilation
effect was now so severe that the warmth of the
ground gave it a false reddish hue. Natural colors were
wildly distorted, well on their way to becoming soft
X-rays; the weird colors which replaced them lent the
land the appearance of hot metal.

He worried about this: sunlight was filtered of most
of its dangerous rays by the Earth's atmosphere; but
the acceleration of time had caused all wavelengths

to shorten, so that infrared became ultraviolet or worse. Cosmic radiation too would be intensified. Within a few subjective days he must expect the onset of burns and skin rashes.

While he had hurried uphill away from the Thames, he had tried to estimate how far out of phase with the real world he had slipped. Days and nights combined lasted only six or seven minutes, an hour after he had set out; halfway to Laffingham, scarcely another hour later, this period had shortened to some three minutes. Like a vast wheel, with the sun, moon, and stars set in it, the sky rolled by ever faster overhead. Incipient dizziness obliged him to walk with his face downcast so he might not see it; then he had to narrow his eyes to slits to shut out the glare of the ground.

However, it grew dark. Winter had come: snow, cold yet glowing dully, mantled all in sullen red. The leafless trees were wisps of hot smoke to his perceptions. The sun, low in the south, barely skimmed the ridge of Windhurst Hill before diving out of sight. He could safely look up at the sky, for now it was frequently masked by writhing masses of shadowy red storm clouds.

But his days continued to shorten. After four hours he descended into the valley of the Wye where the Saxon settlement lay, only to find his progress impeded by the need to pause every ninety seconds for a minute of darkness. His continual fear was that he might have come to the wrong place, or that he might arrive too late and find that the robbers had moved on, leaving him to hurtle helplessly into the future and ultimate dissolution in the twenty-seventh century.

At last he encountered a road and followed it, hoping it served the village. Hardly a track, it was deep in mud. Every few minutes another storm re-

freshed its snow cover, after which the wayfarers that
passed him unseen would beat it into slush again.

Road, river, and valley divided together at a fork.
By now the Wye was only a stream; lower down, where
it spilled into the Thames at Temly, it had grown into a small river. Nilssen studied the wooded hillsides,
aware that the village had to be nearby, and detected
a brighter glow partway up the ridge dividing the two
new valleys. He blessed the color-shift and began to
climb the slope.

By the proximity of dense woods and the village's
small size he guessed it had not been long established.
A generation or two at most. The clearing in which
it had been built still displayed the stumps of huge
trees. Likewise the earthen bank topped with a wood-
en palisade looked too new. And when he walked
straight through the barred gates into the circular
enclosure, he found twenty-eight thatched huts with
ample space for as many again.

The spare ground was partially occupied by stacked
hay and some animal pens; but toward the center of
the village was a larger elongated building that could
only be the hall. While he was studying this, the sky,
the ground, and all around him darkened. Suddenly
he could see people as they went about their business.

They were real people, dashing about but nevertheless visible. At once he knew he had come to the
right place and that the belt at least was nearby. So
much the better if Leofric and Wulfstan still held it
and the sword. The encounter would give him pleasure.

The hall, if anywhere, was the place to find them
once darkness fell. That would be in a matter of hours,
unless he shortened the period by leaving the village
for a while. Direct confrontation at one of the evening gatherings of the menfolk would catch them at
their weakest, loaded with the loot they would be
sure to flaunt in public, and exposed to the censure

of their fellows. No man alive would dare touch an
apparition such as Nilssen knew he must seem. Their
superstitious dread ensured their cooperation; once
he had his hands on belt and sword, he could expect
to leave unmolested. The two hunters would not have
the nerve to attack him a second time, especially in
the presence of witnesses.

Some of the sick dread of the future which had been
haunting him faded.

Time had slowed sufficiently for him to be able to
see animals as well as people as they flitted along the
muddy paths of the village. A dog was visible as a
blur on the end of a rope, leaping about and yapping
furiously as he walked past. In response to the racket
three men wrapped in furs popped their heads out of
the hall's main doors, saw nothing to attract their
interest, and ducked back inside. Nilssen followed
them.

A small blue-white wood fire was burning at one
end of a long, shallow pit dug along the center of the
hall. Flat platforms of earth built up around the sides
of the single room were clear of furniture, although
bedding rolls were heaped against one end wall between the doors that led through to the kitchens and
housecarls were beginning to erect trestle tables in
preparation for the evening meal.

Food, thought Nilssen. *Charred, salty meat, some
gritty bread, some bad beer . . .*

He discovered that he was hungry.

Furthest from the kitchens and nearest the fire
about a dozen men were gathered in a tight group.
Two were playing a board game involving dice and
a square grid of forty-nine holes holding pegs. The
onlookers frequently broke into cheers when one of
the players made a move, at which the other would
scowl and mutter at them.

Nilssen allowed himself to be distracted from his
explorations for only a minute. His murderers were

not amongst the group, so these men were of only casual interest to him. He left by way of the nearest wall to begin a methodical search of the villlage.

Only once in the next few hours did he sense the critical nearness of the belt, when momentarily the huts and people almost lost their half-real appearance. But when he tried to break through a wall to pursue the belt, it resisted him. Forced to detour, he saw the world turn gray and vague again, and he heard the sounds of life fade away to a muffled, high-pitched murmur.

Nonetheless, the near-miss encouraged him.

Snow whirled about the rooftops of the village in flurries. It drifted into corners, spattered rough-hewn doors with white streaks, skittered across frozen paths, piled itself against walls. Thatch caught and clung to it. The night was of snow, the earth of ice, and human-kind lay trapped between the two. And even Nilssen, cocooned in immateriality, responded to the iciness of the season.

All gentleness had drained from his mind as he strode towards the hall. He went boldly, wanting to be seen and heard. The wooden doors of the hall, dark and fingered with snow smears, fell behind him as he walked through them into the unnaturally yellow fire-light within. When the bard and the whole assembled company turned to stare and fearful speechlessness replaced their laughter, he tasted a savage jubilation. Not ten feet to his left sat Leofric, with Wulfstan one place beyond him. Their faces were a joy to behold.

He almost heard the gasp which Wulfstan drew in sharply. The man's mouth dropped open. Ale dribbled down his chin into his beard as his mug hand shook. A palsy of terror seized him as he dropped the mug and crossed himself repeatedly.

The cooler Leofric too lost his nerve, shielding his

face with one arm and pushing himself back as far as he could go on the bench.

The tableau broke suddenly. The bard, who stood hard against the high table, shrilled:

"Who are you? What do you want with us?"

Nilssen spun round to face the man. Angrily he pointed at the cowering pair and yelled, "My property! I want it back; return it to me—now!"

There was an instant reaction from Wulfstan, who leaped up, screaming in a falsetto voice, *"God save me: the devil is come."*

Leofric clamped a hand on his wrist and dragged him back to his seat without saying a word. His eyes, wide and staring, did not stray from Nilssen.

The man at the high table whom Nilssen presumed was the local overlord bobbed to his feet. He squeaked, *"What manner of spirit are you, Wanderer? Are you good, or are you evil? Speak, in Jesus's Name."*

Nilssen decided that the use of melodrama might well impress the locals and aid his cause considerably. Adopting a dramatic stance, he said as rapidly and as loudly as he could through his rebreather mask:

"I am he whom Leofric and Wulfstan slew upon the hill. South of the river there stands a lofty mound, the resting place of a great warrior. This worthy grave they desecrated by murder and by theft. I am here to avenge that vile deed and recover the goods which they stole from me. Give me what I ask and allow me to depart in peace, and it shall not go ill with you."

"Spirit, I hear your words but they confuse me. That barrow is a heathen grave. How can God care so much for one such as he that you should be sent to us?"

The chieftain's face was pale and he had a tight hold on the edge of the table. Nilssen suddenly pitied him. No leader had ever had to cope with such a situation; it was to the man's credit that he could stay and talk when it was obvious everyone in the hall wanted to run.

"God cares for all men," he said, replying in kind. "But I am come on my own behalf. I seek the belt and the sword which were taken from me—and which those two men are wearing even now." He gestured towards the murderers.

"*Leofric . . . Wulfstan . . . Stand forward,*" the chieftain commanded.

Haltingly Leofric preceded Wulfstan around to the open space before the high table. As Wulfstan approached, Nilssen sensed his contact with reality strengthening: his weight returned, and with it the pain in his foot; the taste of the air from his rebreather changed as it began to draw in atmospheric oxygen; colors became richer.

In a deeper voice the chieftain said at almost normal speed:

"This is a heavy charge. And an unusual oath-bringer, to say the least." He eyed Nilssen. "Leofric, where did you get that sword?"

Quickly, almost too quickly, Leofric answered, "It was an heirloom from an uncle of mine. He died last autumn of wounds received in the fighting against the Danes two years ago."

"I see," said the chieftain. His gaze rested on Leofric for a long time. As local justice of the law and leader of the community he would have a shrewd idea of where guilt lay. The trouble was, he would also be obliged by law and custom to prove his suspicions. "And you, Wulfstan, what about that belt?"

"Oh, I bought it," said Wulfstan offhandedly. Leofric's face seemed to stiffen for a second. By contrast the chieftain's expression relaxed.

"Did you?" he said. "And of course you have witnesses?"

"Ah . . ." Wulfstan showed dismay. "That is, I bought it from Leofric."

Leofric's nostrils widened fractionally. Otherwise he remained immobile.

"And no doubt he will so swear. . . . And the stoat will vouch for the fox when the chickens are stolen. . . . Listen, you two: you've got an unhealthy reputation at the best of times; your oath-worthiness is very much in question." He held up his right hand, whose thumb and forefinger were bent round into a nearly closed circle. "*This* much protects you from the noose. So pick your words very carefully."

Nilssen began to see how far the law was being distorted to appease him. They were terrified. Leofric and Wulfstan were as good as condemned.

Suddenly Leofric shoved Wulfstan aside. Drawing the clock-sword from his scabbard, he offered it to his chief hilt first. "My lord Henglaf," he said, "examine this sword. See, it's of Saxon crafting all through. This . . . creature . . . speaks with a foreign accent. How could the sword have been his?"

"That's it," chimed in Wulfstan eagerly. "Can't possibly belong—"

Leofric slapped him hard across the mouth. They glared at each other while Henglaf looked on, smiling indulgently.

At length the chieftain said:

"Wulfstan."

The man looked up. There was a fleck of blood on his lower lip which he licked at slowly. Henglaf said:

"Wulfstan, will you swear the Oath?"

Casting a panicked glance at Nilssen, Wulfstan nodded his head jerkily. "I wi . . ." A sob broke from him; his gaze dropped to the rushes on the floor. "Lord Henglaf, I cannot."

"Why? Have you then a confession to make?"

Leofric seized Wulfstan's shoulders and spat into his face. "Cretin!" he screamed. "You've killed us both!" His right hand flashed to the empty scabbard at his waist, groped there for a second, then fell to his side. A look of resignation made his face sag.

Picking up the sword from where he had placed it on the table, Henglaf studied it without speaking. He hefted it, testing its balance. "Spirit," he said, "your case would seem proven. . . . As and when you wish it, we of Henglafingasham shall return these grave goods to their proper place. I ask only that you leave us quickly. . . . And give a good report of us as you journey back to Hel or Paradise, whichever God has ordained for you."

Nilssen bowed. "Henglaf," he said without mockery, "you are a better man than I thought at first. Give me the sword and belt now and let these men go free; and I shall be satisfied."

"You are welcome to what is your own," said Henglaf. "As to releasing these two I have no power to make that bargain with you. They have broken the law of God and of Man by murder and by treachery. For either they would have to die."

"They must not be harmed!" Nilssen shouted, envisaging the chain of repercussions that would stretch into the future: children not born, deeds not done . . .

"I am the king's high-reeve," said Henglaf. "His law prevails here."

Suddenly Wulfstan let out a manic scream and bolted for the exit. While he was heaving the doors aside, a hush settled on the hall, for Henglaf had raised the sword as though it were a dagger. As the doors swung open, he threw it.

The blade thudded into Wulfstan's back a handsbreadth below his left shoulder blade. A sort of sad sigh escaped, and the man stumbled out into the swirling snow with the blood trickling from the wound, the sword waggling in his back like some obscene banner. As if in reply, everyone in the room seemed to cry out. As one man they leaped to their feet and stormed the doors in pursuit of the dying

Wulfstan. Seeing his chance, Leofric bounded ahead of them.

Nilssen felt the world slipping from him once more. The firelight took on a yellow cast; the men streaming past him accelerated sharply, becoming blurred by speed; sounds turned shrill. His pent-up frustration voiced itself in an involuntary cry as he ran into the night of driving snow.

The quest was hopeless. Losing his way at once, he wandered from end to end of the village, never quite sure where he was, blinded by the darkness, bemused by stray lights, by the snow, and by his own isolation in unreality. When the sun glided into view, he knew he would never find the belt in the village, as it had been clear that Henglaf's one wish was to return sword and belt to the mound so as to be rid of his unwelcome visitor. Up on Windhurst Hill was where he had to go, another four-and-a-half-hour journey at whose end lay no promise of success such as had formerly sustained him.

So because there was no alternative, Nilssen began to walk south.

On the return time regained its exaggerated forward momentum. Winter had gone when he regained the summit of the tumulus. New grass was sprouting. Spring was covering the traces of recent digging. Time slowed for him but did not become normal. He stood awhile, taking in the sight of green shoots thrusting themselves through the earth. A thistle raised its bristling head above the ground. Midsummer had come before he could accept what had been done to him.

Henglaf had caused the belt and sword to be buried in the mound in the mistaken belief that they belonged there. No more than a few feet of earth separated them from Nilssen, but that was enough to shut him out: the soil was too tightly bound to itself for his ghostly fingers to move it.

It was such a simple trap, so innocently laid. Two—no, three—men had died to set it; and shortly, in a millennium or so, one of those men would die again. Reconciling himself to the prospect, he took a walk along the ridge, more relaxed now that he knew what must happen.

Summer green, autumn brown, winter white: he saw the trees changing and imagined what they would be like in the real, slow world. The moving sky no longer bothered him as it had a few hours earlier. At last, freed of his urgent quest, he could find beauty in its black, star-speckled span.

Days shortened to seconds. The sun streamed into a ribbon of light arcing from southeast to southwest that rose and fell with the seasons. Dimly interlaced with it as another band of pulsing luminosity was the moon. Together these marked out the years, the decades, the centuries.

He came to where the Institute's new laboratories would be built and stood contemplating the ghosts of vegetation struggling for life. Trees shot up, with lowlier plant forms foaming about their roots, spread their branches, thickened, became still briefly, then toppled to become crumbling lumps amongst the evanescent surface cover.

A path blinked into existence along the ridge. Side tracks flickered alongside it. Suddenly there was a road whose color changed in patches as the surface fill was varied from decade to decade. Looking back towards the tumulus, Nilssen saw that a small church had appeared beside it and that a low stone wall enclosed both within a churchyard. He decided to investigate.

Before he reached the church it was replaced by a finer building, the beginnings of Windhurst Abbey, showing that he had reached the eleventh century already. Outbuildings sprang up and were incorporated into the main structure.

Then it was a ruin: the Reformation had happened.

Nilssen guessed that he had been wandering the hilltop for almost four hours. The gauge on his re-breather indicated a reserve of twelve hours, so he would live to the end.

A memory brushed against his awareness. Clutching at it before it deserted him, he considered its potential. The somber fog of fatalism into which his mind had plunged was lit by the glimmer of a plan. The mound had survived everything, The War included. That being so, the belt too should survive. . . . No, he had to recover the belt before then else the radioactivity would kill him. Besides, he had still to penetrate the soil.

There came to him a mental image of Saxon grave goods recovered from such a mound. The great age of methodical barrow digging had begun with the nine-teenth century; prior to those times barrows had been shunned by superstitious folk or ignored, except by a few more enterprising souls intent on grubbing out loot.

He ran to the tumulus to be sure it had not yet been tampered with; then he realized he would never see any short-lived marks of excavation unless he stayed near the belt to slow himself, which meant that to catch the signs he would have to risk running out of oxygen.

The ruins were repaired while he pondered this dilemma. Now a grand country house commanded the view across the valley. Down by the river the market town of Bissam had grown from nothing to a sprawl of brickwork and was still engulfing the riverside meadows of the seventeenth century. The sturdy iron bridge appeared; broader roads swept in from north and south to join it. The eighteenth century began to grow old.

He weighed the risks. Anoxia or worse.

Climbing the side of the tumulus, he sat down to wait for the archaeologists to visit Windhurst Hill. Time passed more slowly this close to the belt, so that he was free to appreciate the evolution of the formal gardens on the river side of Windhurst House as successive generations of gardeners expressed the tastes of their equally transitory masters in floral square and topiary beast. By degrees fashions changed; by the mid-nineteenth century, when the owners of Windhurst House were at their wealthiest, the gardens were abundantly embellished. An avenue of cedars arose along the ridge towards Temly ending at a woodland folly in the Doric style, an outbuilding later used by the Institute as a store for dangerous chemicals. The rose gardens Nilssen had known in a much reduced form were established, enclosing the House on its north and east sides. To the south between the old churchyard and the main road an area was walled in and planted with vegetables for the kitchen.

He readied himself for a dash up the mound, sensing that the moment was near.

There was the briefest of warnings. One year the overgrowth of tree branches and elder was cut back; winter came, followed by spring; and trenches sliced into the mound. In the seconds remaining to him he had to reach the top to be near the belt. With a desperate effort he struggled up the mushy slope. Every step made his time sense reel: colors fluttered across the visible spectrum; the sky rolled slower by jerks until the sun showed itself as a hurtling disc and the individual stars traced their own arcs. Then as he reached the summit, a hole opened before him. He fell, heavily, awkwardly, into the top of the mound and struck his head on the handle of an upright shovel . . .

Night. Cool, dark night.

Dizzy from the blow, he was still able to revel in

the sensations of renewed contact with the outside world. Chuckling, he hugged the offending shovel. Stones and earth had a marvelously fine texture; they left the fingers gritty and smelled of pungent mysteries. Too, there were blades of grass and dead leaves in the hole to be touched. And a hapless worm which he fondled with shaking hands as he giggled with hysterical relief.

At length he sobered enough to survey the hole. The belt had to be so near as to be touching him practically; yet it was not fastened about his waist, which was where it had to be to help him. Standing with the aid of the shovel, for his foot was again hurting, he used the implement to poke around in the compacted chalky rubble that formed the floor of the trench. At one end of the hole a tarpaulin had been propped up on poles as a weather screen over the funerary remains of the mound's original tenant, so he worked outwards from these, estimating by the apparent weight of the shovel how close he was to the belt. His gashed right arm too was aching now that the damaged biceps had more strain on it, so his progress was slow.

Nevertheless, within five minutes he had identified the best place to dig and he set to, using one hand and one foot. The rubble had packed almost solid in the thousand years since Henglaf's men had dumped it back into its hole. An extra difficulty was that he had to dig with caution lest he smash the belt with the heavy iron blade of the shovel and repeat the damage Leofric had done to the one he was wearing.

As he dug he could not avoid feeling that he was embroiled in some insane dream that would end at any second. Hitherto he had been too preoccupied with immediate practicalities to bother with mere philosophical niceties. Now that success seemed imminent, his relaxed mind could question the likelihood of what had befallen him. No one could see himself killed and yet rejoin the living world. Where had the material for his copied body and clothes come from? From his "real" body? From nowhere?

He dug and probed and prised and decided he could afford to leave Rhys to do the explaining if they ever met again.

After about a quarter of an hour he found it.

The belt's condition was amazingly good, although the artificial bronze effect had corroded away and the ornamental studs were reduced to green smears in the plastic. The slab-shaped platinum boxes were sound, and even the mark left by Leofric's sword was clearly visible on the control panel. His fingers weak with apprehension, he strapped the belt around his waist over its copy and engaged the buckles.

There was a subtle alteration in the night as his spectrum of sensibility widened to admit the dankness of the pit. Suddenly he caught the faint odor of chestnut blossom mingled with the stronger perfumes of honeysuckle and rose. A screech owl sounded in the woods below the House and was answered from beyond the kitchen garden. Thankfully he climbed onto the muddy grass atop the mound and drew a deep breath of night air.

The sword, he thought.

It would be in the pit still, buried in the claggy muck, hidden because it was designed to evade detection. Degaussing circuits rendered it transparent to magnetometers; echo transponders warped its sonic image to depth sounders; its micropile was thoroughly screened. The entire mound would have to be demolished unless the sword was near where he had found the belt.

Easing himself back into the hole, he attacked with the shovel. Sparks flew as iron struck flints. His hands grew slimy with clay and chalk, his feet heavy with mud. Despite his injuries he dug a hole a full arm span wide and half as deep before admitting to himself that the sword was not going to be found, then or later. Henglaf would hardly have bothered with a second hole. If the sword were in the mound, it would have been with the belt.

Disgusted, he flung the shovel out of the hole.

"*Oi!*" yelled someone out in the churchyard.

Feet scraped on the flinty spoil surrounding the pit. A light shone down on him. "My Gawd," said the same voice reverently. "And who the 'ell might *you* be?"

Nilssen assumed his fiercest expression. "Where's the sword?" he growled.

The newcomer backed away. "Here," he said, "don't you take that tone with me." He sounded less assured. "I asked who you might be. This is private property. 'Is lordship don't take kindly to tramps kipping in 'ere, no more do the vicar."

Nilssen hoisted himself out of the hole and balanced on his uninjured foot.

"No rough stuff, mind," advised the man, "or I'll 'ave the peelers on you."

"Shut up," recommended Nilssen in reply. "Are you part of this digging?"

"Who is it wants to know?"

In confidential tones Nilssen said, "My friend, if you don't stop asking superfluous questions, I propose wringing your neck. Do I make myself clear?"

The lamp dropped away to hang by the man's side. He was a tiny fellow, old and wizened, with a stoop. Nilssen hoped he would not prove violent, for he lacked the heart to hurt the man, who doubtless was doing no more than his job. In the weak light cast upward by the lamp Nilssen saw him staring fearfully. The man swallowed spasmodically. "You don't mean that?" he quavered. "I mean . . ."

"Are you with the diggers?" asked Nilssen.

"Sort of. I'm what you might call the 'andyman round 'ere. 'Do this, do that,' they says, so I do it."

"Have you a name?"

Transparently eager to please now, the man said, "Oh yes, guv. Black's the name, Bob Black. I come to all these does. Always digging round the old bones, I am." He laughed ingratiatingly, then gave a hacking cough.

"And who's in charge?"

"The doctor. Doctor Scott, that is. A great man. Went to Oxford, you know?"

"Then tell me, Bob," said Nilssen carefully, "has Doctor Scott found an old sword on this site?"

Black scratched his head, stirring his wispy hair as if it were lank grass. "He has some tale he tells about an old sword. But not from round 'ere."

"Are you absolutely certain?"

Some measure of Nilssen's concern seemed to infect Black, for his face became still and serious. "As the Lord God's me witness, guv, I never heard tell of one. Not so much as a stiver. And that's gospel."

"I see," said Nilssen. So the sword was lost. He felt slightly sick. The project had failed; someone would have to repeat all the work.

Black was studying him curiously. Nervously he asked:

"Pardon me for saying so, guv, but I don't mark your way of speech. You from these parts?"

"In a manner of speaking I've lived here a very long time."

"You'd be a friend of 'is lordship, maybe?"

"I doubt if he's even heard of me," said Nilssen, vaguely, distracted by the beginnings of a headache. "Bob, I have to go, so let me give you some advice: keep whatever you think you see in the next few minutes strictly to yourself. Better still, return to wherever you came from just now and stay there."

"Can't do that, guv. Doctor Scott says there's valuable stuff in that hole. Has to be watched. Shouldn't be standing chatting to you, really. Come to that—"

And he shied away. "Come to that, I'm not so sure you should be 'ere at all."

"Never you mind," said Nilssen. "I didn't touch his relics. Will you go?"

"Begging your pardon, no. I'll 'ave to see you off the site."

"As you wish, Bob. Will you wait over there for a few seconds, please?"

Black retired to the remote end of the summit trench and waited, obviously uneasy, for Nilssen to accompany him. Nilssen, meanwhile, had hobbled to what he estimated to be the peak of the tumulus. There he steeled himself against the possible failure of the second belt, found Black watching, so pressed his fingers into the recesses

and dropped a short distance, landing painfully on his damaged foot. Skidding down the slippery surface of the denuded tumulus, he bumped to a halt on raw chalk.

Above him was the multihued Fregar dome. Ahead and to his left were grounded fliers. Immediately to his right a technician sat with his jacket unzipped and a cloth cap askew on his head, eating with his fingers from a ration box color-coded as a midday meal. It all looked so normal.

A bell was gonging on the technician's console. He glanced up, saw Nilssen and gasped, "You're back!" Dumping the lunch box on the console, he ran across.

Nilssen sat up and grinned vacuously at him.

"Are you hurt?" asked the tech.

More people were coming on the double. Nilssen shook his head.

"I got stabbed by a bit of grass and murdered." He massaged the back of his neck. "And there's this migraine: the perfect end to a perfect day." The technician's face kept slipping out of focus. "Otherwise I'm fine. I think."

CHAPTER FIVE

Surgeon Georgiana Hartmann was on the Hospital's promenade level planting tulip bulbs when Nilssen padded up behind her in his official-issue slippers.

"Expecting a good crop this year?" he asked, folding down a bench seat beside the plant box she was working on.

Hartmann started, then looked around. "Oh," she said with a frown.

Nilssen leaned an elbow on the balustrade and watched her deftly inserting bulbs with the aid of a small trowel. "I'm told you want a word with me," he said.

"More than one." She put down the trowel and her bag of tulip bulbs and dusted off her hands while inspecting the line of earth mounds. At last she eyed Nilssen sternly. "You're not resting enough."

"After four months in bed I should think not."

Thrusting her grubby hands into the clean pockets of her white overalls, Hartmann studied Nilssen hard. Since his return, once he had recovered his faculties after his bout of radiation sickness, Nilssen had noticed how abnormally solicitous she had been about his welfare. Her concern had been purely professional; and indeed he had been ill; but the two seemed not to match quite. "We've had this argument before," she said. "Don't you ever listen to people? Those bandages around your head aren't there for fun."

He said, "A month ago I was sick—"

"And you still are. Very much so. And if you continue to see so many visitors and sneak off to the computer terminals in the library you'll pretty soon be worse than sick, Jerlan Nilssen—" there was the oddest inflection in her voice "—you'll be dead." She pointed to the plant boxes. "We'll be burying you instead of these bulbs."

"Georgiana, will you stop lecturing me? Considering how healthy I feel, my work load is negligible."

"Jerlan, you shouldn't be working at all. You took an enormous radiation dose on that trip of yours. If we hadn't got you here so fast on your return you'd . . . you'd be a suppurating mess right now. Get me, Jerlan: either you do as I say or I'll have you sedated, full-time."

Rebelliously he said, "I have a department to run. Rudolph Omak can't do everything for me. And there's a second trip to plan; that sword be recovered."

"Rudy Omak is managing splendidly. Rhys can do the planning."

Releasing an angry sigh, he said, "So when can I expect to be cleared for duty?"

"Another month," said Hartmann. "Thirty days, say. Not a day sooner."

"Can I have *any* visitors?"

"If they don't talk shop."

"Very well." He stood, allowing the seat to bang against the wall as it flipped up. Hartmann smiled pleasantly and resumed her planting.

Nilssen thought hard as he stalked off along the promenade.

Rudolph Omak was working when Nilssen phoned him from the Hospital library. His slitted eyes widened on recognizing the image of the bandaged head on his phone screen. "Commissar," he said, "this is forbidden. Expressly."

"Then let's be quick," said Nilssen. "Contact that man Rhys and tell him I'll be out in a month. That makes it mid-February. Allowing another month for preparations, we can go for a second take around the third week in March. Make it a Saturday."

"The twenty-first?" suggested Omak, consulting his calendar off-camera.

"Fine. Next, arrange for one of the special squad to visit me here with a bag of equipment. Here's the list." Nilssen held up a prepared sheet of paper to the phone's camera and waited until Omak had made a recording of it. "Someone reliable. And see they come in civilian clothes."

"Malchek?"

"He'll do. Brief him on the reign of terror at this place so he doesn't fall foul of Hartmann or her minions."

Omak grinned. "And when do I have them storm the main gates?"

"You can joke now," said Nilssen. "Wait 'til you get sick, though."

Clearing the line, he slipped from the booth to the rack of book-blocks and was reading quietly when Hartmann eventually came in.

"You were on the phone," she said icily.

"A social call," he said.

"To a Grade One number."

"Oh, did you try to listen in?"

She compressed her lips. Then she said, "Jerlan, naturally I know what took place on your expedition. I even have some idea of how badly it went for you—for us. I supervised the debriefing mindscan. But at the same time, perhaps because I know it's so serious, I intend to cure you properly. I am *not* going to let you kill yourself!"

Plainly her words had been a signal to the three orderlies who filed into the library. One leveled a hypodermic dart gun at Nilssen. "Go ahead," said Hartmann. The gun coughed; but Nilssen did not even feel the dart pierce his neck, only the swift spread of coldness to his face before he collapsed. There was no opportunity to express surprise, or outrage.

The homebase tech held up his right hand with all fingers spread.

Five seconds.

"Hit it first time," Nilssen shouted. The tech nodded; his left hand ran along a line of switches, setting some, clearing others. His right thumb folded itself across his palm.

Four seconds.

Another rain front came down the valley, pockmarking the Wye. The river was in spate after the sudden spring thaw, so that its water coursed by the new camp like a lithe brown snake. Even the ground within the shelter of the Fregar dome was damp from the heavy winter snow falls. Operators and support staff had to kick mud from their high boots before entering the fliers parked beneath the dome. Only Nilssen envied their lot; he would shortly be pitched into far worse conditions.

Drastic revisions had been made to his equipment in the months since the abortive first mission. Now he wore a modified Fregar generator as protection against repetitions of his accident with the grass stalk. It would buoy him up momentarily; additionally, it was a defense against attacks by bladed weapons.

His timeshift belt, too, had been improved, to the extent that Rhys predicted a placement accuracy of better than one minute. Arrival was planned for the eve of Nilssen's visit to Henglaf's hall.

Privately, Nilssen could not believe that the previous experiment had taught Area Five so much. He preferred to place his trust in the new backup system, a device cryptically identified as "Bluefire." About as elegant as a rope tied around a swimmer's waist, it at least would carry him home, barring major mishaps.

Rhys had explained Bluefire by analogy.

"This device," he said, "is to temporal mechanics roughly what a glider is to aerodynamics. A glider launched from a high place can travel far without an engine by transforming potential energy into kinetic energy: as it falls, it goes faster. With luck, it can circle around to land almost where it started from. Only frictional losses prevent it regaining its original altitude; but with favorable winds it can remain aloft indefinitely.

"Likewise Bluefire. A mass launched from a point within space-time is tied to an original entropy level. It can move into the future, the past, across time, anywhere, provided the entropic disparity between start and finish can be compensated for."

"In practice," Nilssen had asked, "what happens?"

"We create a hole through to your destination and keep it open while you're at the far end. The zone of emergence is marked by a shell of bluish light. Think of it as a personal gate. Because it's keyed to your belt, only you can come back through it; and when you do you'll bounce straight back here. Be warned, though: any anachronistic material with you will delay your return considerably, so wipe your feet and forget about souvenirs."

"And what are the odds of another . . . unforeseen contingency?"

"Slight. Negligible, even, although we still can't be sure what process was responsible for your duplication. Momentary reversal of the belt's stabilizer field could cause a false launch of one of your microline doppelgängers: normally these minutely different versions of people and things coexist as a tightly related bundle of time-lines; but it's possible to split one off. In your case there must have been one or more microlines in which that Saxon's sword triggered your belt's launching circuit before the blowout occurred, while in all the others the circuit remained intact but idle. The upshot was that a version of you survived and replicated itself into all its related microlines."

"But can it happen again?"

Rhys had seemed uneasy. "Possibly. I know of two cases, if this *was* one. Do you remember Gwillem Crewkerne?"

His eyes had been bright, intent, almost feverishly interested in Nilssen's response. The name had certainly been familiar to Nilssen; but though it teased him, he had taken several seconds to place it. It felt as if a gap existed in his memory, a gap surrounded by associations. Then he had it. "Yes," he said, "Yaer mentioned him, I think."

"Right," answered Rhys. Then he flipped a ration token onto Nilssen's desk. "See? Blank. But if I flip it again . . . value face . . . This world's reality status is so precarious that if I continued to toss this token long enough we'd see a significant repetition of the sequence of blank and value faces. In a quasi-deterministic universe like ours anything can happen if it needs to. Today affects the far past, remember. Perhaps your survival, one way or another, was inevitable. Had you thought of that?"

He had not.

Then Rhys added, smiling sardonically, "And so might your end be. Watch your step, Commissar."

One finger: *one second before his return to 880* A.D. The tech's left hand hovered above the abort switch. Then the last and index finger of his right hand folded itself into the upraised fist, Nilssen's skin prickled, and his surroundings changed.

It became nighttime in winter, and very, very cold. He stood beside the frozen river Wye in a valley deep with powdery snow that lifted in dry white fumes and smoked across the ground, borne on a wind so

keen it stole the warmth from his clothes within seconds. A few stars shone through rents in the racing
clouds; as his eyes adapted to the comparative darkness
he saw that Rhys had erred in his choice of site for
the shift. He had to start walking at once and ener-
getically, or freeze to death.

Stepping away from his arrival point, he noticed
the dim blue conic glow of the Bluefire zone, vapor-
ishly vague at its apex but brilliant at its base, where
it cut cleanly into the snow to a depth of several
inches. New snow was drifting into the hole, burying
the brightest part of the cone; but he had been urged
to hide it so it would not be found during his absence.
His belt possessed controls with which he moved the
zone in amongst some trees. Some holly branches
hacked down with his sword formed a dense screen
around it. No harm would come from moving the
zone; it treated space and time as interchangeable
quantities and could allow for variations in either, or
both.

With the Bluefire zone hidden, Nilssen made haste
to reach the village before the confrontation between
his earlier self and the villagers took place. By the
map, he had only half a mile to cover; his deadline
was one hour after sunset, to be safe. But the country
was wilder than anticipated: the memories of the City
people were of a tamer landscape, one freed of the
primitive roads and forbidding forests of the ninth
century. Snow and darkness blindfolded him. The
wind stole his will to press on. Without the inertial
navigator in his sword hilt to guide him he would
have lost his way utterly, for one avenue of advance
after another ended in snow-swathed underbrush or
fallen trees, forcing him far from the direct route
Kwambe's model had suggested. Two hours late, he
blundered onto the road to the village, exhausted and
numbed by the cold, just as snow began falling.

Soon, he remembered, the few soft flakes would

become a blizzard. Half-frozen as he was, he dared not stay in the open much longer, yet he could not make an entry to the village until the storm drove the guards to shelter.

By jogging up and down the road beyond the glow of the watch-beacons he revived some life in his toes. As if to compensate for this slight comfort, his throat and nose became sore from gulping the arctic air. But at last the snowflakes fell thickly enough to hide his invasion.

Reaching the gates he struck out along the outer rim of the ditch, searching for a weakness in the palisade. Finding one, he floundered through the drifted snow in the ditch and scaled the earthen bank. Then he listened. His scrabblings on the icy slope had not been noiseless. Hearing no sounds of guards, he peered over the rough barrier of upright sharpened stakes.

A hut not far away was an amorphous shadow in the whirling snow; the acrid smoke of its fire came to him in whiffs as the wind coursed about its roof and along the ramparts. No one was in sight. Even the tethered dog, which he recalled being near the gates, was paying him no attention. He drew his sword to carve an entrance.

The blade sang under the control of the sword's disruptor pack. Wood peeled off the palisade; it was like slicing cheese. In three minutes he had cut out a panel large enough to allow him access but small enough not to weaken the palisade or be noticed when replaced. He slipped through and down the inside of the bank.

Though many subjective months had passed since his last exploration of the village, its layout remained fresh in his mind as he crept from hut to hut towards the hall. The hazards which troubled him most were the numerous small objects he had not been aware of on his previous visit but which now obstructed him at every turn and made silent progress extremely difficult. Piles of firewood stacked against walls were easily avoided, being bulky and white with snow; harder to see in the blizzard were the water barrels, rubbish heaps, and night-soil pits which abounded in the darker passageways he was obliged to keep to. After treading in one hole he discovered his boot was coated in a sticky mess that defied his efforts to remove it.

Despite these problems he found the hall and took up a position in the lee of an end post where the wind had scoured a small patch of ground free of snow. From there he watched the main doors and listened to the surge and fall of conversation within the building. Occasionally he held his breath on smelling the kitchen odors; his hunger had been sated since his last visit and the greasy stench made his stomach heave.

After a quarter of an hour the storm eased. A guard from the hall wandered around more dutifully than studiously, missing Nilssen in his corner, then retired indoors. Nilssen realized what a blessing the storm had been, for it had blurred his tracks.

Another fifteen minutes in the cold convinced him that a miscalculation had deposited him at the wrong date. Furious with Rhys, he left his hiding place and was crossing the open ground in front of the hall when he saw the ghost.

The vision held him where he was, rapt by the sight of himself as others had seen him: the translucent form of a man in savage dress, his face disfigured by the ugly, inhuman disguise of the rebreather mask, his steps slowed to measured strides by the time dilation effect.

The ghost walked to the doors and sank through them. From the interior of the hall there rang out a scream that woke Nilssen from his near-trance. *This,* he thought ruefully, *is where I came in.* Darting back to his corner, he awaited Wulfstan's fatal exit.

There were loud voices, raised in query then in anger. The wind freshened, bringing more snow with it. Henglaf's deep tones called the murderers out before him. The night became thick with whirling whiteness. Light spilled across the fresh snow; Wulfstan's shadow stretched out towards the nearest huts as if seeking escape; the man himself staggered out into the blizzard, the sword sticking from his back. Nilssen began to run as hard as he could, to wrest the weapon from the wound and be away before the crowd followed.

His hand was on the hilt when he heard running feet behind him. Fearing a guard had spotted him, he turned, only to receive a stunning blow on the side of his head. Pain and confusion hid his attacker; but he saw the expanse of firelit snow tip up and slide away into brief darkness.

No more than seconds later, he could hear again. The crowd was still within the hall, and he had been dragged aside and now lay alone against one end wall of the building. The sword, he found, had been taken.

He stood up. Pushing back his hood and touching his head, he felt blood in his hair. Fortunately the wound was superficial, so he pulled his hood tight about his face. The blow had been delivered expertly and deliberately, that was obvious; which raised a swarm of questions. Nevertheless, the wound and his attacker would have to be dealt with later, for the village had been aroused and he had lost the lead he had relied upon to insure his escape was undetected.

Most of the Saxon warriors had now gathered around Wulfstan's prone body. Others could be heard organizing a hue and cry after Leofric. Torches were being lit amongst the huts. The dog was barking again.

Someone shouted that the sword had been stolen, at which Henglaf emerged from the hall and stooped to examine the body. Nilssen heard him say: "He'll live long enough. Soon as you find the sword, bring it to me. And when you catch Leofric put him in the icehouse with this one. We'll hang them both in the morning—best to do it quickly."

Nilssen resolved to slip away to his prepared exit before he was caught by mistake. The mob seemed to have concentrated on the far side of the village, so if he went quickly he might not be challenged.

He was passing through a dark lane between two huts when right in his path the flap of hide over one of the doors was twitched aside. A young woman stepped out and saw him; they were scarcely two paces apart. He caught his breath. They stared at each other.

"Please," he whispered, "don't shout."

Spellbound, he spoke as in a dream. She was so, so like Eva. Clad though she was in rough, reeking furs, she was beautiful. His urge to run faltered, ensnared by a vision. Beside the wizened creatures he had seen toiling in the village she was a fresh-faced girl, but adult for all that; she demonstrated an immediate self-control he doubted he could have mustered in her place. Her eyes no more than widened and her movements did not stop; they ceased, gracefully. The cry he had dreaded was stillborn as a parting of her lips, surviving only as a slight sound of amazement rather than of fear or alarm.

Raising a finger to his lips, he signaled her to silence. Oddly, she nodded promptly and smiled. Her own left hand made a sign, followed by others.

Astonished, he could hardly answer. In the language of the mute, the artificial code of his own modern times, she had welcomed him as a friend. Furthermore, she had swiftly added the fingerspelling of his own name.

"You know me?" he asked.

Jerlan, her fingers answered. *Always.*

Suddenly he suspected City interference, collusion between Kwambe, Rhys, and Yaer to send a backup agent after him secretly. "So," he said sourly, "they didn't trust me alone. Are you Police?"

She shook her head. Wisps of dark curls escaped from under her hood. Pushing them back again, she said, *You have forgotten me, as you said you would. I am Morwena of Gwerfa Iwrch.*

Stubbornly his memory refused to link her with his past.

If not of his past, was she to be part of his future? Breathing space was at a high premium: a spent second could cost him dear. What to say, what to do; the decision could mean his life. One fact was irrefutable: she *did* know him to some degree. If she was of his future, he could no more than guess what their relationship had been in her eyes. Or was to be in his. All he could depend on were his own instincts; but instinctively he liked her.

Two messages you bade me give you when we met this night, her fingers continued, blending spelling and wordsign. *That you would know me soon. And that you have promised me a second coming. Now, this much I say also for myself: that I wait for none other. So tell me, Jerlan, when do you return?*

Many of the signs she used were the secret symbols Eva and he had evolved privately, recognizing that the mute can be heard as far as the eye can see. The signs were theirs alone, yet he had shared them. Whose opinion could he trust if not his own, he asked himself. Drawn as he was already to her, one day, yes, this girl might excuse him from the commitment to solitude he had made in that shattered building in the far-off future.

But people were stirring in the next hut. The light from the door behind Morwena would reveal him to passersby. Quickly he asked, "What else did I promise?"

Simply that you would name the time and place.

He knew he need only turn and walk away, that she

neither could nor would call the mob down upon him. Simultaneously he told himself he would not have made such a serious contract without cause.

"Then," he said, "if I can, I will return before Midsummer's Day." It was an arbitrary choice of date, but one he was sure would remain independent of calendars. It also gave him sufficient leeway for any revision of plans that might become necessary. He felt he needed the half year. This was all too sudden.

Even as she smiled and pressed his cold hands between her warm ones, he regretted his hasty words, paid over as a sop to expediency in ignorance of his own nature. How could he tell whether the pledge had been sincere? However attractive, this girl was a stranger with a background and personality unknown to him. Her entire story might be a lie. . . . No, his instincts insisted, his renewal of the promise had meant a lot to her.

The conflict of inner emotions and external danger became too great, so that he broke from her gentle clasp and ran. Skidding on icy patches, knocking headlong anything that would move for him, desperate to escape the echoed future, he lost his way. As he circled through the hutments he saw the mob was gathering, attracted by the row. At last three warriors closed in on him, stalking his wary defensive movements by the glare of the torches held aloft.

His mind cleared. He couldn't kill, but he had to scare them off. When he had fought Leofric he had been injured. Now, whole, healthy, and armed with weaponry in advance of his adversaries' swords by at least a thousand years, he did not feel outnumbered. Furthermore, he had a Fregar generator.

Sliding the switch that started his own sword's disruptor, he let out a simulated enraged bellow and charged the nearest man.

The Saxon stepped aside nimbly. His comrades retired, laughing at Nilssen's clumsiness, and left them to fight as a pair. Then Nilssen switched on the Fregar field and their faces fell.

The rainbow shimmer encased him like a suit of light, save for a dark patch before his mouth that was his breathing hole. Its electric tingle renewed his courage as he turned again to face the Saxon. Striding forward with his sword raised for a second blow, Nilssen was upon the man before he had recovered his wits. The Saxon could only bring up his own weapon and block the stroke. His eyes were wide with terror, his legs unsteady. When he tried to run away he slipped in the slush and fell headlong. Only the courage of another Saxon allowed him to escape.

The new man yelled at Nilssen, taunting him and waving his sword, so Nilssen obliged him and left the fallen Saxon alone, glad to have been spared the problem of how to let him go unharmed. He allowed the new man to deliver a powerful downstroke on his right shoulder, a blow that the Fregar field shrugged off; then he returned one of his own that neatly severed the Saxon's sword blade near the hilt.

The Saxon gaped at his truncated weapon. A moment later he and the crowd were running for the shadows. Nilssen was hardly able to challenge the third warrior before he too, after a token gesture with his sword, bolted, howling with fright. Within thirty seconds the scene of the fight was marked by discarded weapons and torches guttering in the snow.

Nilssen switched off the Fregar generator and his sword. He found he was breathing heavily. Though now free to leave he stayed, for he saw Morwena in the shadows. Going to her, he said:

"Are you safe in this place?"

I have the guardian whom you appointed. And Henglaf's oath.

"A guardian?" He guessed that explanations would require more than the breathing space the scuffle had won him. "How good a friend is he to you? Does he understand that you wait?"

Of course. For he waits also.

He had to ask, "Who is this man? Why isn't he out here?"

He lies sick, else I would call him out. . . . My love, hasten away! They return. Her eyes sparkled as she glanced along the alley towards the hall. Listening, Nilssen heard stealthy shufflings and harsh whispers.

More confidently he said, "I shall come back soon," then he left her in the darkness. The noises dogged him to the village gates, through which he carved a hole without remorse or care for the damage done to the defenses. Once on his way he found himself alone, as if no one dared pursue him into the snowbound forest. The village fell behind as he trudged along the road. The wilderness came to dominate both the landscape and his emotions; before long he had halted for want of any clear notion of what his next move should be.

Ostensibly the stolen sword was the sine qua non of his two excursions into the past, yet now the girl Morwena haunted him almost to the exclusion of his scientific objectives. She awoke old traumas, disturbed old scars. Rhys had suggested that his personal future might be predestined, and unexpectedly that idea had become fruitful with many comforting implications. But, of course, Rhys had also cautioned him against overconfidence. The road to destiny might be wearisome and unrewarding, with no happy ending.

His decision—to act as if she did not exist—formed slowly in the course of a minutes-long inward struggle. The spiraling sparks in Rhys's universe-model moved slowly, so slowly that she would surely be there, whatever he did. Meanwhile the sword was all: unless it could be recovered, the mission would fail and the project would suffer a dreadful setback.

So, to expand the limits of his understanding, he must force himself to become dispassionately objective once more.

No fortuitous encounter with a native Saxon had frustrated his mission, of that he was sure. Knocked senseless, yet dragged to cover away from Henglaf's men: these acts were consistent only with the intervention of friendly anachronistic forces. Superficially the answer seemed to be to accept his luck and go home forthwith. On reflection he saw that logic was against that course.

Specifically, possession of an unconstrained time-shifter would have given his attacker the power of on-the-spot disappearance. Thereby freed from fear of capture by the Saxons, he could have stayed to help Nilssen recover but had instead run off at once, despite having devoted precious seconds to dragging his unconscious victim to concealment. So the prominent inference had to be that his escape was chaneled through a particular geographical location, such as a Bluefire zone. The same snow that had complicated Nilssen's journey through the woods could now work for him, by slowing his anonymous assailant's flight from Henglafingasham. Recovery of the sword seemed possible. But was it desirable? He fretted over this question for several minutes, then realized his opposition to the stranger's plans had been counted on. The other man had assumed he would reject all explanations. So be it. The Future, he thought, did not confide in its Past.

Roundly damning all meddlers, he backtracked. When the watch-beacons at the village gate showed blurrily through the snowflakes, he left the road and struck out across open ground to his right, between snow-caked mounds of last summer's dead brambles. If the other man had used Bluefire, he had to have left the village, for the glowing cone could never have remained hidden for long with Henglaf's hue and cry going on. With luck Nilssen would find his tracks soon and could follow them.

As the storm lifted, moonlight began to penetrate the clouds. He glanced towards the palisade, now undoubtedly double-guarded, worried lest he be seen. When he reached the fringes of the forest he felt happier, though the same shadows that hid him would also help to hide the trail he sought.

He did indeed almost miss the tracks, not so much for lack of light to see them by, but owing to their unexpected nature. They were not the deep and close-set prints of a pair of boots. Rather, each print was broad and swept the surface, leaving a recurved smear that ended in a shallow oval depression. Already the marks were being erased by stray flakes of snow; but they were, unmistakably, those of snowshoes. One print even showed a model number molded into the frame, reversed but readable, that identified it as that of a lightweight shoe issued to City agents on winter work. Thousands had been made. Nilssen cursed himself for neglecting to equip himself with some. Then the moon broke free of the clouds. Abandoning vain regrets, he did his best to follow the trail.

The snow made the going heavy. One leg after the other had to be drawn out of the deep soft layer and placed as far ahead as possible without loss of balance. Again he cursed himself, envying his attacker's free stride on the shoes. His guaranteed-flawless Anglo-Saxon clothing was not waterproof and having become soaked early in the night, allowed the snow's chill to insinuate itself into his leggings. Even under the trees the snow was thick. To compound his problems, the wind moved the branches overhead and dislodged dollops of snow on to the trail. The disturbed surface became ever harder to distinguish from the undisturbed, and he realized he was falling farther behind his quarry.

About a mile into the forest the trees ended at a

wide clearing, or dell, through which ran a frozen, drift-choked stream. The trail seemed to enter an isolated copse of silver birches on the near bank.

Nilssen hid behind a tree at the forest's edge and listened, well aware that a City agent could be armed with weapons capable of incinerating a wide tract of forest, and him. Aggressive pursuit, if noticed, might meet with more than a considerate tap on the head.

Branches rattled as the wind stirred them. Snow plopped to the ground here and there. Then from afar there sounded the mournful cries of a wolf pack. He could no longer afford caution. Cupping his hands into a makeshift megaphone, he shouted down the slope in Modern English:

"Hey you! You there!"

After a few seconds he was answered by a wolf-cry, nearer now.

"Come out where I can see you. You can't escape!"

Another minute of waiting convinced him the man had done just that, so he went down the slope as far as the copse. The trail stopped at a circular depression in the snow.

"Bluefire," he said aloud, as if it were a swearword.

The wind was stronger away from the forest. The dell felt too open to the sky. In the few seconds he had stood at the trail's end all he had been able to hear were the silver birches creaking stiffly in the cold gusts laced with snowflakes. Suddenly he appreciated how utterly silent the forest had actually become: he had not simply left its noises behind him; the hush had seemed to follow him down from the trees. Thinking back, he recalled countless scrabblings, a long-eared owl's moaning hoot, sleeping birds shifting nervously on their perches. All had ceased. In their stead was the silence of a watchful wilderness.

He scanned the tree line, seeing the interlaced shadows of leafless branches and the trees themselves, stroked with contrasting white and black. A cloud obscured the moon for a moment, went away. Then, and only then, did he spy the clusters of profounder shadow slinking through the fringes of the forest, encircling him.

Involuntarily his hand went to the switch control-ling the Fregar field. But he refrained from using it; he knew it worked and knew he must husband the limited stored energy supply on which his life might soon depend.

The wolf pack comprised only adults, eleven of them. All were having difficulty with the depth of snow, but Nilssen entertained no hopes of outfloundering them, for they had already closed their circle and were advancing downslope. They appeared in no hurry. The largest, the one he presumed to be the leader, halted frequently to test the wind with its nose. No sounds were made other than the *crump* of their feet in the crusted snow. Their breath came in gusts of vapor that blurred away into the frigid air.

Nilssen caught himself breathing hard too. That night he had walked more than three miles through difficult country, had sparred with two armed Saxons, had been knocked unconscious for a short while. He felt he owed himself a rest. Switching on the Fregar generator again, he sat in the snow.

The leader of the pack paused a few paces off and looked at him out of eyes that reflected the moonlit snow. He waved; it shied away, then crept closer, its upper lip curling back from its fangs.

Fregar, he whispered to himself like a consoling litany, *Field (Repulsor-Excluder) Generator And Regulator. Cancels momentum of physical objects within range. They can't hurt me . . .*

A low gurgle developed into a growl in the wolf's throat and was taken up by the pack. Now that they were closer, Nilssen saw how gaunt they were: only hunger had forced them to prey on man. He remem-bered Kwambe's reassurance on this point, and his appended advice: "If you are attacked by anything but bears, climb a tree and stay put."

Excellent counsel, thought Nilssen, eyeing the tree line beyond the closing ring of wolves. He shivered convulsively, steadied himself.

The pack was working itself up into a frenzy, snarling and yelping. His immobility seemed to disturb them, for when he got to his feet and set a course for his Bluefire zone, they scattered, only to regroup at a distance. Like some nightmare rearguard, they pursued him up the slope into the forest, no longer growling now that the proper order of events prefacing a kill appeared to have been reestablished.

Within a hundred yards of Nilssen's entry amongst the trees they had closed the gap. For a short while he lost sight of them. Abruptly, so fast he hardly saw it coming, the leader darted at him from behind a bulky oak, bowling him over with its lunge. He stared, transfixed, at the beast's teeth biting into the air above his throat as if they chewed on toffee, wisps of coruscation weaving about their points. Their nearness and the wolf's savage fury rendered him helpless with terror for at least ten seconds; without the field around him he would have been unable to protect himself. Enraged by its failure to tear out his throat, the wolf continued to worry at him, straddling his body so that its rank smell became overpoweringly strong and stray hairs fell through the breathing hole into his mouth. Spitting these out, he roused himself to put a hand under its chin. As he flung the animal from him, he struck out at it with his sword; to his delight, though the blade was swaddled by the field the blow startled the wolf and sent it away yelping, its tail between its legs.

At this the pack faltered in their attack. They had held back while their leader fought with Nilssen. Seeing how easily he had thrown it off, they were unsure of themselves and withdrew while Nilssen resumed

his hike, guided by the direction indicator in his
sword hilt.

By the inertial navigator's dead reckoning he still
had two miles to go, so he walked slowly to conserve
his stamina and reduce sweating. The Fregar field kept
him well-insulated, forcing him to breathe deeply and
so lose body heat. Puffing like a steam engine, he
tramped through the snowy forest accompanied by
the wolves who kept exactly level with him. When
he paused to rest, they would usually make an attack;
but these became less determined and eventually
ceased. At length, with only a single backward glance,
from the leader, the pack abandoned Nilssen.

He felt a transitory regret as their gray forms
merged with the gloom of the forest, because though
the experience had been frightening in the extreme
for a while, it had also been interesting. They were
parts of a world he had rediscovered. Its forests and
hills were closer to those of the lost twenty-first century in which he had grown up than were the devas-
tated twenty-seventh's carbonized stumps and badlands.

As he switched off the Fregar field, he noted how
far its power cell had been discharged. The wolves assumed a new guise, that of a potent trap for foolish
travelers. They were not merely the raw material of
quaint folktales; they were real; they could have killed
him. If he planned to continue the search for the
missing sword he ought to recover some of that "loneliness" which Yaer had so valued in him.

Then he remembered Morwena. There was that
about her which made him wonder whether Yaer
would have approved of his feelings at that moment.

CHAPTER SIX

Jerkily Hector Kwambe inscribed a column of minus-
cule crosses in the margin of the top sheet of paper
before him. "Jerlan," he said petulantly, "excuse my
asking, but have you told me everything?"

Morwena of Gwerfa Iwrch and her anonymous
guardian were mentioned nowhere in the eleven pages
of transcript which Kwambe had created from
Nilssen's verbal report. Otherwise, however, Nilssen
had gone to considerable pains to relate his experiences
as fully as possible. The omission had been the outcome of troubled reflection on the encounter, an interim self-censorship while he reviewed the ethics of
passing on uncritically all he knew. In due course, he
appreciated, the fact of Morwena's existence would
be dragged out of him, possibly before he was ready
to let the information go. That reserve was, he told
himself, only a buffer rather than a secret in itself.
The sticking point was, ought he to disclose that
someone quite likely from the City was due to fall ill
during an important mission? That had been his inference from Morwena's words: whoever stayed with
her on that day in Nilssen's subjective future when he
left her his promise to return ran the risk of death
through illness in a miserable Saxon hovel. That
knowledge was guaranteed to deter good agents from
accepting the charge of the girl, under circumstances
when the very best might be barely adequate. As a
slow-moving ship in shallows handles differently from

the same vessel in deep water, so Nilssen sensed in the encounter a brush with wider issues than an interrupted romance; and he was loyal enough to the City to concede the rights of its citizens as taking precedence over his own.

However, Kwambe's terrier instinct had scented information at bay, and unless distracted he would swiftly dig it out. Until he was entrusted with the knowledge, Kwambe could not know of its inherently dangerous nature; thus the evaluation had to be made for him. And Nilssen, in his turn, had to decide on his own behalf how far to carry his obstruction of the City's due investigative processes.

"On the face of it," Kwambe went on, responding to Nilssen's prolonged silence with a show of mild irritation, "between getting clobbered beside the village hall and leaving the place, you appear to have spent a goodish while doing nothing but pick fights with the inhabitants. Why didn't you go while you could?"

"I got lost," Nilssen said, appending a small yawn. "It was black as pitch. And snowing."

Kwambe fingered a line in the transcript after riffling through the pages. "You say here that it was hardly more than a drizzle . . . Jerlan, if there's *any*thing missing from this, for heaven's sake—"

"It's all there, Hector," Nilssen answered him stubbornly. "If I remember extra details, of course you'll get them, in writing. Meanwhile I'm dead on my feet. Eight hours of sleep will help my memory, okay?"

"Sometimes," Kwambe said, "my agents hand in reports while scarcely able to speak, then die."

"But not me. Tomorrow morning—"

"Sometimes," Kwambe said, "they're dead already, in which case we use a mindscan to extract the data."

Nilssen stood over the desk. "Try ordering one for me," he warned, "and find out what trouble means. I'll see you tomorrow. Until then, goodbye."

As he stepped out of the command flier into the mud beneath the temporary Fregar dome, Nilssen recognized that there would be repercussions all the way up to Laheer and back. If he was very unlucky, a mindscan might indeed be ordered, in which case the whole truth would emerge: not only would Morwena's existence be revealed, along with what she had said, what he had felt, and what he had subsequently half-hoped; they would learn of the guardian. There would also be the humiliation of having his thoughts dissected analytically by Kwambe's staff: a mindscan was totally undiscriminating, disgorging fair, foul, fact, and fancy with no regard for feelings. If he was lucky, alternatively, only that which he cared to have revealed would be prised out of him. The degree of mental violation largely depended on whom Kwambe, or Laheer, hired as hatchetman for the interrogation when it finally came.

Once back in the City, he proceeded directly to his quarters, still clad in his mission clothes. A handwritten note on cream-colored heavy card was waiting in his letterbox. His stay of execution had indeed been brief, for the card was an invitation from Laheer to a small impromptu dinner party that same evening. His company, the few lines of freshly dried ink suggested, would be greatly valued.

Briefly an urge to rebel blazed up in him. As it damped down he read the card a second time. The language was polite, almost courteous considering its author; Laheer might have an iron fist hidden, but at least the hand he proffered wore the velvet glove. Unless his star guest failed to turn up, the party would remain in name a social gathering.

Replacing the card in the letterbox, he went to take a shower confident of snatching at least three hours of sleep before Laheer sent someone to fetch him. An innocent mistake: the card had been overlooked; no cause for Laheer to suppose he was not being cooperative—

The phone rang as he entered the bedroom.

"Jerlan, how are you?" It was Laheer, friendly, paternal.

"Tired but well, thank you, sir."

"Kwambe said you were worn out, so I thought maybe that invitation I sent might have been a mistake. . . . You did receive it, I suppose?"

He closed his eyes. "I can't say, sir. It may still be in the box."

"Leave it there, I'll tell you myself." And Laheer proceeded to specify time and place. While the old man talked genially, Nilssen scrutinized his lounge for the camera and found it embedded in a bronze wall sculpture facing the front door.

"Of course I'll come," Nilssen said at last. "No, no bother. I'll catch some sleep. Enough, I hope . . . Thank you for calling, sir."

Replacing the phone handset, he ripped the camera from the sculpture. Some slight disfigurement of the bronze had been caused by the spot welds that helped to disguise the tiny metal shell with its single wide-angle eye. Like a tiny hermit crab sheltering within borrowed armor, the unit was exceedingly fragile; it made a wholesome crunch as his heel crushed it to powder against the floor.

Soon it would be replaced, if it was not already backed up by a better-hidden unit, or units.

Showered and relaxed, he was on the verge of sleep when the bedside phone rang:

a routine call Commissar, exchange here, testing your line, some equipment faulty, all three controlling computers crashed their programs together, sorry to bother you, all-go now . . .

Again, twenty minutes later by the clock, he was roused by the phone:

> Administrator Weston of South Three Parish, thought I might take you up on that promise to come give us a talk, choose your subject of course, so much admired what you've done Commissar, Thursday next week? your secretary gave me your number, you will? most grateful, wonderful . . .

When the phone rang the third time another twenty minutes later, he left it and dressed himself for the evening's event. There were still two hours in hand, but evidently Laheer's friends intended that those too should not be peaceful ones. Groggy with exhaustion, he knew he was in no state to dodge the verbal trip-wires that would be laid for him. Laheer wielded the power of the City, but he had to be defied until Nilssen could be sure it was safe to give in.

Well, he too had friends who in their own small ways had power greater than Laheer's. Georgiana Hartmann, as Surgeon, was largely immune to the Chief Commissar's covert machinations. She had access to intensive sleep inducers that could bestow on him a night's rest in one hour. Much as he disliked having recourse to such artificial aids, Nilssen decided to test her friendship and Laheer's omnipotence.

Chief Commissar Laheer ate slowly, withdrawn from his own table behind a barricade of austere formality. The meal over which he presided was appropriately simple but excellent. It was conducted efficiently; his famous android servitors, whose bodies wore a wood-grain finish to match the dark, lustrous paneling around the walls of his dining chamber, attended to his five guests punctiliously, so permitting them to observe the total control which their host exercised over his private domain. Nilssen in particular was assaulted by politeness and consideration: he had hardly to peer into his empty glass before it was refilled; when he dropped a fork it was retrieved in a trice from the sumptuous rug at his feet and replaced with a clean one of the same style; and always he was the first to be served.

Not deceived, he caught the smirk on Yaer's face. The psychologist, seated on his right opposite Laheer's end of the table, behaved throughout like a cardsharp holding a winning hand: with clinical magnanimity. Left of Nilssen, between him and Laheer, was Maia Kim, who said hardly a word but proclaimed her nervousness by eloquent clumsiness. Facing her, Hector Kwambe also seemed uneasy and expressed it by drinking steadily. Lastly there was Turlough Rhys, sandwiched between Kwambe and Yaer; disdaining small talk and disdained in return as a rude mechanical, he ate heartily and submerged himself below the general level of conversation save for random remarks of no consequence.

By the diligence with which the subject of the mission was avoided, Nilssen concluded that it must be uppermost in their minds and speculated on the parts each would play in the impending unpleasantness. Rhys was a guppy in a goldfish bowl; he was probably present as technical advisor. The others could have almost any rôle now that Laheer had taken command.

Ironically it transpired that Rhys, the person least tainted with mission politics, broke the ice.

Having set his spoon in his empty plate at the conclusion of the final course, he wiped his lips with his napkin. An android whisked plate and spoon away. He frowned. Suddenly he said, half to Nilssen, half to the whole group:

"The more I think about it, the less sense this project makes. Here we have a paradox configuration of two major interlocking fold-backs, with a detached action-locus intersecting both. The available data indicate the presence of a third fold-back; but where is it? What caused the detached action-locus to develop?"

Laheer dismissed the androids by a flick of a finger, then scowled at the scientist. "Doctor Rhys, what the devil are you yattering about?"

Rhys reddened dangerously as if about to answer him back, but was forestalled by Kwambe, who adopted a mock-soothing tone.

"Doctor Rhys is an idealist," he announced. "His models of reality show him everything that's happening. To him the label 'fold-back' categories and thereby defuses a phenomenon that we in the operational departments call by quite another name. Not a nice name at all. We call it a 'worm.' Worms are a nightmare: like the mythological Ourobouros they can swallow their own tails along with anybody and anything riding on them. Mercifully we've lost no more than thirty agents that way; but the jaws can close at any time. Pardon the pun."

Despite being marginally drunk he spoke with tight diction and impassive face. Inwardly, Nilssen could tell, another mood altogether had possessed him; more durable than anger, more positive than despair. His statement had not been a jibe at Rhys, but a plea directed at Nilssen.

"Doctor Rhys," Kwambe added suddenly, "doesn't nature prefer the configuration of least convolution?"

"To a good approximation," agreed Rhys, showing wary interest.

"Topnotch . . . Now, tell us all, true or false: unless the events which establish a worm are enacted precisely right on every pass through its nodes, it can induce acausal reconfiguration of space-time? Or, in English: anybody involved who muffs his lines at the critical moment is liable to find things going wrong around him?"

"Certainly. The Collapse was a case in point. But I wouldn't phrase it so melodramatically—"

"Naturally you bloody well wouldn't! You've never stirred from that safe laboratory of yours. Nor have other people I could name had to make a living imperiling their very existence!"

"Stop this," said Laheer sternly. "Your tiresome interdisciplinary feuds do not interest me. This evening we have a decision to make, a possibly distasteful one concerning the next phase of Project Yardstick. Hector, you will oblige me by leaving that wine alone; you, Doctor Rhys, will forget his ill-chosen words."

Yaer spoke softly, "I imagine Turlough envisaged the possibilities for research that these developments have furnished; and Hector, of course, has the best interests of his agents at heart. The two are not always compatible unfortunately." He kept his eyes fixed on his empty plate, which lay stranded on the brown polished mahogany table with his neatly folded napkin across it. "Oughtn't we to consider the position of the person most directly involved, therefore? I mean Jerlan, here." He nodded towards Nilssen on his left. "He has most to lose in the first instance."

Yaer had to be Laheer's hatchet man. With infinite kindness he would dissect Nilssen's secret soul, would discover Morwena, would decipher her significance to Yardstick, would discard her once she had been recorded in his computerlike intellect. He would understand dispassionately. Nilssen almost hated him in that moment of recognition.

And Morwena's guardian, who had been too sick to come out and meet Nilssen, who laid another obligation upon his discretion—he too risked being betrayed in a far worse fashion. No man so fated should have the news blurted out.

"I really can't pretend to be involved," Nilssen said

under Yaer's penetrating scrutiny. "It was a job that went wrong, that's all."

"Was it?" asked Yaer swiftly.

"I told you I wasn't your man."

"So did I," Kwambe volunteered before Yaer waved him to silence.

"No," said Yaer, "I believe something important happened between the attack and the escape." When he addressed Kwambe directly, even Laheer recoiled from the forbidding expression he had adopted. "Hector, give Jerlan a case history of a worm. So he'll be sure."

"Sure of what?" asked Kwambe.

"Sure that he is wise to withhold information."

Kwambe smiled, but Laheer frowned. "Jerlan, what haven't you told us?"

Why must we struggle through this sham? thought Nilssen even as he shook his head. *Yaer will draw it out of me.* "Nothing," he said emphatically, inciting Yaer to smile mysteriously as he said:

"Hector, tell us about Gwillem Crewkerne."

Everyone sat up. Kwambe ran a hand through his thinning, curly hair. "I, ah, hardly think that's wise—"

"It's a perfect example."

Kwambe laughed nervously. "Well, of course he is . . . was . . ."

Nilssen said, "I thought he was alive still."

At that Kwambe snatched up his wine glass and gulped a mouthful that set him coughing. Laheer paid no heed to this disobedience, apparently preoccupied with what Yaer was saying:

"That's an open issue. Late last year he volunteered for an assignment as yet incomplete. We never expect to see *him* again. What should interest us, however, are his reasons for taking on a task no one else would touch . . . Hector, are you recovered?"

Kwambe shook his head, so Yaer continued:

"Crewkerne was the security officer at the Institute of Hypothetical Physics in early September of 2011, the same month the Commissariat of National Integrity secretly began Operation Damocles there, in defiance of the government's hands-off policy towards the IHP.

"The CNI was obsessed with the idea that if they assassinated all the alternate-world analogues of Jacob Frobisher and Thomas Benyon, the two men behind our successful parachronological research, they would prevent The War from spilling over into our time line. The theory was, we were slightly ahead of the others, or success had worked for us but not for them; but given a while longer they might catch up and export their conflict to us. The CNI were willing to commit any crime to forestall progress in other lines.

"And those acts of violence *were* crimes eventually. The CNI could be allowed a couple of mistakes; they sincerely felt they were at war, in which killing would not be murder. But when it became obvious to the Institute that Damocles was worthless and was rebounding on us, the CNI would not stop. They sent out more assassination squads, compounding the damage they were doing to our world's stability, because the more they involved us with the other worlds, the greater became the pressures on our reality to conform to the general pattern. By October the Changes had started.

"Crewkerne got in the way of the CNI. Details are superfluous. Assume that he had a crisis of conscience. He was that sort. The CNI blacklisted him: for months they had been building this city, forewarned by Frobisher. Which redoubles their guilt, of course; they regarded the risks as great enough to warrant precautions yet they pressed on. That's bureaucracy for you, when it gets bloodyminded. Anyhow, only two million people could be accommodated, so a list had been prepared, a list demanding curious qualifications. Crewkerne's name had been on it; now, however, it was crossed off.

"You may say, so what? He was no unluckier than the rest of the Earth's population of numerous billions. Quite so. Except that certain people felt he was owed something for trying. People such as the girl he almost married, Elsebeytha Cartier, a secretary in the office of the Lord Lieutenant of Middlesex, then head of the CNI. When the world fell apart and Crewkerne was left behind, she initiated a campaign for his rescue.

"For twenty-three years she petitioned the Central Committee on every anniversary of the Purge. That was her way of emphasizing his importance as a symbol of what we all had lost: the CNI had killed him; but in wiping out the CNI in the City we had recovered nothing. Eventually, on the twenty-third try, the Committee relented."

When Yaer paused to take a sip of water—all he had drunk that evening—Laheer remarked:

"Crewkerne should have been satisfied to be so lucky."

"Do you say he was wrong to repay us as he did?" asked Yaer, his voice unmistakably hostile in tone. "And lucky? Don't forget the worm . . . Jerlan, we had to send Cartier back to before her own arrival at the Institute to join Damocles, lest she weaken and warn herself. As a test case of our ability to experiment with time safely, Cartier's movements were rigorously controlled.

"Crewkerne himself could not be salvaged entire. Like it or not, he had to live through the same cycle of events. But we could, and did, extract a microline copy of him—one of Turlough's odder accomplishments.

"The joke was, after all Cartier's trouble this copy of Crewkerne which she brought home had no first-hand experience of how much they meant to each other because *he* had not lived through the relevant period. Cartier is now twenty years his senior. Under those circumstances could *you* have resumed a non-existent engagement?"

A pang of sympathy for the two people stirred in Nilssen, followed at once by one of alarm. The parallel with his own life was too perfect to seem natural. "No," he said with difficulty.

Only Yaer was looking at him, all of a sudden. The exaggerated impassivity of the others warned him to be careful, yet he could not identify the reason. As best he could recall, Yaer's tale was true, and no more than coincidence; the emphasis being laid upon it was apparently that it should be taken as a cautionary tale, not as a snide analogy.

"So," said Yaer, "she lost him and he never had her. Ultimately the one she really wished to rescue was wiped out anyhow. That's the sort of tangle these worms can lead to. Most of the cases aren't half as well documented. Agents usually vanish when they become careless."

Nilssen decided he had been mistaken. Yaer had been lucky in his choice of example.

"Naturally," Nilssen said, "I think they both got a rotten deal, Crewkerne included. But if you want genuine tragedies, join me next time I have to explain to the friends of one of my workers just how he or she became involved in a fatal accident. Flooded hydroponics tanks, spilled chemical reagents, poison gas leaks, building collapse after storm damage. . . . Doctor, these sad stories are all around us. While I sympathize with this woman's predicament and take your advice to heart, I simply don't see the relevance."

Yaer said nothing. Nilssen tried to provoke a reaction:

"Fact one: we had a simple experiment that misfired. Fact two: while I was trying to recover the lost sword, someone, evidently from the City, stepped in and stopped me. Fact three: subsequent searches of the stranger's trail by agents sent out this afternoon have failed to find the sword, even aided by the proper transponder-locator. Fact four: Doctor Rhys says we mustn't intercept the man or we'll tangle the past.

"From those four facts I think we ought to assume that someone, perhaps sitting at this table, will decide in the months to come that it would be best to fill the stranger's shoes himself, so to speak. Bang, the problem is solved."

Rhys laughed sourly. "Facts again, Commissar? How do you know someone from the City nabbed you?"

"The snowshoes were our type."

"I see—so anyone wearing City snow shoes is a Citizen? Just as any Saxon carrying that sword would be? No, boy, we were conned."

"Who do you say was responsible, then?" asked Laheer.

"The CNI, of course," said Rhys.

"*No!*"

They all stared at Maia Kim, who had cried out. Now she clutched at Nilssen's arm.

"No, you're wrong," she said plaintively. "They were all purged—weren't they? I saw the executions myself, down there in Memorial Park: on the gallows where the fountain is now. . . . Oh no, Doctor Rhys, please be wrong . . . So many hanging bodies, all named, accounted for, along with the witnessed list of the Lost." Tears were forming in her eyes as Yaer answered her gently:

"No, Maia, not all. Not the worst of them all. Not Middlesex himself."

"Surely?" said Laheer stiffly.

"He was regarded as Government," Yaer said, leaving the table to fetch his noteblock from his jacket which was draped over an armchair. "That list ought to be on record somewhere still." He tapped the keyplate of the noteblock and skimmed the text presented to him on the small screen. "I have it: one mention only, as a former civil servant funded from the secret bursary . . . Turlough, you may be right."

"Contrariwise," said Rhys, "the CNI may not be involved."

"Dear God," cried Kwambe, rolling his eyes heavenward, "why'd you mention them then?"

"Because they are a distinct possibility."

"There are others?"

"Of lesser likelihood. For instance a Saxon might have stolen the sword but moved the Commissar away from immediate discovery so that when he, hopefully, was captured later, it would be assumed he had taken and hidden it. Thus a smoke screen would be created. Then coincidentally a City agent from our future is sent to track the thief, his snowshoes are mistaken for those of the Saxon, and so forth. . . . I must admit, however, that I wouldn't place much faith in the idea."

"To say the least," answered Kwambe.

"I think we ought to assume the worst," said Laheer loudly, attracting the attention of both men. "Is the worst possibility the involvement of the CNI. . . ? Doctor Rhys?"

"I'll need to evaluate—"

"Damn your evaluations! Yes? Or no?"

"Yes, I'd call it the worst case . . . as a first estimate."

"Hector Kwambe: your professional opinion?"

"Probably, yes."

"Doctor Yaer?"

"Tactically, yes."

About to address Maia Kim, Laheer turned back to Yaer. "Care to explain yourself?"

"I would. In my opinion we have neglected the question of whether or not Jerlan told us everything about his second visit. Without his cooperation our enemy may not only be the CNI, presupposing their survival, but also ourselves. Or, specifically, Jerlan

Nilssen himself may be the enemy of the moment."

"Hard words," said Laheer.

"I deem them appropriate."

"Well, Jerlan?"

Nilssen's heart sank at Yaer's indictment, for it struck at his weakness, his loyalty to the City. Meeting the psychologist's unblinking stare, he said, "That was cruel. You didn't have to say it—"

"I tried to avoid hurting you," replied Yaer.

"Jerlan, is there more?" asked Laheer.

"Yes," said Nilssen. "Yes, there is. I haven't decided what it means; but I met a girl—a woman—in the village, who claimed to be a friend."

"A chance resemblance?" enquired Kwambe.

"No," said Yaer quickly. "She could prove it, couldn't she?"

Nilssen had almost agreed with Kwambe. "She proved it, yes," he said instead. "She was mute, but she used modern sign language, said I had promised to come back to her. She even seemed to know things about me I've never disclosed to anyone in the City. . . . She *knew* me. Is that the pound of flesh you wanted, Doctor Yaer?"

"Not quite all of it. You've come this far. Tell us the rest."

"I've told you everything."

Their eyes remained locked.

"No," said Yaer. "You haven't relaxed yet."

Nilssen discovered to his surprise how tense his face had grown. There was, after all, no magic in the psychologist. Some of the tension eased.

"That's it," said Yaer softly. "Now, did you learn how long it had been since you and she had met, or parted?"

"No more than a couple of years. She talked—signed, I mean—in a way that suggested a short separation."

"How could you tell?" Kim asked suddenly. Breaking free of Yaer's hypnotic gaze, Nilssen looked at her, then away at the table display of flowers.

"Hard to say. Fluent signing doesn't transliterate into spoken language too well; it turns into a stream of shorthand symbols for ideas, idioms that can mean very little to vocalizing people. Relationships affect the choice of symbols, I suppose. I can't be more specific— it simply felt as if we'd not been apart long."

Laheer cleared his throat. "How is it you know this dumb-sign language—" He faltered. "Of course, your wife . . ."

"I was convinced," Nilssen continued, controlling himself, "by her familiarity with some of Eva's gestures, the incidental modifications we worked out together. Through them she expressed what she felt for me. And that, Doctor Yaer, is something private which I refuse to repeat."

"No need," said Yaer offhandedly. "You've told us already. . . . Obviously there is going to be a third expedition; and my guess is that the target date would be . . ." He addressed himself to his noteblock for a few seconds. "The winter of 877 to 878. The area: southwestern England around the Somerset marshes, concentrating on Athelney."

There was a general stir amongst those at the table. Suspiciously, as it seemed to Nilssen, Laheer said, "You sound very sure of that."

"I think I understand," said Rhys, nodding his head. "All these loose ends flapping about in the breeze: the CNI, this woman, the sword, the attack—we can tie them up in one knot. This is the third fold-back. Right, Doctor Yaer? Am I right, boy?"

"Absolutely," said Yaer. "That was the winter when Alfred the Great was on his knees and the Danes were about to chop up Britain, except that he rallied and pushed them back. If the CNI are anywhere around that date, they'll be there in Alfred's camp, subverting his cause, trying to destroy us up here in their future.

It was long enough ago to make a small change suffi-cient, but recent enough to be well-documented. And it fits the data."

"But we don't depend on this line's past," said Kim dubiously. "The War broke the continuity."

"Ah," said Rhys, "but suppose The War never started? Suppose the Danes established a different kind of history? We don't come from one past alone; and one past doesn't lead to only one future. The Danes might win in one time line, and their success could replicate into many others like an infection; it would have to, if it stemmed from a probable out-come."

"And," said Yaer, "it was very much fifty-fifty for Alfred. By rights he should have lost."

"Did someone make sure he won?" murmured Kwambe.

"No," said Yaer. "Alfred's victory is standard in all the histories we've been able to study. If the CNI *are* there, they total no more than a few individuals; and no small group could change defeat to victory, despite the balance. But victory into defeat would be relative-ly simple, for the CNI. Something caused us to visit the years 877 to 878, or thereabouts, because this girl Jerlan met makes that necessary."

"That should please you, Commissar," said Rhys with a wink. "Was she pretty?"

"Does that matter?" Nilssen retorted tartly to hide his twofold triumph. Yes, she was pretty, and more; and the secret of her guardian was still his. To worry over. As intended, Yaer's astuteness had not elicited that last scrap from him; and Nilssen did not intend that it should, ever.

CHAPTER SEVEN

The ringing phone roused him to a headache and the conviction that he had been very foolish the night before. The wan light of early morning illuminated his bedroom curtains, creating a rectangle of insipid flint-gray by whose glow he located the phone, his hand weaving towards the handset and raising it to his ear.

"This is Yaer," said the familiar voice, so calmly that Nilssen could hardly believe it belonged to the same man who had sat up as late as any at Laheer's party. "Listen to me. Do not speak. Please go at once to the museum at the foot of the Spanish Steps. At once. I depend on your discretion." The line cleared, leaving only dial tone.

Partly because he was now awake but mostly because he had never heard Yaer make such a request of any-one in such a tone, Nilssen complied, arriving at the designated spot within twenty-five minutes.

The Spanish Steps were a re-creation of the vanished fragment of Rome that had once been known by that same name. Like their prototype, they wound up be-tween high flanking walls. This was a district of the City noted more for its quaintness than for its state of good repair. In fact, the peeling stucco and chipped stonework were tended constantly by the refurbish-ment squads and were an integral part of the district's bohemian air. Here were many of the craft workshops and hobbyist display arcades, deserted and a delight to wander through during the working week, bustling with pleasure-seekers and barterers on the weekends. At the foot of the steps, beside an archway opening onto a piazza where a fountain played, was the museum Yaer had mentioned, an architectural afterthought crammed with wood carvings and slender pillars supporting high-springing, domical vaults.

No natural light penetrated far beyond the beaded curtains across the door; within was only the artificial radiance of phosphorescent mosaics, encrusting every permanent surface with vivid colors. Woods that by day would have been beautiful became, in this Aladdin's cave, sublime; shapes that had been imposed upon wondrously veined and patterned raw timber were transmuted by fugitive reflections into a catalogue of mental states, haunting the peripheral vision like things in dreams that will not rest but must always be changing.

Few people cared to subject themselves to a second visit, so the museum was frequently empty, even on the busiest of days, save for its proprietor, an elderly one-eyed man whose hobby it was when he was not engaged in the upkeep of the civic woodwork in his Parish. Nilssen had met him once a long time back, and nodded to him when he pushed through the bead curtain into the rainbow interior.

The old carver nodded back, then stood aside as if to imply Nilssen should precede him toward the rear of the long narrow space.

Yaer was waiting in the workshop, leaning against a workbench littered with knives and chisels and the crisp shavings of the proprietor's morning labors. There were no mosaics here, only a pair of plain white lamps on multijointed booms whose glare revived Nilssen's headache at once.

"I'm afraid the lights are necessary," Yaer said. "They baffle any cameras Laheer may have planted here."

"And the secrecy?" asked Nilssen, shielding his eyes and thereby gaining some relief.

"Doubly so. Laheer would not want us to meet; he would suspect my motives. You go tomorrow—did you know that?"

"So soon?"

"Laheer would have sent you today, Sunday or no, except that Kwambe told him the special crew had been sent home after your return yesterday. And Maia Kim insisted on six hours for your imprinting."

The psychologist stared at his feet.

"So?" prompted Nilssen.

Yaer looked up. "You won't be going alone," he said. "I want to go with you, if you'll let me."

His unwonted humility lessened the impact of his words. Nevertheless, Nilssen was surprised and, when he thought about the implications, offended.

"I can't take—" he began.

"You can. You will. Jerlan, you have to!" Yaer's demeanor had reverted from the supplicant to the authoritative. "I was wrong to think that mental quality was sufficient. It's not; your accident—a silly blade of grass, for the Cause of Shazol!—demonstrated that a man alone is a ready victim for any mischance. So a second man has to go with you."

"And suddenly you become suitable for duty when you failed to volunteer last time someone was needed?"

"You were first choice," Yaer said. "I was your understudy."

"Then why are we meeting here, hidden away from Laheer?"

Yaer's gaze wandered about the room, avoiding Nilssen.

"All right," Nilssen said, "you have your reasons for wanting to accompany me. But I have mine for preventing you. The winter of 877 and 878 was one of the severest for many years, even by the standards of an age when exposure to the elements was taken for granted. Houses were drafty; waterproof garments were almost unknown; in winter whole communities could perish from starvation or cold. . . ."

"And if I came, I'd be a liability, that's what you're saying?"

Nilssen had not wanted to put his objection in so many words.

"How old are you, Doctor?"

"Old enough not to count years when judging a man," said Yaer.

"How old?"

"Forty."

"I've always wondered about that slight huskiness in your voice. Someone said you'd had TB when you were younger."

"Actually it was diphtheria—from which I made a complete recovery. . . . Jerlan, if it's a medical certificate you want, I have it right here in my wallet." Yaer fumbled in an inside pocket.

"Put it away," Nilssen said, disguising his anger by emphasizing his genuine concern. Yaer always had an answer ready. "Are you set on suicide? And on taking me with you?"

Yaer considered his question carefully. "I believe not," he said. "My responses to psycho-suggestion tests on suicide are negative, so presumably my drives are healthy. As to 'taking you with me': your doubts are reasonable, though I must protest your choice of expression."

I've cracked the shell, Nilssen thought, amazed.

Out in the display room the bead curtain clacked and rattled. A young woman spoke quietly. A male voice answered her. At once Yaer held a finger to his lips and went to spy through the partially open workshop door. Nilssen saw him relax; then Yaer beckoned him over to look for himself.

The proprietor was proudly guiding a young couple around the carvings. By their appearance and behavior Nilssen classified them at once as trainees from different disciplines; evidently this particular Sunday had yielded coincident days off work, a chance they had seized on for companionable relaxation. Their hands remained loosely linked as they strolled after the old carver, their faces politely attentive, demonstrating the interest that lovers can discover for anything when in each other's company. They were no threat; after a few seconds Yaer quietly shut the solid door.

"You were saying?" he asked.

"It's a form of words," Nilssen said, recapturing his argument. "An exaggeration, maybe; but how else can I phrase it? You belong in the City."

"With my nose to the grindstone?"

"What do you mean?"

Yaer shook his head. "Nothing much, only—" Stretching himself, he said, "I grow so tired sometimes. Not physically, but mentally. Those two out there in the museum: I wonder what they do for a living. His hands are calloused; perhaps he's one of your lower-ranks laborers. And hers are pale, but her face is tanned: a farm girl, I expect. What they do now is unimportant; they could swap jobs any time. Our ecumenic socialism guarantees that right to every citizen. But you and I, Jerlan, are stuck where we are. Imprinting can only lend knowledge; it cannot impose the requisite personal characteristics, so the great are trapped by their obligations to the small. Didn't your heart beat that fraction faster at the promise of escape, that night when we discussed Project Yardstick in your office? And when you saw the living countryside again, didn't you taste a quality of life the City owns no part of? That's what I want to see: a world in which history still matters, unlike this City of ours, this museum full of fossils." His face and voice became imploring: "Jerlan, please don't obstruct me in this."

Uncomfortable at being confronted with weakness in someone he had long thought totally self-possessed, Nilssen defended himself feebly:

"Doctor Yaer, we have to be objective. You and I are valuable assets to our community. Removing me is bad enough—there has been chaos in my department these last few months; Omak has been seriously over-loaded with work—but removing you also is crazy. Anyone who comes with me has to be expendable. You don't qualify."

Yaer replied, "There's an old saying in management circles, to the effect that a good manager can disappear and not be missed. That being so . . ." Even though shadowed by the lights at his back, his grin was conspicuous.

"So I overstated the problem."

"And there *are* others who can stand in for me."

After a decent interval Nilssen asked, "Can you brief me on the mission?"

"Thank you," said Yaer.

"I didn't ask for thanks."

"Have them anyhow," Yaer answered. "As to the mission: King Alfred had a reputation for being keen to talk to foreigners, which suggested an opening. Unfortunately, for the best part of eighty years Britain as a whole had been having trouble with foreigners, so to gain time for questions the locals' curiosity has to be aroused by some distinctive feature of the disguise."

"Don't tell me," Nilssen remarked, "you and I are going as the two halves of a pantomime horse."

Yaer sighed. "You don't want me along. You told me so; I heard you; I understand. But if I am, after all, to be of assistance rather than the hindrance you expect, we must not be enemies. Last night I bore down on you hard, yes; but because it had to be done. We—" Evidently he revised whatever he had been on the verge of saying, for when he restarted his sentence

the "we" seemed to connote a different group of people. "We have to cooperate fully."

"You and me and Laheer, for instance?"

"Could we leave that to later?"

"Why do I trust you?" commented Nilssen dispiritedly, at which Yaer nodded without explaining himself.

Resuming his didactic tone, the psychologist said,
"Most foreigners in Britain during the ninth century
were light-skinned. If it weren't for the possible presence of better-informed CNI refugees in Alfred's camp,
I might recommend melanization: black men would
have been a hit at court. But we have to avoid anachronism of that sort. Instead, we'll be going as Arabs—"

Nilssen could not stifle his laughter at the incon-
gruity of the notion. In common with most folk his
mind had long since compartmentalized the ancient
world into segregated cultures that coexisted no more
closely than did the parallel worlds with which he was
familiar.

"Why not Chinamen?" he asked. "We could take
along a few rockets."

"Do let's be serious," said Yaer. "In about fifteen
minutes a City-wide search for you will start when
Maia Kim cannot contact you for your imprinting.
You and I both have to go our separate ways shortly,
until the morning."

"But Arabs?"

"Your course will cover Old Arabic and the culture
of the Mediterranean peoples up to 880." Yaer allowed
a malicious smile to spread across his face. "Oh, and
afterwards the dentist will replace those fillings of
yours with false dentine and enamel."

"That," said Nilssen, "is taking seriousness too damn
far! The Saxons can take my fillings as part of the
disguise. Arab doctors had a high standing; check your
own data files."

"I have," replied Yaer. "And if the CNI are as closely in touch with our affairs as we think, they can too. Dental work of that standard was beyond the Arabs, according to the records. And, since we're doing it by the book on this cover story, those fillings come out. Or would you rather have a CNI man peering into your mouth someday soon?"

Nilssen capitulated without a word.

"Good," Yaer said. "When you go from the museum, take a bit of wood with you. I strongly recommend the one titled 'Anxiety'—he carved it after his last session with me." More soberly, he said, "Jerlan, will I be seeing you tomorrow?"

"And the day after, I expect," Nilssen replied.

CHAPTER EIGHT

Exhausted by his last night in the City, Nilssen would have slept through the entire journey to the secret site in Somerset but for Yaer's constant interruptions. Lately there had been far too many long days and short nights; true, the night just past could have been an exception; and perhaps he ought to have spent it alone. The miracle was, he realized, that he was bearing the strain far better than a man of his age ought. He wished Yaer would either cease worrying about details or do so quietly. For a while he had been folding and refolding an unmanageably large-scale map of Somerset and Avon, rustling it loudly. Suddenly he said, "There's an awful lot of water here."

"Poor drainage," Nilssen muttered, half-opening his eyes. The maps were probably wrong, anyway. Aerial surveys had been prohibited lest the CNI see the flying drones, thereby forcing the Geodetic Survey department back onto reconstructions and interpolations of parallel worlds.

"I know that," Yaer answered testily. "How do we make a dry transfer?"

Overnight Yaer's equanimity had weakened considerably, as if his nerve were failing him now that he had got his way over going. Though tired, Nilssen was not so enervated as to be indifferent to this change; but for the moment he could conceive no remedy better than leaving Yaer to find his feet alone. Yawning, he said, "The technicians will have explored the far end for us."

Drowsily Nilssen regarded Yaer through half-closed eyes, thinking what an odd Arab the psychologist made. To a Saxon, the small man would appear slightly undersize but well-fleshed, though Nilssen saw him as lean and well short of the City height average. His clothes comprised a hybrid mess of Saxon and Arab styles: baggy blue trousers under a grubby khaki tunic, over which was a patched gray djellaba which bulked his torso out disproportionately to his lower body. His boots were of thick leather nailed to wooden soles, one of which had lost a large chunk near the toe, while his timeshift belt masqueraded as a nondescript cracked leather strap about his waist with a clumsy buckle that housed the mechanism. Had there been a mirror in which to compare himself with Yaer, Nilssen knew he would be no more impressed by his own appearance; the intention had been to depict two over-traveled strangers down on their luck, on which account he had no complaints against the costumers.

Yaer took up his clipboard of final briefing notes. "Have you read these?" he asked Nilssen.

"Twice," Nilssen said.

"Why do you suppose Alfred was able to build his camp at Athelney in only a week: Friday the fourteenth of March through to Good Friday of 878? At the end of a long hard winter, too."

"You work fast if your life depends on the finished product," said Nilssen. "A disciplined army can achieve wonders: the Romans used to establish a new camp with palisaded walls every night. Besides, the few men Alfred had with him hardly required more than a couple of shacks to sleep in; and the marshes would discourage the Danes until the spring."

"But if we're going to arrive on the twenty-ninth, they'll not have built spare quarters for visitors."

"We're *important* visitors. Alfred won't leave us out in the open."

"You hope."

"I'm beginning to trust my luck," Nilssen said. He was interrupted when the door into the pilot's compartment of the flier opened to admit a brief babble of radio talk and Varno Malchek, the expedition's Director of Operations.

Gravely Malchek strapped himself into a seat beside Yaer. Though about Nilssen's age, his added six years had brought with them gray hair and wrinkles in abundance. Police life could be hard. However, his voice still contained authority and his mind was still keen.

"We land in five minutes," he said, "after which, Doctor Yaer, you're on your own. If the Chief Commissar catches you . . ." With a small shrug he looked away, out of the window at the rising ground below. Eastward there was a glimpse of the Mendip Hills and Glastonbury Tor, a lone summit amid the mudflats of the Somerset levels. Clouds flitted past the window, darkening the sunlight from yellow-white to watery gray.

Making a mental note of Malchek's willingness to oblige Yaer illegally, Nilssen borrowed the map and opened it across his knees. He had difficulty in arranging the folds of his trousers so they would not foul the scabbard of the dagger at his waist but managed to spread the map wide enough to show the general area around Alfred's camp.

"We were discussing conditions at the far end," he said to Malchek. "What can you tell us?"

Malchek peered at the map, his head held at an angle that puzzled Nilssen until he remembered the man's defective left eye.

"About here," Malchek said, touching the pattern of blue and brown with a manicured forefinger. "Most of the country is peat bogs and deep water. They had a high rainfall the previous autumn but subzero temperatures for the past three months, so the ice will be safe. It took the weight of a ground crawler drone, at least; and they weigh more than a man. Here and there are islands of higher ground, one of which is big enough for a safe transfer. For extra security you will arrive at night; at dawn you will follow a route traced on rice paper which you will later eat or allow to disintegrate once you have sighted the Saxon encampment."

"Have you any pictures of it?" asked Yaer.

Malchek shook his head emphatically. "Photo-drones show far too high a profile. Orders were to stay hidden. The crawler found a route, logged it, and that was that."

The flier came to earth gently amid drizzle and a field of mud. As the hatch opened, a force field canopy was developed above them and they disembarked for a short walk along a raised walkway that led into a larger, temporary Fregar dome. This spanned a circular patch of mud over four hundred meters in diameter on which had been erected numerous prefabricated huts and a network of walkways. Off to one side a grounded communications flier had extended a telescopic antenna mast through the dome. Still farther towards the perimeter were four small unarmed scouting fliers; these appeared to have been idle for some hours, as their landing skids were awash with mud and no heat haze rose from their engine vents. Next to them was the contrastingly nonaerodynamic shape of a mobile power station from which billowed a gale of hot air that was the heat supply for the entire field station. Already a crust had formed on the mud and the humidity within the dome's compass was uncomfortably high.

At the middle of the dome was an oval platform to which the newcomers were conducted. The mandatory clear zone around the launch point was delineated by a fluorescent orange circle, so that from above the platform resembled an eye whose empty iris stared up from between corneal segments crowded with equipment and its operators. Embroiled though he was in pre-transfer activity, Nilssen observed that the narrow strips above and below the "iris" remained deserted; and, furthermore, that anyone who had cause to cross them did so hastily.

"Look over there," said Malchek when Nilssen asked about them. "An armed flier has its sights laid across that circle." The squat black arrowhead sat motionless, its flare guns deployed but inert; in his mind Nilssen extrapolated the field of fire and saw that only the invulnerable Fregar dome was in the way. "Laheer thought you might be captured," said Malchek. "Doctor Rhys has constructed those belts so they'll revert to these spatial coordinates, one second after your departure time, no matter where or when they start from at the other end. We want to be sure that only the right returnees leave that circle . . . alive."

After the weighing and measuring was completed, Malchek took Nilssen aside and said, "There's someone in the communications flier wants a word with you."

"What about Doctor Yaer?"

"He only asked for you."

Yaer was not far away, sitting on the edge of the platform with his hood pulled over his head to hide his face. Nilssen considered calling him anyway; then he decided not to. If Laheer had found them out, he would arrest whom he pleased and hear testimony later. Yaer would be picked up at the proper moment.

The "someone" was Kwambe; and he was alone, playing a game of solitaire on his noteblock. Nilssen shut the flier's hatch behind him and regarded his friend steadily. "Hello, Hector," he said.

"Ah," said Kwambe, cheerfully. "I have a present

for you." He removed a long thin parcel from a locker. "Surgeon Hartmann says she doesn't really understand why you want it but adds that she can trust you to appreciate its effectiveness. Does that mean anything?"

Double relief suffused Nilssen. In his haste to leave the City he had totally forgotten his special request of Hartmann, phoned through to her answering service on Sunday afternoon. In the absence of any reply he had assumed her refusal. "Thanks," he said, hefting the parcel and estimating its weight at five or six pounds. "This may prove very useful." The Hospital workshops were accustomed to urgent orders for hardware, so a plastic tube disguised as a staff would not tax their resources, although the dozen rounds of anaesthetic darts might have raised a few objections from the dispensary stores.

Kwambe clicked his teeth together impatiently. "Jerlan, either open it or hop it. I dislike mysteries."

"Live with this one, Hector. The fewer people know about my secret weapon, the sounder I'll sleep where I'm going."

The other man's mouth turned down at the corners. "Am I a suspect also? Then to hell with it; damn your secrets." Seizing the hatch lever, he swung it across to "Unlocked"; humid air rolled in as the hatch opened.

Nilssen pulled it shut again. Had the shock absorbers not foiled him, he would have slammed it. "Hector, use your brain for one second!" he said. "An hour from now I'll be in enemy territory with one solitary companion, rejoicing in the reasonable prospect of being caught and killed by any of three rival factions. Namely: the Danes, the Anglo-Saxons, or the CNI. Given a lot of luck, the Anglo-Saxons will get us first and restrain themselves long enough to ask our names. Having—somehow—made friends with them, we have to learn who, of all the odd bodies we're liable to meet, is connected with the CNI. Once we've found the

enemy's people and established that they don't belong
to that era, we must quietly subtract them from it.

"Now, Hector, do you imagine I'm going to shorten
the odds in our favor by telling the world what my
methods will be? Before you answer, recall that *someone from the City* is due to attack me in 880 and steal
that sword. We still have no idea who, only a fuzzy
photo of a tall figure in loose clothes. Think about it."

"Kick me sometime," Kwambe apologized. "Whatever your secret weapon is, I hope it works."

The parcel remained unopened, though Nilssen car-
red it with him everywhere, through the final checkout
and to the platform, exciting inquiries from several
people, not least the technicians whose task was to account for all mass transmitted through the timeshifter.
Eventually the cuffs and belts were fitted and the
stabilizers built into their clothes were activated. Yaer
and Nilssen waited alone at the center of the launch
circle. The signal to proceed was given; and the guns
of the flier twitched, correcting their aim.

"No second thoughts?" asked Nilssen quietly.

"None. Just press the button," said Yaer in an unsteady but peculiarly eager voice.

Dawn of Saturday the twenty-ninth day of March,
year of grace eight hundred and seventy-eight, came
upon them slowly.

It began as a paleness in the mist which lay low
upon the frozen marshes. Directly overhead the sky
was clear, shot with stars in constellations that Nilssen
found immediately recognizable. Towards the horizon
the mist thickened into a dewy haze whose lowest levels reduced their world to a circle hardly larger than
that from which they had embarked in the far future.

Finding themselves upon a grassy islet, they had
agreed to stay put, though the mist had not then
formed. Mile after mile about them lay a land rigid

with ice, blanched by a sliver of a waning moon. In that labyrinth of channels winding amongst tussocky islets ringed by the husks of bearded sedges they would lose themselves too easily. A bitter frost had rimed the dead rushes that choked the pools and rivulets; a fitful breeze stirred these and brought from across the icy miles the faintest hint of dampness. The conditions were ideal for fog.

Huddling down in their cloaks, they stayed awake by talking in low voices, discussing plans that were founded, Nilssen felt, more on optimism than sense. Seen denuded of plant life, the mudlands of the twenty-seventh century were no threat, however huge and depressing. The selfsame area in the ninth century was a swarming wilderness, a land strange in every respect, the home of people for whom the City and all it implied did not exist. Two intruders surely could not but fail. When Nilssen unwrapped his parcel and explained the purpose of the mock staff, Yaer showed no more than dull interest.

"Twelve darts?" he said. "You can't knock out every enemy."

His apathy perturbed Nilssen as another sign of the change that had begun before the shift to the ninth century. Maintaining a tactful cheerfulness, Nilssen said, "Oh, but we don't have to. Only suspects will be dosed."

"That won't prove a thing," Yaer objected with slightly greater animation. "If it falls asleep, it's hostile, yes?"

"No. Think: even if the CNI refugees came through the old cargo gates, their bodies will still be better attuned to *our* time than this. Therefore a CNI agent will retain the drug overdose significantly longer than a local, who will quickly lose it. So if it *stays* asleep, it's hostile."

Yaer's reply was a sarcastic laugh and a long sullen

silence at the end of which he asked, "Could we make a fire?"

"Danes might see it."

"On a night like this?"

Intuitively Nilssen saw that Yaer was not asking questions to be enlightened, since Yaer was as well-informed as he by virtue of the same imprinting course. His innocent inquiries smacked of a corrupt Socratic interrogation, intent upon argument for its own sake, a truly odd turnabout by the customarily dispassionate peacemaker.

"Why, on any night," Nilssen replied casually adding before Yaer might protract the dispute, "The Anglo-Saxon Chronicle makes frequent mention of Danish winter marches, as though the pirates were so hardened by their continuous warmaking that the weather was a trivial thing. Even as we sit here—" he gazed towards what he guessed to be the northeast, though the thickening mist had begun to confuse his sense of direction "—several hundred of them are camped at Chippenham. That's only forty-five miles. God knows how many are wandering loose on foraging sweeps, besides those spying on Alfred's doings."

Yaer sighed and was quiet a while longer. Later, when the mist was so dense in the channels that their island seemed afloat on it, he sighed again. "Nowhere," he said.

The puff of vapor he had exhaled with the word drifted away.

"Who cares?" he asked in a despairing tone. "I mean, who cares?"

"About what?" replied Nilssen.

"Look." Yaer fumbled in a concealed pocket and struck a match. The scrape, pop, and fizz of it were startlingly loud; but it burned invisibly, hidden by his cloak, and what little smoke it gave off was swallowed by entropic reversion. When he dropped the blackened stick on the frosty grass it sizzled briefly, then disappeared.

"That match was real," Yaer said. "It didn't belong here, so it had to go. All this around us is false; I cannot believe in it. All I believe in is you, me, and that match. How long before we too must disappear, Jerlan?"

Baffled by Yaer's behavior, Nilssen could think of nothing to say.

"Thanks," Yaer said abruptly.

"For what?"

"For not interfering."

"The match? Don't thank me. If I had any idea—"

"That also. Mostly . . ." His djellaba cast an impenetrable shadow over his face, so that only his chin could be seen in the wan moonlight, bobbing as he talked. Nilssen imagined he bit his lip. "About Laheer, and his objections to my coming along. Thanks for trusting me."

"You *do* owe me an explanation," Nilssen reminded him.

"True; but would you mind revealing why you refrained from going to Laheer?"

"Because Laheer is an ignorant umpire for his experts. He bases his decisions on precedents and rules. Rhys showed me there were few rules worth a candle; and this project surely has no precedents. Furthermore, I asked myself why he'd be so strongly against you going onto field work and remembered his irrational gut-objections to my first excursion. My silence was an act of faith. Was it a mistake?"

"I'll tell you about Laheer," said Yaer with passion. "He's sick, sick with a paranoid delusion that when his back is turned everyone he relies on will desert him. You, me, Kwambe, Kim, even Rhys. Every morning he demands from the personnel register a listing of his key officers' whereabouts, which he reads and checks with that trick television of his before break-fast. Hartmann held you incommunicado in hospital longer than necessary to protect you from his harass-ment. That, Jerlan, is the man who runs the City."

"And you've told nobody?"

"I couldn't."

"It was your duty—"

"Will you take my word on it, Jerlan, it was out of my hands!"

"But the one person who could depose the Chief Commissar unaided is you, Yaer. A single memoran-dum is all it would take."

"Oh, physically it could be done," agreed Yaer with caustic heartiness. "Politically it would make me a hero for a few days. But if I did . . . if I did . . ." Air whistled between his front teeth as he sucked hard. . . . "The repercussions . . ."

Then he said:

"Does your disguise please you?"

Nilssen hesitated, then answered in Old Arabic, de-liberately affecting a poetic style:

"It is written that each soul is hostage to its own deeds. That which I am, I am always; no garment can change me. Therefore, that which I seem is neither pleasing nor displeasing; it is me. Before you stands Ibrahim ibn-Haroun, traveler distressed by misfortune, seeking succor of a kindly king whose Christian charity may smile upon even such as I appear to be."

Yaer snorted and answered sourly in Old English:

"You sound born to the part. As to who you seem, every lie should contain seed crystals of truth for it to be credible. . . . And *my* disguise?"

More carefully, Nilssen answered him, again in Arabic, "As with all new cloth, time will shape it to you."

Persistently Yaer continued with the twanging gut-turals of Old English as though by his choice of language he threw down a challenge to the rasping Arabic. "You have doubts. Speak your mind."

Reverting to Modern English, Nilssen said, "You need a second name in case someone insists on knowing it."

The hood of Yaer's djellaba rustled as he shook his head. Though he copied Nilssen's adoption of the modern tongue, yet he remained inflexible. "Khaled is enough. It was a deliberate restriction."

"Like your real name?"

"What do you mean?" he asked tightly.

"I've always called you 'Yaer,'" said Nilssen. "Thinking back, I can't recall ever hearing your first name. Nobody uses it."

"Not important."

"Don't let's be so formal, especially here."

"Here you'll address me as Khaled. The locals will expect it."

Tentatively Nilssen asked, "Do these questions bother you?"

"No."

The denial sounded automatic, the product of a defense that Yaer had long ago constructed in himself and long ago lost control of.

"Are you sure?"

"One name is all I want," Yaer answered hotly. "Will you leave me alone?"

Nilssen made no rejoinder. A sensitive nerve had been stimulated; before long Yaer would have to soothe its itch, which he shortly did in a curiously innocuous, deadpan voice.

"Yaer is a false name," he said. "When I was twenty-one and free to make some decisions for myself, I took it to escape the man who was my father, Chief Commissar Laheer."

Several seconds passed before Nilssen thought to draw breath again.

"You are *Laheer's* son?" he asked weakly.

"Didn't I say so?" retorted Yaer. "That's why I don't care to add another name: one lie in a lifetime is enough, when it's so large. Jerlan, Laheer is the man you say I should have thrown out of office for mental incompetence. Very well, suppose I did. If I moved against him, do you imagine he would stay quiet? It amuses Laheer to keep my secret, because it gives him a sort of power over me. And if that power were broken, he'd invoke another: the power of conventional family morality. It's strong in the City, Jerlan; let the news of what I did to my own father become public knowledge and I'd be a pariah. Nobody would trust me. My life depends on manipulating people. I'm good at it; but to be successful I must be trusted. Without trust I have no job, no life. And Laheer relies on that weakness."

"Did you have to change names? A famous father—"

"—can be a curse. Laheer interferes endlessly. By changing names I hoped to make him understand that what I wanted was to be myself, rather than some part of his shadow. Instead he seized on the anonymity it gave me to advance me through the City's hierarchy faster than he might otherwise have dared. That dear father of mine, who can do no wrong in the Council's eyes, is a born fixer. He fixed Malchek, for instance, when Malchek wouldn't cooperate just once, by freezing his promotions for eight years. I'm not stupid, Jerlan. Transgress that invisible boundary and Laheer will get you, whoever you are. The only way out is to be better than he is. When I have an independent voice, then people will listen to me without hearing echoes of Laheer in what I say."

"And participation in the final defeat of the CNI would do it." Indeed, the chance must have been an irresistible lure to someone desperate to win personal glory, possibly to the extent that Yaer would forget that theirs was meant to be a team effort.

Yaer neither agreed nor disagreed; but he said, "I left a note."

"Oh, terrific!" Nilssen exclaimed, visualizing a court martial and the inevitable consequent tinkering with his mental processes. "You had to be sure of making trouble, didn't you?"

"No, I had to be sure he'd leave us alone," said Yaer earnestly, "prior to departure at least."

"And after?"

"Now it's different. We're here and we can do the job. My belt is no longer slaved to yours; there's no way you'll persuade me to risk the guns of that flier."

"What *did* you say in that note?"

"A few home truths about his past."

"Yaer, I'm done with messing about! What did you say?"

"I reminded him of a certain evening before the Collapse, when we had a special visitor to our house. Even at the age of twelve I knew enough about the world to disbelieve his pretense that he held down an ordinary job. Few of my friends' parents could have afforded private cars the size of ours, or our home, or the numerous smaller luxuries we took for granted. That night I eavesdropped from the first-floor balcony. Very little was audible, save for when the visitor was putting on his coat to leave. Then, in the few seconds he was alone with my mother, I heard him say, 'My dear, the Lord Lieutenant does not demand miracles, only loyalty. Please, encourage him.' A few weeks later my mother left us. She wrote to me a few times, then we heard she had been arrested for treason. In those days they still shot people, so I never saw her again. But I think she had discovered something she could neither live with nor keep to herself. Much later I connected these events with the CNI."

Incredulously Nilssen asked, "And so Laheer is Middlesex?"

"Of course not," answered Yaer. "That woman Cartier who used to work in his office would have recognized him as would dozens of others. All I'm saying is that Laheer had a part to play in that business. Keeping quiet about it is worth his life to him; and mine to me, before I had objective proof. Unhappily, that proof lies in the guns of that flier, which will fire accidentally as soon as anyone appears on the staging. While you were closeted with Kwambe, I asked around; one of the technicians said the flier arrived in a hurry minutes ahead of us, which would fit tidily into my estimate of when Laheer must have found the note and acted on it."

"So you've closed our line of retreat. Thanks a lot."

"Jerlan, nobody is asking you to do more than was agreed. The night after you came back from the village and we talked about the CNI around Laheer's table, I watched his face. When Alfred was mentioned, it went white. So there *is* something here that can't bear investigation. We need only find whoever is hiding at Athelney and use their link with the City to get home. There must be a link or Laheer wouldn't be so concerned."

"Wait," said Nilssen. "Anything that is due to happen in these times is firm fact by the twenty-seventh century. Laheer is helpless. If we won, we'll win; if the CNI won, it'll make no difference."

"Exactly," said Yaer pleasantly. "*That* is why he's worried. He has probably been advancing some scheme all these years, then suddenly it falls apart in his hands. At every turn he has tried to obstruct Project Yardstick, only people won't do as he wants. Something has fouled the works: your brush with those hunters; the theft of the sword; Rhys's success with his timeshifters; you and that girl, Morwena. It is as though one string has been pulling every piece together, so that the whole weight of coincidence has been caused to collapse on Laheer's head. I'm tempted to agree with Rhys and his ideas about predestination. Nature takes the easiest course most times."

"And you don't mind profiting from it?"

"Not in the least. My presence here may be a prerequisite. But you'll not find me weeping when the day of Laheer's downfall comes, when we enter the City by the back door."

"I wonder," said Nilssen. This new Yaer was strange to him, more competent and more sinister than the old. "You could have warned me."

Sighing with apparent irritation, Yaer said, "I didn't want an accident all of my own, Jerlan. Everyone I told was a security risk. Now at least I'll have company." In the darkness it was hard to tell if he had been attempting a joke.

Nilssen inspected the sky. A veil of mist obscured the stars, transforming them into fuzzy blotches; but in the east there was a hint of morning. "The wind's stronger," he said. "We ought to start walking."

Stiff from their cold sojourn on the islet, to begin with they made clumsy going of their cross-country march. Fortunately the early part of the route was simple, for it consisted of following a wide channel. However, by dawn the wind had subsided once more, bringing down thick mist that forced them to halt. Although the ice on the marsh pools would have borne them and there was no risk of stumbling into quicksands or sloughs, they had become dependent on landmarks. One mistake could send them wandering far from the path picked out by the drone crawler and far from shelter. Already they were tired and shivering, and their food supply was finished.

Their new island sanctuary boasted a pair of storm-twisted willows. Yaer amused himself by studying them. Crowns of lesser plants nestled amongst their upper branches, including ferns and brambles dormant within coats of hoarfrost. One tree was smothered to half its height in ivy, while the other sported a scum of ferny lichen like a fur coat.

"This countryside must be wonderful in fine weather," Yaer said. "There's a clump of bob-myrtle by these roots—'Sweet Gale,' some used to call it, for the aroma of the leaves in summer. And there's self-heal by that bank there, with three kinds of star sedge."

Nilssen had taken shelter by one of the willows to escape the strengthening breeze. Misty billows swirled past as he peered around at Yaer, saying, "You sound as if you're enjoying yourself."

Yaer plucked a fragment from a clump of frosty plants and rubbing it between his fingers, sniffed at it. "Cross-leaved heath, I do believe," he mused. "No, I haven't forgotten our problems. But I never waste myself in worrying when it won't help. . . . I'd love to come back when there's no fighting going on."

"Idealist," remarked Nilssen, his teeth chattering. "People have always been knocking the stuffing out of each other around here. Go back to prehistoric times if you want peace. Twenty thousand years should do it. There mightn't be too many humans squabbling over the hunting grounds then. That would take you to the end of the last ice age, so the winter sports should be first class."

"Then I won't bother," Yaer said, exhaling a long plume of vapor into the icy air. "Look, the mist is dispersing."

Nilssen stood up. It was so: there were wide gaps in the mist, exposing vistas of winter-crisp marshlands and salmon-pink skies to the east. He pointed away from the sun into the retreating night. "Our last landmark: there, the birches beyond the line of alders by that small lagoon. Keep them in sight and we can dispense with the guide notes. The ice will support us. Once on the ridge we should be able to see Alfred's camp."

In the dawn light a path was easily found. Shortcuts across the misty ice eliminated meandering detours. They left plants flattened in windrows as they trampled onto and off the creaking ice, heedless of the intricate beauty of the frozen rushes. Air that had earlier smelled clean now burned their nostrils. All that mattered was to find shelter.

Yaer was first to the birches. He immediately mounted a tussock of snow-crowned purple moor grass, steadying himself against one of the silvery trunks.

"There it is!" he shouted back to Nilssen. Quieter concern displaced his exuberance; his pointing hand fell. "Shazol be my witness," he said, so quietly he was nearly inaudible, "I had no idea . . ." Nilssen came abreast of him. Yaer's expression was one of alarm. "Jerlan, it's too big. Far, far too big."

Two miles away on a spit of dry land running roughly northeast was an oblong fort so large, its steep earthen walls rose directly from the ice on three sides. Fifty yards wide, two hundred yards long, it gave ample cause for concern by its amazing size and by its elaborate construction.

"How can this be?" breathed Nilssen. "Alfred's a fugitive. He had nothing like this."

Even allowing for the inland seventy-five yards given over to livestock, the fort had to be more than a mere refuge. A major military work built after the Roman pattern, its earth banks like city walls had been carefully packed with turves, topped off with palisades of stakes, and girdled with a zariba of sharp downward-angled wooden prongs. Saxons patrolled them, armed with shield and spear, or sword, and clad in leather overmailed by bright byrnies, their heads encased in shining helmets. One roof at the heart of the camp dominated the shingled roofs of many buildings set in orderly rows. Two storeys high, it was resplendent with carved gables picked out with gold that glittered in the rising sun; it in turn was overtopped by an enclosed watchtower more than twenty yards tall. From every roof, it seemed, ascended the smoke of vigorous cooking fires; and from the camp as a whole came an animated murmur.

Yaer stepped down from the tussock. "So it's wrong," he said. "But it's real."

Slowly Nilssen replied, "Any doubts I had about the CNI being here are gone." He blew on his hands to warm them. "Come on, Khaled, we should go and introduce ourselves."

CHAPTER NINE

Nilssen and Yaer had exchanged hardly a word throughout the long day. On arrival at the camp they had been greeted with suspicion and instant imprisonment in a small drafty hut, where they had sat, sustained by philosophical fortitude. Their general plan of action had been agreed beforehand; having committed themselves into the hands of Alfred and his forces, they now had no option but to learn whether the king would permit that plan to work its way through to the hoped-for end.

Their reticence was also prompted by the real risk of their being overheard. The hut, in common with many at Athelney, was of flimsy wattle-and-daub, more effective as a weatherbreak than a prison; and their custodian, a mournful-faced Saxon wielding a nicked and pitted sword the length of a man's arm, was never far from the door.

Nilssen had considered the use of what he thought of as "modern" English; the fear of intruding yet another element of anachronism into their situation dissuaded him, as did the chance that their guard might not be totally ignorant of the language, given the presence of the CNI. Arabic, in which their imprinting course had made them fluent, was available and probably safe. Still, he felt, that ought to be held in reserve. Then he realized on reflection that there was nothing he really wanted to say.

By degrees it grew dark. The short March day, itself chilly, shaded into the still colder night. Their guard brought in a small pottery oil lamp which he slung by a cord from a hook in one of the ceiling crossbeams. Nilssen tried engaging him in conversation.

"What hour is it, friend?"

The man gazed at him solemnly. A half-inch scar at the corner of his mouth gave him a disdainful expression but he answered civilly enough. "After sunset," he said and went out, bolting the door behind him.

"I think they've forgotten to let the king know we've come," remarked Yaer.

Nilssen said nothing. He could hear the guard walking around outside, his feet crunching in the freezing slush as he sang to himself in a hoarse baritone about some woman who had jilted him when the sap was in the greenwood-oh. After a while the man stopped singing and began cursing softly as he stamped his feet vigorously and slapped his arms to keep warm.

Sunset might well have been a signal to all in camp to hide themselves indoors. As the temperature fell sharply the everyday sounds died away. A great peace descended. Nilssen's world contracted until it was filled by the smoky light of the oil lamp, revolving slowly on its cord, its flame wobbling at the lip. The lamp gave no real heat but it did hold back the fearful pressure of lonesomeness that the night brought with it, so that it warmed him spiritually.

These, he thought, staring into the yellow eye of the lamp, *are the Dark Ages. All over Europe, as you sit here, men of violence are threatening to extinguish a light no less frail than this. Scholarship is a precious thing; pray that our Alfred is equal to his future responsibilities, whatever changes the CNI have brought.*

Yaer stirred and wrapped his cloak closer around himself.

"What do you suppose the time is, actually?" he asked in Old English.

Reflexively, Nilssen answered in the same language:

"Who knows?" He shivered violently and gritted his teeth to prevent them chattering. "Feels like midnight. Can't be much after eight, though."

"I wish they'd get a move on," said Yaer miserably. "Wouldn't it be a laugh: to come all this way, then die of frostbite!"

"You don't often die of just frostbite," Nilssen said absently, distracted by Yaer's subordinate demeanor. Then he caught the other's intent and gave him a conspiratorial wink, now fully aware of the cessation of movement outside the door. ". . . Or so the travelers from northern climes I have spoken with attest," he added for the benefit of the listening Saxon guard.

Yaer replied promptly, "But we'd be of little use to the king's cause without fingers or toes."

As it transpired their playacting was given no time in which to take effect, for almost at that same moment they heard men approaching. Two new voices spoke with their guard. The bolt was drawn; the door creaked open and the light of a torch, held high by one of the newcomers, snaked into the hut to flicker on their faces.

Nilssen got to his feet stiffly. "Now?" he asked.

The man with the torch nodded. "The king will see you. But you alone. Your companion stays here."

"No," said Nilssen firmly, seating himself once more. The chill had settled into the bench in the few seconds he had been standing, so that the cold nipped at him. "We are together," he said. "—Bound by an oath," he added swiftly, seeing the man gather himself to use force.

The torchbearer looked to the other newcomer, who shrugged and said, "Let *them* explain it."

"Very well," said the torchbearer to Nilssen. "But if the king asks . . ."

"No blame to you," agreed Nilssen, emerging from the hut. Their erstwhile guard surveyed the interior of the hut to see that all was in order, extinguished the lamp and followed them.

By the flaring torch the camp was a maze of shadows, blackest black, rimmed with silver fire where starlight and torchlight flashed on hoarfrost. Gaunt against eaves were pendant skeletal fingers of ice which caught and refracted the glow as they passed by. High overheard Orion burned bright and steady in a sky that seemed to suck all warmth from the winter land beneath it.

The prisoners went ahead, urged on by touches of their guards' swords, deflected to left and right along pathways slick with ice that cracked and squeaked underfoot in the dry cold. Once they were challenged by a squad of heavily armed soldiers: the night watch going their rounds, on the lookout for Danish infiltrators. Up on the stockades Nilssen picked out the silhouettes of more soldiers pacing out their slow patrols. Here and there yellow glimmers escaped from chinks in barracks buildings.

Soon they were at the foot of the enclosed watchtower they had noted on first sighting the camp. Nearby was the high building with the gilded gables. This Nilssen guessed to be the meeting hall, Alfred's grander version of Henglaf's mead-hall, for there came a babble of voices from within it. Twenty yards long by ten wide, like the tower it was of wattle-and-daub, with a roof of wooden slats. Some effort had been made to render the hall draftproof: the plume of smoke which issued from the roof did so in only one place; and the wisps of vapor which issued from gaps around the double doors midway along it gave warning that the atmosphere inside must be warm and humid.

. Their guard of the day plodded off to a door at the foot of the tower. King or no king, he said, he was going to thaw out in the guardhouse. Nilssen drew comfort from this sign that the remaining two men scarcely amounted to more than guides.

Then, with a rush, they were surrounded by four villainous-looking ruffians. Each was armed with sword, axe, shield, and spear and was seemingly ready to use any or all. Their leader, whose right hand dandled a massive double-headed war axe as if it were a featherweight, blocked their path.

"No further," he said, the fingers of his left hand prodding Nilssen hard in the chest. His friends held their weapons in full view while he inspected the City men in turn by the light of the torch.

Eventually he sighed and demanded of one guard: "Well, Coelric? And what, exactly, are *these*?"

"The travelers," said Coelric meekly, ". . . sergeant."

The word was mispronounced but unmistakable. *Sergeant,* he had said; even disguised by the twanging Saxon accent it could be no other. Suddenly Nilssen's attention was riveted on the squad leader. Could this be one of the CNI's men? If so, they had infiltrated deeply.

The sergeant gave Nilssen a disgusted glare. "Christ-save-us-sinners-all," he muttered. "At times like these the king bothers himself with wet-eared wave-waifs. . . . Stay there while I make the announcement."

Beyond the double doors a comparative hush had settled. A single tenor voice held sway, occasionally breaking into near-song. Plainly the words were loaded with tragedy, though the walls muffled their detailed meaning; and just as plainly the sergeant cared little for them. He seemed to take great pleasure in interrupting the bard's poetic flight, flinging the doors wide and declaring, in a bellow that drowned the verses:

"My lord king, the Saracen travelers."

There was a startled silence. Nilssen stepped into the smoke-scented hall, conscious of the scrutiny of at least forty pairs of eyes. All he could hear was the swish of his own garments, the crackle of the fire, and the slow susurrus of breathing around him.

Down each of the long sides of the room there ran a raised earthen bank, broken on the nearer side for the doorway. On this bank and on that section of it which traversed one of the shorter sides were trestle tables at which sat the wildest assortment of uncouth nobility he had ever seen. Henglaf's men had been farmer-hunters with some skill in arms; but these were warriors all, bearing the airs and accouterments of warriors, scarred and proud, distinctively dressed, gilded with brooches and jewels that were their main wealth apart from the lands they could not carry with them on campaign.

A long, narrow fire pit between the banks was heaped with blazing wood, the heat of which stung Nilssen's face and forced him to shield his eyes with one hand as he skirted it in his approach to the high table opposite the doors. Suddenly he was cold no longer but sweating. As he halted he found his mouth was dry. He wanted to sit down.

The trestle table came level with his chest, so that as he raised his eyes, he saw King Alfred gazing down upon him.

The unblinking gaze frightened him more than anything he had braved in the ninth century. He understood why it was that some folk feared ghosts: the past, once dead, ought not to get up and walk. How brave indeed had been the high-reeve Henglaf!

For a minute or more the king studied him, a quizzical smile on his face. He had a pleasant expression, marred solely by a white scar on the bridge of his long, narrow nose and continued on the left cheek. By contemporary standards he was clean-shaven; the stubble which darkened his cheeks and somewhat overlarge chin represented no more than a day's growth. His hair, dark brown and falling to his shoulders, was held back from his hazel eyes by a white linen headband embroidered with gold zigzags. Hair and headband appeared clean but his fine linen clothes were stained with mud and grease, and his short fingernails were limned with crescents of dirt.

He took a slow draft from his drinking-horn, then set it once more in its silver stand.

"Well, well," he said at last, "so these are the frightful heretics."

An answering snicker of mirth circled the room as Alfred leaned forwards and looked along the table to his right.

"Hey, Werferth?" he prompted.

A lean man in monkish habit swallowed a mouthful of meat he had been chewing at the time of the interruption and wiped his fingers fastidiously on his hem. His movements were rapid yet precise.

"Their perilous nature, my king," he replied in a voice as dry as last summer's leaves, "lies in their hearts, not in their faces."

"So you say," agreed the king matter-of-factly. "So you say." He faced Nilssen again; he seemed to have forgotten Yaer, who remained silent as had been agreed. "However, even the devil possesses knowledge the holy may safely use, so by your leave I shall reserve judgment for now." There was more laughter, to which the monk's only reply was a renewed assault on his food with a knife.

The king touched the shoulder of the man on his immediate right. "Eorhic, my dear friend, will you as a kindness to me alone give way to this honoured guest"—here Alfred seemed to become aware of Yaer, for he gave the small man a penetrating glance—"and his companion who have come so far and at such peril to their lives in order to share this evening with us?"

The man so addressed appeared reluctant to comply but thought better of it and in turn urged the man beyond him to move along the bench. The side-shifting progressed until two places had been opened beside the king who then saw to it that Nilssen and Yaer were well supplied with cuts of beef and mugs of sharp-tasting ale before yielding to the curiosity Nilssen knew must be like a pain in him. Even so, his first inquiries were confined to haphazard questions about their health and their comfort, until he tired of filling the time and said:

"Good sir, both of you know my name. May we not know yours?"

A comment drifted along the table from Werferth: "The devil has one name and one nature." Alfred scowled at him but held his tongue.

Here we go, thought Nilssen. The chunk of roast beef he had been given suddenly lost all flavor and became a slab of warm greasy rubber in his mouth. Simultaneously his stomach forgot its interest in food as it tightened in panic.

So that all in the room might see and hear him, he stood up. As he quelled his fear he noticed the bard whose ballad had been cut short by their coming: the man sat slumped on a low stool at one end of the hall, with a wolfhound asleep at his feet and his four-stringed harp cradled in his arms. *Sooner you than me,* Nilssen thought. Then he began to speak the lines he and Yaer had rehearsed so carefully.

"Your majesty," he said, feeling not unlike an after-dinner speaker at home, a comparison which somehow steadied his nerve, "my name is Ibrahim ibn-Haroun. That of my companion is Khaled, who has no other name, having forsworn all joys of wife, of family, and of inheritance until his homeland is freed from the tyrant who now rules there."

An outburst of table-pounding and joyous yells interrupted his speech. Some positive response had been anticipated; this much was most gratifying. Nilssen guessed that they had seriously underestimated the depth of feeling the Danish invasion had aroused in the Saxons. Still, it was all to the good. When he had their attention again, he continued:

"We are of different nations, he and I, but chance and adversity have thrown us together. For nigh on eleven years we have journeyed in company. It is our great good fortune that Allah, the Compassionate, the Merciful, has guided us to this place and the hospitality which is so rare in times as troubled as these."

Now the reaction was hardly more than a subdued show of polite interest.

Damnation, thought Nilssen, *they didn't like that allusion to a foreign god.*

However, Werferth seemed content to say nothing, as if relying on Nilssen to dig his own grave.

Hurrying on, Nilssen said, "Far to the south and east of here, as you know, is the Mediterranean Sea, whose shores are blessed with a fair climate and many rich lands. I am from one of those lands, the Kingdom of the Aglabids, which lies along much of the mid-northern coast of Africa. It is a region of dryness whose fields and groves are few and, for the greater part, close by the sea. Well inland is the camp-city of Kairouan, given over to the army of the king, where I was born, the third son of a cavalry officer.

"Raised as a soldier, I entered service as a scribe with authority over supplies, a post of great importance to an army always on the move—"

"We could've used you at Nottingham," someone remarked on the far side of the hall, a comment that elicited from Alfred a moody frown.

"—for without supplies the fighting men starve, their weapons grow few, and their cause may be lost.

"In the Year of Jesus's Nativity 867 I was stationed in Sicily when the order came to us to make ready for a seaborne attack upon the island of Melita, for which in due course we set sail. Ours was a fleet of fully five-score ships, that should have won us victory. Alas, no sooner had we sighted the coast when a violent storm scattered us far and wide. The flagship—where I was—became wrecked. Only with the greatest of good fortune did I escape drowning; but the next morning I fell into the hands of the Maltese when peasants came to search the wreckage.

"By virtue of my scholarly abilities I was not cast into prison with the rest of the survivors but was taken into the service of the governor of that island. . . . If I may, I shall pass over this time, which was one of shame for me."

"No shame in being captured," said Eorhic, the one who had first been displaced from his seat. "So long as you go down fighting."

Nilssen thought he detected a jibe but let it pass.

"No," he said, "it wasn't that. I hope you will inter-pret me correctly if I say simply that customs vary from land to land, that the Byzantines are more given to luxuriation in perversion than your people or mine. The governor was one such; it was not for my skill in arithmetic or algebra alone that he valued my services."

There was a long silence. Someone began to laugh. At once the king cut in angrily, *"Enough!* This man is my guest." The laughter died. "Do continue with your story in your own way," said Alfred kindly.

Nilssen bowed low, relieved that the ploy had worked. Henceforth he could safely gloss over any details that might be checked by skeptics. Few would dare to voice doubts.

"The king is more honorable than even his repu-tation suggests," he said. "There is, in any case, little to tell of my stay on the island. Within weeks there came news from spies that my people were massing for a renewed and more determined attack; and the governor decided to evacuate himself and his retinue until all was safe again. Naturally I, as a valuable prisoner and, ah, friend of the governor, was required to accompany him aboard his ship when it sailed for Constantinople.

"She was a well-found vessel. Her two tall masts were augmented by ninety pairs of oars in three ranks. Besides the crew and slaves, there were numerous fighting men, since the governor had a high regard for his personal safety." Nilssen allowed a pause while he refreshed himself from his mug of ale. A housecarl hurried to refill it. "But for all his wisdom in matters of government he was over-proud and cursed with the peculiar stupidity of the arrogant. On the fourth day of the journey I happened to be with him on the high stern of the ship, whilst he dictated official letters, when the lookout hailed us from the masthead saying that another vessel was crossing our bows from the east, making slow going as she tacked upwind.

"At this the captain requested permission to alter course, to give the other vessel a wide berth. The governor demanded what kind of ship she was; on being told she was only a coastal trader, he ordered that we should run her down—you must understand that the war craft of the Byzantines commonly bear huge spikes, or rams, at their bows, with which they crush enemy vessels.

"Reluctantly, the captain obeyed. As we came closer we saw the other to be an Arab ship, probably of the Caliphate of Bhagdad; and the governor rejoiced loudly that God Himself had arranged the encounter.

"However, if the Hand of Allah was indeed at work, He showed little love for the governor, or for his followers. We were no more than a ship's length from collision when the other craft swung sharply round and, running before the wind, came abreast of us as we overtook her. Men ran about her decks with ropes and grappling irons; lines were cast and made taut.

184 ANDREW M. STEPHENSON

Before the duty-guard could be called out we had been boarded and a bloody slaughter began, not the least of which was effected by the liberated galley slaves.

"When it was finished I was taken before the leader of the attackers, a man of the Ethiopians whose skins are sometimes so dark as to seem black. He questioned me closely concerning my origins. When I explained that I had been a prisoner of the Byzantines he replied that I was now free, if I wished, provided I was prepared to accompany him and his crew into exile. All were fugitives of one sort or another: runaway slaves, political refugees, army deserters, along with common criminals who had evaded punishment.

"I answered that I would rather be free and hope to see my home some day, even if that day might be many years hence, than rot in the sickly embrace of the Emperors of Byzantium. And with that, I became one of them.

"We resumed the westward journey they had been pursuing, though in the captured ship of the erstwhile governor, now deceased. Within weeks we reached the port of Tortosa which serves the eastern coast of the Emirate of Cordova. There we disembarked and took our leave of each other. From that day to this their fate is unknown to me, save only Khaled, here.

"Whilst yet aboard, Khaled and I had become fast friends, so that whereas most of our company split up, he and I remained together. His practical knowledge matched my more clerical bent. Together it seemed we would make a useful pair, in which we were shortly proven correct, as we made the acquaintance of a Jewish merchant in need of a warehouse supervisor and shipping clerk. So began our career in exile.

"It was not an unhappy time. That part of the Muslim World as often as not is in conflict with the remainder, with the result that cordial relationships exist with several nearby Christian countries. Many communities of Christians and Jews exist within the Emirate also; thereby the realm is enriched to the benefit of all; and nobility and citizenry alike profit from the free trade that proceeds with all parts of the civilized world.

"Some ten years elapsed. The old Jew who had befriended us died and was succeeded by his son, a young man of imagination who was determined to enhance the family business so that it would outrank all other mercantile concerns.

"The young man explained that he had it in mind to steal a march on the merchants of Byzantium by proceeding directly to the source of supply with which they trade in the far north. It seems that the Ruotsi, a people of the frozen lands, presently convey their produce down the rivers which meet the sea near Constantinople. Thus, not only must their goods be subject to the natural hazards of the way but also to the tribute of two cities, a levy which considerably diminishes the merchants' profits and elevates their prices. Worse, this route is controlled by the Byzantines.

"What he planned was to sail an exploratory expedition south and west, going past Tarik's Mountain into the western ocean—as many coastal craft already do—after which it would turn north and try for passage to a town he had heard tell of: Hedeby, in the land of the Jutes, where it is said the warehouses bulge with wealth. There he hoped an agent might be found, from which small beginning would flow a river of benefits.

"Khaled and I were impressed by his spirit of adventure; he was the true son of his father. Thereupon, he asked us to lead the expedition and foolishly we accepted, not knowing how perilously close to death it would bring us, nor what privations we would endure. For the soft-tongued Northmen with whom he had talked in the harbor had neglected to mention the plague of Vikings which infest these waters.

"Though we set sail last summer, so long was spent in mapping and maintaining supplies against possible scarcity that autumn was on us before we had gained the eastward sea. Our captain began to fear lest we be forced to over-winter in the north; he had heard that thereabouts even the sea died and became stiff with cold. Then, as we rounded the last headland and saw open horizons to the east, foul weather found us. A huge storm bore us north away from land, so that we did not doubt that we would be lost in the endless fogs where the djinn are said to eat the souls of men. For two days we were carried by the waves, helpless, our crew afraid to remain on deck lest they be washed overboard, as some were, yet afraid to remain below lest they go down with the ship when she foundered, as few doubted she must ere long.

"Then, like a miracle, the storm eased. The wind hurried the clouds away into the western sky and there, rosy-red in the sunset, were cliffs of chalk and beaches of shingle upon which a ship might safely be run ashore, and green grasses, with the promise of food and dry wood for fires. Truly, we gave thanks to God. Then we bent our backs to the oars whilst the captain raised what sail remained, and we made our way towards this welcoming landfall."

Nilssen took another draft of ale. Not a cough broke the hush his tale had induced. Only the wolf-hound, whimpering in its sleep, reminded him that the world had not been altered in any real way by the story. The dog probably knew full well that once its masters had begun to talk in a certain fashion it was wisest to stay quiet; but that later there would be more noise, and bones to chew.

Well, let's give them all something to chew on,

thought Nilssen, preparing for the final chapter, the one that would most likely trip him of any.

"Though we were not to know it, the land we had sighted was an island, the name being White Island, or some such—"

"Wihtland," said Alfred.

"Thank you, my lord," said Nilssen, unable to tell if Alfred was volunteering information to ease the flow of the story or to trap him.

"Nearing the southern shore, we observed that it would be wisest to let the wind bear us westabout, so to gain the lee of the land and a sheltered anchorage in which to make repairs. Accordingly, we followed the cliffs until they turned north and east, where a line of rocks runs out to sea. To our horror we found we had blundered into a nest of pirates."

Grim looks from several of those opposite him convinced Nilssen he had some sympathizers in his audience. "I see by your faces," he said, "that you have guessed what next transpired. These northmen, these godless manslayers, clambered aboard their animal-headed craft and came at us from where they had themselves sought shelter. Four, five, six ships: long and low, wide-sailed, many-oared, with foam boiling from sleek prows and sunlight flashing from tenscore sharpened blades. These were ships of war, not slow freighters like ours; and they were fresh, not set to sink from storm damage. So swiftly they seemed to fly, they bore down upon us as we wallowed towards the coast that opened before us to the north of the island. There, we hoped, we might find safety.

"The captain held hurried counsel with Khaled and me, saying that the ship and cargo were lost and we ought at least to save our lives by running the ship aground and escaping on foot.

"This we agreed to. It hurt us to think of our wealth of spices, glass, and silk falling into the foul clutches of pirates, yet we relished still less the prospect of ourselves becoming prey to such monsters. We saw a long beach of mud and stones, backed by dunes where coarse grasses grew. Heedless of the damage done to our keel, the captain did not slacken sail but drove us hard aground. Thereafter, we made our separate ways across the mud.

"The night was so near that the going would soon be hazardous. Only the fear of our pursuers enabled us to struggle on. Before long we had outdistanced the pirates. In any case, I do not think they wanted us so much as our ship. Once they had her, they preferred to stay and plunder.

"Overnight we regrouped. By dawn the ship's company was complete save for a few; and those we expected not to see this side of paradise, for none had been a fast runner. Then we debated what to do.

"The coast where we had landed is a dreadful place. Inland there are tracts of gloomy woods and open sandy country full of thorn bushes. A wind blows that cuts through to the soul. There we found ourselves, without knowledge of the people or their customs and only a merchant's grasp of the language.

"The captain suggested that once the pirates had looted the ship, they might abandon her. If so, we might manage to cross the eastward sea to the shores we knew from our surveys. As this seemed sensible, we returned to our landing place, only to find the spiteful wretches had chopped holes in the hull and used the torn sails to fuel their fires.

"What can I tell of the months which followed? We headed east and were attacked by a roving band of these same pirates; only Khaled and I survived. In time we learned from peasants who helped us that our best hope lay in finding you, my lord king, the one man whose love of law best accords with ours, whose cause had been made one with ours through the

murders of our shipmates, and who might advise us
how we should regain our homeward path.

"This is my story."

The wolfhound awoke and raised its head, then
lowered it onto its paws again when it sensed that
the special-talk was not yet done.

Alfred fingered the scar on his cheek. "Yes," he
said at last. "Interesting. You learn quickly."

"My lord?"

"Languages," said the king. "I see you too have
the gift of memory."

Carefully Nilssen said, "I believe dire necessity is
an excellent tutor, albeit I have always possessed a
flair for tongues."

"You do yourself no credit by such modesty," said
Alfred. "But what of your companion?"

Nilssen and Yaer exchanged quick glances. Yaer's
right eye closed fractionally: *yes,* he was saying; and
he stood up.

"I'm not so good with words," he began in his
cultivated bad accent. Nilssen smiled inwardly, recol-
lecting how much of his own speech had been planned
by the psychologist to play on nuances of phrasing so
as to train the minds of his listeners to accept what
they were being told. "Where I come from people
mostly know what they think and come straight out
with it. No fancy talk. I'm from away over east. My
home was in the port of Basra; still is, come to that.
One day I'll go back and make the bastard who's
running the place eat dirt like he did to my family
the day his soldiers walked in and took over.

"That was twenty years ago. I was sold as a slave
when we couldn't pay the taxes. About a year later
I made a break and joined the Zanj, in Persia, where
the authorities had their hands full with a war on
their own doorstep. That lasted a couple of years before the soldiers hit us and I was on the run again.

"Four years of wandering brought me to Antioch,

near the border with Byzantium. You get a lot of odd
characters near frontiers, especially around there:
smugglers, freebooters, men on the run, even a few
spies. I got mixed up with some fellows who were
planning an escape overseas. They wanted someone to
size up the ships in the harbor, a few miles away at
Seleucia. Idea was, there were always a good score of
ships in port. Of those, a couple should be ready for
a new voyage, so they'd be fully provisioned. My job
was to guess which would be ready when we were. I'd
had a bit of experience that way, see, from my days
in Basra where my father ran a ship's chandler-shop.
You could always tell when they'd refitted and were
loading, because they threw the offcuts of old rope and
such overboard and some of it would lie about the
quayside. All you had to do was stroll along and look
for recent rubbish of that sort, then hang about watching the provisions dealers. As soon as they loaded the
drinking water, that was it.

"We got a ship. Not a bad crate but not the best
that ever sailed either. She'd hold out the sea, I reckoned, until we got somewhere safe. I slipped my gang
the word and that night we crept aboard, mugged the
guards, and were off on the tide about twelve hours
earlier than the owner had planned to be away. It
was neat, if I say so myself.

"So we sailed along and met up with this glory-boat
bound for Constantinople. They tried to ram us. You
know the rest."

And he sat down abruptly before anyone could ask
questions. Nilssen spoke up at once to cover for him:

"So, my king, we are here, as you see. And though
we would dearly love to go home as soon as possible
we have an unsettled account with certain Danes. Our
services are at your disposal."

Drily, the king said, "I'll bear your offer in mind."
Conscription into the standing army, the fyrd, was the
order of the day; Nilssen had only hoped to imply

their goodwill, not suggest that Alfred had no alternative source of troops. "But for now," the king said, "I am intrigued by what you say of the fighting in the Mediterranean. Is it true that the Muslims make war on Rome?"

Yaer stirred uneasily. *"Be very careful,"* he whispered in Arabic, and coughed. To the Saxons it would sound as if he had cleared his throat.

"It is true that raiders once attacked that city," Nilssen admitted, "but that was when I was scarcely more than a boy; thirty years gone or longer. And they were pirates."

Suddenly Werferth said, "Listen to me, my king. These heretics will repay your kindness with hacksilver. Their sort never deals in whole coin."

"I hear what you say, Werferth," said Alfred. "What then, Ibrahim ibn-Haroun, of your warlike activities in Sicily? Is that not part of Rome's dominion?"

"No, my lord. No more than Mercia is of yours."

The air seemed to freeze. Alfred nodded slowly. "As you say. And no doubt the worthy Werferth would support you in that."

"My king," said the Mercian monk, "I would count you a kinder overlord than any Muslim blasphemer, as would most of my countrymen."

"Still, it is the law that matters," replied Alfred. "You have made your point . . . my friend," he said to Nilssen.

Jumping up from his seat, Werferth came around the remote end of the table and strode along the line of diners until he stood before Alfred. Pointing at Nilssen and Yaer, he said, with controlled rage making his jaw muscles stand proud of his sunken cheeks:

"They have sacked and desecrated the Basilica of Saint Peter and Saint Paul! Even now the Holy Father, Pope John himself, pays tribute. . . . How can you eat in their presence without choking?"

A wave of muttering seemed to run along the tables,

break at the ends, and roll back again. Nilssen stood up to gain the attention of the assembly. There was every chance the king might not be able, nor care, to control the ill will the monk's righteous fury had stirred up. He chose his reply and spoke:

"Sir, are you a believer in the deity of Jesus?"

"I am. As you are not."

"We shall see . . . Will you answer me this: is not your God one Being?"

"He is."

"Therefore, according to your creed, is not Jesus part of God?"

A wariness haunted Werferth's face. Guardedly he said, "Yes."

"And is not God the greatest Being of all?"

There was a noticeable delay before Werferth assented. "That is so."

"Would you deny that we Muslims hold Allah to be the greatest Being?"

"Of course I cannot deny you your blasphemies!" snapped the monk. "My king, may I be excused this catechism of the damned?"

"Words alone cannot hurt you," said Alfred, "provided you hold fast to the truth. . . . Besides, I suspect our guest would not knowingly espouse heresy under this roof. You shall stay and hear him out."

The monk almost argued. Then he lowered his eyes and sighed. "Say on," he whispered.

Nilssen licked his dry lips. "So far we are agreed that Christians and Muslims each worship a god whom they hail as the greatest Being. As the greatest cannot, by definition, be inferior in any aspect or attribute to any other being, your God and mine must be one and the same, and our dispute over His nature must spring only from our imperfect perception or comprehension of that nature. Sir, if you are obedient to your God, then we are true brothers in Islam, whatever men may pretend."

Werferth's tonsured head gleamed in the firelight as he looked away from Nilssen, then back at him. "You are the devil's advocate indeed," he hissed. "*Retro me, satana!*"

Alfred coughed softly. "I see no heresy in what he says."

"It reeks of it!"

"Perhaps. But can you fault his reason?"

"No. And that is what distresses me: my wits have been seduced by wizardry! Alfred, if you fear God, let me quit their presence, else I am lost forever!"

"Go if you must," said Alfred; and Werferth ran for the door. The king waited until the night had again been shut out before announcing in a voice that carried clearly for all its quietness, "Nor can *I* fault that argument. And because of that I find I am afraid." His eyes moved to watch Nilssen. "Could it be, I am asking myself, for all that the question is abhorrent to me, that the Danes are not wrong to worship Thor and his bloodthirsty tribe, and that men are fools to raise graves in the name of religion?" He blinked and frowned. "My friend, I trust you not to make a custom of such doubts whilst you bide with us."

With absolute sincerity Nilssen answered, "That, my lord Alfred, is the last thing I want to do."

"Good," said Alfred. He snapped his fingers at the bard, who jumped up and began to lead the assembly in a rowdy drinking song. The dog stretched itself hugely before questing along the tables for tidbits.

With the tumult at its height the king leaned over to whisper in Nilssen's ear, "Otherwise, my friend, whomsoever you may *truly* be, I shall not hesitate to have you killed if you seem likely to weaken our stand against the Danes." So saying, he smiled pleasantly, raising his drinking horn in a toast.

* * *

The feast proceeded, roaring with song and valiant boasting by the assembled leaders. The fire was maintained by relays of housecarls bearing logs, filling the confines of the hall with its heat and smoke until the visitors had to loosen their clothing in imitation of the less heavily dressed Saxons. Food was brought when demanded; but when bellies were sated with meat the calls were more often for drink, over whose dispensation the king watched with an indulgent eye.

Alfred, Nilssen noted, was careful to play the moderator rather than the overlord. The Saxon way was to elect their kings, at least in theory. It mattered little that Alfred's succession to the throne of Wessex had virtually been a foregone conclusion; kings retained their power by public approval and the support of followers. Alfred's brother, Ethelred, had been king before him and ought to have been succeeded by his son, Ethelwold, had the natural heir not disqualified himself by his inexperience in government and battle, and by his casual attitude to responsibility. It behooved Alfred to guide his lords in their cups; stern discipline was for sober men. With drunkenness had come argument; after the prefatory outburst there would be a lull in which the king would appeal to one man or the other, and usually his understanding of their characters would be sufficiently astute to subdue the dispute. If it persisted, he would rally support from disinterested onlookers, so that their combined weight of opinion could quash it. It was, Nilssen decided, an admirable display of the art which Yaer practiced. The psychologist would do well to beware of the king.

The thought evidently had occurred to Yaer also, for he leaned close to Nilssen after one argument had been resolved and murmured in Arabic, "It would serve us well if Khaled the Homeless were not as stupid as we planned. I cannot hope for a faultless performance. That man will assuredly trip me."

"Then lack only learning," Nilssen replied, "and affect rudimentary courtesies. That will suffice."

"So be it," said Yaer and resumed his conversation with Eorhic, who had expressed an interest in eastern weapons.

Nilssen continued his pretense of drinking. Having stretched his ale further than any of the locals, he had even been outpaced by Yaer. Inevitably, with the last dram drained from it, his mug returned empty to the table.

Alfred noticed. "Finished so soon?" he inquired with a lopsided grin that warped the scar on his cheek. "My, my, you Saracens are lusty guzzlers." He beckoned to the housecarl who had charge of the drink, and the man hurried to top up the king's horn with the remainder of the ale in his jug.

Alfred frowned at him. "Not me, idiot," he said. "Him." He jabbed a finger into Nilssen's empty mug.

The carl's face fell. "This pitcher is dry, lord. Another must be brought."

"Do it," said Alfred, "and smartly. No, where's Osric? That lazy devil . . ."

"Steward Osric fetches more ale also. The demand has been great."

As he spoke, the second steward pushed through the curtained doorway from the kitchen with two earthenware jugs, one of which he deposited on the floor by the wall and covered with a square of muslin weighted at its corners. Someone seemed to be beyond the curtain attracting his attention, for, turning back, he pulled aside the cloth and gave an order. And for a moment Nilssen saw Morwena.

He had missed her keenly, he realized, his breath catching in his tightening throat. Her eyes were on the steward while she lingered in the doorway, the curtain draped gracefully over one shoulder and down her arm. Surely she had already stolen inquisitive glances at the two foreign visitors? Perhaps; but so far they were less than nothing to her. Through a trick of a twist of time she was presently indifferent to his attentions; yet he felt reunited and happier, determined that before long the mockery which had been made of precedent by his expurgation from her mind would be remedied. History could not be so fluid that some effort on his part would come to nothing, given such an auspicious start. Here he was, an honored guest; and there she was, working for the king's household. One could easily meet the other in a place the size of Athelney.

"A handsome woman," said the king in an undertone.

"Your pardon," replied Nilssen, facing him quickly. Alfred lowered his eyes and twitched his head from side to side, not quite shaking it.

"You must ignore her, my friend. Any other woman, perhaps, may be yours to bed, if you find favor in her heart. But the Welsh girl is forbidden—even to me, were I unmarried and free to choose her."

Struggling to maintain his playacting, Nilssen asked, his voice breathless all of a sudden, "Why? Is she of unclean caste?"

"That I neither know nor care," said the king. "She is good enough for one of my companions, that I do know; and he is good enough to see she is not shared. Look there to our left by the second roof post from the corner. That sullen giant is her guardian. Learn his face well, mark those hands of his that have choked a Dane apiece, imagine the fury that is his when crossed. And remember his name: Sigewulf, the Wolf of Victory, the one madman I tolerate in my army by virtue of his loyalty to our cause. Offend him, my friend, and I cannot save you, since to save you I would have to kill that man, which I will not do."

"That brute is her lover?" asked Nilssen with dismay so pronounced that Alfred laid a hand on his sleeve and said, "Do not be distressed. I can see the girl has taken your fancy; and after all the self-denial you have endured who can blame you? If it's a woman you want, something can be arranged." His smile verged on being a filthy leer.

The king was being hospitable. "No, I thank you," Nilssen said politely, his eyes straying to Sigewulf who was burying his scarred face in a quart-size leather tankard. "That man hardly seems . . ." His vocabulary failed him. The old writings had tended to be sketchy when discussing sexual matters; the teaching machines in the City could not impart unavailable knowledge. Nevertheless the king caught his meaning.

"Oh, there's no question of *that*," he chuckled. "Sigewulf hasn't so much as glanced at a woman since he arrived at court. Or if he does he keeps close about it. No, his love for her is of the sort the ancient philosopher Plato preached: pure and free of carnal intent." Alfred tossed back some of his ale. "Myself, I think he's a touch soft in the head."

"Yet he keeps her for himself?"

"With a vengeance . . . Look, here's your ale. Drink up, my friend, forget this futile longing by nursing a morning-head." Snatching the jug from the housecarl who had just then returned, the king himself poured Nilssen a generous measure. The housecarl departed, to be hailed by another reveler farther down the table.

But Nilssen had lost interest in the celebration. His immediate requirements of food and warmth had been supplied; the king appeared willing to harbor him and Yaer; now he must concern himself with the business that had brought him to Athelney, not the least of which in his own estimation was the suddenly doubly difficult question of Morwena of Gwerfa Iwrch.

"My lord," he said, not touching the mug, "I fear

I have already drunk all that I am permitted by my faith."

The king's eyebrows rose. "Are you forbidden ale? By God, that *is* a harsh religion; no wonder Bishop Werferth hates it so." And he burst out laughing, so loudly that several nearby revelers stopped their merrymaking to listen to what was being said at the High Seat.

"Intoxicating beverages are not prohibited, my lord, merely the overindulgence in them. I know my limit."

The king evinced disappointment. From beyond Yaer, Nilssen heard Eorhic say:

"More than your companion does. If he goes for a leak the marsh will rise and drown us."

"Rubbish," said Yaer in very poorly enunciated Arabic. "Filthy son of a camel. I gotta lot better stuff'n this inside me 'fore now, and held it."

"What does he say?" asked Alfred.

"You want't in Saxon?" Yaer slurred. "Right—" But Nilssen shoved him back against the wall and hissed in his ear, "You're drunk, man. Shut up."

"Not for you!" yelled Yaer, reverting to Arabic. Nilssen had never been so glad of the tendency for machine-taught languages to supervene when an agent was under stress. The small man paused, took a deep breath, and yelled again: "I'm as good as you anytime. You don't tell me when to shut up. I'm the brains here. Don't you forget that, you . . ." Unhappily for the general effect, Yaer's inexperience with insults caused him to falter. Alfred interposed himself smoothly, though his bemused expression showed that the ourburst had gone over his head.

"Your companion would seem to lack your respect for religious observance."

Yaer stopped shouting. For about two seconds he sat bolt upright, frowning slightly as if puzzling out the king's remark, then collapsed forward across the table.

This graceless withdrawal from the celebrations aroused not the assembled lords' disapproval, but their ribaldry, as if they had been expecting it. One of the bulkier warriors elevated his tankard and, with a sardonic and slightly contemptuous grin, called out, "Hey, Saracen! *Waes hael!*"

Nilssen nodded acknowledgment without replying to the toast. He was trying to close the container of anaesthetic darts beneath the table, for the one he had used on Yaer was still three-quarters full and he disliked wasting valuable weaponry.

The king, however, nudged him gently. "You must respond," he said. "Else he will be offended."

"And if I do?"

"Well," said Alfred casually, "I expect he'll desist. Of course he might have decided to test your capacity. You never can tell with Eorl Sarnvig."

"Tell him I'm not interested."

"Here, my friend, a man speaks on his own behalf."

What would Yaer have done? Nilssen asked himself, considering his friend's snoring form. *He'll sleep for hours; no point in asking him for advice.*

Gingerly he held his mug out towards Sarnvig whose eyes lit up at the acceptance of the call. "*Drink hael!*" replied Nilssen; and together they drank from their vessels, watching each other sideways. Sarnvig gulped down his ale first but waited for Nilssen to finish before saying in a half-shout that left no one in any doubt as to what was afoot:

"Your turn, Saracen: You won't deny me your good-will, hey?"

So Nilssen returned the toast for the sake of good form and was obliged to respond to Sarnvig's reply, which necessitated his reply, and so on for another dozen mugs until both men were having difficulty in downing the ale for lack of space to store it.

"Hoy, but you're a brave drinker," Sarnvig declared after one of his challenges had been satisfied. "Let's take a break."

They trooped outside into the freezing air and returned to cheers. However, it was plain the assembly had tired of the contest and Nilssen saw his opportunity to end it. Before they separated to regain their seats, he said to the huge Saxon, "That was a good night's work. We must drink together again some day."

"That we must," agreed Sarnvig, obviously glad to be rid of the need to uphold his reputation amongst his fellows and sorry he had picked on Nilssen. "Where did you learn to drink that way?"

Nilssen doubted if the man would have believed the truth: *oh, hanging about bars in London, New York, Singapore, Melbourne, not to mention the Officers' Mess on Kittywake Island where there was damn-all to do but booze the nights away.* So he simply said, "I had a thirst."

Sarnvig could not have been accustomed to false modesty, for he completely misunderstood. "Then have a care we do not meet when *I* am the thirsty one," he cautioned Nilssen. Suddenly he mellowed. "Saracen, I am prepared to be your friend. What do you say?"

"Why, I am of course flattered," Nilssen managed to reply without smiling. Sarnvig could not have been much older than twenty; the king himself was not yet twenty-nine and looked far more timeworn than his eorl.

"Then it is done. . . . Do you ride?"

"Horses?"

Bewildered, Sarnvig said, "What else?"

"We also ride camels where I come from," Nilssen answered quickly to cover his mistake, for nobody rode horses in the City. "When I was much younger my father taught me. He was an accomplished rider, so I am ashamed to say that little of what I learned remains."

Sarnvig dismissed the objection with an airy wave of the hand. "I can find you a suitable mount. In the morning, if the king has no need of me, you and I shall venture out awhile. Naturally, if anyone asks, we shall be patrolling." He winked conspiratorially after insuring that the king's eye was not on them. "The Sabbath's a perilous dull day around here."

They parted before Nilssen could ask about the Danes who were supposed to be harrying the land; and Alfred could not be asked directly. Yaer, who was still unconscious, made a good opening gambit.

"I must apologize for Khaled," Nilssen said to the king. "The long journey has combined with the sudden wealth of drink to intoxicate him. Mostly it is tiredness, I am sure. He is not usually so ill-mannered at table."

"It's nothing," said Alfred. "Bide awhile; we'll be lucky if half these oafs can find the door by sleeptime. Most will pass out like your friend there . . . which brings me to where you two will lodge whilst you are with us."

"But, my lord, we already have a hut."

Alfred studied him. "I can't believe you're serious," he said. "The gaol is no place—"

Nilssen's ears tingled. "The gaol?" he asked, finding the mixture of Old and Modern English clumsy on his tongue.

"A word I picked up," the king explained. "It means a place of temporary imprisonment, such as for men on a charge." Again Modern English obtruded itself. Nilssen managed to nod. The king continued, "My army is growing. Recruits need discipline. We find it helpful to have a mild punishment in reserve; it's better than a firing squad."

"Your pardon," Nilssen said, "I fear you have spoken so technically I have not grasped all you said.

May I inquire, is the art of warfare so altered lately? Have the Danes perhaps brought new words into Britain? I cannot recall so much novelty being talked of in our travels hither."

"Later," said the king. "We have your quarters to find. By a fortunate coincidence several of my officers have recently departed on a special mission, so there is a room available near mine. I would be pleased if you would use it."

By the hard stare accompanying the offer Nilssen saw it was not one to be refused. "You are too kind," he said.

Alfred's pensive expression conveyed a disturbing hint of agreement, which vanished as he asked, "Sarnvig's taken a liking to you, has he?" His former cheerfulness had returned. "An excellent friend. One of my most loyal companions. Stick close to him and you'll come to little harm."

Without warning a blankness came upon the king's face. His eyes rolled up, exposing their whites, and his mouth dropped open. A moment passed. Then he seemed to regain awareness of his surroundings without realizing what had happened. "I'll tell you now, so you won't worry about a habit of his: he likes to steal away for some excitement of his own making. If he invites you out for a ride, especially if he takes along his war-gear . . . Ibrahim, you stare at me."

"Did you not experience a strangeness just now, my lord?"

Alfred frowned and devoted himself to his ale. Harshly, he said, "Yes, Sarnvig's a sound man to have at your back. But when you are with him there is some advice I would give you, who are a stranger to this camp. Overlook any oddities in his behavior. They are unimportant, and they offend him."

"I understand," said Nilssen, chastened. "You speak of Sarnvig, yet not of him."

"Just so."

"Then, my lord king, I would say that in my own land it is not uncommon for men—great men—to be as Sarnvig, or others of whom we might be speaking. We see no shame in it. Had I the wit the sooner to comprehend what my eyes told me, I would not have remarked on it. Customs vary. Men are alike. I will not mention it again."

"That would be for the best." The king's face softened. "I keep forgetting that you are not a Saxon, nor an Engle, but from farther afield than most men here have dreamed of. It is hard not to judge you as I would a subject. Tell me true, Saracen, is it so that amongst the Muslims there are doctors who can cure this affliction?"

"A baseless rumor, no more," said Nilssen. *Surgeon Hartmann could fix you in half an hour. Epilepsy isn't what it was in these days.* He so badly wanted to advise the king about the precautions that could be taken; an ever-present wariness of anachronism prevented him. "Their skill is no greater than that of the army commander who relies upon proven observation instead of blind belief."

"Does God's Will play no part in their cures?"

A cleft stick. Nilssen cursed the disguise that required him to pretend a theolatry foreign to his common sense. This man needed honest advice; all he could risk offering was superstitious gibberish. Still, he could attempt a balance of one against the other: "If it is truly Willed, then man cannot but submit. Yet Allah is not cruel; for most of our lives He leaves us free, so that salvation or damnation is truly earned. Men fall sick often in their lives. Is it not reasonable to suppose that there are means whereby the necessary cures may be aided? For we know there are sicknesses of cold weather, of the summer heat, and of bad food. If there is to be harmony in nature, there must also be benign forces we may call to our aid."

"But none that you can command?"

"No, my lord."

Alfred's acute disappointment showed; and Nilssen hoped the king had not placed too much faith in his visitors or their treatment might undergo a change for the worse.

"Well-a-day," said the king calmly, "it is a small thing. I thank God it is not as severe as it once was."

"The falling, lord?"

"And the kicking . . . yes." Alfred drained his horn. When it had been refilled, he stared down into the dark ale. "You seem to be a civilized man, Ibrahim ibn-Haroun. A mystery, yes, and perhaps still a danger until we know you better. But you are welcome to stay until this business with the Danes is resolved and we have time for more worthwhile pursuits." A wistfulness entered his voice. "All my life I have sought to understand God's creation. In hunting I have experienced His natural order. In the few books I have had read to me there has been another order, that of a wondrous yet obscured vision. I would discover that which is hidden. There must be more than is written in the books the ancients bequeathed us. The Greeks and Romans cannot have taken their knowledge with them to the grave, nor—forgive me— can God have given all wisdom to the Infidel. *What remains?* I ask myself; must all of life be spent in fighting a useless war against unteachable savages? Can we not aspire to purity of thought, having washed off the slime of war?" Slumping back in his seat, he sighed. "You must find me strange company to praise peace upon the eve of battle."

"Not so," said Nilssen forcibly. "I am amazed that you have given yourself so fully to war whilst it must be waged, yet remember the virtues of peace."

"Able advisers, that's all," muttered the king through clenched teeth. "I would dismiss them to their homesteads tomorrow if I could. This entire camp I would erase by fire, so that its flaming timbers might be seen as a sign that war was ended forever. But that must wait. Soon, when the weather is fair for us, we shall march upon the Danes. Then their bones shall litter the downs; their blood shall re-enrich our soil. I swear, as I am king of the Engles and Saxons, that no pirate shall escape the sword for what they have done in Britain. Before they came to pillage and murder, we had a land unequaled in Christendom for wealth and learning, excepting only Rome herself. Now we struggle to live. Every second year the crops are laid waste by the Here or rot whilst the harvesters fight. Our priests can barely pronounce the Latin, let alone interpret it for souls in need of enlightenment. As God is my Witness, I would slay them all myself!"

Throughout his statement he had slowly been rising to his feet, while his voice had swelled to a roar of virulent hatred that silenced even the wolfhound's whine. His breathing was deep, his face flushed, and the tendons stood out on the backs of his hands, which were curled into fists planted on the table before him. Not a person moved until Eorhic too stood and said, so quietly he seemed not to be addressing the hall:

"Our king has spoken. Let us learn by his example. *Waes hael!*"

He waited with his mug held aloft. And the reply exploded from those still able to stand:

"*DRINK HAEL!*"

"Tomorrow is the Sabbath," continued Eorhic, with not the slightest hint of an allusion to the presence of Nilssen and Yaer. "Let us remember in our hearts what our king has said when we come to God."

The evening ended in anticlimax. No more seemed to have been left unsaid that night. When Nilssen was escorted to his quarters by three guards, two of whom carried Yaer slung between them like a sack of turnips, they all went in silence, abandoning the hall to the sleeping drunks and the firelight.

CHAPTER TEN

"I saw her last night."

Yaer sat back on his heels on the prayer mat and squinted up at Nilssen against the light from the open door. "Morwena?" Nilssen nodded. "Sooner than you expected," said Yaer. "And what will you do?"

"Nothing for the moment. She has a guardian, a thug called Sigewulf who apparently lives up to his name."

"And are you asking my advice?"

Nilssen turned to lean against the uneven surface of the door jamb. "After what I did to you?"

Yaer pursed his lips momentarily. "Maybe I earned it," he said. "I can't recall what I was saying."

"Quite a lot. Most of it in Arabic, fortunately. It was pretty ripe."

"Forget it then." Yaer prostrated himself to mumble a prayer before sitting up again. "I think you ought to wait. Eventually it'll work out for you."

"No," said Nilssen, "time is mutable. Rhys insisted on that. And he's been right often enough." He faced the outdoors and the strangely quiet camp. Mass was in progress on the parade ground; Bishop Werferth's dusty voice would whisper and be answered by several hundred hearty bellows. Otherwise he could hear only their guard shuffling his feet a few yards away and seagulls squabbling over scraps near the cookhouse. The night's frost had been followed by a day of surprising warmth, so that the paths in the camp were paved alternately with ice and thawed mud where bars of shadow and sunlight lay across them amongst the huts. The quality of the sky too was changing, from the deep blue of winter to the hazier watercolor blue of warm weather. Time was indeed mutable; every year held at least four seasons.

"Then make friends with this Sigewulf," said Yaer. "It's likely he has several girls, if he's such a gift to women. He might not miss this one."

"Not a hope. From what Alfred says about him, I think the man's schizo, or very nearly. Morwena is his sole love-object."

Yaer delivered himself of another prayer. "That one," he said, "was for you. You have problems. Stay well away from them both. Don't even try to make friends with Sigewulf, because the moment he discovers your real plans he'll very probably try to kill you. Just wait."

"How can you say that?" asked Nilssen, puzzled by the resentment in him against Yaer's objectivity. "She's an important segment of the loop we've come to trace. If I don't meet her in Henglafingasham, we don't come here."

"Is that your only incentive for hunting an introduction?"

Nilssen delayed answering but said, finally:

"You know it isn't."

"Of course I do. But do you?" Aggressively, Yaer went on without a pause, "If you don't understand your own motives clearly, it could be bad for us both. So, Jerlan, out with it: do you love her?"

Embarrassed, Nilssen looked away. "What a stupid question," he said. "How can I answer that? Two minutes of whispering in the dark on a winter's night, with snow blowing down our collars—"

"I'll phrase it differently," Yaer said. "Can you swear that you don't?"

Uneasily, Nilssen admitted, "No, I do feel something."

"Fine. That's the first hurdle. Next, does it bother you that Sigewulf has her?"

He was surprised to realize it did not. "It shook me at the start. Now I'm rather glad she has someone like him, for protection."

Yaer pinched the tip of his nose between a thumb and forefinger, an idle motion that somehow made his smile the more sinister. "Say no more. Leave it to me."

"What are you going to do?"

"The same as you: nothing for now. But . . ." The smile drained away; his voice too lost its warmth. "We may have to arrange Sigewulf's disposal . . . No," he said, seeing Nilssen's consternation, "I'll not be so crude as to murder him; there are limits. There's a way of letting him decide for himself. Don't ask me what it is, because I won't tell you. It's between me and him."

"And her."

"An interesting ethical conundrum," Yaer mused. "*I* know that she will warm to you if I act in a certain way; I also know that you love her—"

"I never said . . ."

"There's more to a message than words, Jerlan. . . . So, ought I to favor dubious means to a worthy end? Assuming the end to be worthy, of course. Or, should I permit that end to remain unrealized by default? In either eventuality I am liable to censure. Being the person I am, therefore, I will select my own future and allow Sigewulf the same option. . . . That is what Shazol preached and what I myself believe. Jerlan, you can't dissuade me. Don't try."

With that, he resumed the simulated prayer in which they were obliged to indulge five times daily for the benefit of their disguise. Prevented from interrupting lest the guard's suspicions be aroused,

Nilssen seethed; when it was apparent that Yaer would sabotage further argument, he went out for a walk to calm himself.

Their second guard fell into step beside him. Nilssen recognized the man as one of those who had been on duty the previous night.

"You are Coelric, I believe?"

"Coelric of Æglesburg, late of Batha, yes." He seemed pleased to have made an impression. Almost diffidently he asked, "Is it so, that you are come from Hierusalem bearing fragments of the True Cross hither to aid us?"

"Wherever did you get that idea?"

"Is it then a lie?" Coelric's face was full of eagerness. Nilssen hated to disillusion him as he had the king.

"A rumor, I think," he answered.

"Ah, it was too rich a hope to be wholesome," said Coelric sadly. "What then are you come for?"

"The enemy bars our return home."

"You also?" The Saxon nodded understandingly. "I too am a wanderer, as are many of us. My home is Æglesburg really. But when the Danes overran Mercia and drove out King Burhed, I would not serve their puppet-king Ceolwulf. He was a stupid man. And stingy. He had a bad name even before he let the Here foist him on the people. Only fools follow him." He spat a gout of phlegm into a semifrozen puddle. "I went to Batha where I have relatives. Later I joined the army."

"Do you like it here?"

"It's not bad, considering."

"Considering?"

"The dampness and everything. Those who've been here all year round say it's a taste of Purgatory when the summer flies come out."

"How long have they been here?"

"Ever since God created them, I suppose." Coelric squinted at Nilssen. "What's it to you?"

It was Nilssen's turn to stop and think. "I meant the permanent staff, not the flies."

"*La!*, I thought it queer you should ask after them. Mark you, some are as big as bumblebees. And with the arrival of the horses, now we've the blasted cleggs to ward off too."

Nilssen hesitated. It might be risky to press the question. Then Coelric recollected himself. "Some soldiers have been stationed here almost four years. Before them it was artisans and a few special guards—that was the same summer King Burhed fled to Rome. And the first garrison was moved here about the time of the Long Siege of Wareham . . . You know, we had that cutthroat Guthrum cooped up in his camp between the rivers, all set to run him and his through, when he turned church on us and swore oaths left, right, and center. If we'd had those extra men to back us, we'd not have had all this trouble since." He spat again.

They had now crossed the camp to the northern embankment and were faced with a choice of directions. Suddenly Coelric suggested, "There's a good view on top." With a thumb he indicated the ramparts ten feet above their heads. "And a better smell." Wrinkling his nose, he drew Nilssen's attention to the ripening odor emerging from the thawing mud and its trodden-in refuse.

The inner face of the embankment was stepped so that an energetic person might swiftly mount the palisade anywhere. The individual steps were upheld by woven screens of withies behind stout posts. Seated on one of these posts, they discovered Sigewulf sunning himself with his eyes closed and a blissful smile upon his broad face.

The huge man blinked as they approached, though

they had hardly made a sound, and eyed Nilssen fixedly. Then he spoke. His voice too was huge and deep and stimulated sympathetic vibrations in the pit of one's stomach. His accent was foreign even to Nilssen's ignorant ear.

"Saracen," he grumbled, "I got you here." His right hand swung up like the jib of a crane; and clamped between his thumb and second finger—the first finger appeared to have been chewed off at the base—was a hazelnut. Finger and thumb tightened their grip. The nut shattered and a fragment of the shell flicked Sigewulf's stubbled cheek, drawing blood; but he did not flinch. "Look good at this. Not at my woman. I do not teach outlander another time. Good?"

So much for caution, Nilssen decided, even as he nodded. "Yes, very good."

Sigewulf became thoughtful. From a small leather bag at his waist he extracted another hazelnut which he also cracked, though more carefully than he had the first. This he proferred to Nilssen. "This also good. You will show that we are friends."

Nilssen chewed the nut while the giant prepared two more for Coelric and for himself. The taste was pleasant though insipid compared with the cultivated nuts he was accustomed to.

"Next," said Sigewulf, "I have a message for you. Must think, wait." His brow crumpled into a frown. "Yes: *your house is founded upon sand; the storms will wash it away.*"

He did not so much as blink as Nilssen stared at him, tense and afraid. "Is that all?"

The giant nodded after considering the question.

"Whose message is it?"

Sigewulf shied away like a horse from a snake, going as far as to shift his position on the post. "No," he grunted, "nobody."

"Somebody must have sent it," Nilssen insisted, "unless it comes from you."

"I am forbidden to tell you," said Sigewulf. "But the message is not of me. I am your friend." Concern mingled with utter guilelessness in his expression.

"Of course. And I am your friend," Nilssen assured him. Even so, I must learn who sent the message. So I can answer."

Sigewulf snorted, balked, finally nodded. "You will tell me. I will tell him."

"Tell your friend—" It was then that the awful significance of the message became clear to Nilssen. Meaning no more than it said, it had been a form of words to test his disguise. By finding meaning in the words he had failed the test. Who else but the CNI and men of the City would know of timestorms and what they could do?

Sigewulf was waiting patiently for the reply.

"Tell your friend that I would be his friend. Say also"—*how could words lure an alerted enemy into the open?*—"that time heals all wounds."

Sigewulf held his head to one side for a full minute, reciting the words to himself. Finally he said, "That is not so. Some wounds never heal."

"It's a way of speaking," said Nilssen. "Will you convey it to him at once?"

"When I may," replied Sigewulf, yawning. "Later. Now the sun is hot. I will enjoy it. Farewell."

Thus dismissed, Nilssen disconsolately walked on around the ramparts accompanied by Coelric. The Arab disguises had not been expected to survive indefinitely, but to be unmasked within twenty-four hours was a shattering blow to pride and confidence alike. Were there a traitor in the City, the CNI could have been waiting for them. But that was unlikely, for all who were privy to the secret had everything to lose by betrayal, so the damage had been done accidentally. A small mistake. A word; a glance. The CNI had sense enough to stay vigilant and appraise any newcomers on the basis of "guilty until proven innocent."

All in all he became poor company for Coelric, who responded by hustling him back to the hut as soon as Mass was ended.

Yaer listened to Nilssen's report and agreed that they could now only hope to deceive the genuine Saxons.

"We do have an advantage, though," he said. "Our quarry knows who we are."

"That's a strange sort of advantage," said Nilssen.

"True. One I could do without, actually. But we benefit because our quarry cannot help but react to our presence. He will know that we know more than we pretend; therefore he will try not to let us know that he knows more than he pretends to know. Are you with me?"

"Just a second . . . Yes."

"Inevitably he will react to us: he will either make a detectable mistake or—more likely—he will act out of character in front of his local friends and arouse their interest. They can find him for us."

"You keep saying 'he' and 'him.' "

"If Sigewulf said exactly what you have relayed to me, there can only be one person of any consequence. Review his words: Sigewulf meant to consult a superior of some power who was not immediately available for consultation. Sigewulf did not delay for the sake of it but because he had to. He's only a pawn. An isolated one, I rather suspect. Yes," he concluded with satisfaction, "I think we can concentrate on one man."

"You wouldn't happen to know his shoe size, I suppose?"

"I do believe you're jealous," Yaer said.

"Not at all," said Nilssen huffily, irked to have been analyzed correctly on top of being outthought. "We shouldn't make drastic assumptions from hints and the statements of a near-idiot."

"An idiot who has earned the king's respect, may I remind you," stressed Yaer. "Who is observant and alert. Who has survived years of fending for himself in the wilds of Wales as a brigand, then moved to Wessex to fight for spoils on the king's side because he gauged correctly that the war would swing against the Danes."

"Have you been talking to someone?"

"The guard," said Yaer. "While you were out taking the air I was beating him at draughts. Repeatedly."

Nilssen clucked his tongue softly. "Sigewulf is a man of many hidden talents."

"Well-hidden."

"I think I shall become afflicted by a recurrence of my old war wound," Nilssen said. "That which I received at Melita." He lifted his staff from its niche by his bed-mound.

"I wouldn't," advised Yaer. "You'll fall flat on your face. Sigewulf can't possibly be Middlesex; and Middlesex is the only one we're after, in the end."

"It would be nice to be sure."

"I am sure. The guard claims that our brigand makes a habit, widely known in the army, of going into battle stripped to the waist with no more than a cord to hold up his breeches. No wrist bands or personal jewelry. Quite out of character for our man. Put the darts away."

Nilssen did so and subsided onto the heap of straw and furs which composed his bed.

"I was so certain."

"Yes, it would have been convenient," Yaer said. "Both problems solved at once: ours, and yours."

Disregarding the taunt, Nilssen asked mildly, "And who's your suspect?"

"No one," said Yaer. "Give me longer than half an hour in a stuffy hall to study the prospects, will you?"

"But will the CNI?"

"Ah, that's the great imponderable. Not if the sender of that message has us as tightly as he seems to think. That, of course, is another clue to his identity. A common soldier wouldn't show his hand so early; but a powerful man—say, one of Alfred's companions—could afford to."

"So he was in the hall last night."

"Indubitably." Yaer raised his head to listen. "Someone's coming," he said quietly. "I doubt if even Arabic is secure anymore. We'll talk later."

Osric the ale-bearer rapped on the door frame with his knuckles and waited to be admitted, although the door was open wide and all three men were in full view of each other. Once recognized, he said formally:

"My master the king commands that you be invited to partake of meat with him in his chambers, it being the hour of noon."

The City men rose to their feet to obey, Yaer muttering in Arabic, "Mind you leave those blasted darts in their box this time."

Nilssen repressed a smile, saying in Old English for the Saxon's ears, "Indeed, my brother, we must be sure of that." To Osric he said, "For us it is also the hour of prayer. Shall we be delayed?"

"The king dines lightly at noon," replied Osric with ill-concealed disdain for the demands of heathen custom. "Will you follow me?"

They were taken to a low building adjoining the hall and connected to it by a covered passage. Here, as elsewhere, the floors were of rammed earth strewn with clean rushes, and though the decorations were richer than in those common buildings into which they had looked, the furnishings were sparse. Alfred had come to the camp not long since, to live without his wife and children, they being safely hidden in Cornwall, so that his Spartan temperament had been free to express itself in permitting no more than necessities in the royal apartments.

In a room some ten feet wide and fifteen long was a narrow oak table set with a pewter jug and two oil lamps on ornamental, gilded stands. Though darkness filled the ceiling recess and draped the walls, enough light was cast by the lamps to show that the rest of the furniture consisted of three carved chairs around the table. There were no fire, so the air was damp, edged with a chill that was the worse for being tainted with an unhealthy smell that reminded Nilssen of a grave he had once dug.

When the king joined them he wore outdoor clothes to which the dirt of travel still clung. He greeted them pleasantly, though coolly.

"Good morrow," he said. "I shall not restrain you from your devotions long. There is some information I desire, after which I trust you will be free to spend the remainder of the day as you prefer."

"My lord," Yaer replied, "it is our constant pleasure to assist you. Allah knows we praise Him in our hearts. He will not turn His face from us so readily."

Nilssen expected Alfred to discern the sarcasm in the reply. Of course, Yaer the atheist was striking two blows: at the king's piety, and at his own disguise. That was his game. But too audacious a game by far.

"We are practical men," he said with a reproving glance at Yaer. "It is written that there shall be no compulsion in religion; and again, that Allah knows the evildoers. You have called us to you for a purpose, lord. I pray you declare it to us."

"My purpose is to break my fast," answered Alfred, clapping his hands. As they sat, Alfred at the head of the table, his guests to either side, Osric returned with a tray of bread-platters—small hollowed pastries about the size of a spread hand—and a bowl of steaming beef-and-barley. They ate quickly, following the example of the king, who limited his conversation severely until they had finished and eaten the last of the bread.

Then he patted his stomach and belched discreetly. "It is an ill thought to transact serious business on an empty belly," he declared. "Come." Pushing back his chair, he conducted them through a series of dark rooms to the open air.

They had entered a small compound whose existence Nilssen had not suspected even with the benefit of an overall view from the palisade that morning. Surrounded by buildings and a wall of clay-caulked posts, it could only be a place of imprisonment. A surge of panic gripped Nilssen, subsiding only slightly when he saw a man tied by his wrists to a ring stapled high on the north wall, where the sun lit him clearly.

The man had been stripped to the waist and beaten. The beating had been severe, but so skillful that he hung sufficiently conscious to groan yet too weak to support his weight on his legs. Thus the strain imposed on his wrists by the leather thongs which bound them went unrelieved. Otherwise his appearance was of a man who had subsisted in the open without the comforts of a settled life while preserving civilized personal values. His baggy calf-length linen trousers were worn but neatly repaired; and his long fair hair would have been clean but for the blood that had run onto it from the coagulating crust smeared sideways from his nose. More blood was on the bindings at his wrists, fresh and constantly renewed by seepage from deep wounds in which the thongs rode slickly as he moved. The blood trickled down his bare arms, cutting red tracks through the filth caked on his chest. Across his pale upper torso were numerous whip weals.

And his eyes were open.

"Behold our enemy," said Alfred contemptuously.

The weight of food in Nilssen's stomach moved. The roof of his mouth went dry. "A Dane?" he asked to divert himself from nausea.

"You need ask?" said the king. "Didn't you say his kind have harried you from Wihtland to this camp?"

Yaer, who had been massaging his temples vigorously, finally spoke:

"Blood is the same the world over." He sounded ill. "All that may be said is that this man cannot be a subject of yours."

There was censure in his tone. Even Alfred's habitual urbanity could not overlook it, Nilssen suspected, so he was not surprised when the king stood over the shorter man and asked quietly:

"How so?"

Yaer was not to be cowed. "Because, *my lord,* no king would serve his subject thus."

Alfred smiled. "Does his condition trouble you? If so, you shall dispatch him yourself." And he presented his own long sword to Yaer. Four soldiers who had been standing aside all the while stepped forward to hover at Yaer's elbow as he accepted the weapon. Alfred moved back, opening the way to the prisoner.

Yaer faced Nilssen and asked in Arabic, "What would you do in my place?"

"Kill him," answered Nilssen. "Quickly. Save him the pain. These maniacs don't care how much he suffers. They'd let him hang until he dies."

With an amazing reversal of mood Alfred screamed, "Speak so we can understand you!" Just as suddenly he was calm again. "We need to anticipate the subtlety of your method, my friends. I have heard how skilled you Saracens are in putting prisoners to the question. Please, demonstrate this skill."

All the Saxons were now grinning; no doubt, Nilssen thought, sharing the joke of discovering that the heretic had a weak stomach.

Yaer took a steady grip upon the sword and stepped up to the Dane. His purposeful stance must have warned the king that he intended making a quick job of the execution, for at a sign the four soldiers disarmed him. The relief on Yaer's face was beyond disguising.

"No guts, man?" said Alfred as his sword was returned to him by a soldier. "Then let me show you how we treat these northern swine." In six rapid steps he stood by the prisoner. "First—" the sword chopped at the thongs. "—we cut them loose." The Dane cried out at the sudden relaxation of the tension. Falling forward away from the wall, he tried to protect his damaged face. Too slow, he dashed his elbows on the stony ground and doubled up, whimpering.

"Next," said Alfred, hoisting the Dane to his feet with one hand, "we insure that they comprehend what is being done and why. . . . *Pirate, do you hear me?*" he shouted. The Dane mumbled; his head fell forward. Alfred brushed the hair aside to shout directly into his ear, saw that it had been cut off, and made an impatient sound. "You and you," he said to two of the soldiers, "hold him up."

"Now," he continued, with a Saxon on either side of the prisoner to insure he stayed on his feet, "shake him."

After much jostling and face-slapping the Dane opened his eyes to gaze blankly at the king.

"Do you hear me, Dane?" demanded Alfred.

"I hear you," said the Dane in a weak voice. His accent was strongly foreign but his diction good.

"You were taken prisoner this morning whilst scouting our defenses. Yes or no?"

"You know I was," the man muttered. "I've denied none of your charges. Kill me; you've no further cause to keep me alive."

"Only when you have begged for my mercy," said the king, "the mercy of my sword."

"I do not beg," the Dane protested with renewed energy. "And you have no right to demand—"

The king's fist smashed into the Dane's mouth and withdrew with bloodied knuckles. The man's nosebleed had started again; but he merely kept his head up and breathed through his mouth. Enraged by this defiance, the king hit him repeatedly until the man could not stand without assistance from the soldiers.

"No Dane defines my rights!" Alfred said through clenched teeth. "I will reduce you before I let you die."

"Alfred Cerdinga," said Yaer harshly, "are you a king?"

Slowly Alfred turned, smiling horribly. "At last," he said, "you begin to declare an interest."

"Not in him," said Yaer, "but in you. Are you really Alfred, son of Ethelwulf, whose lineage includes Cerdic and Woden, and whom some call the Great?"

One of the soldiers made a hissing sound with his teeth. Alfred waved him to silence. His eyes rested on Yaer for some seconds. "I have been so hailed," he said, once more the confident gentleman of the previous evening. "And who are you, little man? A sparrow blown into my camp of war by the winter winds? An outlander, bred by men whose ignorance of our customs is matched by their own barbarities? Do the people of your golden cities sneer at us from their untroubled climes? Don't ask after my kingship, Saracen; don't ask by what right I so entreat this filth. Don't dare to open your mouth, lest I begin to regret my hospitality."

"For God's sake," whispered Nilssen in Arabic, "make peace with him!"

"You," snapped Alfred, "hold your tongue or I'll make you eat it . . . Little man, what is your answer?"

Yaer displayed no fear as he folded his arms and looked up into the king's angry face.

"I'm nobody special. Not like you. But in my travels I've seen kings and princes and overlords of every cut and class. And I've seen how they go on, good and bad. Only a fool could believe that a king is other than a man, breathing the same air as lesser men, moved to rage or pity like them, and to courage or cowardice. The sons of Adam are scattered throughout many lands and many estates, yet they are of one blood. That's what I have seen. That's what I have to start by saying.

"So I know you're just a man, my king. Common sense tells me that. But it also tells me how much you care about the welfare of your kingdom, given into your charge more by chance than by birth. Your people are oppressed by this Dane's kin, who spread havoc like a running fire in the harvest stubble whilst they laugh at the anguish they inflict. The blood price they owe you grows by night and day; there is no end to the slaughter in sight. And because you are a man with breath in him you know that it is natural to claim some small portion of this debt when chance permits. For this I do not judge you, Alfred Cerdinga. You are a man and a father; you love your children and the lands they will rule one day.

"Nevertheless, aren't you also a child of God? And if you disregard His plain commandments, wouldn't you expect His hand to smite you? It is written, *Thou shalt not kill*—this, in the holiest book of the Christians; as also is written that the Sabbath is consecrated to God. Therefore, though one part of you screams for revenge against this pirate, the nobler part ought to be mindful of its royal duties and the example which is set before your subject peoples, that family whose life is guided by your royal hand. King of the Engles and Saxons, if this man must die for his deeds, see that it is done decently so that no blood may stain your soul. Be just. Be stern. And, in the manner of the truly kingly, be merciful."

Alfred crossed himself. "I should have your throat cut," he said in a subdued voice. For some seconds he was wrapped in thought. "Take the sword. If he is to die quickly, you must do it. I cannot give him the release you plead for, not with my own hand."

With many expressions of doubt fleeting across his

face Yaer accepted the sword for the second time. His
hands, indeed his entire body, trembled as he neared
the Dane, who watched him calmly all the while.
When Yaer raised the yard of steel and placed its point
upon the man's bare chest, dimpling the skin over the
heart, the pirate spoke to him.

"Wait," he said.

The two guards tightened their grip on the Dane's
arms. He looked at each in turn, smiled, and addressed
Yaer.

"Friend, I would ask to borrow that sword, except
that these men would prevent it." He blinked away a
drop of sweat from his left eye. "If I tell you what to
do, will you be guided by me?"

Yaer lowered the sword. "I can do it," he said un-
certainly. "Close your eyes."

Nilssen noticed Alfred raise his face towards the sky
as if he preferred to watch the clouds cruising by overhead than be involved in the drama before him.

"No," said the Dane. "I am already in your debt but
if you are a man of custom you will grant me this
small favor more."

"I know where to strike," insisted Yaer.

"Any sokeman knows how to butcher a hog. Since I
came to manhood in my twelfth year I have been
obedient to Thor. No matter where you are from,
friend, will you deny me the death I have earned?"

"Hurry up," called Alfred suddenly, "or I'll make
damn sure he gets what he's whining for."

"What must I do?" Yaer asked. The king's interference had increased his nervousness.

"You must memorize my name: Jokulbjorn Kveldufsson. I beg you to remember it most ardently." He
allowed Yaer some seconds in which to repeat the
name under his breath. Nilssen also tried to commit it
to memory. The king looked disgusted. "At the next
full moon, repeat it seven times within the shade of a

holy oak. Thereby Thor will understand that he is to
speak for me at the *Hel-thing*. Odin cares only for
those who die in battle; I think I shall need Thor on
my side. Will you do all that for me?"

Yaer nodded jerkily. "If I am able," he said.

"No man can ask more, in reason," said the Dane. "I
thank you. As to my death, hold the sword upright
with its hilt upon the ground. . . . Will you let me
fall on it?" he asked the two guards. They looked to
Alfred, who nodded peremptorily.

With the sword pressed into the hollow below his
chest the Dane kneeled and studied Yaer's face intently. "What is my name?" he asked.

"You are Jokulbjorn Kveldufsson," said Yaer; and
the Dane fell forward, forcing the sword up through
his diaphragm and into his heart. A wet gasp burst
from his lips which reared back from his yellowed
teeth in a ghastly grin; from his wide open mouth
there came a choking gargle. Then he slid still farther
down the sword, so that it erupted from the muscles
at the base of his neck to jut from his left shoulder,
filmed pink with fresh bright blood. The corpse kicked
spasmodically. The left hand grasped feebly at open
air.

Yaer staggered away. Nilssen caught and held him
while he tried to retch. The king strolled to the body,
rolled it onto its back with his foot, and pulled out the
sword. Handing it to one of the soldiers, he said,
"Clean it." Then he came over to Yaer and Nilssen.
"This morning," he said, "I was considering your disposal . . . along with his. But I thought you deserved a
chance to prove yourselves."

"And did we pass the test?" asked Nilssen bitterly.

"There was no test," said the king, seemingly surprised by the suggestion. "I pride myself on being a
judge of men. You, I am sure of; but your friend puzzled me. Until now. Now I know where you both belong in my schemes, so I can allow for you."

"Is that all?" asked Yaer. "You had me kill a man to dispel a doubt?"

Alfred chuckled deep in his chest. "No, my wind-blown sparrow, not to dispel a doubt. To be sure of it. Those travelers' tales with which you entertained my companions last night make fine listening whilst the ale flows free; but morning sheds a new light on them. I needed to be sure you were worth the trouble it will take to corroborate your story. Now I am sure. Until the proof arrives you may remain alive." Moving away, he added cheerfully to Nilssen, "Eorl Sarnvig presents his courtesies but regrets he will be unable to take you riding as promised, being detained upon the king's business for some days to come. . . . In his absence, I trust you both will accept my hospitality this evening?"

Nilssen and Yaer walked from the king's quarters like men half-dead, mentally reeling from their experience. As they trudged through the mud, Yaer said, "I see why he made us eat with him before . . ." The rest he left unsaid.

Nilssen nodded. "Yes, he's qute considerate in his ham-handed fashion."

"I never thought the Danes were like that."

Suddenly Nilssen found he could not recall the prisoner's name. "I've forgotten already," he said.

Yaer bit his lip. "Me too," he said. "Does it matter so very much?"

"It did to him."

"But he died believing he'd be saved. That should be enough."

"If he was wrong in his beliefs, yes."

"A conundrum worthy of Shazol himself," Yaer observed.

And that, thought Nilssen, was Yaer all through. When the life that had to be lived became too uncomfortable, he could always take refuge in his mental games room. People could be made subservient to strategy; facts could be reduced to factors. Free will was the interaction of preplanned processes: outcome defined; algorithmic reality. *One day, Doctor Yaer, you'll run short of computing capacity and a problem will swamp you. What instincts will you rely on then?*

CHAPTER ELEVEN

The horsemen rode out of the southeast, ahead of slaty clouds threatening snow. Piling upon themselves, rearing into the evening sky, those clouds stood opposed to the sunset's radiance; already they had conquered the eastern hills by shadow and by premature night; soon they would engulf the marshes too.

Both horses were willing but exhausted. Saliva flecked with foam clung about their lips, and their feet failed to obtain the firm purchase on the thawing ground they would have found when fresh. Reined in to await the opening of the gates, riders and mounts alike swayed before the east wind. Nilssen, far along the ramparts, could hear the horses' heavy breathing and see their heaving flanks.

To Coelric, his personal escort and dedicated shadow, he said, "That looks much like the Eorl Sarnvig."

Coelric leaned over the palisade to follow the riders' progress through the gates. "Aye," he said, "and Eorhic of Æsces-dun. Not a scratch on either, what's more." Withdrawing from the edge, he settled his collar tightly around his neck. "It's a mercy they made it back so opportunely, before that storm strikes. I freeze. Let us go indoors."

Nilssen was not so eager to shut himself away, although he felt Yaer ought to be warned their hour of trial had come. For the past six days he had been dreading Sarnvig's return, certain that the man would report his total inability to trace the Saracens' movements.

Coelric had relayed camp gossip quite frankly. Everyone expected that the Sabbath eve would be enlivened by a pair of summary executions, Nilssen and Yaer to take the starring roles. Someone had been putting it about that Alfred had humored his guests for the sake of their novelty and the diversion they furnished to all, but that once proof of their duplicity was in his hands he would let the law prevail and treat them as the rogues they doubtless were. This rumor had been readily believed, such being the antipathy towards foreigners nursed by most Anglo-Saxons in Alfred's retinue. The few Welsh and other immigrants from the fringes of the British Isles were divided; but most adopted a pragmatic view, that it would not hurt to be safe. Coelric had several times been obliged to calm his comrades' overt hostility in the last day or two. Now Nilssen wondered how much of the man's shivering was a contrivance to usher his charge out of public view and last-minute harm.

"It's getting to me too," he said.

Coelric quickly seemed to forget his coldness as they went by back ways to the hut.

Yaer was stretched out on his bed beneath a pile of furs, snoring softly. He sat up when Nilssen nudged him with his foot.

"He's back," said Nilssen.

"Sarnvig?"

"Yes. I couldn't tell from his face what the news is, but we'd be wise to be ready to run for it." He began to load his staff with anaesthetic darts.

"Those won't help us," said Yaer. "If the word is bad we'll have to bluff. Meanwhile, keep hoping that Malchek did his job right."

"I'm not thinking of this for any escape." Nilssen loosened his belt and dropped his secret cache of bread and salted mutton into the pockets sewn into the lining of his cloak. "The CNI might show themselves. Three darts will kill by overdose; I think I can put five into one target within two seconds. If I have to die, it'll be for a reason this time."

"This . . ?" Yaer began. Then he understood.

With his preparations complete Nilssen sat on his bed and started wolfing down the last of his food stock. Through a mouth full of bread, he said, "Eat what you can. Wrap up well. There's a blizzard coming, so if we have to run we'll have full stomachs and warm clothes."

Hardly had he spoken when there came a heavy pounding on the door, the latch was lifted, and a squad of hall-guards pushed into their small room, led by the sergeant who had challenged them their first night in camp. He greeted Nilssen with mocking familiarity.

"Feasting alone, my Saracen? Why, this is not fitting. Come, there is a king who longs for your company, over that of all the eorls who presently wait with him in the council chamber. So great is his wish to see you, he has sent us as your honor guards." The five soldiers packed around him hardly bothered to smile. "So if you've broken your fast enough to give strength for this short walk, would you both care to step outside?" The squad retired to the hut-run; and Nilssen saw the first snowflakes fleck their armor.

The council chamber was merely the feast-hall without its trestle tables. A smaller fire burned in the pit, and the air was cool enough for all present to wear their outdoor garments without discomfort. Most of the crowd stood on the earth banks; but a few ornamented seats had been set where the high table normally would be. The best and central one, the king's, was empty. On either side sat the most influential of Alfred's companions. Two seats off to the right down by the fire were for the recently returned riders, who sat drowsing over mugs of mulled ale.

Their fatigue suggested the worst to Nilssen. They had driven themselves and their horses hard to bring home the news. Good news traveled by slower mounts.

Yaer displayed no emotion at all when Nilssen caught his eye. Instead he averted his gaze to the rear door of the hall by which the king would enter. Nilssen copied him, leaning carefully on the armed staff, his finger near its trigger.

When Alfred arrived he hurried through most of the formalities with one short speech.

"Friends," he said, standing before his seat, "these two men came to us a week ago, claiming to be ship-wrecked merchants, besides a number of other things we have no means of checking. In times like these, a reliable man is worth more than gold. Accordingly last Sabbath-morn I sent the Eorl Sarnvig and Eorhic of Æsces-dun to that part of Hamtunscir lying this side of the water. Their brief was twofold. One portion was war-work, which we will speak of later. But whilst they were there, they were to determine what truth there might be in the claims of these foreigners, or what deceit.

"Therefore I call now on Eorl Sarnvig to stand forward and give an account of their findings." He sat while Sarnvig levered himself from the seat into which he had relaxed and came to stand between the king and the City men.

"Lord Alfred," he said, "we did as you commanded and rode fast for the south coast. Three full days it took, without sign of the Dane though many of his handiwork. Common folk fled when they saw us coming. One man we caught said the Here had foraged that way earlier in the winter but that they had gone north before Martinmas. We asked about the fyrd—"

"Later," said Alfred.

Sarnvig ducked his head. "On arrival at the coast, near Cristescirice, we struck out eastward, letting our horses rest while we examined every piece of wreckage on the shore that resembled what we sought. For more than half a day we thought our journey wasted. Then, at about noon—"

Nilssen's skin prickled as all around him the crowd stirred, moving to see what the foreigners might say or do when confronted with the damning truth.

"At about noon," Sarnvig repeated more firmly, "we chanced upon the hull of a ship."

The hall filled with muttering: this was not the anticipated outcome. What right, the crowd seemed to be asking, had Sarnvig to rob them of a spectacle? The king called for silence. Nilssen had the impression he was not displeased by the news. Inwardly he was cheering their luck. Geodetic Survey department had been asked to locate a wreck to fit their cover story. Two years earlier, a storm had caught the viking fleet off Swanage: some one hundred twenty vessels had been destroyed and their wreckage now littered the shores for miles. But it had been by no means certain that Sarnvig too could find the right remains.

Sarnvig continued, "It lay in the proper place, though more deeply embedded in sand and stones than expected. The currents along the coast there are said to be fierce, which may explain it. Our conclusion, after examining this wreck, is that it could well be the one that brought these two to Britain, for its style is as foreign as any I have seen and its condition acceptably poor, considering the bad weather we have had. I say they seem not to have lied."

"My thanks to you," said Alfred. "Eorhic of Æsces-dun, do you concur?"

Eorhic got up slowly, pushing against the armrests of his chair with both hands. Nilssen watched him anxiously. If he said "yes," all would be well. If not, the balance of opinion would be against them. It all pivoted on one word: all the future, all the present, some of the past. That man of middling height, of no special nobility of feature, with hair of the same brown as many a Saxon, dressed in clothes no better or cleaner than any worn by the mass of decisionmakers of ninth century Britain, could make or break a world by one word. *Be lucky,* Nilssen prayed, invoking a god he had just discovered in that moment of painful attention, *be mistaken.*

Their eyes passed across each other's face, did not linger, dropped as if aware of what might have been communicated in the event of contact.

Eorhic took a breath. His nod was minute, his single "Yes" brief. But the impact on the hall's occupants was lasting. Without meaning to, Nilssen let go a sigh; and he heard Yaer's breathing resume with a soft gasp. Loud whispers began but trailed off when Alfred spoke:

"So be it. I declare these men free of suspicion. Whilst they bide within my realm their wergild is set at that of an eorl. I shall myself be their protector.

"However," and here he addressed himself to Nilssen and Yaer in particular, "they must count themselves bound to observe the courtesies due to hosts who wage war, by refraining from interference in our preparation for and conduct of battle. I hope they infer my meaning."

There came a rasping cough from Bishop Werferth. The priest left his seat to stand before his peers. "Alfred," he said, "this error is the gravest of your reign. By their nature these men can intend you nothing but harm." His bright eyes fixed on Nilssen. "There are some who would pretend that time heals all wounds—"

You? was Nilssen's shocked thought even as the priest spoke on:

"—as though the indissoluble enmity that exists between his kind and ours will diminish if endured for long enough. No simple circumstantial evidence can establish their good intent. Only the obliteration of this affront to God can cleanse us for the fray. Alfred, my king, my friend, hear what I say. Love of learning cannot justify the jeopardy into which you plunge your kingdom . . . and your followers."

From the outset Nilssen had recognized the priest's hostility. Given contemporary religious intolerance it was predictable and had been allowed for by Yaer. But few revelations could have disconcerted him more than a link between the old man, the king's long-time bishop and counselor, and the CNI.

Alfred waved Werferth back to his seat before answering.

"Werferth, I do not care to hear more on this subject. Moreover, I am persuaded by what you say to declare a special peace within this camp, save for the purposes of war against the Danes. I therefore remind you of the penalties prescribed by the law, for violence committed near the king's person. If my purposes seem obscure, recall how often I have sought your trust in the past, and how rarely that trust has not been redeemed an hundredfold. Companions all, this is a modern age upon which we are embarked: new times deserve new wisdoms. Do not heed your prejudices. They have always favored stagnation and feared innovation. Werferth, tell me, have these men preached heresy?"

"No," the priest allowed with very bad grace. "They don't have to. Their presence—"

"—is therefore none of your business . . . Sarnvig, what news of the fyrd?"

The eorl inclined his head towards the City men. "With them present?"

"Best they know now, not later. Withhold details."

"Whatever you wish."

But Sarnvig's worried sidelong scrutiny was lost on Nilssen, whose mind was taken up with the single thought, that the bishop was their target. Or, that the man pretending to be the bishop was really Middlesex. That meant history had already been changed by the replacement of a genuine participant by a calculating fraud. The bishop glared at Nilssen when he dared to turn his face that way, so he pretended interest in what Sarnvig was saying.

The eorl was mentioning isolated trees where they had posted messages in rotten hollows and those from which other messages had been retrieved. It went well in the south and west, he said; the land was mustering its strength for the spring offensive; by the first week in May they would have an army powerful enough to challenge even the hardened campaigners of the Danish Here. As the good news was told, the crowd's enthusiasm became roused, eyes shone, teeth gleamed as grins spread from face to face. Only the two City men remained subdued: they, and the CNI, were aware that victory was not inevitable.

"An absurd suggestion," said Yaer.

"He did send the message," Nilssen reminded him.

Patiently Yaer enumerated his objections, halting beneath a lighted window to mark them off on his fingers. Snow flitted past as he talked; a figure deformed by a hooded fur cloak sidestepped them on the path, bidding them a grudging good night.

"For one thing," said Yaer, "Bishop Werferth is an historical figure, a known associate of King Alfred. The CNI cannot have invented him as a cover—"

"I'm well aware of that," Nilssen burst out. "An actor—"

"But Middlesex could not hope to impersonate him. The depth of characterization to be emulated would defeat the most expert of actors. Finally, the age disparity is too great—"

"I disagree. Middlesex wasn't over thirty at the Collapse. Werferth must be an easy fifty. Twenty years is ample time to build an alias. How long has Alfred known him anyway?"

"Will you be guided by me?" asked Yaer. "Dammit

to hell, Jerlan, there is *no* way the bishop could be our man. All that muddle over the message via Sigewulf has blinkered you."

Nilssen, rebelliously unconvinced, avoided the psychologist's eyes, which he knew would be full of patronizing concern. Yaer saved him from further damage to his self-esteem, however.

"You'd do better to suspect Eorhic," he said.

"But he saved us."

"I know," agreed Yaer. "It makes no sense, taken at face value. But when the bishop flung your message back at you, Eorhic jumped as if someone had pricked him."

"I didn't notice."

"He recognized that anachronism. Perhaps you saw how he stared at you?"

"I thought he was just interested in us, after the king backed us."

"Out of character . . . Let's walk on." This they did while Yaer talked. "And he was giving the bishop odd looks later, too. Eorhic of Æsces-dun is someone I'd dearly love to have under a mindscanner. His age is right; he has the position of power you'd expect; his actions to date have not cleared him, however friendly he may have seemed. Jerlan, if you must go hunting tomorrow, go after him, not Werferth."

"Why not both?" said Nilssen.

Their footfalls squelched wetly in the slush while Yaer mulled over the suggestion. "No," he said finally, "don't plan for it. If the opportunity presents itself, obviously you take advantage. Meanwhile you must condition yourself carefully, commit your whole effort to one target."

"Are you being profound again? Or just obscure?" He suspected Yaer of indulging himself in another of his one-upmanship ploys.

Yaer might have blinked in the darkness. He sounded hurt. "No, Jerlan, I am being professional;

working for my ticket here, you might say. If a technical reference will reassure you, on your return to the City you may ask the Library for the text of my doctoral thesis, *Identification of Decision-Reflex Mechanisms in Multivariate Psychostress Environments, their Isolation, and their Stimulation, with Applications to Extratemporal Personnel Evaluation.*"

When Nilssen failed to reply, he chuckled.

"The trouble is," he went on, "you can't tell when I stop being serious. Maddening, isn't it?"

"I don't see why you try so hard," Nilssen replied.

"Someone has to."

"Is that a criticism of me? Or another of your smug attempts to show how highly you regard yourself?" Seizing Yaer's baggy sleeve, Nilssen whirled him around so that their faces almost touched. "I've watched you change since we left the City, and I can tell you I prefer Doctor Jekyll any day. Yaer, if it's an admission of your superiority you want from me, you can have it: yes, you're almighty clever with your tricks. And quite possibly you could talk sense into a stone. I yield to you on that score. For the sake of the mission I'll concede any petty advantage you've set your heart on. But I want something back from you. One tiny thing. So small a sane man would hardly notice it. Want to know what it is . . . Doctor Yaer?"

Yaer's jaw worked stiffly within his cheeks. His nostrils flared slightly. For a few seconds his lips trembled, half opened, shut firmly again.

"I'll spare you the shame of asking," said Nilssen, so coldly, he surprised himself; and some of his righteous indignation left him. But he held to the path he had chosen. "All I ask is that you *pretend* to be what you're supposed to be. Just that: play your part. Is it a deal?"

He released Yaer's sleeve, and the small man drew back a full step before swinging around and walking away into the darkness. His pace never slackened while he was within earshot.

Nilssen drew several deep breaths to clear the tension in him. His chest felt tight. Gradually the cold air tempered his anger, hardening the surface memory of their quarrel. *Tomorrow he'll hate me but will pretend not to,* he thought. He sighed. The City abounded with professionals full of their own importance. The saying that the worst-shod man in town was the cobbler applied as much to Yaer as to any other tradesman. *But how to convince the vainglorious little squirt?*

He leaned on his staff, thinking it over.

His reverie was ended by footsteps from the direction in which Yaer had gone. They were too loud to be those of the psychologist. When Sigewulf appeared in the weak light Nilssen was not alarmed, for he had half expected a renewed approach by the bishop or one of his minions.

The Welshman pointed at Nilssen, then back along the path. His other hand made a sign for silence by covering his own mouth. He beckoned.

Nilssen weighed the risk of accompanying the giant and falling into a CNI trap. Were the bishop Middlesex, his evident hold over Sigewulf meant Nilssen was now in great danger, for one blow by a huge fist could leave him to die of exposure amongst the hutments without soiling the CNI's cover. Yaer would still be alive but uncertain whom to blame; and already he had discounted Werferth.

"Where—" Nilssen began to whisper but was silenced by Sigewulf's emphatic repetition of the mouth-covering sign. The violent gesture was ameliorated by a gentler, almost pleading, signal that Nilssen was to come quickly. Won over, he went warily.

Sigewulf led him almost to the foot of the southern rampart where he expertly opened the door of a hut like the one Nilssen shared with Yaer. There was no

sound as he lifted the hinged panel and swung it clear
of the earthen floor. Dubiously Nilssen followed him
into the darkened interior. The door was returned to
its closed position and Sigewulf said:

"Light."

At once a cover was removed from a lantern and
the darkness was dispelled, taking with it the horrors
Nilssen had expected. In their place stood Morwena.

She was reaching up, offering the carrying loop of
the lantern to a hook on a crossbeam, so missed his
frank stare. So too did Sigewulf, who was shambling
away from him, shedding his voluminous outer fur
jacket. Man and woman were dressed in similar homespun cloth and dressed skins; but on her they seemed
softer, kinder. Her hair hung free in a black fan
across her shoulders, and her bare arms were pale in
the lantern's glow. Then she turned to face him.

She showed no special interest. Politely she drew a
three-legged stool forward from a corner for him,
after which she seemed to forget him as she bent to
revive the embers of the fire in the middle of the floor.

Meanwhile Sigewulf had taken from a shelf a dark
piece of sacking wrapped tightly about some long,
narrow object. This he brought into the light. Taking
another stool, he urged Nilssen by a sign to join the
gathering, saying, "We have talk to make. The woman
will not trouble us. No speech." To emphasize his
point he inserted his left forefinger in his mouth just
as Morwena dropped an armful of peat on the floor
with a thud. The pile toppled and Sigewulf assisted
in the restacking of it.

While his hosts were distracted Nilssen examined
their home. He did so guiltily, aware of how much of
an intruder he was. Later ages would have disdained
it as a hovel and its poor furnishings as sticks of rubbish. There were two rush bed-piles, the stools the
men occupied, a brass-bound chest by one wall, numerous items hanging from hooks. The fire was neatly

delimited by a circle of small stones. He was impressed by the tidiness of the hut and by its cleanliness. He sensed a loving care. Morwena and Sigewulf worked well together.

With the peat again in order Sigewulf unwrapped his bundle, exposing the burnished blade and jeweled hilt of a broadsword to the light. Rocking it slowly so that sparks of brilliance danced up and down its length, he watched for Nilssen's reaction.

"A lovely weapon," Nilssen said.

Sigewulf smiled. "I fight good for this. Killed a king to get it. Welsh king, yes, only four-valley king, but king. And many soldiers. Good fight."

Morwena turned her face to him and smiled warmly, as Nilssen had seen her smile in Henglaf's village. Sigewulf reached out a huge hand to stroke her cheek. "But biggest treasure I get is this woman. Save her. Very good night." He made a sign towards the wall, and she fetched for him a chunk of sandstone which he began to pass lovingly along the sword blade's edge. "Soon I need this sword more. Much big fight, Alfred says: kill all Danes in spring." He peered at Nilssen from beneath his overshadowing brows. "Some folk say you come for this battle."

Jerlan, don't imagine things. "They may be right. We came because we heard the king shares our cause. If a battle is due, well and good."

Sigewulf licked his lips and spat on the stone. "But the priest, he wishes curses on you."

"Bishop Werferth has nothng to fear from us."

"But he sent me with his words. And he would not make peace. He is afraid, yes."

"I can't help that."

The big man rumbled deep in his throat. "Frightened man becomes stupid man. In fight, out of fight, all places. The priest will be stupid soon."

"Are you warning me?"

The slow scrape of stone against metal ceased.

Sigewulf sat still, watching the small flames licking at the peat in the firepit. "Yes," he said. "Yes, Saracen, I warn you. Maybe I am wrong. Maybe right. Priest says that heathen is not a man, can be killed without sin. But king says you must live. To kill you therefore is treachery against king. That is sin, yes?"

"How right you are," answered Nilssen, releasing a relieved breath.

The grim-visaged giant returned to polishing his blade, deftly stroking the edges so as to hone them to the keenest, cruelest pitch without folding the metal or warping it with too much pressure. He worked as a craftsman, without fuss.

"So," said Sigewulf, "you have care. Priest says I must kill you. I will not tell him not, so he discovers late. But when he does, I think another will be sent."

"Who do you think that will be?"

"Any fool." Sigewulf laid aside the sword, swaddling it tenderly in the sacking, placing the stone beside it on the floor. "Many men will hear the word of God in what he says. But I am not stupid. God-talk is stupid; so much anger for nothing comes." He paused. All of a sudden, he stood up, stepped to the door, and, with a sudden burst of speed, dashed out into the night.

At this Nilssen leaped to his feet to follow, convinced of a trap. But Morwena's hands held his wrist tightly, forcing him to halt. Her eyes implored him not to go, as did her frantic shaking of her head. His panic faded. He touched her hands with his free hand and she released him. He sat again. She scrutinized him more intently than she had earlier, as though reading his face. Suddenly she settled herself by the fire with her legs tucked beneath her and fed twigs to the flames.

"Do you know why I trust you?" he asked her, admiring the fall of her hair about her neck and the deft movements of her fingers.

She looked at him and shook her head.

"You will."

Her eyebrows requested an explanation.

"Not yet," he said. "Morwena, before long . . ."

Her face was transformed. The twigs scattered as she scrambled to her feet. Eyes wide, teeth bared, she backed towards the door.

"What have I said?" he demanded. "Morwena, I'm on your side, yours and Sigewulf's. Don't go. If he comes back . . ."

His fear of what the giant would do seemed to communicate itself to her. She stopped at the door, her face alive with suspicion.

"Morwena—" he said, and she jerked. "That *is* your name?" he asked, aghast that he might after all have found the wrong person.

She nodded slowly, relaxing. Then she pointed to him. Again her eyebrows asked a question.

"Me?" he said. "I am Ibrahim . . ."

Her hair flew wide as she shook her head. Her lips shaped a word.

"If only you could use better signs," he said. "Morwena, what—"

Once more she pointed; sharply, violently.

She mouthed a name: *M—*

"Morwena?" he asked; and she responded with a gentler hand sign. "Why is your name so strange to you?" he asked. Then she came nearer to the fire, and by the shifting light of the lantern he saw a tear on her cheek. By a sign she expressed silence spread over the name.

"I still don't understand," he said as Sigewulf entered carrying a body in his arms.

As the big man swung around to kick the door shut, Morwena hurriedly composed herself, flashing Nilssen a look that begged his discretion. By the slightest of nods he assented, discovering that the signs he had employed daily when a quarter century younger were still to hand, as if a second side to his mind were re-awakening and reaching out to participate in his life.

The first barrier between them had been breached.

Then Sigewulf intruded his body into the space beside the fire.

"This is yours, yes?" he said, in his arms the limp form of Yaer, on his face an unreadable blankness.

"Have you killed him?" Nilssen cried out, starting up.

"You must speak to me plainly, Saracen," said the Welshman. "I do not know your tongue."

In his confusion Nilssen had reverted to Arabic. He repeated the question in Old English.

"If yes, he died quick," said the big man. His thick fingers, curled easily about the smaller man's body, added explanation as they shifted for a better grip. They were like the armored talons of an eagle but tipped with grubby, broken nails instead of claws. The tendons which cabled the backs of his hands were like metal rods encased within leather. A blend of man and machine, if he killed, he would kill swiftly. "But I go to catch for question. I think he sleeps."

They laid him on one of the bed-piles so that Nilssen might examine his head, where Sigewulf had hit him. Blood was in his hair and the scalp was swollen. The corners of his eyes were already pink, confirming Nilssen's tentative diagnosis of concussion.

Covering Yaer with a fur, Nilssen said to Sigewulf, "He's badly hurt."

Alarm filled the Welshman's face, as though he was mindful of the king's edict. "He dies?"

"Not necessarily." Sigewulf looked happier. By comparison Morwena continued to show concern for Yaer by tucking the fur around him as she listened to them talking. "It's not far to our hut. Nevertheless, it would be well if he could stay here undisturbed, at least until tomorrow noon."

He had no doubt that Sigewulf could have carried

Yaer the short distance without increasing his injuries;
but there were several benefits to be derived from
leaving him where he was. Nilssen felt no shame at
seizing the opportunity. The next morning all able-
bodied warriors who were off duty would be expected
to attend Mass, a chance to revisit the hut which Nilssen had no intention of letting slip. Presumably
Yaer's injuries were part of the loop they were tracing
through time. Within a few days he would have recovered fully. The enforced rest would keep him
quiet, and the wound might gain them some sympathy from Sigewulf. In the meantime the giant could
stand guard over him.

Sigewulf sat, hunching his shoulders as he leaned
his elbows on his knees. "Once I see a man hit on the
head—another did it," he added quickly, "—and he
lies sleeping for many days. Then he dies."

"That's called a *coma*," said Nilssen. Surprisingly
the only word which came forward from his imprinted
memory was Arabic. Evidently the Anglo-Saxons chose
not to record such medical oddities or failed to distinguish degrees of unconsciousness with exactitude.
A functionally minded race, he thought: a man was
awake or asleep; all else was rhetoric.

Sigewulf gave up the effort of mastering the word
after a couple of attempts.

"Don't concern yourself so much," said Nilssen,
well aware that this consolation would inhibit Sigewulf from talking the matter through without calming
him. The giant was too directly involved with life to
defer worry until the time for action arrived. It was
oddly appropriate that it should have been Yaer whom
he knocked out.

But why had Yaer been there anyway?

"Sigewulf."

The man raised his head from staring at the fire and
waited patiently for the question.

"What was he doing?"

"Listening, I think. I hear sly creepings outside, I go as you see, I run, I catch. He fights, so I hit him."

"I heard nothing."

Sigewulf merely smiled as he fed another twig to the fire.

"You're a man of the mountains, aren't you," said Nilssen.

The other nodded. "High mountains, above trees, with rocks and bears. No people."

"A hard life?"

"Uh-huh . . ." It could have been agreement or denial.

"But a good one?"

"No. Bad."

Nilssen felt a touch on his hand. Morwena was shaking her head at him, apprehension in her eyes. But he had to know more, so asked, "You weren't always a fighter, were you?"

Sigewulf's head swung around until his eyes could both bear on Nilssen. The rest of him remained still. "Sigewulf always fights. This sword—" which he now picked up and laid across his knees "—is my arm. Its blade is my mouth. Its blood is my blood. We drink and eat together. Before, before I am in the mountains, I am dead: I am a not-man."

He could not tell where the danger lay but felt compelled to go on into the thicket of the man's past. "Do you mind talking about it?"

"There is nothing. I do not care about nothing." He spoke defensively.

"Then, do you remember nothing?"

Sigewulf resumed honing the blade with the stone gripped tightly in his white-knuckled fist. Morwena tapped Nilssen sharply on the hand; this time her eyes were angry and her lips tightly set. Nilssen acknowledged Sigewulf's reluctance to talk about his origins by a nod, a sign which Morwena accepted by withdrawing her hand.

After they had sat in the firelight listening to Yaer's stertorous breathing for some while, Sigewulf raised the sword and sighted along the edges. With a grunt of satisfaction he said:

"Saracen, when you come here, to this camp, you tell your saga. I listen good, because always there is wisdom in another man's life. Maybe small. Maybe big. Always a little at least. Sometimes in strangeness there is new seeing of custom, like coming to outland place in the mind. In Cymru, more than in Britain, our bards tell of times so strange they are not real for me. In Britain they always tell of fighting. Every song is of shadow-people: made up in bard's head. Real is very good, because real—" Licking his lips, he rubbed his right thumb across the remaining fingers of that hand as if feeling the texture of what he wanted to say. "—Real is full of life. Are you understanding me?"

Nilssen nodded, aware of the woman's attention and of Sigewulf's painstaking attempts at self-expression.

"Good. Because I listen close to your words, Saracen. And something whispers in my head that you lie. There is shadow everywhere in your saga, with shadow-people, shadow-places. You and him, there on the bed, both speak of shadows. Why, Saracen? Why is your life to be hidden? Is there shame in it?"

The first reaction had been a flush of adrenalin that sent the blood through his head in a dizzying series of hammer-blows; counterreaction brought its wake of numbness. His answer began with a helpless stammer, "We're not—" He had almost told Sigewulf the truth, the full truth. "We're not quite what we seem, that's true," he said, recovering rapidly but despising his lack of control. Sigewulf did not so much as blink. "But the life we led before coming here would seem so strange you would at once accuse us of deceit anyway. We devised those stories to placate the curiosity of anyone we met."

Sigewulf pondered this notion. Morwena got up

and brought to Yaer's side a bowl of water and a rag
with which she began to bathe his brow. It must have
been more than an act of kindness, possibly a signal
between the woman and the man, for Sigewulf gave a
slow smile. "We will not ask all your secret," he said.
"But can you say truth for us?"

Were he to reciprocate the big man's trust, Nilssen
realized he would be acting on behalf of both himself
and the injured Yaer. Yaer himself had ruled out
Sigewulf as a suspect, which seemed to leave the way
free. However, the whole truth would be beyond the
comprehension of any ninth century warrior, regardless of his apparent mental resilience. Yet too far
diluted it might lack conviction.

"We seek an enemy," he compromised, "in order to
kill him."

"Aha!" Sigewulf's mouth widened into a huge grin.
"When I first see you I think: this man is a hunter,
he follows a spoor. I tell the woman. Woman, is this
not so?"

Morwena glanced up from her ministrations and
nodded while looking at Nilssen, before bending her
head to Yaer again.

"Unfortunately," said Nilssen, "the face of our
enemy is unknown to us. Only his ways can betray
him. But we believe he is here in this camp, deceiving
you as well as us."

"You have not found him?"

Nilssen regarded Sigewulf levelly. "Not yet. We
will, though."

"Is it written as his fate? You speak as one who can
see the future."

Was Sigewulf taunting him with the evidence of
his gullibility? Had he made a dreadful mistake?
"Nothing is written that cannot be erased," said
Nilssen, adding for the sake of his disguise, "except
what God ordains. I say we will find him because
failure cannot be accepted."

"Ah, he is very bad?"

"He was . . . a tyrant." The word he used meant, literally, *people-hater*. To Sigewulf it would imply more than its later counterpart would to speakers of Modern English, for it embodied paramount treachery of a ruler against his people. "Beside him, the pirate host are honest soldiers engaged in open war upon a clear battlefield."

"And he is here now," marveled Sigewulf, seemingly impressed by such concentrated wickedness in one man. He reached a decision. "Saracen, I cannot say if you tell full-truth, or part-truth. But you do not lie. So I will watch close for what will happen. Maybe I will help later. Maybe I will fight you. You have enough enemies now."

"Will you keep this secret?"

"We will." Sigewulf held out his right hand towards Morwena, who clasped it with hers, a response that brought a pang of envy to Nilssen.

"Even from the king?"

"If it does not hurt him."

"Agreed." He stood up, sure of Sigewulf's trustworthiness. "If my friend may remain with you, I shall go now to sleep. Tomorrow I shall return to see how he fares."

"The woman will tend to him," said Sigewulf. "She commands good arts of healing."

"I'm sure she does," said Nilssen. He corrected himself. "I'm sure you do." They shared a smile. Casually he said, ostensibly to her but in hope that Sigewulf would rise to the bait, "I wish I knew your name."

The big man stood to put away his sword.

"No man knows her name," he said; and it was as though a bolt of lightning had struck the hut as Nilssen's mind filled with a sudden terrible understanding of what Morwena had felt, hearing herself addressed by name from the mouth of a stranger whose home lay far away. "The king I killed said she was booty from a raid. All her family dead. He did not know her name. So I do not. And she, she cannot talk." He held open the door for Nilssen and clapped him on the shoulder. "But no matter. What is a name? You are what man you are. She is my woman. I am me. That is enough."

But when Nilssen looked back and caught sight of her face through the closing door, he saw that it was not so. The door might close on him that night; but she would see that it stayed open rather than endure the locked room of silence again.

CHAPTER TWELVE

Wind sifted through the watchtower, rattling a loose tile on its roof. Across the gray hutments below it hurried flocks of smoke and stray snowflakes that fell from the clouded sky in errant flurries. It gusted, fell away, came on again. *The land is breathing,* thought Nilssen, leaning on the parapet of the sentry platform, watching the celebration of the Mass, wishing the soldiers with him would turn their backs long enough for him to try his staff against the bishop.

Werferth stood not far away in terms of yards, yet in a world of his own that presupposed a God triumphant bestriding the faithful at prayer beneath His throne. Despite the coldness of the day he was afire with zeal. His was no gelid piety. The furs which hung about his clerical vestments flapped with every gesture of his arms. From his mouth there issued a constant torrent of vapor as he preached or prayed, calling the martial ranks of worshippers to salvation. Nilssen regretted not knowing Latin better than he did, for here was a performance worthy of an audience. Haplessly, the verses rising from the parade ground might be meaningful to the god to whom they were dedicated, but to Nilssen—and, he suspected, most of the congregation—they were so much impressive noise.

Coelric crossed the platform, his wood-soled shoes clunking on the rough planks. "Enjoying it, Ibrahim?" he asked.

"Beyond my expectations," replied Nilssen. "It was

kind of you to permit my presence. . . . Tell me, who is that man yonder—in the dark furs?" Selecting a warrior at random, he pointed to him with the staff, keeping his fingers away from the trigger-bar.

The Saxon squinted towards the parade ground, even as Nilssen allowed his aim to drop and settle on the bishop's neck. The staff was perfectly balanced, the sights set; he had only to touch the bar—

"That one?" asked Coelric, taking hold of the staff and swinging it up again. Nilssen felt it kick, heard the *chi-click* as it reloaded and cocked itself automatically, saw snow spurt up in the open ground between priest and congregation.

Controlling himself, he said, "Not him. The man next to the tall swarthy fellow in the third row, on the left."

"Oh, Wistan the Elder. A clever wight with an axe. The tall one's his son. Why?"

"He has an interesting face." *Let it fall casually . . . Onto the neck . . .*
Chi-click . . . chi-click . . .
Werferth's tirade ended in a yelp of pain. His hand flew up to slap at his neck; he peered at the specks of blood on his palm. The darts would strike, pump in their cargo of anaesthetic, then, with a last gasp of gas pressure in their tanks eject themselves from the wound so rapidly, only close scrutiny would catch them at work. Once on the ground they would disintegrate within forty seconds.

The priest's outcry brought members of his congregation to his aid. Foremost was Sarnvig, who caught the priest about the shoulders as he began to sway. More helpers crowded close, hiding both men, and Coelric uttered an oath that Nilssen was sure was not Christian.

"I always said he'd go astray, carrying on like that," said the Saxon. "All those invocations of God's wrath. One of us had better call the sergeant . . . Eadwald!

On your way—quickly now! . . . Ibrahim, it would be best if you were not found here. This trouble might be blamed on you. Let Eadwald conduct you down."

Obediently Nilssen followed the soldier, exaggerating his false limp and dependence on the staff. Emerging into daylight from the darkened body of the tower, he was able to mingle with the milling crowd. No one knew quite what had taken place. Speculation was fermenting the simple facts available into a fine brew of nonsense, which ranged from the supposition that a Danish attack had started to the assertion that God had finally tired of Werferth's acid sanctity and had made a public example of him.

This last rumor puzzled Nilssen, although it conveniently laid a misleading trail away from him. Far too elaborate to have arisen naturally so quickly, it might almost have been manufactured to fit someone's needs. He had not started it; and Yaer was lying semidelirious in Morwena's care, vomiting whenever he tried to move.

Someone shouted that Werferth was awake again; and Nilssen slipped away, conscious of his failure to find their enemy, who now would be alert if he had not been alerted already.

Morwena answered his knock and admitted him to her hut. Exchanging smiles with her, he squatted beside Yaer's bed, shaking him gently by the shoulders.

The other man's eyes opened, revealing bloodshot whites. He stared at Nilssen without focusing on him.

"Khaled?" said Nilssen. "Do you hear me?" He spoke Arabic.

Yaer blinked. His brows and cheeks grew mobile, bringing expression to his face at last. "I hear shouting," he said, also in Arabic.

"I potted Werferth."

"And . . ?"

"He fell over."

"So you were right. I apologize. . . . You know, I

was coming back to do that last night, when I saw Sigewulf leading you away."

"Thanks for the thought." Nilssen was glad of the explanation and their reconciliation. Yaer's smouldering resentment would have been one handicap too many. "Unfortunately, he got up again almost at once. You'd better have those apologies back: I bungled it."

"Ah, well," said Yaer drowsily, as though his plans could accommodate this minor upset. "He's an old man. I expect the drug was in him long enough. . . . The test might still be useful. . . ." His eyelids fluttered as he struggled to stay awake. "What else?"

"I'll tell you later."

"Now, please," he slurred. "I want to be thinking what to do."

So Nilssen repeated the rumor he had overheard and summarized his own inferences: that the CNI had taken advantage of Werferth's accident; that inadvertently it had helped them.

Yaer nodded, winced. "Strategically, it's advisable to suppose . . . though it doesn't have to be our man. Could be a local opportunist. But play safe, yes?"

"Right," said Nilssen. "Get some sleep. I'll talk to Sigewulf."

He left the hut. It was Sigewulf who intercepted him, near the parade ground. "Saracen!" he whispered urgently from the gap between two huts.

Nilssen slipped aside from the path. "I was looking for you—"

"Well-met, then," said Sigewulf in a secretive but hopelessly loud voice. "Bishop Werferth cries your name like a man with the madness. He asks folk to bring you to him. He weeps and prays. I think you should not go."

"He really wants me?" said Nilssen, struck by a pleasant thought. "Would you say he's had a vision, perhaps?"

"I do not know. He is . . . different." Sigewulf looked baffled. "I do not understand these priests."

"Who can ever understand them?" agreed Nilssen. "Take me to him, please. Our troubles may have eased themselves."

Muttering at the folly of needlessly entering the lion's den, Sigewulf complied.

The bishop's rooms at the rear of the royal chapel were packed with the curious and the concerned through whose ranks the giant bulled a path with scant regard for the dignity of those he displaced. Nilssen expected trouble; but when they saw him they fell back of their own accord, respectfully he thought, though he observed traces of fear also.

Bishop Werferth lay swaddled in furs on his bed; a real bed with a wooden frame and a mattress stuffed with horsehair. He was fenced in by anxious acolytes and well-wishers whose candles and incense burners raised such a fug Nilssen was at a loss for breath. Catching sight of him, the priest let out a sob. Scrambling to his knees atop the bed, he seized Nilssen's hands and lowered his bald head to touch them.

"My brother," he wheezed in a voice broken with anguish, "in persecuting you I have sinned most grievously. And God has punished me as He did the sinner Saul. Grant me your absolution, unworthy though I am to receive it, that His wrath may not visit me twice."

Startled by this greeting, Nilssen could barely raise a stammer. "Why, of course," he said, trying to disentangle his hands from the old man's clutching fingers. "It was a misunderstanding. Forget it—"

"*Never!*" cried Werferth, weeping afresh. "As much as I have sinned, so much also must I atone. Brother, command my penance. Say what it will be; these present shall witness that it be performed in full."

A score of serious countenances took in Nilssen's indecision.

Out in the unconfined air the priest's change of heart had amounted to a delightful joke, a piece of serendipity too sweet to be the prelude to his current predicament. The onlookers lived their religion and would expect him to exact penance or forfeit his credibility. And its degree had to be calculated to a nicety, in accordance with their scale of values.

Pulling a hand free, he laid it flat on the bishop's head. "It's not right," he told all present, "that I, a man, should interpret the will of God. Nor that I, as great a sinner as any here, should be this man's judge." The audience's censors, which had been allowed to fall still, swung on their tasseled cords again. The witnesses approved; the air smelled fresher in his imagination. "Rarely is it given to us to see our lives for what they are. So often we live out a delusion. Bishop Werferth, many would not have admitted their fault as you have. In confessing your sin without pride you have done penance enough."

Besides, he told himself ruefully, *we can't afford to rearrange history.*

Tears beaded the old man's eyes as he raised his head and kissed Nilssen's hands. Hardly able to speak for emotion, he choked out, "Henceforth you are my son, if you will have me for your father."

"By all means," said Nilssen, blushing hotly, unable to escape the penetrating stares of the onlookers. "Let's leave it at that, shall we?"

The old man was helped under the bedcovers. Once the furs were drawn up around his chest, he seemed more composed. "Saracen," he said, "in all truth, I cannot approve your faith. But I think it not devoid of virtue."

Nilssen felt ashamed. He had never planned to involve himself in ninth century religions beyond learning how to use them to his advantage. After all, the locals were born into their culture whereas he was only a tourist. Nevertheless, lately he had grown sympathetic to that which he once would have regarded as foreign to his nature. The old priest's sincerity seared his conscience painfully. "God send you swift health," he said as he departed from the crowded room.

Aimlessly he wandered through the camp, arriving eventually at the north gate. This was guarded by the usual complement of eight common soldiers. That morning their wariness was well-nigh tangible, to the extent that one soldier crossed himself and caused three others to follow suit.

Nilssen veered off along the eastern limb of the ramparts, avoiding the group. From his vantage point he had a good view of the thawing marshes. At intervals he encountered more sentries, all of whom demonstrated some aversion to him, behavior which he ascribed to that morning's excitement at Mass. One man went so far as to step down from the upper level until he was well past.

Nearing the farther end where the north and east walls met at a small roofed platform like that surmounting the watchtower, he found one who did not move away. This was Eorhic, and he seemed to have been waiting for him.

He gave Nilssen a slow, grave nod. "Will you talk awhile?"

"I will." Nilssen joined him at the parapet. "What brings you out on such an afternoon?"

"The same as you, I fancy."

"Which might be . . . ?"

"The chance of a respite from folly."

Nilssen smiled. "Then you know yourself better than I do."

"I find it pays. . . . My congratulations, by the way."

Frowning, Nilssen glanced at him sidelong. "For what?"

"On humoring the saintly fool. Nobody thought you could carry it off."

"So I've been discussed?"

"Take my word on it, friend. The king was hearing counsel from his Witan on whether to test you for witchcraft. Your presence in the tower was noted, you see." He gave a short pitiless laugh. "Poor Coelric."

"I hope no one has harmed him."

"Not yet; and not likely to, if he watches his feet. He's been rewarded with a place in tonight's patrol towards Glastonbury. What with the thaw and this fresh snow, there'll be some deceptive rotten ice on the bogs now."

Somewhat relieved, Nilssen surveyed the marshes, checkered green-brown and gray. Doubtlessly Coelric was acquainted with the character of the land.

Eorhic leaned back against the parapet, folding his arms across his chest. "When I alluded to folly a moment ago," he said in a businesslike tone, "you appeared to agree."

"That depends on the folly you had in mind," said Nilssen.

Raising an eyebrow, Eorhic pouted at him. "Surely my meaning isn't so opaque? Dear God, man, I'm talking about that ass in priest's clothing, Werferth, whom you so neatly put in his place today."

Alarm stilled Nilssen's tongue. Recognizing the effects of his machine training, he accepted the warning it provided. When his mind was clear, he said, "I am poorly versed in your customs. It would have been stupid of me to exact some real penance."

"Hah," said Eorhic. "I'm sure we understand each other."

"Be sure that we do not," said Nilssen firmly. "If your meaning is of such great consequence, you must enlighten me more thoroughly."

Eorhic scratched at his right earlobe. "Perhaps it's nothing after all. . . . You know, I was truly surprised that Sarnvig and I were able to locate your ship. That story of yours was so wild and fanciful it quite put to shame the regular fare our bard serves up."

"Then I suggest you recruit a new bard," said Nilssen as calmly as he could in the aftermath of the question about the penance. Of all those he had met Eorhic best fitted the preconceptions he had concerning Middlesex, save one: he seemed too bold for a man on the run.

The corners of Eorhic's mouth had turned down. He shook his head. "The king likes him too much. A family retainer for twenty years, he served Ethelred when he was alive; and Ethelbert before him and Ethelbald first of all. Now, were the decision mine . . . However, that's another battle altogether. What I want to know is: now that you've been here a couple of weeks and seen what we're like, have your plans changed at all?"

He's fishing. In Nilssen's gut was a tightness that would not ease, try as he might to calm himself. *This could well be him: Middlesex, head of the CNI. I can't keep fooling him. Cut it short.*

"Our plans?" asked Nilssen hesitantly. "Such as they were, they still depend on the king."

"Indeed?"

"On his success in battle, I ought to have said."

"Oh, quite." Eorhic's remark hung unexplained while Nilssen imagined he heard the man's brain whirring through plot and counterplot toward some fatal question that would pin him helplessly. "That will be a brave battle, don't you think?"

Nilssen decided to take the initiative.

"If the two sides fight as hard as folk promise, there can be no doubt of that. . . . What outcome do you foresee?"

A smile flickered on Eorhic's lips. "Why, victory," he said; and he watched Nilssen. "One side must win. But I fancy it will be we who hold the place of slaughter by sunset."

"You are very confident."

"No." Genuine doubt seemed to dim Eorhic's pleasure. "Only Mother Church knows which stars are fixed and which will fall, and even her priests are not privy to the full secret. We ordinary men must muddle along, making do with good judgment. And I choose to guess at victory for Wessex."

"But you advise the king."

"I attend the Witenagemot, yes; I am not *of* the Witan, though. Is that relevant?"

"If you have the king's ear, he might be swayed by what you say."

Slow to answer, Eorhic did so with evident irritation. "If it causes you concern, yes, I talk to Alfred. As do a number of his companions. But he keeps more advisors than those in the Witan . . . some of them up here." And he tapped his own head. "Whatever is wrought in the king's name is done by his wish."

"And the whole of Wessex is in his hand?"

"Or those hands he trusts."

Nilssen studied the crudely trimmed stakes forming the parapet. "Men are the same the world over," he said. "Caliphs have their emirs, who have their wazirs, and so down to the commonest of goatherds' helpers. A long chain of trust. If every link is perfect, it will hold; but should there be rust to eat at any one of them . . ."

"What do you imply?" asked Eorhic, stepping close. "Face me, Saracen, and tell me what it is you want to say."

Nilssen stared at him in return; but the man's rank breath forced him to avert his face quickly, saying with revulsion, "I implied nothing, save that the king is lucky to be so well served. Many a crowned head has fallen prey to a follower's incompetence."

"Or worse," said Eorhic. "You are right." He drew

back far enough to let Nilssen breathe freely, though he seemed to remain on edge. "We were all lucky."

"We . . ?"

"We share the good fortune his leadership has brought us. Without his forethought none of this would have existed." With a sweep of one hand Eorhic pointed to the camp below them. "Only the foul marsh would protect us from the enemy. And the fyrd would not now be gathering all across Wessex, readying for the day of balancing."

Doubts like cawing rooks flapped through Nilssen's thoughts, disrupting with their clamor of irrelevant speculations what he had planned to say. Did no one wish to admit authorship of these military preparations? Alfred attributed them to "advisors"; Eorhic credited Alfred; Sigewulf and Sarnvig were lost in loyalty to their great king; Coelric observed no more than any soldier serving his time cared to see; Werferth cared for God's works and nothing less. And as for the remainder of the camp, they were a complete mystery. Yaer had been certain that Eorhic was Middlesex, as had he for a few real and frightening moments; but Yaer had not talked privately with the man.

"Nothing to say?" asked Eorhic.

Nilssen shook his head. "Except that I wish the old priest had not selected me for his confessor."

"Have no fear, no one who matters imagines you were involved."

"Those soldiers on the wall do." Nilssen indicated the remote end of the north wall where the guards had clustered as if reluctant to come near.

"Peasants," sneered Eorhic. "Give them a spear to carry and what are they? Spear-carriers. They don't matter, man. All they are is the dirt beneath the feet of real people."

Reproachfully Nilssen asked, "What then am I,

the youngest son of a minor officer of cavalry? Or you, Eorhic of Æsces-dun?"

For an instant the man's eyes glazed and his mouth clamped shut. Then, licking his lips slowly, he answered, "You and I are what we have made of ourselves. *They* will never amount to anything. Now I must go; the king wants a report of our talk."

"The king?" echoed Nilssen as Eorhic bounded from the upper level towards the hutments below. His pace did not slacken; he seemed not to have heard.

If, Nilssen reasoned, *he is not Middlesex, I may be safe and all that we discussed will not be discounted. Or if he is Middlesex and if he has not penetrated my disguise, I may also be safe; or if he has discovered my identity and has his own plans, likewise. And even if he knows who I am, he may still be unable to hurt us; for the king appears to want us safe for reasons of his own . . .*

If . . .

CHAPTER THIRTEEN

Nothing untoward happened. The king continued to welcome Nilssen to his hall; and when Yaer was well, he too sat at meat and drink like any of the royal companions. From time to time Nilssen fancied he detected in one person or another some hint of their adversary, so that suspicions waxed and waned with the moon throughout the month of April. Meanwhile the weather warmed to the brightening sun, and the marshes bloomed with spring grasses and clumps of flowers amongst the islets. Save when squalls of rain blotted the heavens, the sky remained a blue-and-white dome spanning the marshlands, innocent of smoke and other war sign. Everyone seemed well content to stay in the camp throughout the summer, apart from those who fell foul of the flies which now swarmed about the fetid alleys and refuse dumps.

Friendships were reinforced. Sigewulf became the inspiration of numerous outdoor amusements, taking the City men on far ranging rides through the sprouting willow brakes or on furtive mallard hunts amongst the sedges. On occasion the nobler Sarnvig would show them how deer were caught, journeying east into the western fringes of the Selwood that lay between the Somerset levels and the chalky uplands of Salisbury Plain. On forays into remoter parts, particularly those to dry lands, the guides would issue warnings about the Danes, for the northmen were expert in fieldcraft and capable of cunning ambushes. However, all Nilssen and Yaer suffered were sore muscles and backsides from jogging on horseback and bramble scratches and stings from the burgeoning nettles in the undergrowth through which they learned to creep in pursuit of game. The invaders might as well not have existed.

Quite by accident Nilssen discovered that Sigewulf was eager to overcome the silence Morwena's muteness had forced on her and looked to him for the means. Eager in principle, that was, until he realized that a large proportion of the language-signs Nilssen used were based on a skill he lacked and probably would never master. Sigewulf could not read, neither could he fingerspell.

Morwena, it transpired, had been partially educated while a captive of the Welsh king whom Sigewulf had killed. Her future role in the palace was to have been personal secretary to the queen, a lady educated by nuns but with too high an opinion of her own status to deign to dirty her hands with ink. Accordingly Morwena was aware of the significance of the letters of the alphabet, although her schooling had been interrupted before she could learn more than a few of them.

This suited Nilssen's purposes admirably. He had only to teach her the modified system of finger spelling evolved within the City to augment the rapidly expanding vocabulary of whole signs which she was committing to memory. She proved a brilliant pupil. Before long she had attained a fluency that allowed her to hold her own in conversation as one person to another.

That other person, however, continued to be Nilssen. Sigewulf was a painfully slow learner and a moody one. Largely he observed Nilssen's monopoly of Morwena without overt disapproval; but sometimes he would intrude on one of their conversations bluntly, dispensing with even those few signs he had learned and speaking aloud to Morwena as he had formerly, waving aside her signed replies or ignoring them completely.

At such times Sigewulf behaved as if prey to incompatible desires, simultaneously determined that Morwena should benefit from all that Nilssen could teach her, yet anxious lest she outgrow his own company. He was clinging to a treasured past. Subsequently, once his displays of pique were done with, he would put on a clumsy show of repentance and redouble his pathetic efforts to learn.

Oddly none of his unhappiness was turned against Nilssen, who had been scrupulously open in his dealings with Morwena, being mindful of Yaer's admonition regarding Sigewulf's mental condition. The giant never revealed any awareness that Nilssen alone could talk the new language of signs or that his elimination would restore the old relationship. Those thoughts, if they existed, he kept to himself. Morwena did not exploit his lenience; but often she and Nilssen would go about the camp in broad daylight conversing silently, a feat no Saxon would have dared for fear of arousing Sigewulf's jealousy.

Often Nilssen wondered what the giant really thought, what maelstrom of bitterness might be churning behind the naïve façade of his broken English and indelicate manners, what action he would take come the day when the Saracens left Wessex and Morwena made her choice between them. Sigewulf must have anticipated that day. Nilssen was of the impression that his course of action had already been decided; and that it was to be neither gross nor trivial.

CHAPTER FOURTEEN

Leather creaked. Clothing flapped. A continuous, gelatinous, sucking splattering arose as a hundred pairs
of heavy feet trod dewy marsh grass into mud. Interlaced with these sounds were the jingle of ring-mail
corselets and riding harness and the sporadic muttering of burdened soldiery hastening through the pre-
dawn twilight. The air was moist and dankly cold—
so cold as to render bare metal well-nigh untouchable
—and smelled tainted with vegetable decay. Many
memories were evoked for Nilssen as he rode along:
route marches with the Air Force; hikes with friends;
the feeling of being lost on a minor jungle-choked
island in the Far East.

And the date of the day itself was cause for reminiscence, for it was a special Monday—the fifth of May,
his own birthday.

He paid no special heed to this once he had realized
how meaningless it was in that context. Better to live
from day to day. That it was a Monday was due to
the devout king's insistence on celebrating the Sunday
mass at Athelney with his companions and bodyguard
before following in the tracks of the two hundred soldiers who had preceded them.

The delay had meant they must hasten to their
appointed rendezvous with the fyrd. The place fixed,
a victory memorial known far and wide as Egbert's
Stone, lay more than thirty miles east of Athelney, on
the Keysley Down overlooking the Blackmoor Vale. It

would be a march of one-and-a-half days over rising hilly ground, made worse by the cumbersome combination of cavalry and infantry, and by the earlier movements of troops along that route. Haste would improve their chances of evading the Danish patrols who had undoubtedly been alerted by the growing troop concentrations and would be expecting an imminent foray by the king.

The Thursday gone, the two hundred had marched quietly out before dawn, leaving the rest to simulate full occupancy of the camp. Extra cooking fires had been lit and May Day honored with the strewing of flower petals at the four gates; and in the evening there had been rowdy celebration by the troops, though Alfred's abstinence from more than a minimum of intoxicating drink had been copied. Likewise Friday, Saturday, and the Sunday itself had resounded with feigned activity in a largely resting encampment. By the Monday everyone professed relief at the prospect of some real action.

An officer galloped by, spattering soldiers with mud flung from his horse's flying hooves. High on his own mount close behind the king's party, Nilssen escaped the worst of it, as did Yaer on his left. But someone on foot cursed the officer for his lack of consideration. Overhearing the abuse, the officer reined in his mount to favor the column with a furious scowl, then wheeled about and advanced to join the king. Rapid reports were delivered, after which the rider returned, showering the men with more mud.

Yaer remarked in Arabic, "Interesting. With the institution of a clearly defined officer class Alfred has also given his army the us-versus-them syndrome."

"No," said Nilssen. "Some arrogant bastards are born, not made."

Yaer laughed softly, as though at a secret joke. They rode on towards the east where blue-gray clouds were backed by a pink sky.

Over an hour earlier, while it was still night, the army had picked its way across the River Parrett on a frail pontoon bridge, aided by torches; now it wound across the marshes between that river and the Cary to the north, seeking higher ground. At Aller, whose royal vill lay empty and cold on its wooded hillside, they had been joined by a score of foot soldiers led by a minor thane who had come south with the news that the majority of Guthrum's Danes still lodged at Chippenham, though the countryside generally was beginning to fill with their patrols. The sudden movements of Saxon troops evidently had alarmed them to the extent that they had dispatched reinforcements southwards to Bratton Castle, their outpost on the northernmost lip of Warden Down where Salisbury Plain plunged hundreds of feet into the Avon valley.

Alfred had smiled on hearing this and had rubbed his hands. Both from his knowledge of history as it had once happened and from their premarch briefing, Nilssen deduced that the Danes were falling in with Saxon tactics. The battle would be on ground of Alfred's choosing, not Guthrum's: high on the flat, dry turf of the downs where the improved Saxon army might exert itself fully against the traditional methods of the vikings. Alfred might well grin as he blew on his hands to warm them. His army no longer belonged to the ninth century. It had borrowed from all ages, anticipating Cromwell's New Modern Army by some eight hundred years. Every man was plainly but soundly equipped; the emphasis had shifted to functional efficiency and group effort. The common foot soldier carried a round wooden shield almost three feet in diameter with a stout central boss and a rim of bronze; also a broadsword fashioned with blade-breaker slots, a conical helmet with slatted neck and ear guards after the Chinese pattern, a toughened corselet, and a spear. Furthermore, in his pack he kept a field-green woolen cloak, a full waterskin, some dried bread and meat, linen strips for bandages, a short-handled spade, and two wooden stakes which, Roman-style, could be incorporated into his one yard of overnight or battlefield fortifications. Some men were armed with crossbows instead of spears; and about fifty had longbows. And whereas the Saxons had formerly employed horses solely for transport to the fight, dismounting on arrival, a cavalry now existed as a force in its own right. Even here there were innovations: Nilssen had seen mounted officers hurling weighted nets at volunteers on the Athelney parade ground, following through with blunted spears on captive lines; the complaints of the test subjects about their bruises proved the practice had been no idle game. Warfare had altered its character, Nilssen told himself; whoever was behind the changes had surely inscribed his mark too deeply for it to be erased.

The disruption of history had been aggravated by associated social reorganization. The old system of loyalty to a personal overlord had been supplanted by one of obedience to any superior officer. The king still commanded all, and amongst the officers the pecking order was established by traditional methods; but gone were the clusters of housecarls trailing after individual nobles; and gone was the anarchic temporary banding together of a peasant levy. The new army would survive the present war in the same way the Danish Here would, whether smashed or not, for it existed as a state of mind, not as a network of allegiance dependent on the men at its nodes. In comparison with what Nilssen had expected to find it was disquietingly efficient.

The sun rose. To the south the Parrett was succeeded by the River Yeo. Scouts came and went; but the flies came and stayed. The mounts which the City men had been given, placid beasts resembling Welsh mountain ponies, were much troubled by horseflies and not infrequently leaped and quivered when bit-

ten. The foot soldiers were constantly batting at invisible tormentors. With the flies came the miasma of
the marshes: as the water warmed, so did the mud,
releasing methane gas in bloated bubbles that popped
and puffed out their stench above the drifting waters.
Now and then by way of relief a breeze would spring
up, bustling through the bright green heads of rushes
along the margins, setting myriads of tiny flowers nodding and winking, blue, white, yellow. Redstarts and
reed warblers hunted insects about the pools; some
late golden plovers were surprised by an outrider
around midmorning, exploding into flight and scattering themselves amongst the waste of grass and
knobbly trees. And overhead, like an aerial escort, the
occasional gull would wheel watchfully, then dip a
wing and cruise away across the marshes.

Towards noon Sigewulf rode back to report in a
loud voice that they ought to bunch up. Larger trees
in greater numbers, he explained to the king. The
order was given: the column shortened, two lines becoming four in a gradual compression of the ranks
that was complete before the last of the boggy ground
lay behind them. By early afternoon they were approaching the Selwood proper.

Skirting the wooded knoll of Cadbury Castle on its
north side, the army followed a tributary of the Yeo
up its valley to a ridge deep in trees. Instead of a halt
for a midday meal a cook-camp had been established
temporarily, from which rations were doled out as
the column passed. Water was available from a spotty-
faced youth who drove a pair of pack mules along the
line. Relief was gained by stepping aside, then hurrying to catch up. Rest stops were few and none lasted
longer than five minutes.

Routes had been scouted in advance and marked
with tree-blazes. Now woodsmen fanned out into the
dense cover on both flanks while the army proceeded
with drawn sword and raised shield. For mile upon

mile they traversed glade and thicket in a cool twilight without a single alarm from the outriders, stepping briskly along beneath trees that had been old
when their forefathers invaded Britain, scattering deer
and wild boar alike in their bold progress. Confidence
expressed itself in upright backs and earnest, eager
faces that almost pleaded for a brush with the enemy.

But there were no encounters that day; and when
they made camp beside a stream, the Cale-by-Pensel-
wood, the king walked amongst them, praising their
stamina, flattering their egos, and promising that soon
their blades would draw enemy blood.

Nilssen and Yaer compared notes. History might
still be said to be on course. Nearby lay the Penselwood, an offshoot of the Selwood, so if they headed
east next day for the rendezvous at Egbert's Stone, the
day after could well see them encamped at Iley Oak
which was supposed to have been near Warminster,
close to the foot of the Summer Down.

After a restless night beneath furs that were barely
enough to ward off the cold they were roused by
Sarnvig, who whipped away their coverings in darkness and left them to deduce that it was time to re-
mount for another day's march. Rank-and-file soldiers
were grumbling volubly about the discomforts and the
cold breakfast, all thoughts of heroism having been
frozen out of them overnight. Eventually, once more
chivied into being an army, they took to the road,
shaking aches from sleep-sodden limbs as the dawn
filtered down into avenues of green trees, speckling
the turf, spearing the brown shadows with gold. Gradually the night withdrew into the undergrowth and the
day grew sultry. The birds ceased their morning racket, until only the call of a cuckoo haunting the
gnarled colonnades or the alarmed chatter of a blackbird showed they were still there, all around the army
that squeaked, clashed, muttered, and stamped
through the dewy stillness.

Frequently Nilssen was amazed by their guides' skill. The lean weathered men who advised the king and his officers seemed to interpret every twig as a unique signpost. They knew, almost to the minute, how soon a landmark would be reached, where there would be water for the horses, the condition of the ground, the best detours. If, as happened twice, someone became lost, he was quickly found and brought back into line, mocked gently by his rescuer's assurance in that wilderness.

Around early morning the word was sent down the line to halt and keep silent. By now they had left the Selwood, indeed had almost crossed the Penselwood, and indications of downland were plentiful. The shorter trees were more widely dispersed and woodland species were giving way to hardier sorts, particularly yellow-blossomed thornbushes; and exposed soil was often pale with chalk.

A guide trotted up on silent feet to speak with the king. "Danes," he announced, his voice low, the sort of voice that does not carry far. "Two miles ahead, perhaps less."

Alfred looked over his shoulder at the column of soldiers, who were paying close attention. Without noticeable alarm he asked the guide, "How many?"

"A score-and-three."

"A patrol, do you suppose?"

"No more than that." Smirking, the woodsman drew his knife from its leather sheath at his hip and displayed its bloodstained blade. "I caught one to demand his business. Alas, he spoke no English."

"Did the others see you?"

His smile drew cunning, but he sounded offended. "Nay, my lord. And I hid the body well." Then he laughed softly, almost tenderly. "They will fear that a wild beast took him."

"Good," said Alfred, adding regretfully, "I do not think we could catch all. Were one to escape, our stealth would be wasted. We ought not to hold this course lest they come upon us, or we on them."

"There is another way," said the guide. "More roads than the Long Lane lead to Egbert's Stone." He pointed southeast, down into the crowded trees of the Blackmoor Vale. "Yonder lies Shaftesburg and the road out of Portland. The fyrd of Dorcan-ceaster will have come by that way. We must seek the valley road, turning north with it. Though it is longer and leads to climbing, we will be free of these Danes."

"The extra exercise won't hurt the men," said Alfred, "albeit I expect they'd rather stay to argue rights of way."

The king's mounted companions laughed at this pleasantry; the foot soldiers simply set their faces and plodded after the officers.

The descent into the valley and the wearying ascent of the chalk ridge at its northern end added a full hour to their journey; but well before noon they found themselves again on the uplands amongst tussocky grass, flowering gorse, and ash trees. A peewit was wheeping from somewhere out of sight. Ahead the blue sky was banded by the rising smoke of campfires. Men could be heard shouting as a horn summoned them to arms. Abruptly over the crest of the hill rode Sarnvig, his face flushed with excitement.

"My lord!" he cried. "They are all here: all of them —and more! Besides your own ten score there are six score Somerseatas from Old Sarum with nine score south-men out of Dorcan-ceaster. And your own city of Wintan-ceaster sent no fewer than fifteen score, gathered from all across the southeast. Even the battered East Angles have sent a few!"

Visibly moved, blinking away tears of joy, Alfred urged his horse to a canter. Alone he went to the crest of the hill, halting in dark silhouette against the brilliant sky as a roar of cheering broke from the as-yet hidden host. Again and again they applauded their king, drowning the skylarks with their clamor of yells and horn-blowing.

The king's party caught him up, and at last Nilssen saw the army. Hundreds of men were arrayed in irregular ranks on either side of Alfred as he walked his horse between them, waving his sword whose every flourish elicited cheers. His face was that of a crusader exulting in certain victory.

"Look at them," said Yaer, speaking for the first time in hours. "Most are peasants fresh from the fields." That much was true: too many bore mere sickles or firewood axes; a few brandished weapons that must have been heirlooms for generations; fewer still wore oddments of armor. Although he took no pleasure from the knowledge, Nilssen felt less anxious, seeing that the odds against the Danes were more favorable than he had supposed. It restored some order to the situation. Yaer, meanwhile, went further: "The poor sods, the vikings will butcher them."

It had been so since the apemen, Nilssen wanted to reply. The farmer was the brigand's ancient victim; only determined self-sacrifice by the valiant would turn back the predatory sword. But he felt no better for thinking it and was sure it would help Yaer not one whit more.

Thus the three hundred expert soldiers of Alfred's own band had been augmented by another six hundred assorted troops, of whom perhaps three-quarters could be described as fighters of any worth. The rest were semiskilled battle fodder whose principal value lay in the support they could provide: making and tending fires, feeding horses, generally filling the menial void. As darkness fell these farmers huddled together around their fires, scorned by the experienced warriors who sought out their own kind and boasted of how gloriously they intended to outshine the heroes of the past, given half a chance. So the camp divided into two castes of soldier; and the nobles stood aloof from

both, in their turn. Guards were set. The evening meal
was eaten. In due course sleep claimed commoner and
lord alike.

Camp was struck as dawn broke. One by one the
fires were smothered with shovelfuls of earth after
coals had been safely lodged in fireboxes for the march
to the next camp; baggage carls gathered loose gear
and orders were bawled above the hee-hawing of don-
keys and the rattle of arms. Ranks formed, four-deep;
the king cantered by in hasty review, preceded by the
dragon banner of Wessex; a ragged leftface was executed; and they stepped off smartly to the measured
beat of a drum.

They had but seven miles to go that day. The king's
wish was that every man should be well rested prior to
battle, he said. The truth was, Nilssen suspected,
though scouts reported great activity by the Danes, the
king was not yet certain as to where the enemy would
make their battle line and preferred to give them a
while longer in which to commit themselves—and tire
themselves with digging.

The army proceeded slowly, reveling in the May
morning and the warmth of the sun. The fresh wind
that in foul weather scoured the exposed downs, de-
forming the thorn trees so that their branches appeared to stream before it, heartened them after the
humidity of the marshes. Crossing the Keysley Down,
a farmer armed with no more than an axe began to
intone the refrain of an ancestral song, a song of the
heathen past when, as everyone knew, all men were
heroes and there were dragons and ogres in the earth
and many famous deeds were done. . . .

A warrior on his way to battle came upon a linden
tree in which two watchful ravens roosted. Gladly he
greeted them, knowing they were sent by Odin the
One-Eyed, the Father of Battles, to be his guides. . . .

The words were taken up, the chant pulsing along
the ranks, the caesuras booming out in time with the

drum and the ground-shaking tramp of almost a thousand pairs of feet. Eyes were aflame with battle passion, teeth bared, hands tight about the hafts of spear and axe, swords slapping at leather-girt thighs, sunlight sparkling from polished armor . . .

Insatiable and far-ranging revenge was the theme, a wild delight in war as retribution. Harshly the warrior boasted of how his armaments were kept bright, as bright as his anger, which no wergild could assuage. . . .

Every few lines, as if at a signal, those bearing shields pounded them furiously with their fists: . . . boom . . . *BOOM* . . . boom . . . *BOOM* . . . The shocks rang out across the downs like a challenge to skulking Danish spies.

Bishop Werferth was most displeased. "Disgusting," he repeated as he jogged along on his skinny horse. "These are no sentiments for Christians. What if they should die unshriven? Their souls, laden with godlessness, would sink into the Pit of Tartarus as surely as—"

"Werferth," Alfred said suddenly, shifting in his saddle to look at him, "some have waited since childhood for this revenge. Can you not find it in you to forgive them this one rebuke to the heathens?" Werferth displayed puzzlement, so Alfred explained patiently: "They are laughing at the Danes."

Before the priest could reply, Eorhic insinuated himself. "Nevertheless, my king, His Holiness may have a point. Did I not once tell you of the great tribal chieftain, Czar Nicholas, whose carelessness nearly cost him his head at the hands of the subverters of his people? Your men strike me as being too confident; better if they were scared of defeat—in moderation."

Nilssen felt his lingering doubts depart. This was their enemy. When Alfred submitted with a grave nod and thoughtful frown, there was no responsive show

of gratification from Eorhic, who simply waited for
the king to order a more suitable Christian song replace the pagan one. Then he said:

"Lord Alfred, never be tempted into contempt for
an enemy." King and bishop listened obediently, demonstrating beyond question how the man had wedged
himself into the political hierarchy of Wessex. No
overt bid for power, merely good advice, had won
him his seat at Alfred's board.

In the Old World the CNI had used information
as a telling weapon in the war of international espio-
nage. There it had formed a whole department of the
government. Reduced to one man as it was, its methods would not have changed. Eleven centuries of hind-
sight was a weighty advantage. A man trained during
the twenty-first century had much wisdom with which
to overawe one of the ninth.

Nilssen eyed the back of Eorhic's head as they rode
across the downs. *So we've found Middlesex, Lord of
the CNI. This is the man I must take back or destroy.
. . . But has he found us? And who will eliminate
whom first?*

Shortly afterward they descended into the Wylye
Valley whose river cut through the uplands from the
east and bent sharply south again at the site of the
future town of Warminster. They found the ruins of a
farmstead sacked by pirates months back before the
winter. Already the fields surrounding it were furry
with green shoots of barley and bere as though the
farmer still worked them. Men in the ranks frowned
and some shook their heads, cursing the invaders in
voices gritty with hatred.

Though it was yet morning, camp was made on the
slope overlooking the inner bank of the river, for the
day was too far spent to seek battle and they would
have been inviting trouble were they to cross the
water and spend the hours of darkness on the enemy's

doorstep. The afternoon would not be wasted: plenty of drill practice could be put into effect, and the army's traveling smiths could beat a few more of the peasants' plowshares into swords.

The campsite had been selected to reutilize some prehistoric earthworks which, though badly eroded, still provided the makings of an admirable enclosure. Northeast of these diggings, almost directly across the valley, were the similarly ancient hilltop fortifications of Battlesbury and Scratchbury, twin tributes to forgotten wars.

Westward of the camp lay an oak grove, one of the many fingers of the Selwood that groped at the periphery of Salisbury Plain. While the Saxons were preoccupied, Nilssen asked Yaer to come over to the trees away from the crowds. Unhurried they strolled out of the camp, Nilssen leaning frequently on his staff to make their movements appear less furtive. However, once they were beneath the canopy of the branches, he quickened his pace.

Though late, the spring had flourished since the thaw. The oaks were bushy with leaves, so that daylight was soon reduced to a green gloom. Fifty yards into the wood Nilssen found himself a seat on a mossy root and said, "Middlesex is Eorhic."

Yaer squatted nearby and shredded dead leaves. He greeted this revelation offhandedly. "Of course he is. I said as much weeks ago."

"That was a guess and we both know it."

"Proof *has* been hard to come by," Yaer conceded.

Nilssen said, "I think we should take him out now before the battle. We might yet wreck the CNI's plans."

"With the staff?"

"Yes."

"No." Yaer slapped his hands to his thighs, dusting leaf fragments onto his baggy blue trousers and pushing himself to his feet in the same movement. "Absolutely not. One mysterious attack of unconsciousness can be blamed on divine intervention. Two would call for a human agency. And you and I top everyone's eligibility list. So unless Eorhic sets himself up as a target in ideal circumstances, don't risk a charge of witchcraft. It could be made to stick."

Desperately Nilssen asked, "And what if it all goes wrong for our side simply because we didn't dare take a chance?"

"The Danes will kill us, I expect." Bending down, Yaer picked up a rotten stick which he began breaking into fragments as he had the leaves. Rolling a piece between his fingers, he tossed it into the undergrowth, where it brought debris pattering onto the dead leaf cover.

"And the City? If history goes wrong too, the transfer our people made from the twenty-first to the twenty-seventh century would be prevented."

"Perhaps." Yaer took a deep impatient breath. "Why fret about it now?"

During the two-day journey from Athelney they had exchanged few words. Yaer's accident with Sigewulf had restructured their relationship: Yaer gave every sign of being less sure of himself, as if he were now nervously aware that intellect alone was insufficient defense against the physical hazards of the ninth century world; Nilssen, by contrast, embraced the strangeness of the past, though apprehensive of its influence over the future. He perceived that Yaer was unconsciously begging for reassurance, for Yaer had never been one to indulge in finger-twiddling surrogates like leaves and broken sticks.

"We have to worry about it," Nilssen said. "Now as never before. Whatever Eorhic has planned for Wessex will take effect in the next few days. So far he has me baffled completely. Why should he help Alfred? That only strengthens law and order in Britain; chaos would fit his style better—" Dead leaves rustled.

"What a depressing opinion you have of me," said Eorhic, emerging from the trees to stand not five yards away. He nodded back along his path. "Excuse me, I've been eavesdropping. Not polite, true, but most informative . . . You seem surprised." A false smile complemented his tone of triumph. "Before coming to these times I acquired as many languages as I could. Old Arabic was practically compulsory."

"You've saved us a lot of subterfuge," Nilssen replied with a calmness that belied his mental turmoil.

"Ah," said Eorhic, radiant with comprehension, "yes. I gather you were debating whether you should commit mayhem on me with that staff of yours. Well . . ." Running a forefinger over the stubble on his throat, he sighed. "You might as well be warned: Sigewulf has been delegated to guard you both discreetly until the battle. He showed me where you were." His smile renewed itself, becoming malevolent. "So the three of us are on our best behavior. You understand me?"

Disappointed, Nilssen gave a nod. Sigewulf would come running at the first hint of a fight. Eorhic looked to Yaer.

"And you, Khaled?" he asked.

"Are you Middlesex?" replied Yaer bluntly.

Eorhic seemed taken aback. At last his smile faded. "Once," he said. "Yes, once I was."

"And here you are again, repeating history?"

"No!" Eorhic took a step forwards, saying angrily, "I'm correcting it. The others caused the Collapse. I was totally innocent!"

"That's an easy claim, now." Yaer discarded the stump of the stick with which he had been fiddling. His empty hands fell to his sides, to hang still. "I don't always concur with the law's decrees on titular culpability, my Lord Lieutenant"—Eorhic winced, faintly yet noticeably—"but the case against you is remarkable for its mountain of supportive evidence. You author-

280 ANDREW M. STEPHENSON

ized Operation Damocles; you pushed it ahead; yours is the responsibility."

"Obviously there's no changing your mind," said Eorhic. "So brand me as you wish. Remember, though: here, in Wessex, in the ninth century, I have power. I am respected. The king listens to me. So too do most of his eorls. Neither of you can block me because no one would recognize the crime you've accused me of—it doesn't exist."

"They'd recognize it," countered Nilssen. "Except that here they call it treason."

Even in that shadowy place Eorhic colored perceptibly. "It would be so simple," he said, "to arrange your death."

"Very melodramatic," sneered Yaer, though Nilssen had gone cold momentarily, aware that Eorhic had made no empty threat. "You've picked up the local ways quickly. What a shame you never studied their system of justice. Cause must be shown before any execution is permitted."

"There are ways around laws."

"For those who don't care to abide by them."

Eorhic seemed to bite his own tongue. His right hand reached across his waist to fondle the hilt of his sword.

"Don't forget Sigewulf," Yaer chided, and reluctantly Eorhic released his weapon. "We ought to be practical about this, Middlesex. You and we are opponents. Enemies. Someday we shall try to kill each other, I expect. Temporarily we are forced to coexist to survive the Danish threat. Leave it at that."

But Eorhic had ceased to pay attention to Yaer. He asked in a strained whisper, "Did you hear something?"

"Don't play that game with us—" said Nilssen loudly. Eorhic turned on him, hissing, *"Shut up!"*

Yaer tilted his head to listen. He too whispered when he asked, "Sigewulf?"

"No. He was to whistle. It must be Danes."

They peered into the depths of the wood surrounding them.

"Back to the camp," Yaer suggested.

"You were fools to come here," said Eorhic as they stole along the path. "Their spies must be all over this area."

"You weren't forced to follow us," said Yaer softly.

A branch creaked. Not far away something solid plopped into a bed of leaves; there came a scurrying overhead.

"A squirrel," sighed Eorhic thankfully.

Then a man spat out a curse. There was a shrill porcine squeal, a thud, a resounding clang, and the sound of a heavy body crashing through undergrowth. Quick feet fled into the distance.

A different male voice was whimpering with pain. The one who had cursed was comforting him. Within a minute only the occasional groan was audible to the three listeners.

Eorhic's face was set in a frown as he nodded. His lips shaped a word: *Danes.*

Nilssen replied with a look of inquiry, holding up a hand and extending one, two, three, fingers. Eorhic shrugged.

Yaer pointed toward their camp. The other two nodded; a patrol could come after whoever had fallen foul of the wild boar, along with his companions. Crawling stealthily from bush to tree to thicket, they resumed their retreat, acutely conscious of the attentive silence that had pervaded the woods. The outbreak of sounds had been too brief and the woods too dense to permit an estimate of the Danes' position. Furthermore the enemy scouts, aware that they had been carelessly noisy, would now be applying all their guile to finding their human quarry before the alarm could be raised.

A triangle of sky came in sight. The clamminess of the inner woods was dispelled by the warm, sweet air of the unconfined downs. Cow-parsley crowned with full white floral heads stood thickly in the long grass a few paces away. Nilssen could hear a lark singing above the wind-rippled field beyond the trees.

With shocking suddenness two Danes leaped from cover to their right. Brown-clad with soot-blackened faces, their braided hair was tucked beneath dulled iron helmets. Their hands were heavy with swords. Their movements resembled the gait of hunting cats as with balanced paces they closed the gap between themselves and the three.

"Scatter!" Eorhic yelled, diving aside when the leading Dane hewed at him. Rolling, he came to his feet with his own sword in his hand and parried the second thrust smoothly.

Meanwhile Nilssen had bounded behind an oak, placing it between himself and the second Dane. Yaer scooped up a handful of twigs and flung them into the man's face before vaulting a bramble brake.

The Dane paused, sneezed, compared his chances with Nilssen and Yaer, and came after Nilssen.

They circled the oak, feinting to left and right. Moments later Eorhic's duel came to a bloody end. Lunging in response to a pretended opening in Eorhic's guard, the Dane trod awkwardly on a root hidden in the grass, stumbled for a second, and received the edge of Eorhic's sword across his belly. He doubled up, his hands struggling to hold back the blood spilling from the wound, and fell on his face into a bed of nettles. Seconds passed. Then he toppled off his knees onto his side, his hands releasing their convulsive hold on his stomach. All around him crumpled plants protruded from a pool of his blood. In front of him a purple-red, glistening, convoluted mass gradually spread itself, slowly pushing over a stick of cowparsley until it stood strangely askew.

The surviving Dane curled his lip at Nilssen, cursing him foully in accented English. Still speaking, he dived forward against the tree, catching his weight with his left hand and stabbing at Nilssen with the sword in his right. The point pierced the hem of Nilssen's djellaba. Jerking away, he barely escaped the powerful sideswipe with which the Dane followed through.

Then Eorhic ran over, breathing heavily from his first fight but shouting abuse, so that the Dane was obliged to push himself clear of the tree and fall back several paces. The two men stood in confrontation a moment too long:

"Leave him!" commanded a stentorian voice. Sigewulf loomed over them, seemingly materializing in their midst.

Eorhic stared longingly at the Dane, then yielded.

"He's yours," he said.

Sigewulf advanced on the pale-faced northman, whose eyes were wide and whose lips trembled at this change in his fortunes. The transformation of bravura into palsied terror was complete. Suddenly he bolted for the cover of the deep woods.

Lithely and virtually silently Sigewulf pursued and overtook him. The giant's sword flickered through an arc that intercepted the Dane's neck, and the helmeted head flew on by itself. Reboundng from a tree with a meaty thump, it tumbled down the swell of the trunk to jam itself upside down between two roots, surprise on its inverted face. Pulsing blood from its headless stump, the body fell prone. Soon the heart was stilled and the red flow ceased.

Sigewulf wiped his blade on the decapitated Dane's rump, retrieved the man's sword, and rejoined his friends.

"Bad men," he told Nilssen. "Many near here. Come to the camp now." Without another word he led them home.

When Nilssen thanked him, Sigewulf began fidgeting. "Saracen," he said, "I think you will repay me soon."

284 ANDREW M. STEPHENSON

"How can I pay you for my life?" asked Nilssen.

"The woman." Sigewulf knew her proper name but had never taken to it.

"Morwena?"

The man grunted agreement. "If I am killed, she must be cared for."

"Who says you'll die?" asked Nilssen. "A man of your prowess—"

"No. Wyrd takes all men, even the heroes. But I do not think you die soon. You have the far-wyrd."

"Whatever that may mean, I am only a man," said Nilssen.

"I feel death close," Sigewulf confided in a low voice. "If it touches me, you will guard the woman?"

"I will. She is very dear to me."

Sigewulf studied him for a disconcerting interval. "Good," he said finally. "But only if I die."

Nilssen nodded. They understood each other.

Abruptly Sigewulf walked away.

The clamor of the camp reasserted itself in Nilssen's awareness. Voices and the clash of smiths' hammers; horses galloping and the scrape of whetstones; these were the dominant sounds. As a background the wind stirred the downland grasses to a hissing, a rustling, the faintest of moans. And beyond these the curlews and the larks. By degrees his conscious appreciation absorbed them all, rejecting only the incomprehension of Sigewulf's readiness to undergo death so calmly.

The babble around him quietened. "Daydreaming, Ibrahim?" asked King Alfred from what seemed a great height. Refocusing his eyes, he saw the king on his horse and Eorhic beyond him, also mounted, his face expressionless.

"I was giving thanks for our deliverance," he said.

"So indeed you ought," replied the king. "We stand at the enemy's gate. Don't give yourself to him." Inspecting the clouds in the sky critically, he went on, "Tomorrow will be fine for battle. You and Khaled will hold yourselves in reserve, well back from the front line. Eorhic will guard you."

"My lord!" protested Eorhic, rather weakly, Nilssen considered.

Alfred raised a hand. "Eorhic, ever since you fought by my side at Æsces-dun, you have been my companion. This once I require of you a service that will seem demeaning yet is not. Often you have said that the legendary Alexander of Macedon won his empire by the planning of whole conquests, not single battles. Now I am doing exactly that. So be consoled, my friend, and if fools disparage your bravery or mock your prowess, bear their taunts for me. Can you do that?"

Most of the speech plainly had been aimed at the troops within earshot; but Eorhic's face sobered. Submissively he said, "If it is your wish, of course I shall obey."

"Excellent," said Alfred. He pointed a gloved hand at Nilssen. "And you will aid him by staying out of the woods." With that he wheeled his horse around and cantered off toward his tent.

Eorhic remained behind. Calmly he said, "You do realize that it's too late?"

He was still speaking Old English, so Nilssen answered in the same language, quietly to avoid being overheard, "By being here we've disturbed your plans. By talking to the king, to his lords, to his men, we've altered conditions."

"But in ignorance of the effect. I joined the king seven years ago: on the fifth of January 871, to be precise. They were calling it the Season of Slaughter. Battle after battle, with Ashdown about the only indisputable victory. I showed Alfred how to stretch his resources. Over the years I've worked on his army to the extent that even I couldn't undo the changes. So you don't bother me, Ibrahim. History rarely hinges on isolated events; every strand is a twist of thousands.

That's the strength of my strategy. Here we are, one day away from what could be the most decisive battle of early British times, and you haven't a clue what my intentions are. Isn't that beautiful?"

His horse whickered and stamped a forefoot. Eorhic patted its neck, talking soothing nonsense to it while he watched Nilssen for his reaction.

Nilssen said, "When did we give ourselves away?"

"Hard question, that," said Eorhic, so softly that his reply was almost lost in his horse's breathing. "I was only sure when I caught you scheming in the woods. You were marked for investigation the night you reached Athelney. Some gall you had, telling a tall story like that. Don't forget that I've supervised hundreds of interrogations. I can smell out most lies unless the liar is in the master-class. Which you aren't quite, though your friend certainly is. Your disguise was far too good—and far too superficial; you hadn't got properly into character or you'd never have dared refute Werferth as you did. Your theology was too modern, even for these progressive times." He treated the squalid encampment to a sardonic smile. "But I must admit you laid a first-rate smoke screen." The Modern English word clanged amongst the Saxon syllables. "I'm almost prepared to admire your will to win. It's helpless of course; you stepped in far too late. Forward planning, as the king reminds us, pays. As to what you said about treason in the woods, well, obviously you believe it. I won't hold a grudge on account of your stupidity."

"Are you making an offer?"

Eorhic toyed with his horse's mane. "A truce," he said. "My work is over. If I have missed my objective I won't get another opening. And if I've won, you'll have to stay here. Either way we can stop being enemies."

"Except that you are who you are."

"I am Eorhic of Æsces-dun," he answered mildly.

"Eric Halvey, Lord Lieutenant of Middlesex, Commissar General of the Commissariat of National Integrity, died on Monday the seventh of November, 2011. Why do you insist on resurrecting him? Haven't we all had enough?"

"Convince me of the worthiness of what you're trying to do here," said Nilssen. "Perhaps then I can give you my answer."

In a vehement undertone Eorhic said, "I want to wipe out the future which gave rise to The War, the Collapse, the Exodus—"

"And the City?"

"That above all. A clean slate. Time travel is a false hope: a Pandora's Box containing only troubles. It's a rotten tree, Ibrahim; I mean to cut it down."

Taking a firm grip of his reins, he gave a mocking salute. "I'll tell you if I win."

Yaer had no ready answers when Nilssen repeated what little information Eorhic had volunteered. Though he listened gravely, he did snap his fingers in annoyance on hearing how they had been detected.

When Nilssen was finished with his account, Yaer said, "I feel that he's bluffing us. It's May the eighth tomorrow, a Thursday. Thor's Day: propitious for Danes in battle. Superstition counts for a lot on both sides. A clever fellow like our Eorhic wouldn't assume it was all cut-and-dried, for all his reorganization."

"So the battle's only half of it?"

"More like a quarter, I'd say," answered Yaer.

CHAPTER FIFTEEN

From the grassy rampart which encircled the summit of Battlesbury Hill one could see a long, long way, Nilssen discovered on scrambling up out of the enclosure to face the wind and the slanting rays of the morning sun.

A mile and a half distant, across the shallow, sloping valley which lay to the north, the enemy stood in battle array behind their trench. Cutting across the crest of the Bishopstrow Down in a nearly horizontal line, the renewed trench was white and crisp like a wound slashed in the green turf. In silence the northmen observed the progress of their lone herald as he rode through the lush, dewy grass of the lower slope to meet his Saxon counterpart. This much was ritual; this much had to be done properly, even in a confrontation so fraught with foredoomed violence, in order that both sides might feel justified in shedding blood.

Nilssen slowly surveyed the panorama visible from his vantage point. Due west the rounded peak of Battlesbury Hill just blocked his view. The downs and dales of Salisbury Plain extended to north and east beyond the armies, with the forested trough of the Wylye Valley they had crossed that morning running away to the southeast. Southward and as far westward as he could see rose waves of woodlands lapping about green-capped hills. Green predominated, be it the somber green of primeval forest or the verdant green of grasslands. Overhead the sky was hazy with moisture that still rose from hollows in fugitive wisps, routed thence by the wind and the sun's burgeoning heat. Already a few swallows swooped across the downs, and the larks were up, warning off rivals from their territories with twittering liquid song.

The heralds met and exchanged demands. Those of the Danes would be simple: gold or silver in exchange for their promise to go and harry another king's realm. Those of the Saxons would be simpler still: unconditional surrender. Within a couple of minutes the two riders had parted and were hastening back to their armies.

At daybreak the battle-horns had roused the Saxon camp, summoning men from their beds in shambling half-dressed hundreds, strapping armor and arms to themselves as they fell into line. The king had ridden out before them, his war shield slung on his back, his polished sword held aloft to catch the dawn light and glitter against the last stars in the frosty sky. The pirates, he announced, had left their stockade at the Ethan-dun and overnight had entrenched themselves three miles away; what had the warriors of Britain to say to this challenge?

A joyous roar had answered him from the ranks of the professionals and been imitated by a weaker cheer from the peasants. At this, he had marked their northward line of march with his sword as pointer, before sheathing it and slapping his horse's flanks with his high boots to urge it forward to the head of the column.

However, there was now obvious uneasiness amongst all ranks. Even the officers, who had most incentive to put on brave faces, had been seen to pick at their breakfasts. The Danes defended a strong position. There were many of them. And evaluating the Saxon force objectively, one could not help but question the military worth of so many of the undernourished and ill-equipped part-time soldiers who waited, trembling with cold and fear, for the signal to advance. Few could ever have seen a Dane in the flesh at close quarters prior to the deployment along the near slope; in all likelihood they regarded the enemy as supranormal beings to be shunned through headlong flight, not as mortal men susceptible to defeat in battle. That psychological barrier alone would have cost Alfred dear throughout his lengthy preparations.

Eorhic was standing not far to Nilssen's left, his arms folded, his face screwed up in an expression suggestive of combined satisfaction and doubt. Yaer, on the other hand, sat on the grassy rampart with his legs splayed out down the outer incline, plainly not asleep although he had hardly moved for some time. A stalk of ryegrass between his lips bobbed as he chewed on it. He would, Nilssen thought, be meditating on words they had exchanged during the battlefield Mass half an hour before. . . .

Eorhic then had not yet taken up his post beside them. Three ranks of infantry had been extended across the face of the hill, one yard of turf to a man, two hundred and thirty men to each rank. On either wing were the dismounted cavalry, divided evenly between Sarnvig's troop on the left and that of an unidentified officer on the right, totaling ninety-eight. Away to the fore stood Werferth, conducting the service with his brown habit billowing in the wind, his words snatched into the sky beyond the hearing of most soldiers. Prayers ascended in an asynchronous babble, prayers for deliverance, prayers for courage, prayers for the stamina to be preeminent in the slaughter of enemies.

Nilssen had suggested that courtesy and prudence made it advisable for them too to be seen at prayer; and Yaer had acceded with surprising readiness.

But once on his knees Nilssen had found that he was unable to carry the pretense further. The Islamic prayers they had learned by heart seemed to mock the

292 ANDREW M. STEPHENSON

occasion: he, an unbeliever, could not ape sincerity nor mime the orisons of the devout without a sense of guilt. Instead he contemplated the dual images of cloud shadows sweeping across the downs; and of the sunlight caught upon the myriad points of spear and sword. Shadow and light, night and day, history leavened with human blood, impaled uopn a drawn-out moment before battle.

This was not abstract history. This day was a part of his own life: had been; would be; would remain, whatever the version of time's uncoilings that gave birth to it. Without it he would not be who he was. Nor would Yaer. Nor would Eorhic. Nor would any man, nor any point in space and time out to the ultimate nothingness enclosing the revolving whirlpool Rhys had shown him once in replica. A life was not a single thing.

"Is anyone out there, listening to all these prayers?" he whispered. *"If there is, these people believe in You. Don't let them down."*

"And what about us?"

He found Yaer looking at him and blushed.

"It's part of their way of life," Nilssen said. "Until now I hadn't realized how intensely they believed. Not the way we technically advanced people imagine; the literal blood-and-thunder religion that Werferth preaches is an abnormality. They laugh at him for it, behind his back. But you have to believe in *something* to exist here."

Yaer closed his eyes and nodded. "Otherwise you lose everything, yes."

"But tell me, does the god matter? Take that Dane whom Alfred made you kill, for instance: he thought there was a God; but he prayed to Thor, not Jehova. He knew where his world turned and who controlled it; and he knew where he was going after death. What have *we* got, Yaer?"

Yaer doubled himself so that his forehead neared

the ground. Desolately he said, "We have our knowledge of the past. Our personal, uncertain past."

"So which of us is right? Is our god any better than theirs?"

Yaer straightened and looked directly at Nilssen. "Us? You know I was never a believer."

"Not even in Shazol?"

"The creed of Shazol is a philosophy, devised by a man, and named after him. It is not a god."

"Yet you worship it for the constancy it offers while all else changes." Yaer doubled up again, acting out his public devotions, as if trying not to listen. The drone of prayer continued unabated on the slopes below the earthworks. "Yaer, take a lesson from them down there. We're the same: we depend on that unchanging point of stability. Remember how you condemned Laheer that night we talked on the marshes? Did he betray you; is that why you hate him?"

"Why should that be any concern of yours?"

"Because I have to be at peace with myself and can't see how. Show me. Or tell me if my search is pointless. It's for me, Yaer; and maybe for you too. If we outlive today, we must have made up our minds, be ready to act decisively, so as to outwit the worm we're riding."

"You'll live," said Yaer. "You can depend on it, for all of Hector Kwambe's horror stories. And you'll get the girl. And together you'll live happily ever after. Even Rhys would bet on it. No call for you to worry about me either; I hate Laheer because he's a bastard, not because he symbolizes any kind of flawed godhead. Remember who you're talking to, Jerlan, when you invent theories of that sort."

"And if it does all go wrong for us, you'll hold on?"

"What else can I do?" Frowning, Yaer interlinked his hands in his lap. "Jerlan, if it helps, try to understand that what I believe in is quite simply this: the world exists as it is; nothing else needs to be real."

His frown smoothed itself out. "I'm very durable. You won't lose me so easily. And while you have me . . ."

Nilssen saw the stark truth to which Yaer had led him. Yaer had been his mentor throughout the mission; Yaer had anticipated the evolution of simple loneliness into fear of loneliness once Nilssen had been exposed to a vital human society that owed nothing to the City. Yaer had seen through him and his superficial adoption of this world of the past. Perhaps he had anticipated the fear as long ago as their first consultation in Nilssen's office; perhaps Yaer, in comprehending the flaw, had accepted the concomitant burden of responsibility, even as Nilssen had accepted his necessary rôle in the original Project Yardstick. Yaer might have been playing a multilayered game of such exquisite subtlety that no one but he might ever be able to trace its convolutions. But Yaer would never volunteer confirmation; his art required secrecy of its practitioners.

At last Yaer blinked away the tears the cold wind had brought to his eyes. He sniffed. "Ah well," he said, as though they had shared far more than unashamed silence. . . .

As the heralds rejoined the ranks, the two armies stiffened. Of course, Nilssen reminded himself, Yaer was a wilful enigma, a man who kept and concealed his own counsel. So frequently right that he was trusted, he did not confer with his equals, whose existence his demeanor denied. Enclosed by his aloofness, he chose to be useful because that satisfied him. An amoral philanthropist, almost, Yaer would be well able to steer a productive course between overt self-gratification and self-inconveniencing benevolence, the Scylla and Charybdis of the hypocrite—

Was that fair? Perhaps Yaer was nothing worse than a benign pragmatist, which would accord with Shazol's teachings, the guiding light of his life. But since he could maintain a false front better than could most

people, that makeshift character profile was unlikely
to be improved on.

Eorhic cleared his throat. "Here we go," he said.

Officers and NCOs along the lines were rapidly
marshaling their sections into distinct blocks while
the two cavalry troops galloped off, one left, the other
right, toward the flanking limits of the battlefield. A
horn blatted and the infantry commenced a leisurely
but steady march straight across the shallow valley.

It seemed they were intent on engaging the western-
most flank of the Danes, so at once the enemy responded by sidling along their trench.

Nilssen was moved to ask, "All they've got is that
little ditch. What's to stop our side from walking
around to the other side?"

Eorhic spared him a superior smile. "And what's to
stop the Danes from stepping over their 'ditch,' as you
call it?"

"Fair enough," Nilssen admitted. "But that would
only work if all the attackers stay on one side; suppose we surrounded them?"

"What with? Fresh air? The Danes—and most other
armies, come to that—will only start a battle in this
order if the numbers favor them. Here the two sides
are about balanced, so any encirclement will weaken
our side's weight of arms at any given point. With the
'ditch' to their front the Danes' strength is considerably enhanced. Don't discount that trench of theirs so
readily, however simple it looks."

The Bishopstrow Down was deeply indented in at
least three places. Opposite Battlesbury Hill the most
prominent of its headlands rose some two hundred
feet above the floor of the valley over a distance of
about half a mile. The Saxons had no real excuse to
slow down; yet before long they were advancing at no
more than a crawl. The left flank certainly benefited
from following the contours of the higher ground at
the head of the valley and so had to hang back to keep

the front line straight; but had Yaer not asked the reason, Nilssen would have risked another lecture from Eorhic.

"Is it so obvious?" replied Eorhic, intent on the spectacle. "I hoped the Danes would interpret the slowness as caution or conservation of effort." He seemed content to confine his reply to that vague statement.

The army was still some distance from the Danes' trench when the enemy began singing. Their chanted words came in wind-shredded scraps across the valley, a menacing incantation glorifying a foredoomed victory.

Yaer said, "Psychological warfare, I suppose."

"Definitely," said Eorhic. "Somewhat defused, however."

"How so?"

"The Here have used that song before every one of their battles for the last two years. So I had Alfred order that our recruits be taught to sing it during training sessions. All the Danes are doing is helping our men get into the spirit of the occasion; one or two are even singing along. . . . In a minute—ah, yes, there it is: the horse's head."

A solitary Dane had leapt the trench and run out before his fellows, carrying a long pole on whose upper end the bleeding head of a horse had been impaled. This he waved from side to side as he jogged along the line, displaying it as much to his own side as to the Saxons.

"An intriguingly economical token," continued Eorhic. "Both an insult to us and a good omen to them. The horse was sacrificed to Tyr at dawn. Now they sing his praises, calling on him to accept the blood of the animal as a promise of the blood of men to follow if he will aid the Danes today. . . . And if you look up there in the sky, you'll see some carrion crows.

The damn things always appear when there's a battle. The superstitious fools regard them as Odin's ravens. A confusion of *Corvus corone corone* with *Corvus corax*. Or a dose of wishful thinking. More the latter, I suspect. The vikings throw horseflesh to them to hedge their bets by currying favor with Odin too."

"And the insult?" inquired Yaer.

"Implicit in the sacrifice of an animal. A *real* opponent would warrant a man. A prisoner, naturally."

"Have you fought the Danes often?" asked Nilssen. "I mean, personally."

"A dozen or more times. In war, every man fights."

"So you're an experienced hand-to-hander?"

"Average-to-middling."

Yaer looked worried.

Nilssen asked, "When you're in there, and a solid wall of men is rushing at you, and you know that every last one of them wants to kill you, how do you feel?"

Eorhic grinned. "Scared shitless."

Even Yaer smiled, momentarily.

More thoughtfully Eorhic added, "My first experience was at Ashdown. I wanted to impress Prince Alfred, as he then was, so stuck close when he charged the enemy. It was a stupid risk he took, but his companions went in with him; and where they went, I went. After that there wasn't a lot of choice: fight or be hacked to bits. The Danes pressed us hard, frantic to kill the Wessex heir and his brother the king in one go. They kept on coming. I'd scavenged a shield, and when I swore fealty to Alfred he'd given me a sword. With those I blocked and chopped until the enemy soldiers began to look alike. If I cut one down he seemed to run at me from another angle—"

A shout rumbled along the battle line. Steel thudded into wood and flesh as the first flights of spears were loosed between the armies. Firefly-like, they winked in the sunlight. Men screamed with pain and gratified bloodlust. Arrows whickered along arcing trajectories. The armies met with a roar.

"Strangely," said Eorhic, "there was no reassurance in the knowledge that the Saxons would win the Battle of Ashdown. Like today, my survival wasn't guaranteed. And I'd never killed anyone with a sword. I wasn't sure I could."

Yaer showed surprise but very quickly nodded in comprehension.

"The way it happened, it turned out so easy. Not what I'd anticipated, of course. A man rushed at me: an ordinary fellow about my size, sweating a lot, bruised on his left cheek. As I swung up my shield to protect myself, I saw his left side was unguarded. Left-handed, he was. Tired, and growing careless too, I suppose. So I stuck my sword into him."

Eorhic gave a nervous laugh. "The blade wouldn't go in. I'd imagined it would slide in, like into butter. You have to push hard, you know; then, if you've missed the ribs, it begins to cut the clothing. Suddenly there's very little resistance." A shudder added tremolo to the last word. Closing his eyes hard, Eorhic breathed deeply. As he swallowed, his Adam's apple wobbled. "He tried to speak but blood bubbled out of his mouth. It spattered my face. Then he collapsed . . . God, that was frightening: I was hemmed in by vikings and my only weapon was stuck in a corpse. One of theirs. Kicking him over onto his back, I tugged that sword out of him and at once had another fight on my hands. That's how it went, hour after hour. Occasionally there'd be a lull and we could rest for a few seconds. Then you could depend on some bird-brained ass getting up and bragging about his score of kills. He usually got his in the next charge. Take it from me, if you dispatch more than four you're doing well. Damn well. Hardly any deaths are immediate. Bleeding, gangrene, crippling, exposure:

these account for far more. Out there you try to keep a whole skin, between trying to chop holes in someone else's. Actual death is irrelevant. Battles are trials of strength . . . No, I'm wrong: trials of nerve. You see, the side that wins is the side that dares lose most. . . . Funny, isn't it?"

Nilssen met his glance. "Now and always."

"There's a lesson for us all," said Eorhic.

Yaer coughed and asked, "How did it end?"

"Ashdown? Their line broke. They ran. Afterward we went around finishing off their wounded. . . . If I could, I'd forget that part; I don't think I ever will."

"And what are today's prospects?"

"A win for us, God willing," muttered Eorhic, frowning at the mêlée on the far side of the valley. The opposed lines were buckling: on the wings, where the more experienced Saxon force had been stationed, the Danes had been pushed back from their trench; but in the center the predominantly raw troops were in serious difficulties, their attack on the verge of collapse. Bodies were piling up, cluttered with broken weapons and the gear of the fallen, so that the survivors could be seen stumbling over them. The loudest uproar of clashing steel came from a core of Saxons slightly off center towards the right wing where the king and his banner defied the Danes from behind a shield wall of the royal companions. Here was where the enemy vented his fury most diligently, throwing wave after wave of sweating, bloodied vikings against the Saxon swords until the grass was slippery with gore and blades became blunted from hacking at deep-notched shields.

Eorhic appeared to turn restless as the minutes went by. All of a sudden he growled, "Where the hell are those cavalry? Our men are being slaughtered—"

He was interrupted by the faint but confident ululation of a horn which, according to the reaction of the combatants, was as yet hidden by the Down.

There was a pause in the fighting as friend and foe sighted upslope to learn whose arrival was being announced. Hoofbeats drummed on the firm ground, and, reinforced by a chorus of bloodcurdling yells and whoops, the two troops of cavalry swept over the hill and down upon the place of battle.

"You were asking," said Eorhic, "why we didn't surround them. Behold: new weapons, new tactics."

At once the Danes were in a quandary. Not only were they outflanked, but they were unaccustomed to fighting against mounted men. The habit of the Germanic and Scandinavian peoples hitherto had been to fight on foot. The advent of the new Saxon force with their handfuls of darts and their weighted circular nets must have overtaxed the Danes' resilience, for their response was to regroup in a circle with their shields outwards in an unbroken wall. Now they were on the defensive.

Many Danes were lost in this simple maneuver. Smartly executed by the majority, the move caught out the tired ones and those bewildered by the appearance of novel reinforcements. Stragglers late in joining the redoubt were set upon by gleeful, merciless Saxons who then enclosed their enemies with a constricting ring of relentlessly probing blades.

Eorhic seemed well-satisfied. "After all that guesswork," he said, "we carried it off. Years ago I read that the vikings in Gaul were intimidated by Frankish cavalry. I gambled that we could break their nerve the same way. And we have: the battle is ours; and with it the war against the northmen!"

Yaer asked doubtfully, "Do *they* know that?"

"The defensive ring is a recourse of desperation," said Eorhic. "They know it. Even our peasants know it. The great change that overthrew conventional warfare in our twentieth century was enhanced mobility. Battlefronts were diffused by the freedom to relocate forces rapidly; by coincidence they grew comparable in size to the real frontiers in dispute. What you see here is the prototype of the Flanders trenches, only here the lines are measured in hundreds of, not miles, but yards. Nevertheless, they share a common principle. As in the Oriental game of Go, the fronts are symbolic. The ground held is a measure of one's success. And the closed circle is a precursor to the vanishing point."

There came three blasts on the horn. In reply the Saxons swiftly retired some ten paces from the Danish enclave. Puzzled, the northmen did not break ranks in pursuit but stood fast in expectation of some new ploy. Their throwing weapons had been used up before the first bout of hand-to-hand fighting, so they had no option but to stay where they were, sullenly confronting the Saxons.

"Watch closely," said Eorhic softly, eagerly. "Secret weapons rely on their surprise value, so it is instructive to observe their initial impact. This, for example, is the first known application of hand grenades. Not the explosive kind of course," he reassured Nilssen and Yaer. "We couldn't collect sufficient barnyard nitre or procure the sulphur. But the substitute is an impressive stopgap."

Horrified, Nilssen groped for words to match his feelings.

"Eorhic," he gasped, "you mustn't change war like this! These people have no defenses, military or mental. Do away with the rules and you do away with the point of it all."

"Which is?" demanded Eorhic. "What point has there ever been in wholesale killing?"

"It proves who is stronger," said Nilssen. "It proves, between people who recognize it as a test of superiority, who has the right to govern. This is a formal contest between nations who trust in human strength, not technical prowess. If you break their rules you prove nothing: you leave shame and anger, a resentful determination to strike back another time. Our kind of war is *not* theirs!"

"The code of gentlemen," Eorhic sneered. "Live here a while longer . . . Oh, I keep forgetting: you were going home to that City of yours when this is over. Think again, Mister City-man. Look over there and tell me I haven't obliterated your future."

Prominent above the heads of the foot soldiers were several of the cavalry who were riding closer to the Danish ring. In their fists were torches from whose ends flapped banners of smoky flame; and from their saddles hung nets full of globular objects that might have been bloated animal bladders. Halting immediately behind their own front rank of infantry, they steadied their mounts and prepared themselves to use their new weapon.

In a concerted movement every man touched a bladder to his torch and flung it amongst the close-packed Danes. Before the first barrage had landed, a second was being lit. Bladders burst, strewing flame. Terrified burning men threw themselves about, spreading confusion and fire even as more of the oil-filled sacs fell, fueling the growing conflagration. Shrieks rose with the sooty smoke. The toughest Saxon could hardly have taken pleasure from the sight of fire-sheathed human shapes rolling on the ground, howling in agony. It seemed the Saxons' battle fury had been overwhelmed, for when the Danes broke formation rather than be incinerated with their comrades, only slow advantage was taken of their disorder. By then the cavalry had halted their bombardment, evidently reluctant to continue.

"Gutless cowards!" Eorhic raged, unheard by those he cursed. "Wipe them out! They'll get away!"

"You bloody butcher," Yaer groaned. "You drove them too far."

Nilssen shivered despite the sun's heat, but forced himself to witness the end of the battle.

Fierce fighting broke out anew between the armies, and the Saxons began giving ground to the desperate Danes whose massed thrust rapidly directed itself up the hill. Despite their losses, or perhaps because of them, they stayed shoulder to shoulder and seemed likely to leave the field in good order. Their base camp was only three miles away at the Ethan-dun; the Saxons had not gone unpunished in the battle and might, if the Danes held close, be persuaded to desist from harrying them. But the smell of charred flesh that wafted even to where Nilssen stood must have overthrown convention; or there was a new mood, a taste for victory, in the Saxons; for they shook off their bemusement and set off after their retreating foes. Of some eight hundred Danes who took the field, scarcely five hundred left it; and these were hotly pursued by the cavalry, who cut them down with spear and sword as they ran, transforming their ranks into a rabble, so that the trail to the camp was marked from start to finish by corpses.

Eorhic's fury soon subsided. "Outmanned, out-maneuvered, and outgunned, by God!" he exclaimed. "Let's get our horses and follow."

Mounted, they galloped across the valley: past the bloodied, trampled grass of the battle-lea where hundreds of the wounded begged them for aid, for water, for some surcease from pain and the heat of early afternoon, and where flies crawled on dead, sky-staring faces and smoke churned upward from sputtering, greasy fires; on, past horses that kicked helplessly where they lay, wounded by weapons aimed at their departed riders; past heaps of shattered weapons and lost shields; past a crow that lifted heavily on slow-flapping wings, abandoning its feast of sightless eyes; past the prone, half-naked body of a powerfully built man—

"Wait!" Nilssen shouted, reining in his horse so savagely it neighed. Dismounting, he ran to the body.

Gently he moved its head to see its face. Sure now, he turned the whole body onto its back.

In death, as in life, Sigewulf had retained his dignity. His eyes did not stare. As he cooled, the lids might open slightly, drawn apart by rigor mortis; but for the moment he seemed asleep, at peace with his fate. The broken haft of the spear which had taken his life still protruded from his belly. Nearby, the jeweled sword that had been his pride jutted from the chest of a dead Dane. His horse had fled.

Nilssen brushed aside a lock of hair from Sigewulf's eyes for a better sight of his whole face. A footfall told him Yaer stood close.

Quietly Nilssen asked, "Could the expectation of certain death make a man like Sigewulf careless, Yaer?"

"If he saw it in his wyrd."

"And did he, Yaer?"

Hesitantly: "I'm not sure. Do you think I talked him into suicide? All I told him was, if the Danes were utterly destroyed in this battle, Morwena would be safe. That was all. I swear."

"You *swear*? . . . So he'd fight all the harder, take senseless risks . . . Yaer, you might as well be told, now or never, that I despise the games you play with people's minds."

Yaer did not reply.

Slow hoofbeats caused Nilssen to look over his shoulder. In the same glance he saw: Eorhic approaching, impatience proclaimed in every angle of his posture; and Yaer, eyes squeezed tight shut, his face distraught.

"You'll learn," Nilssen said. "Being told the first time hurts. Worse than physical pain. I've been there too. Just turn it over inside you. Absorb it. Use it."

Eorhic contemplated them from his horse. Flatly he remarked, "So someone finally got the better of Sigewulf. That's too bad." He glanced at Yaer. "What's wrong with you?"

Nilssen answered for him. "We both lost a friend."

Eorhic looked northward to where black smoke belched up in billows that scudded across the skyline. "Alfred will take it hard. I'll tell him. Do you want to stand guard?"

Opening his eyes, Yaer regarded Nilssen without blinking.

"I'll stay," said Nilssen. "I need to think. Alone."

"I'll come back later," said Yaer.

During his vigil Nilssen cleaned Sigewulf's sword meticulously, scrubbing the blade with wads of grass moistened with spittle, finally tearing a swatch of cloth from the Dane's tunic with which to polish it. When its steel shone and the jewels had recovered their sparkle, he placed the hilt in the dead Welshman's right hand, curling the unresponsive and stiffening fingers close about it so that he seemed less defenseless. Subsequently, yielding to second thoughts, Nilssen laid the sword on the corpse's chest, the blade toward the feet, the arms bent with their hands upon the hilt. The Dane he dragged over to lie like a footstool against Sigewulf's feet. The composition struck him as being more fitting for a warrior than a haphazard charnel sprawl.

But inevitably he found himself unable to distract his racing mind with useful activity. Sigewulf was dead and therefore Morwena had passed into his care. He had promised Sigewulf.

Why, he wondered, did the prospect unsettle him? Was it the remorseless unfolding of his own wyrd which had caught Sigewulf and might yet catch others also? If only Rhys had been available. Rhys would know.

A cloud crossed the sun. Light and shadow, he remembered: natural laws contrasted with the totipotent forces behind nature that the City tapped, forces neither good nor evil, mindlessly dedicated to universal stability.

306 ANDREW M. STEPHENSON

With that he comprehended his fear. He was not afraid of death of body, but of death of will. If the universe demanded of him a certain attitude of mind, he would adopt it whether it was rational or not. Doubts too might be a link in the causal chain which, when completed, would bind together scattered events. He saw free will as an illusion. His own people, in trying to deflect the flow of causality, had been slapped down by the Collapse, an acausal cataclysm. No matter how secure the City seemed, it too would vanish if it ceased to be a necessary part of reality. That was what Rhys had tried to convey the day Nilssen visited him in Area Five. Nature would not tolerate redundant elaboration.

The sounds of the battle in front of the Ethan-dun fort diminished during the following half hour. Thereafter, four riders came to where Nilssen waited, flogging all possible speed from their mounts. They were Alfred, Eorhic, Sarnvig, and another eorl. Leaping from his horse, the bloodied king flung himself upon Sigewulf's cold body and, hugging it, began to sob like a child.

"You too, dear friend?" he wept. "At the victory-tide do you leave me?"

Sarnvig drew closer. Huskily he muttered, "Many a Dane lies in Hel tonight because of him, my lord. He bought our victory with his life; but it was a hero's parting, not a death of sorrow."

"Sarnvig, pray God may teach me to believe you!" said Alfred. "Then I may face Guthrum and take pleasure in his downfall!" He raised tearful yet fierce eyes towards Nilssen. "But I fear that Sigewulf meant it to be so, else he would not have come last night to beg an holy oath of me—two oaths, I ought to say."

Nilssen's throat was dry as he asked, "What oaths?"

Alfred kissed the corpse of his dead companion on both cheeks. Then, wearily, he released it from his embrace and stood up. Slipping Sigewulf's sword from

between the stiff fingers that enclosed its hilt, he tilted
it in the afternoon sunlight so that it returned a
glorious display of colors and the elusive, lambent
sheen of lovingly polished metal.

"I swore that this treasure should not pass into the
grave. So it was he worded the oath; and so it was I
recited it, never dreaming how apt those words should
be. Afterward I swore also that you, Ibrahim ibn-
Haroun, should be sole heir to Sigewulf's two greatest
treasures, and that I myself should stand as oath-
supporter in any dispute. These were my oaths, witnessed only by God, yet oaths by which I shall abide
as I fear God and as Sigewulf was loyal to me, to
death.

"Accordingly, Ibrahim, this sword, the lesser of his
treasures, is yours by right of inheritance; and the
one whom he counted dearest of all he guarded, the
woman Morwena, is in your keeping also. Use the first
wisely; and ward the second well." There was no kindness in his voice: the pronouncement in law was also
a threat.

Nilssen sought some means to satisfy the grieving
king. Eorhic, out of Alfred's sight, smiled at Nilssen's
discomfort.

Suddenly the king reversed the sword and thrust the
hilt hard into Nilssen's midriff. "Take it," he snapped.
"Mind well what I said . . . And attend me in my
tent tomorrow with Khaled." Remounting, he said
to the nameless eorl, "See to it that Sigewulf lies in
the place of honor on the funeral pyre. Cover him
with my purple cloak. And set my bronze-chased shield
by him; also my war-spear that is inlaid with gold and
niello. I shall set the first brand."

Kicking his heels into his horse's flanks, he rode off
to rejoin the army with the eorl and Sarnvig close
behind. Eorhic stayed only long enough to say:

"You've been greatly honored. That sword should

have been Alfred's—*heriot,* they call it here: the lord's
death-duties. Make sure you earn it."

Then he too departed.

Nilssen stayed until gangs of supervised Danish
prisoners arrived to construct the funeral pyres that
would purge the field of battle and make it fit for
legend.

He walked his horse along the down toward the
smoke and sounds of revelry, oppressed by forebod-
ings. Now he felt the tendrils of responsibility closing
on him, constricting his freedom of movement. If the
future were to be reshaped, that would be done soon.
He hardly dared anticipate the moment, so fragmentary were his plans, for the battle had gone as history
recorded and theoretically all that remained was the
agreement of terms with Guthrum, a task for Alfred
not Eorhic. The CNI appeared to have let slip its
opportunity. Somehow Nilssen could not believe that
anyone of Eorhic's ability, experience, or poise would
permit outsiders to compromise his long-laid plans
simply by their presence. That Yaer had missed the
crux of the plot was proof positive of its cunning;
that it conformed so well to the orthodox line of historical development argued likewise for its simplicity.

Nilssen fingered the reassuring weight of Sigewulf's
sword at his waist and speculated on whether the dead
man had foreseen its usefulness to him as more than
an ornament.

The Ethan-dun in which the Danes had taken
refuge was an Iron Age fort. It had been renovated
by the northmen and was clearly one of their important minor outposts. A double ring of earthen banks
twenty feet high, separated by a ditch almost as deep,
enclosed several acres of exposed ground on a promon-
tory of the downs jutting out into the Avon valley. To
north and west it was protected by vertiginous grassy
slopes four hundred feet high and steep enough to
make the rashest attacker take thought. To the east

the approach seemed gentle only in comparison. On the south side, where an expanse of level turf might have encouraged an enemy to rush the timber gates, an outer wall resembling a barbican shielded the principal defenses.

So many Danes had been lost in the battle that they had been obliged to retreat to the inner ringwall, abandoning the southern enclosure to the Saxons who, defying the Danish archers and spearmen, rampaged through its shacks and animal pens, burning at will and driving off the cattle they found there. Afterward, as the exhausted defenders manned their ramparts in expectation of an assault, the Saxons instead settled outside, pitching their tents and bivouac shelters, lighting their fires, and contenting themselves with posting sentries along the outer bank and around the foot of the downs.

Later that afternoon scouts were sent north along the Avon valley to watch for relief forces from Chippenham twelve miles away. Otherwise the Saxons did not spend themselves in storming the fort, for rudimentary logistical estimates predicted a short life to the siege. The enemy bodies gathered for burning were all undernourished, so Guthrum's men had been short of food even before their livestock were captured. Nigh on five hundred battle-shattered, hungry men deprived of firewood, water, and fresh meat would not long endure the cold May nights atop a windy hill, aware that their foes grew stronger outside their gates.

As the sun set, drawing shadows across the hills, drowning the valleys in darkness, the downs lingered awhile in daylight. Southward, brown smoke spiraled up from separate funeral pyres. One was for the Saxons, another for the Danes. In rising, the smoke encountered the more democratic winds aloft. Its tattered ribbons were mingled and dispersed into invisibility across the blood-red sky with which the night was rounding out the day.

CHAPTER SIXTEEN

"Ibrahim, wait!"

Nilssen allowed Eorhic to catch him up, then resumed his steady stride through the busy camp toward the king's tent, leaving it to the other to broach his business.

"I want to make you an offer," Eorhic said quickly.

"Not interested," Nilssen answered. "Unless you're surrendering." His answer seemed to amuse Eorhic. "I mean it: come back with us quietly—"

"For a hanging like the others got?" Eorhic asked sarcastically. "You must take me for a damned idiot." With evident effort he recovered his pleasant manner. "Listen, we can work together. This infighting wastes us all. You, your friend, and I: we can each carve out as much as we want from this world with our special knowledge . . ."

"Why this sudden generosity, my Lord Lieutenant? Are we beginning to tread on your heels?"

"That's a stupid idea."

"Not according to your change of tack. Recently you were patronizing us; suddenly you're crawling."

Pursing his lips, Eorhic adopted a forthright tone. "I've always been a practical man—"

"A pragmatist, you mean."

"And proud of it." There was the briefest of pauses. "You've won. All I want is enough to live well—"

"And who's keeping you from it?"

Drawing a slow breath, Eorhic said, "Obviously

I've been too soft. This idealism of yours would be ludicrous if it weren't so bloody dangerous. One way or another it has to be controlled. And will be."

"With a knife in my back?"

"Not *your* back. I'll not risk incurring Alfred's anger, much as I'd love to be rid of you and your friend. I had someone else in mind. A hostage to your good behavior."

He laughed at Nilssen's incredulity.

"But not yet," he added. "She won't be touched if you cooperate."

Nilssen could feel his self-control slip away. He did not try to retain it but fed on the rising rage until his caution was overwhelmed. All he wanted was to choke the arrogant confidence out of the man.

Almost too late Eorhic forced out a cry for help as Nilssen's fingers dug into his throat. Struggling to reach his sword, he was pinned to the muddy ground by Nilssen's weight. He kicked ever more feebly and his face darkened while his eyes bulged as though in disbelief that this should be happening. His hands raking at Nilssen's sides and back became weaker.

A muscular arm slid under Nilssen's chin and pressed back against his windpipe. A knee gouged his back cruelly. Bodily he was dragged away from Eorhic and dumped in the mud while Eorhic gasped air noisily. A crowd of rank-and-file soldiers stared down at them both.

"Your pardon," said one deferentially, as though he meant to be polite and was not simply affecting manners to mock them, "the king has banned fighting. Cost us our ears, t'would, we stand idle."

"That's how it is, all right," said another. The voice struck Nilssen as being familiar. Twisting around, he looked up at a face he had thought never to see again.

"Leofric!"

Leofric of Henglafingasham stared back boldly.

"I'd not reckoned we'd met," he answered Nilssen. "But that *is* my name." Pointing to Eorhic, now sitting up massaging his throat, he said with a wink to his fellow soldiers, "As obedient subjects of the king we ought to report this fight. . . . Might cost us dear if we didn't. You take my meaning?"

Nilssen noticed how crafty greed enlivened the stolid soldiers' faces.

". . . Of course," Leofric continued, "any reward Alfred would likely offer us would hardly be worth our effort, considering the trouble the report would cause—"

"Here," wheezed Eorhic, holding out his left hand to Leofric. "Take this for your conscience, parasite."

Love of money mellowed any resentment Leofric might have felt at being so addressed. Cheerfully he took the gold coin. Saluting, he remarked, "I always said Alfred was a leader who attracts a good sort of follower. Generous; like master, like man. Your health, lord Eorhic." Again he saluted with insulting precision. "And you, kind sir," he said to Nilssen, "I'd like to remember you also when I drink to absent friends."

Ignoring his mocking smile, Nilssen said contemptuously, "You'll not remember me. "So clear off before I remember you to Alfred."

Leofric's joviality deserted him, dropping away like a mask.

"I've heard about you Saracens," he said nastily, "and all of it seems to be true. If—"

A sudden move by Nilssen made him retreat a pace.

". . . Next time we meet," the man finished, "be very careful." He and his friends left, proclaiming brave boasts.

Then Nilssen looked at Eorhic.

The marks of fingernails showed white on both sides of his windpipe; the skin would be badly bruised in

314 ANDREW M. STEPHENSON

the morning. His eyes were round with fright, his mouth drawn taut, and his hand trembled as it explored his throat.

"Merely a warning," Nilssen said. "Try it and you're dead."

"What have I got left?" Eorhic asked in a low, shaky voice, getting to his feet. "Everything I am or own is here. I've lost two home worlds already. Now you want to take this one as well. Can you blame me for trying to stay alive?"

"Morwena is no part of us," Nilssen answered. "She belongs here; and when we go, she stays." The mad fury had left him, freeing his mind. "But you, you don't belong. Don't fool yourself that we'll leave you behind to muddle the future. Either you come with us or you take the consequences." He could not quite say, *or you'll have to be killed.* Five minutes earlier violence had come naturally to him, a disquieting reversal of mood that was akin to discovering a stranger in his own head.

"Hobson's choice," Eorhic muttered, raising an echo in Nilssen's memory, that of Rhys presenting options.

"Not at all," said Nilssen. "We've outgrown revenge by now—"

"And when is 'now?'" asked Eorhic. "For how many years in your City's culture has my name been a byword for monstrous evil? I escaped . . . early on, when at least I was hated for real crimes, even if I was innocent of them. But the story will have been embroidered since, because the people always need a scapegoat. The CNI made a good target, didn't it? Handy, monolithic, mysterious, dripping with so many dirty deals a few extra credits for villainy hardly mattered. . . . In our original world I expect that Russian fellow, Lenin, would have got short shrift too, had he returned from the grave—from 1917 onward the Menshies flung every failure of their five-year plans at his memory and that of his Bolsheviks; yet it was he—

and not Kerensky—who gave them the guts to get their Reformation started. The man who tries and loses is always rewarded with a stinking obituary. Suppose our own Revolution had turned out differently, hey? Would 'republic' be a dirty word?"

Nilssen walked on, ignoring this diatribe. Eorhic trailed him at more than arm's length.

"What would your bribe have been?" Nilssen asked suddenly.

Promptly Eorhic replied, "Keep out of my way and I'll see you set up for life."

"Money?"

"Money, gold, jewels, land, titles—name it."

"And how long do we have to . . . keep out of your way?"

"A month at most."

"So," Nilssen said decisively, "your plan is to sabotage the negotiations."

Eorhic's enthusiasm subsided. "Damn your eyes," he said.

Nilssen smiled. "Did I promise acceptance?"

"I suppose," said Eorhic, "if I returned with you the same double-dealing would apply." He loosened his sword in its sheath. "Your free ride is over, Mister City-man. Nobody can save you but me; and if I get the idea it's not worth my while . . ." Though he stood well clear, he convinced Nilssen that the truce was ended and that he was not afraid to fight the matter out.

However sensible passive noninvolvement had once appeared, Nilssen now knew it would not suffice, else Eorhic would not have asked it of him, so whatever service the king might require would have to be rendered in the hope of rapidly gaining some influence at court. When, a few minutes later, he stood with Yaer and Eorhic in the king's tent, he appreciated the urgency of Eorhic's bid for his cooperation.

"I?" he asked, on being informed of Alfred's wishes. "My lord, is this a serious suggestion?"

"Not you," said Alfred. "It's him I want: Khaled." Yaer's eyebrows twitched but otherwise he showed no surprise. "In all my life I have met no man with his skill for juggling words. If we are finally to beat down these wily Danes, he must be at hand when they come to make terms."

Yaer coughed. It was a hoarse, bronchial noise, a throat-clearing rather than a polite means of drawing attention to himself, yet it served both purposes. "The king flatters me," he said, and Eorhic nodded, his first contribution to the discussion. Nilssen had been unable to warn Yaer of the end of their noninvolvement policy and tried signaling, unsuccessfully. "The customs of the northmen are strange to me," Yaer said, "so what little skill at argument I may be master of would be wasted on them. It might even work against the Saxon cause."

"Nonsense," retorted Alfred, interrupting Eorhic. The king paused. "Ah yes, Eorhic. Your silence has been deafening. What do you think?"

"I would agree with Khaled. Superficially, yes, he would seem ideal . . ." Yaer glanced at Nilssen, caught his concern, and frowned. ". . . but as to insuring that those scum pay in full for all the damage they've done us, well, only a Saxon can know what to demand. These outlanders can't possibly feel as deeply as we do."

Alfred scratched himself. "There's sense in that."

"On the other hand," Yaer said, "my undue modesty ought not to deprive you of my talents which, I confess, are not insignificant. For years I've found it pays to fake stupidity; that way you can win all sorts of arguments. Even before I met Ibrahim, I'd haggled with folk of every kind and clan. In all honesty, my lord, I cannot deny I could help you, provided you call on me as an advisor only."

"Why?" asked Alfred, apparently not displeased at this about-face.

"Because the Danes will be surrendering to Saxons—and Engles. Their pride will not tolerate too much humiliation. Foreigners of our sort ought not to be the ones to present terms—"

"A good point," put in Eorhic. "And it could work, too, if Khaled remains hidden, well back from the confrontation. If you wish, I could be his intermediary. His mouthpiece, as it were."

Alfred looked to Nilssen for comment.

"Khaled?" Nilssen said, yielding at once to Yaer's signal.

Yaer said, "The spokesmen should all be warriors whom the Danes remember from battle, so as to command their respect. Unfortunately, Eorhic was with us at the rear, otherwise he'd be a natural choice."

"I am forced to agree," said Alfred glumly. "My deepest apologies, Eorhic. No disgrace to you, you understand."

"Full well, my lord," replied Eorhic bitterly, casting a malevolent look at Yaer who continued to smile attentively at the king.

"So it is settled," said Alfred. "But Khaled, I expect you to inflict a due penance on them. No misplaced charity is to sway you."

"Have no fear," said Yaer. "I know exactly what to ask."

Bowing stiffly to the king, Eorhic excused himself. As they too left the tent, Nilssen asked Yaer in Arabic, "Can you remember all the terms of the Peace of Wedmore?"

"No," said Yaer blandly. "But the details will be thrashed out in the weeks to come. The crucial meeting is the first, where the tone of the negotiations will be set. That's what mustn't be upset."

As the siege prolonged itself they went about armed, as a pair; they rested, ate, and slept in trusted company, ever vigilant against Eorhic. It was a period of grave danger. Their enemy was never without his sword. When they chanced to meet, Nilssen was conscious of the man's vitriolic hatred, and his desire to break the stalemate with violence.

Others noticed the ill will that had, it seemed, arisen spontaneously between them on the morning after the battle. For a day or two the gossips stirred up sympathy for Eorhic with the story that guarding the Saracens had robbed him of his due battle-honors. Many a wounded soldier who had discovered he would live to brag about that day agreed this to be just cause for a grudge until Alfred let it be known that the foreigners' skills were to be used against the Danes, whereupon Eorhic's dudgeon was at once ascribed to jealousy, an emotion the Saxons also comprehended but held in low esteem. At this news Eorhic's stock immediately fell, while that of the Saracens rose. Privately Nilssen was of the opinion that Yaer had somehow engineered even this reverse of Eorhic's fortunes. It was like him to rub salt in the wound.

For nigh on a fortnight the Saxons watched the Danes and were watched in return. Idle, the army became restless. The farmers complained that their steads were being neglected, the warriors that the Danes were up to no good behind their walls and ought to be rushed before they could recuperate from the hammering they had been given. Increasingly frequently the king had to intervene in quarrels born of boredom. More than one otherwise fine soldier was made an example of. Discipline was maintained, though at cost to the king's health; had the Danes not decided to give in when they did, Alfred might have been forced by illness to leave the siege in less capable hands. As it was, he was stricken by two well-concealed fits. Prolonged hardship had toughened only his will; and the frustrations of holding together an army that was foreign to the natures of those who comprised it, in the face of an enemy believed to be on the point of surrender, was a heart-rot in a leader longing for peace.

Daybreak of Thursday the twenty-second day of May was cold. Windborne dampness hinted at rain in the clouds assembled along the southern horizon. Dense air buffeted the tents and bivouacs of the Saxon and raised trails of sparks from freshly fueled fires. Gritty-eyed men leaned into it as they shuffled about the camp, and in the animal pens the horses and cattle huddled close for warmth.

The king stepped from his tent, buckling on his sword belt and sniffing the wind.

"Rain," he remarked to one of his guards.

"Before noon," the man agreed, stifling a yawn.

"When does your watch end?" asked the king, making small talk as he often did, for it eased tempers wonderfully.

"Within the hour," said the guard, adding so as not to seem a weakling, "yet truly I am as fresh as though the night was not half-spent."

The king shook his head at this boast. "The wise soldier," he reproved the guard gently, "tends his strength no less diligently than his weapons." He waved at the Danish fortifications. "See, they know we will wait forever for them to come out, so they set no watch."

The guard blinked. "Those walls were manned a moment gone."

The second and third royal guards confirmed this. . . .

That, at least, was the official story related by the bards: how the keen-eyed king was first to espy the bare walls; how it was he who ordered the call to arms; and how he stood ready while his army assembled behind him when, alone and helmetless, King Guthrum, leader of the viking horde, mounted the battlements to offer his surernder. . . .

Nilssen's recollection differed in a few details. The discrepancies were trivial, undoubtedly introduced by the bards to improve the dramatic flow of the narrative. . . .

Shortly after dawn the horns began to wail, taking up the alarm one from another as the heralds rubbed sleep from their eyes. Nilssen and Yaer were sharing a tent with Sarnvig and another officer, who at once bolted from their beds, grabbing boots and armor, swearing at each other for being obstructive, falling about as they dressed themselves in the cluttered confines of their shelter. NCOs could be heard raging at their underlings for daring not to be ready for action at a moment's notice. People ran and shouted. Pandemonium prevailed for at least ten minutes, after which Nilssen ventured into the daylight to find the army drawn up between the fort and the camp. If not exactly alert or fully prepared to repulse a Danish sortie, every Saxon was facing the enemy, and only a handful of stragglers still trickled onto parade.

There was then a hiatus that lasted another five minutes. Officers kept looking to Alfred for orders. Unresponsive, he remained staring to the fore, disheveled and ill-tempered, the cross-gartering of his leggings awry to an extent Nilssen was sure would have cost him a lecture from Maia Kim, had she been present. The king was not, it seemed, about to disband his troops without giving the Danes ample opportunity to explain themselves.

Eventually a single Dane peered over the palisade. Ducking down at once, he was succeeded by a bolder individual in a black cloak who showed himself as fully as the chest-high line of stakes allowed. Awed Saxon murmurings identified him as Guthrum, king of all the Danes in Wessex—and, it was widely held, of those elsewhere in Britain too. At any rate, this was the man whose decisions counted for most amongst the infamous Here.

Guthrum was a sharp disillusionment for Nilssen. In his fifties and already succumbing to old age, his long hair hung to his shoulders in two lank gray plaits. and his beard and moustache, though bushy, were mostly white. The faded hair and weathered face looked out of place; Nilssen had been raised to believe in hearty, axe-swinging viking chieftains resplendent in gilded armor and horned helmets. He had to remind himself that this apparently decrepit man had outlasted some of the most violent butchers of the ninth century—the three sons of Ragnar Lodbrok for example: Ubbi, Halfdan, and the frightful Ivar the Boneless, himself no mean strategist and a cold-blooded killer by reputation—and furthermore that the pirates picked leaders for their ability to find them victories and loot. If Guthrum seemed a dotard, that would be a misconcetpion fostered by him to gain his own ends.

Abruptly, with an outstretched arm Alfred silenced his own troops. Then he pointed to Guthrum and let his hand drop.

Guthrum stirred, flicked aside his cloak so that it hung down his back. Revealed were black-enameled chain mail and a black leather tunic studded with silver ornaments. An involuntary hiss of admiration was drawn from the Saxons, who had heard of the wealth amassed by the vikings but hitherto had only glimpsed it in the battle shambles.

The pirate grinned. His teeth were as white as his beard. Then in one curving movement the eye could not quite trace, he raised a spear horizontally above his head, gripping it with both fists. Even at that distance his wrist tendons could be seen to bulge with the ferocity of his grasp. When the spear snapped and the dry *crack* of its rupture followed swiftly, no one betrayed surprise; and when he flung the fragments over the parapet into the charred ruins of no-man's-land, the silence was sustained. Even in defeat he had captured their respect with his ritual gesture.

There was a pause, a period of recognition of the new political reality, before Guthrum shouted, *"Ælfred!"*

"I hear you, Guthrum Dane-king," answered Alfred.

"I will to talk with you."

"Agreed. It is long overdue."

"My man comes—soon, yes?"

"We are ready for him."

So Alfred gained his victory. The king who turned from his vanquished adversary bore tranquility in his face. As he gave orders for the reception of the Danish delegation, he spoke softly. When an hour later the single viking ventured from the fort, clearly prepared to run for cover, the king himself met the man and put him at his ease.

The introductory contact was no more than an exchange of declarations of intent, politely noncommittal. Penance had not been forgotten; the vikings were not forgiven. Alfred was exercising his natural courtesy. In sum it was agreed that negotiations would commence the next day, once Danish hostages had been bartered for limited supplies of food and water. The emissary departed as sheets of rain swept down out of a gray and joyless sky.

CHAPTER SEVENTEEN

For three generations and more the viking northmen had terrorized western Europe with their predatory rampages. Prayers and palisades had failed to turn back their tide; like the sea whose spume-crowned waves were roadways for their longships, they beat repeatedly upon the shores of less warlike peoples. The Christian world cursed their name into nethermost hell. Kings bought them off or saw their realms ruined. Their popular image was of an irresistible horde roving from land to land, insatiably devouring all that was good or godly, for havoc's sake alone.

It was unfortunate, perhaps, that this was only a half-truth. Hailing from a folk who year-in year-out fought against scarcity—of land, of materials, of comfort—the men deserving of the name *viking* were true pirates hunting an easy living. Amongst them there traveled others who knew the worth of toil, whose dream in life was of their own farmstead, who went a-viking because they saw no better way to gain what bad luck had denied them. Younger sons or impoverished sokemen, they sailed outsouth to the fruitful lands, fell in love with the rich earth and the balmy winters, and resolved to stay. In northern Britain and its offshore islands they settled quickly, in thousands, even while their brothers ravaged southward and across the sea into Frankland. By the spring of A.D. 878 they were almost ready for peace, for by then the contest had altered, from a struggle for gold to carry home, to one for the right to remain where they were.

Thus Dane and Saxon recognized what it was they bargained for when they met in Alfred's conference tent. Thus also they understood that any agreement must be durable, fit to last forever if need be.

As was most fitting, neither faction's leader attended the preliminary meetings. Renewed hostilities were still barely a careless phrase away; the emissaries must needs be expendable. Nor would it do for a king to soil his pride in bartering with an enemy until that enemy had proved himself desirous of reconciliation.

Three Danes came, loaded with war finery, girt with gilded ring-mail and brass-bound iron helmets, draped in embroidered cloaks, and hung about with costly jewel-inlaid sidearms. Guthrum had sent *jarlar*, sober nobles who bore their wealth as a birthright and their armor as working clothes. Surrendering their splendid Frankish damascened swords and silver-chased skeggöxes, they remained warriors. Their firm speech neither stumbled nor hastened as they measured out their offers and responses, giving no heed to their tactical inferiority, it seemed. The Saxon representatives found themselves closely matched. Often it was hard to say from the bargaining alone whose had been the field victory. Neither side gave away any advantage.

The cautious battle of words filled the Friday while rain drizzled outside the conference tent and puddles swelled amongst the Saxon lines. The armies, sheltering from the weather, were tensely expectant. When it was decided to prolong the talks by another day, there was much covert sharpening of blades; no one wanted more fighting, but if no agreement could be found, that would be the outcome, regardless of how many hostages the Saxons held.

Yaer secretly reported to Nilssen all that had been said. At the outset the Saxons had demanded heavy fines as restitution for war damage in accordance with Alfred's wishes. The king being unable to press the point in person, the Danes persuaded the Saxons to admit the impracticality of this, suggesting instead a long-term pact of mutual association, of trade, of amicable coexistence. Unsure what to make of this notion, Buhrwit, leader of the Saxon delegation, retired to consult Alfred. The king furiously commanded him to go back and repeat the original demands, until Yaer talked him out of it, counseling moderation for the sake of progress. Resentfully Alfred conceded that even the total extermination of the Danes—itself an impossible undertaking—would not make adequate amends; and Buhrwit returned with Yaer to the conference. For the remainder of the afternoon they haggled over generalities, circling inward towards a consensus.

"It was eerie," Yaer said. "I sat listening, pretending to be a scribe, while they argued for hour after hour. At any moment I could have spoken up and told them what the result would be; but I couldn't, because it had to be worked through with every false trail explored so both sides would realize where their common ground lay."

"Any conclusions?" asked Nilssen.

"So far Guthrum will have to accept Christian baptism, which fits with history. Buhrwit is still insisting on them giving up all of Mercia and East Anglia; I expect that'll be dropped tomorrow, as we know the Danes will hold London until 886—"

"You hope."

Yaer pursed his lips, nodded, and broke into a fit of coughing. "This damp air," he explained huskily.

"Are you well enough?"

"To carry on? Easily." Yaer lowered his voice to a whisper, although they were talking in Arabic. "From what I hear, Eorhic hasn't given up. He's trying to incense Alfred and Buhrwit against the Danes. Even Sarnvig seems to be listening to him."

"What is he saying?"

"That the Danes are being allowed to get away with murder—literally as well as figuratively. It's exactly what a lot of them want to hear. Our friend Eorhic must have been working this line for years; one gets the impression he has a name for being a retributionist."

"A what?" queried Nilssen.

"Werferth's word. He was becoming quite irate with Eorhic because he sees himself as the Saint Augustine of the Danes and doesn't want his golden opportunity of saving souls wholesale to slip away. As a good Christian, Alfred keeps agreeing; but at once Eorhic reminds him how often the pirates have taken baptism to preserve their skins, then reneged. That man is an accursed pest."

"At least it's not going all his way," Nilssen said. He thrust a hand out of the tent, palm uppermost. "The rain's easing. Shall we look in on them?"

But at that moment Sarnvig and their other tentmate stamped in, drunk and angry, so they adjourned all activity for that day. Lying awake under his odoriferous furs, Nilssen speculated on why the failure of the talks should be so desirable to Eorhic. A period of calm, such as the forthcoming Peace of Wedmore would bring, would allow Eorhic to live out the comfortable life he claimed to want; Alfred would see to it that his loyal companions were rewarded after the fighting was over.

Feet squelched in the mud outside the tent, proceeding toward the confrontation line. Over in the Danish camp someone was singing. The words were incomprehensible, but the cheerful tone was as old as humanity, as old as homecoming.

Evidently the Danes still hoped for peace.

The same delegates met on the Saturday at sunrise. The rain clouds had drawn back into the northeast, exposing clear skies. As if responding to the brighter weather, the Danes were more accommodating, the

Saxons less demanding, so that by noon Buhrwit could inform Alfred that the basis of a treaty had been arrived at. The king managed to be forebearing when informed of the terms. For all that the Danes had done better than he had planned, no realist could claim the Saxons' victory had been militarily complete; so winning from the still-powerful enemy half of Mercia and numerous side benefits was enough to start with.

Hearing the news, Nilssen sought out Eorhic. He found him west of the fort, seated on the down's edge, contemplating the flat, forested reaches of the Avon valley. Hailing the man by name, he was ignored. So he sat himself nearby to share the view.

Some minutes elapsed. Riding the steady draft that welled up from the valley, a kestrel climbed from the woods and glided along the slope, either unconscious of the two humans higher up or oblivious to them. Eorhic broke his silence with a languid laugh.

"There," he said. "That's me, hunting a free lunch while you people watched. Does your victory give you pleasure, City man?"

"My name is Nilssen."

"At last, a real label. I never could call you 'Ibrahim' without a qualm—one feels so silly, prolonging a failed charade. . . . What did you want from me, Nilssen? Scope for a good gloat?"

"No," he said.

"Indulge yourself," urged Eorhic. "You've earned it. You and that—What's *his* name incidentally?"

"Yaer."

Eorhic regarded Nilssen sidelong. "Uncommon one that . . . but familiar," he mused. "Oh, yes, of course: from the old days. There was a CNI department head by that name; had a wife who abandoned him with a young son . . ." He shrugged. "However, that's all in the future. Someone else's future."

Nilssen absorbed the new datum on Yaer's schemings. And on Laheer's past.

"Does the future still interest you?" he asked.

"Not much, now." Eorhic reclined on the grass to view the passing clouds. "Alfred has promised me extensive estates in the liberated territories. Should I accept?"

"I wouldn't recommend it."

"Oh? What rival offer can you make to tempt me? A billion hectares of radioactive desert? . . . Come off it, Nilssen, what sort of an incentive is that? You've won your game in stopping me; now go home before I bury you."

"But have we won?" Nilssen asked hoarsely. "You can't be trusted!"

With a snap the kestrel folded its pointed wings and, stooping upon the long grass of the hillside, snatched up a wriggling mouse. Eorhic missed the capture; but when the bird flew off, calling *kee-kee-kee*, he sat up to observe its graceful curving descent into the trees far below. When it had plunged into cover, he answered.

"That bird has its own nature. I have mine. You have yours. Each of us works the way he's made. Now where in God's name does *trust* figure in that?"

Smarting under the reproof, Nilssen corrected himself:

"If we leave you here, how can we know you won't try again?"

"That's better," Eorhic said. "With my track record, I might. But stop and think. Subjectively, I'm almost thirty-eight years old. Here in the ninth century I'll be lucky to make seventy—very lucky, with my predisposition for embroilment in roughhouse politics." A self-deprecating smile crinkled the corners of his eyes. "So I ought to be dead by, say, A.D. 910." He tried to revive the smile; instead he looked haunted by the prospect. "I don't foresee many second chances. Do you?"

"The later Danish wars?"

"Governed by bulk effects. Of all the sociological processes at work around us only the formal institution of the Danelaw is sensitive to interference. And even that took seven years to derail . . . only to be corrected at the eleventh hour by a comedy team of ham-fisted amateurs."

"Thanks," retorted Nilssen.

"Don't grab all the credit. Not infrequently I suspect there's a force at work in the world which holds history true to form." A featherlight touch of *déjà vu* brushed Nilssen's awareness; intently he listened to Eorhic's calm deliberations. "Destiny? Could be; the northmen say the Norns are the ones who weave the world's future, and the Greeks had a similar idea.

"I admire the Greeks: clear thinkers. But the northmen have the measure of fate's coldness, the mechanical process that balances event against event without regard to virtue. Nilssen, I *have* tried to fight this force, but all I've proved is that we humans will always fail if we challenge it. I'm no threat. Can't you see that?"

"If you'd explain what you were after, maybe I could learn to . . . live with the idea."

"I'll try." Eorhic resettled himself in the rank grass, reflected a moment, and launched himself into a speech throughout which Nilssen sensed emotions bubbling beneath the placid crust of words. It seemed the man bared his soul no less than his secret ambitions, as in a confessional.

"Alfred," he began, "is a romantic idealist. He sees himself master of an all-conquering army, one day driving the Danes back into the North Sea without giving or asking quarter. He wants this land for the 'Engle-Race' and no part of the Danes or their doings. His loathing for them, as you have seen, sometimes verges on hysteria.

"On the other hand is Guthrum, a realist, an exceptionally farsighted viking. He'll tolerate even the indignity of Christian baptism to gain his political ends. Over the years some one hundred fifty thousand of his nation have settled in England, so that he now holds about a third of the country. And that is enough for him, for now. What his sons or his successors do is up to them; Guthrum wants peace so he can consolidate his gains. Knowing the dangers of overextension, he'll wait until what he holds is his, land, stock, and population.

"Compare him with Alfred, so different from the super-king we were taught to revere at school. Our earnest, wild-brained Engle-king would go against a people who now think of this land as their home and drive them out, no compromise. Does he understand what he asks of his forces? Has he heard of genocide? Of the fierce defense of *lebensraum* these Danes will put up?

"And yet Guthrum could not do without Alfred; and Alfred needs Guthrum. Opposed, just *so,* they balance each other at a critical point in the social evolution of Britain. Without Guthrum to keep his mind concentrated on the military health of his kingdom, Alfred would abandon himself to scholarly works and social reform; and within a score of years he'd be displaced by some ambitious eorl whose mind is focused on more earthy matters than justice or good laws.

"Conversely, Guthrum would destroy the unity of his own side were he much stronger. It's enough that he should have forced a truce at Edington—and, mark me, some of Alfred's followers will interpret this deal as a defeat. Now Guthrum can go to his jarls and ohtors and use it to save face while he counsels a time of recuperation. Should they demur, he can threaten them with Alfred who, though badly mauled in this clash, could gain a devastating victory at their next.

"So each side wins what it needs, and the two halves of a developing proto-nation can grow toward maturity for the few years that are required. And there, Nilssen, is where you destroyed me: I'd have tipped the balance in Alfred's favor, not Guthrum's. Followed through, this weak victory could have become a resounding triumph for the Saxons.

"Thereafter . . . Well, Alfred would be by far the more unstable of the two leaders, easier to control once he anticipated endless peace. I could have taken command of the army, like *that*; and believe me, matters would have gone very differently with me in charge."

"I do believe you," said Nilssen, awed by Eorhic's ambition and the apparent ease with which he might have succeeded. "And what of the army now?"

"It will degenerate into its old ways: a rabble of yes-men dying for their favorite lords. It failed, Nilssen; they won't want to retain my newfangled nonsense now."

"It might have worked."

"It might. Nevertheless, it was I who failed to seize the advantage, I who should have known that an army is worthless without its appropriate leader."

Eorhic plucked a grass stalk and stripped away its leaves until no more than the bare, pale-green stem remained. This he threw down the slope like a spear. The wind frustrated his aim, tossing it wide, far over the flank of the hill.

"You threatened to change the future," Nilssen said, "as though it meant a lot to you."

"Scare tactics."

"Was that all?"

"Oh, if the City were wiped out, so much the better."

"But you came by way of the City—"

Eorhic frowned.

"—so if it vanishes, so do you."

"Maybe that's why I failed," Eorhic said, his voice sugary with sarcastic wonderment. "Do you suppose I haven't been over my tracks thousands of times? Re-

considering all my moves, racked by second thoughts.
. . . God, I remember—" Shaking his head, he stopped
himself.

"What do you remember?"

"Private memories."

"If they have a bearing on our problem, you ought
to air them."

"November the seventh, 2011?"

"Oh," said Nilssen, more calmly than his own refreshed memories warranted.

"Any other day," said Eorhic bitterly, "but something forced it to be *that* particular Monday, the one
after Republic Sunday. No other day would fit so
well: when in an eyeblink cities were transformed to
ashes at the onset of the final breakthrough; when the
Changes spread like a racing cancer, remolding our
world into the one we would have lived in, had we
not discovered time travel and averted The War. . . .
God knows, Nilssen, I can never forget that, though I
swear I was blameless."

"Shall we stick to facts we can agree on?" said
Nilssen.

"Fact one, then. I was in Oxford for the holiday.
Around dawn the CNI contacted me through the local
office. Their scraps of news matched far too well with
a report I'd handled only months earlier. A physicist
called Frobisher—"

"I know of him," said Nilssen drily. "You might say
he's a civic hero . . . headed the Theory Section at the
Institute of Hypothetical Physics. Right?"

"The same, yes. Frobisher had an idea we were due
for trouble and went so far as to characterize it. 'Massive faulting in sequential time' was his formal word-
ing. Spontaneous imprinting of parallel world-lines on
our own, and a general collapse of statistical processes. Some electronic components would no longer
work properly—Zener and tunnel diodes, for example.
Gamblers would have fantastic runs of good and bad

luck. Freaks of weather and waves at sea. His list ran to several pages. He argued that we should prepare an escape route using our time-travel technology.

"I had learned to take Frobisher seriously, so we did what he said. By the onset of the Collapse we'd quietly shipped out most of what was thought useful to the colony that we established in the far future and away from our time line. That Monday I knew *that* was where I had to go.

"Of course, I'd never visited the new sanctuary—your City—but the IHP was where the gates to it were hidden. Despite the refugees choking the roads away from London, Windhurst Hill was the place to start looking.

"I remember: I'd gone to the Oxford CNI Ops Room and a sergeant had just handed me a cup of coffee when I made my decision. *'Keep it hot for me,'* I said, loudly so everyone could hear, then I walked straight out through the duty room and down to the armory.

"There was a siren wailing; it sounded like the one on the Bodelian roof. No one guessed I was deserting. No one questioned me when I signed out a rifle, nor when I requisitioned the only vehicle left in the motor pool. Coordination was falling apart, like the whole world.

"The staff who'd stayed at their posts were the loyal ones. The rest had decamped with whatever they thought would keep them alive. The antiquated van in the garage must have seemed fit for scrap, too ruinous to reach even the open road. But I knew—because I made it my business to check the records—that it was one of our surveillance hides, outwardly a wreck, inwardly well-maintained and only short of a cylinder of gas. That I got by flagging down an ambulance in the street."

"They had one to spare?" asked Nilssen uneasily.

Eorhic's explanation was blandly rational, as though

he fully appreciated the unlikeliness of this eventuality. "Well, I did have to take it. I shouted to the driver. My uniform must have reassured him because he pulled up to ask what was wrong, which was when I shot him. Had to be done, otherwise the van would have been no good to me."

"And I suppose you shot the patients too?"

"Oh no. They were all melt-cases, caught on the fringes of a big Change. Scarcely one whole limb between all six. No sense in hurting *them*. . . . Anyhow, the van failed me again a few klicks outside Oxford and took some fixing. What with that and some other bother, my arrival at the IHP was delayed to mid-afternoon.

"Fires had burned out the woods around the Institute. Most of the site was rubble, apparently abandoned. That was when I began to worry. I was convinced it was finished for me; after all my trouble, I had no idea how to find the escape gates. The only promising place was a multistory building still in good shape; but there were bars on every window and armor-glass doors that would soak up more rifle bullets than I possessed."

A peculiar calm had settled on Nilssen as the tale of callous murder and selfishness progressed. He could not determine quite when he began to recognize its pattern; all that mattered was that when Eorhic paused for breath, no more really needed to be added. He was convinced that what remained unsaid was already painfully familiar.

But Eorhic was engrossed in reliving his last days as Eric Halvey. Unaware of his peril, he actually smiled as he recalled subsequent developments.

"Old Frobisher had promised miracles. Good ones, bad ones. That day he delivered all kinds. Nilssen, unless you're a gambling man you won't credit this, but I had the most incredible bit of luck. I'd been walking around searching for about an hour, just long enough to be considering suicide as a way out, when two late-comers turned up."

"A man and a woman?" Nilssen asked woodenly.

"That was a good guess."

"Plenty of staff members or people temporarily posted to the Institute went home for their families. Most never returned. A few missed the boat. Largely the successful escapees were individuals. It happened so fast."

"Yes," said Eorhic agreeably, "that makes sense."

"And then?" asked Nilssen, to be sure of his man.

"They were running for the modern building when I spotted them. Obviously they had a key to the doors, a key I had to have. Within seconds they'd be safe inside, so I ordered them to stop. When they didn't obey me, I fired at them."

"How neat and logical," said Nilssen. "Did anyone ever praise your determination?"

Scornfully Eorhic said, "For thirty-eight years it has kept me alive and whole. Until you've tried it—"

"I'm not knocking it, truly. For twenty-six years a very special determination has kept me going. In this respect we two do share a common interest."

Eorhic seemed about to ask questions, so Nilssen said, "Do finish what you were telling me."

Eorhic appeared reluctant to continue, so that Nilssen had to prompt him:

"Obviously you stopped them."

"I hit the woman."

"Why did you shoot?"

"They were almost inside—what difference does it make now?"

"One's attitude to the taking of life always makes a difference. Especially human life; for some reason we humans prize it most highly. Do you suppose that man dismissed her murder so quickly?"

"It wasn't murder . . . But I didn't say I killed her!"

"Oh, but you did. How could you not? An expert like you. You'd make a point of being good with any weapon."

"Yes," Eorhic admitted. "Yes, when she fell, the signs were there. He dragged her inside. Luckily he abandoned his pass card in the checker, so the doors were still unlocked when I reached them.

"I searched that building, starting at the top. Later it dawned on me that I should have followed the blue lights I saw everywhere. By then I'd lost time. Almost by accident I found the woman in one of the offices, dead. She was so beautiful. Nilssen, I tell you, I cried at what I'd done. The CNI was no band of saints, but we never did anything without a reason. And killing her . . . one more pointless death; they should have waited!"

"It was a stupid, stupid waste," Nilssen whispered. "I cried also, Eric Halvey, down inside me, for twenty-six years. For twenty-six years I waited for you; but you never came. I wanted to meet that man who murdered my wife, planning what I'd say, what I'd do.

"Now that I've found you, I'm too late. Almost eighteen centuries late. You happened so long ago I can't decide what would make amends. You are right; her death was pointless. An empty gesture, Halvey. So maybe my killing you would be also. It's a funny old world."

Eorhic's face was white with shock. It twitched. His cheek muscles bunched themselves in a palsied jitter; his right hand reached to press into the grass for support while his left hand crept up to scratch at an insect bite on his chin. The left began to shake. He thrust it between his knees, trapping it.

"You must hate me," he said.

"Must? Or ought? Do you want me to condemn you?"

"God in heaven!" cried Eorhic. "How can you be so cold-blooded?"

"Because I don't dare to hate you after all. That would make it personal."

"Isn't your wife personal enough?"

"I'm not allowed your luxury of selfishness. My people are owed you. Your debt goes way beyond me." He wanted to laugh to drive out his disappointment. "And that's worse than never finding you. Until today, this minute, I could have taken you back for execution, as ordered, and felt I'd achieved something important."

"So that stuff about a pardon was a lie?"

"Who mentioned pardons? I said we'd outgrown revenge, Halvey. The City requires a balancing of the account, that's all."

Eorhic shuddered. "And I thought the CNI was methodical. . . . Listen, would it help if I tried to make up for it?"

"Unless you're being insulting, there's only one way to do that."

Momentarily Eorhic was nonplussed. Then he jumped to his feet, red-faced, yelling, "Get up! If what it takes to clear the score is my neck, you can damn well fight me for it!"

Standing, Nilssen rested his left hand on the hilt of his new sword. The temptation was acute.

He took a step forward. Eorhic drew his own sword and bent his legs, balancing himself for a leap either to left or right, his free left arm spread wide as a counterweight to the mass of steel in his right hand. Another step by Nilssen brought Eorhic within a blade's length.

"How old are you?" Eorhic asked. "Thirty-five? Forty?"

"Forty-seven."

"My compliments to the City doctors. . . . By now,

if my reckoning is right, you and I have traded age handicaps. I've become ten years younger than you are Nilssen; and we've both grown older since the old days. My guess is you've spent your life behind a desk, getting soft. But mine has been one long slog of war and hard living. I'm fit. And I'm strong. Don't make me dirty my blade on you.'"

Throughout the years since Eva's death Nilssen had cherished an image of a faceless man in a corner, cowering away from retribution. Now that man had a face; but it was a brazenly unrepentant face that taunted him. Eorhic was a man without a conscience, a perpetual citizen of the selfish present, incapable of lasting remorse or fear. For him punishment was the abstract creation of an alien morality, a weapon he employed without understanding its purpose or true power. Fear, pleasure, anger, sorrow, all were the short-lived catalysts of decisions he made on a cerebral level. He did not, could not, identify with the feelings of another person, even if that person was himself of another day or hour. His show of sorrow had undoubtedly been synthetic. A man of that sort could not be punished.

"You are afraid of me," jeered Eorhic.

Nilssen welcomed the insult as an excuse to ignore his wiser instincts. His silence provoked Eorhic to goad him further.

"Your woman would have been proud of you. It calls for real cunning to back down at the proper time, so you can keep her memory alive year after year, bravely defending it with words. Such a shame you lack the guts—"

Straight-armed, Nilssen struck Eorhic a whipcrack blow across the face with his open hand. The impact stung his fingers. Beard stubble rasped his palm. But Eorhic's head snapped right, then left, his eyes rolling as he reeled back. His feet tripped in the long grass, and the sword spun out of his hand, spearing the turf several yards away. With a thud he fell heavily on his side. Then he groaned.

"You understand," said Nilssen, "that this changes everything. I intend to dispose of you personally. Properly, in a duel. The memory of Eric Halvey is already discredited; all that remains is to do the same for Eorhic of Æsces-dun. There'll be no one to tell of your great deeds, your lof-daedum around the mead-hall fire, because you'll have been erased from history within a decade. No saga for you; only a shabby ending."

Rubbing his left cheek, Eorhic took a deep breath and spat bloody sputum onto the grass. "A square fight?" he said.

"With rules."

"Then I can't wait."

"Your kind of rules," Nilssen amended.

"What the hell does that mean?" There was the edge of panic in his voice.

Nilssen turned away about to leave. "Don't ask me," he said. "Ask yourself." Now he sensed that his enemy was learning fear; and he was, in part, satisfied.

CHAPTER EIGHTEEN

Slamming down the lid of his treasure chest, the king pounded its iron-cased oak with a white-knuckled fist.

"In God's name, *why*?" he demanded of Nilssen. "Why must it be blood? All this I have offered you: three times the wergild any wife of commoner might command in law; safe conduct to the port of your choice; passage therefrom to Frankland; and a handsome bursary besides. I can do no more, Saracen. Why lust for his life?"

Doggedly Nilssen repeated himself:

"I seek the right of trial by arms against Eorhic of Æsces-dun, in settlement of the blood debt he owes me by virtue of his slaying of my wife seven years ago. Will you grant me this?"

Releasing a huge sigh, Alfred dropped into a chair.

"I thought to have found in you a fount of Christian charity, for all that you worship heresies."

"This is no cause for charity."

"Nor is any slaying, Saracen, whether in war or peace. These ancient feuds are no fitting answer to the bereaved relations, dividing stead 'gainst stead, town 'gainst town. They are the devil's instigations. Our Lord commanded us, Saracen, that if a man offend you seventy times seven, yet shall you forgive him."

"We revere him as a prophet too," said Nilssen with stubborn calm. "But often the Mosaic law commends itself better to human needs—and sensibilities."

"What are you saying?" the king asked severely. "Why that sly regard towards the door?"

They were now in Aller, having removed thence from the Ethan-dun rather than to the comparative hardships of the Athelney fort. Fort and vill were only a few miles apart; but the greater altitude of the vill lifted it out of the flyblown humidity of the summertime marshes. The extra thickness of the overlapped plank walls and reed-thatched roofs gave shelter from the soporific temperatures of a three-week heat wave. Too, there were more creature comforts, like fresh food from the farm and proper lodgings. Reacquainted with civilized living, already the royal retinue were beginning to liken the recent battle to the feats of ancestral valor. Heads were stuffed with bards' tales of courage and vengeance, leaving no room for latterday softheartedness. Nilssen had only to add, "The folk are of a mind to see bold justice done, my lord," for Alfred to recognize the ineffectuality of his objections.

"Then by all means let us talk of justice and the law," he said with a languid coolness that gave Nilssen pause. "Your part in this feud, for example. How was it you forebore to declare it to me on your arrival?"

"I—" He clamped his mouth shut, frantically considering how to escape the trap. There were dire penalties for not declaring feuds, for the king's vicinity was sacrosanct. Quickly he extemporized, "Eorhic was not at once recognizable. Only after the battle was he unmasked."

"How convenient. And in the interim he befriends you, when one might in reason see his blade held to your throat as surety for your silence. How is this, Saracen? One—no, two—of your kind traveling free amid Christendom ought to kindle remembrance in the dampest memory—and his, we learn, is tinder-dry. Suddenly he rails against you as a long-lost foe, a

monster of revenge, the archetype of infidel savagery."
His mouth turned down at the corners as he bridged
his fingers before him and eyed the golden signet ring
he wore. "Am I a fool, Saracen?"

"Not in my estimation, lord Alfred."

"Why, then, must you both entreat me as one?"
Brown eyes, intelligent, quick to perceive facial signals,
steadied their aim on Nilssen.

"Both of us?"

"As well you know." Waiting. Watching. A dry,
shallow laugh: "I think you do . . . Eorhic has rarely
been one to start a quarrel. Now he comes with naked
murder in his hand, begging no less than you: the
right of final settlement. There's a weirdness, wouldn't
you say?"

The truth, even a part-truth? The easy solution. An
explanation to reunite the shattered fragments of the
feud. So hazardous too—an explanation bound to be
taken as an affirmation of madness, absolute excuse for
dismissal of his case. No, Alfred was no Sigewulf. The
untutored brigand had discerned honesty; the cultured
king saw only justice.

"When the leaf falls from the tree, my lord, can
man say where it will rest? Rest it must, though borne
many leagues by the tireless wind. A weirdness there
too, perhaps, that it should chance upon this spot
rather than that? Its travels dwindle, in summary, to
but a few words—that it fell to earth far from its
parent tree. Thus also are the lives of men."

"How prettily you play with words," murmured
Alfred. "But leaves are not lives. Do not ward off my
questions with kennings, Saracen."

"Then I can say only that it is a story with many
byways," Nilssen told him bluntly. "We each have
agreed the feud exists, that in his youth Eorhic came
on pilgrimage to Rome where I and my wife were,
attendant upon the Aglabid ambassadors; that he
there did take her life. An accident it may have been,

yet he fled from investigation. Now we are met, his terror of never-failing pursuit has nerved him to meet my challenge. This is agreed by all."

"Yes," admitted Alfred. "But it stinks of Khaled's deceits." Withdrawing into his thoughts, he finally said, "Go, then, and fight. It seems the price of peace is never paid in full."

Bowing, Nilssen said, "Thank you, my lord."

"Stay a moment," said Alfred, causing him to halt at the door. "King Guthrum will be here tomorrow. Since, by custom, three nights must pass before the duel, you will postpone it until he has gone. It would be unseemly to entertain the Danes with our disputes."

"How long must we wait?"

"Tomorrow is the fourteenth day of June and the Sabbath eve. The Sabbath itself will be the day of baptism. We leave for Wedmore on the Tuesday. So, the day after?"

"Wednesday the eighteenth will be perfect," said Nilssen.

Five days. Five sunsets. Five dawns. Five nights of thinking: will it be me? As he left the king's presence, he was shaking with the onset of a fit of terror that did not fade away for several hours.

During the past winter Aller had naturally been visited by bands of Danes. Finding it deserted and provisionless, they had gone their way without firing it so as to avoid drawing trouble to themselves. The Saxons controlled most of the marshlands and were swift to hunt down intruders. Come the spring and Saxon victory, therefore, the vill had quickly been revived as domestic staff and livestock drifted in from their refuges. With the arrival of the royal entourage, the halls again gleamed with treasures, the walls were coated in costly hangings, and the stagnant odor of desertion was displaced by a pervasive aroma of woodsmoke.

Wandering through the bustling stead, Nilssen came upon Yaer by the goose pen. The psychologist was leaning over the low withy fence, winning the honking acclaim of the pen's inmates with chunks of moldy bread.

"Doing your bit for the vill, Yaer?" he asked dispiritedly.

Yaer put a finger to his lips. "This is a controlled experiment. Please keep your voice down."

Nilssen had wanted a heart-to-heart talk with Yaer but was curious to learn what he was up to. "Geese like bread," he whispered. "Surely you knew that?"

"Not these."

"They're eating it."

"Look closer. *Some* are; they're the ones who've learned in the last couple of minutes that the stuff's edible. The gooseherd tells me they always get mash or, more usually, go out to graze in the fields. The noisy ones are those who suspect they're missing out on something, resent it like hell, but haven't plucked up the courage to try this new food."

"They've got sense. I wouldn't touch that stuff, myself. Why don't they test a bite?" For the moment Nilssen had forgotten his problems.

"That's the experiment, to see how well their initiative relates to their place in the pecking order, which I've already established by observation before introducing this variable element. So far the brave ones win on both counts."

"Are you surprised?"

"Not especially."

"So why do it?"

"To check my guess."

"You never stop," said Nilssen. A couple of feeding geese raised their heads; and after a moment's thought Yaer copied them.

"This world is full of intriguing questions," he said. "So *alive* . . ."

"But a death trap for us. And a mindkiller; look at Eorhic, alone and scared, haunted by the world-that-will-be." ·

Yaer shook himself from his trance. "Though he'd deny it, Eorhic wants to return. He might have come with us if you hadn't warned him what to expect in the City." Tossing another gray-green chunk of bread at the geese, he asked: "What of the duel?"

"The king agrees."

Yaer licked his lips slowly. "What decided him?"

"Your point about the popular mood."

"I feel I ought to be pleased." Another handful of breadcrumbs was scattered. "You'll reconsider taking the staff with you?"

"No. It stays in your hands. . . . Yaer, I've sent for Morwena. Afterward, if necessary, will you see her safely to Henglafingasham?"

"I'll do what I can—but why are you so bent on risking yourself, Jerlan? Allow me to go home for help—"

"No. You'd reappear in front of Kwambe's guns. If Laheer's sympathies do lie with the CNI . . ."

"It was always only a possibility."

"But a real one. This muddle can't be stretched to include another loop through time."

"Have you forgotten Eorhic's skill with the sword?"

"He will lose."

Yaer raised an eyebrow.

"Call it faith," Nilssen said. "Or logic. Kwambe's worms can help us if we keep our heads. We're tracing one that leads beyond this fight through several futures, through my own past at least twice. I won't be allowed to lose."

"And does Eorhic suspect?"

"I think he does. But he's not the sort to take it seriously."

"So." Yaer impaled the residue of his bread on the fence above the reach of the geese. "May I borrow your sword?"

Nilssen drew it from its scabbard with a dry, slithering sound. Sunlight blazed from the exposed blade as he passed it across.

"What a blessing to be certain that God is on your side," said Yaer.

"Are you being sarcastic?"

"Who? Me?" Yaer gave an amused snort, then remarked, "I rather think these Danes will make eminently practical Christians."

Tartly Nilssen said, "I hadn't given it much thought, actually."

"You should. Faith is a rotting ladder worth frequent examination: useful at first, one day it may not bear your weight. Christ will join the Norse pantheon; he won't replace it outright."

"An insurance policy—the best of both?"

"Precisely . . ." Yaer swung the sword experimentally. "Weeks ago, when you accused me of treating Shazol's doctrine as my religion, I failed to grasp your meaning. Even you, I think, missed the point. Age reduces the human mind's tolerance of imprecision. As it grows less flexible, it prefers certainties, whether warranted or groundless. Hence faiths. And systems, generalizations, summaries, codes of conduct, rules-of-thumb. Gods too: we worship those which suit us. Frequently a multitude of gods go by one name. The vikings' Christ is not King Alfred's, nor Bishop Werferth's nor the One we learned about as children, by whom Eorhic swears so casually. The Muslims whom you and I impersonate see him from another angle altogether. In just the same way history is stripped of its circumstantial oddities so it will fit comfortably in books to please simple tastes.

"But we, Jerlan, we of the City dare not hold too great a faith in any god or doctrine. Being portions of Reality, they are illusions. Believe what you wish about intangibles. Draw comfort from them. But don't rely on them to save you despite yourself.

"I agree that Eorhic seems doomed. I do not agree that you will necessarily survive. In Henglafingasham Morwena only reported words you were supposed to have said. Anyone could have briefed her. Your life is not charmed. Nor is mine. We are candles in a hurricane."

So bleak. So uncompromisingly cynical. In his imagination Nilssen walked again through the village, through the wintry darkness between the huts. Morwena's joy had warmed his spirit then, though it had perplexed him. Incredulity had been too much a part of it, as though she had already seen—

"Impossible," he whispered. "She would have said!"

"If she knew you had died?" asked Yaer. "Why should she? A dying friend swears to return; when he does, do you waste time telling him what happened?" He fell silent a moment. "You're besotted with this fantasy. Fatally so. Eric Halvey is not an honorable man. He'll fight dirty. Treat him accordingly: catch him unawares and overdose him with drugged darts. Then vanish to safety."

It was reasonable counsel. It ought not to repel him; yet it did, for all that Eorhic was no saint. He said, "The Saxons regard a man's reputation as his chance at immortality. Tell someone that his fame will live forever and you praise him highly. I find myself drawn to that idea. If I have to go, it'll be as myself, not as a subscriber to Eorhic's ethics."

"Think about it," Yaer insisted.

"I have. And the decision is made."

"By you, yes. But not by me."

Nilssen wrested his sword from Yaer and resheathed it with a crash of steel on brass. "Keep out of this fight, Yaer."

"Only if you'll listen to my advice."

"Advice? Is that your euphemism for the string-pulling you've indulged in since Yardstick began? You listen to me for a change: Morwena may only have been the trick that got us here, but to me she's not expendable. Sigewulf threw away his life because of us. Without him, hers will be worth next to nothing amongst people who exploit mutes as idiots. That's a debt we clear before we go. I don't care overmuch if you don't help; but if you interfere, I'll cheerfully break your neck."

"Fair warning," said Yaer. "But you do realize, Jerlan, that Morwena isn't Eva?"

There was a blade of ice in his chest. It had slipped in so smoothly that the cut at first gave no pain; only when Yaer twisted his question did the psychic wound open to the cold air.

"Saving one will not save both—you understand? Do not pretend to yourself that by transferring compassion from Eva to Morwena you can eradicate your past failure through present action. As you told me yourself, Eorhic shot Eva; that is part of you. Morwena is one of the world's abundance of pitiable wretches. Reality is compassionless. Don't try to edit your life. Let yourself become involved and you'll be eradicated; brood on it and you'll go mad, as mad as some City agents I've tried to cure. As to the debt: wasn't Morwena happy in Henglafingasham?"

Nilssen leaned on the fence and stared at the geese which loitered in front of him emitting occasional hopeful honks. Offended by the mycotic stench of the bread, he hooked it off its post into the enclosure, where it was efficiently reduced to crumbs by the birds.

"Why did you have to come?" he groaned. "I knew where I was going."

"You were lost and going nowhere," said Yaer. "That's why I had to come. I came to be your guide, to retrieve you from a maze into which I had let you wander. A dreadful mistake was made, Jerlan, when I selected you for Yardstick: a flaw in myself made me blind to the same one in you."

"But you said I was ideal."

"I said you were the best, the best available at that time."

"I don't feel flawed."

"Nor did I; it doesn't show up like that. The flaw was, and remains, that you and I had made a discovery. We'd found the way out of the City."

"There's no escape from the City," said Nilssen, touching the slabs of his stabilizer belt through his djellaba's folds. "Not while we have to wear these things."

"Escape is a state of mind. In time it can become a state of being. Eorhic got away. His biggest adjustment was to local ways; but he seems to have managed. Others could too, even if they had to wear stabilizers."

"That," said Nilssen after some thought, "is a very dangerous idea. Could it be so straightforward?"

"With the aid of a pair of cargo gates it would be still simpler," said Yaer. "A lot of people would be tempted to try it."

"And you thought I hoped to stay here?"

Yaer shook his head. "Not consciously. But there were bound to be powerful distractions. To compensate I had to talk you into letting me come."

Exasperated, Nilssen asked, "Have I made *any* of my own decisions?"

"Enough. Most in fact. The truth is, my professional advice has been my least important contribution. I came along as an irritant, Jerlan, to keep your mind on your work. Eorhic wasn't the only person to think up the complement-of-types configuration: most of what he said about Alfred and Guthrum being constructively antagonistic applies to us as well."

"My God," said Nilssen. "I thought you were just being bloody superior at my expense." The humorous aspect of the situation undermined his resentment of Yaer and he began to laugh. Yaer joined him. The geese appeared nonplussed.

Sobering after a minute or so, Nilssen said, "But that still leaves us with Eorhic."

Yaer looked at him. Nodding, he said seriously, "And Morwena. Take my advice, will you? Leave for Henglafingasham tonight with her."

"And you?"

"I'll deal with Eorhic."

With his tears of laughter still cold on his cheeks Nilssen found all vestiges of humor had left him. "No," he said firmly. "He shot Eva. As you said, that's part of me. But don't you see, that makes this duel part of *her*, the last and only contact we can ever share. If either you or I must execute him on behalf of the City, shouldn't I be the one?"

"You only *think* you want to do it!" said Yaer.

"Has my free will been rigged, then? I worried about that once, before the futility of fighting the system settled my doubts. So maybe I've been programmed to want a fight with Eorhic; and maybe your job is to argue against it. Personally, I agree with the motives I've been given and am happy to oblige. How about you? What does it feel like to be inside an experiment for once, Doctor Yaer?"

A minute passed. Then, wrinkling his nose, Yaer glanced at the geese. "Peculiar," he admitted. "If true."

King Guthrum led thirty of his noblest lords into Aller before noon the next day. Though all were mounted on strong horses and had managed a swift journey, they were nonetheless travel-weary and anxious to refresh themselves. At once they were engulfed by Alfred's determined hospitality and vanished from public view until the Sunday morning, when they reappeared, shorn of their barbaric finery. Their armor and weapons had been exchanged for plain white linen trousers and belted, open-necked shirts, as be-

fitted humble candidates for baptism. Meekly they
marched into the chapel, and closed the doors behind
them. The eaves rang with the hosannas of Werferth's
ministry; the reek of incense was strong, far down-
wind. Afterward when only their brows, bound with
white linen bands to protect the anointed portions
of their earthly bodies, betrayed their salvation, they
surrendered themselves to renewed feasting in Alfred's
hall, where they praised the Saxon ale and ogled the
Saxon women, all the while proclaiming everlasting
brotherhood.

In person Guthrum was an urbane, approachable
fellow, lacking in the studied deceits of courtliness
but invested with ample innate subtlety. His English
served him without adornment. His humor was that
of a man of flint and steel: hard and sparkling, quickly
quenched in the cold pool of his self-reserve. Those
with him, although individually recognizable as distinct personalities, were of his kind. In conversation
they were discreet without quite being so rude as to
be secretive; in pleasure they were wholehearted, yet
never overindulgent. As Yaer observed to Nilssen, the
Danes were still their own masters; Alfred had a shock
coming to him if he thought them tamed.

But the Danes were short-term guests at Aller. The
holiday was soon over and the combined entourage
of the two kings readied itself for the remove to Wedmore, north by some fourteen miles and away from
the humid marshes. There the weather would be
cooler, the air fresher and more conducive to clear
thinking and detailed treaty-making.

The column of dignitaries, soldiers, baggage mules,
and sundry servants was on the point of departure
when Nilssen and Yaer were summoned to attend
Alfred at the vill-gate. From horseback he studied
them. He looked the complete king in his royal garb,
armed and decorated beyond the ambitions of peasant
folk. A new purple cloak hung from his shoulders,

casting shadows in which gold and silver fittings gleamed on silk-trimmed linen tunic and dark red leather belt; the golden buckles which fastened the cloak at his shoulders were inlaid with rubies and black enamel. His new boots, which extended up to his calves, were also of red leather, soft but thick. He had been freshly barbered and smelled of scented oils. The regard with which he fixed Nilssen was one of purest contempt.

"Saracen," he said, his lower lip trembling, "we shall not, I trust to God, meet again in this life. Chance we do, one of us shall quit it forthwith. I cannot judge whether you have spat upon my charity, so have prayed to our Lord that justice may be done. Nonetheless, should you survive, it is my wish that you do not trouble my kingdom further. There is about you an unwholesomeness that steals slowly upon the sensibilities of good men, else I doubt not that Sigewulf would never have bound me to yield that sword to you—it grieves me that it should come to be the instrument of peril to my loyal companion Eorhic.

"The housecarls now have orders to supply only your simple needs. Sarnvig will remain to see fair play at the duel. Furthermore, for reasons I cannot unravel, the woman Morwena also wishes to linger in your company.

"So be it. May God grant you such mercy as He deems fitting. I can leave you only my ill will."

"My lord—" Nilssen protested too slowly: the young king had wheeled his horse about and was noisily galloping out of earshot. In a tumult of hooves and feet and jangling armament the column moved off after him. Passing faces turned and stared uncomprehendingly at the pair of bedraggled outlanders who stood so forlornly by the gate. Blithely, two nations marched out to shape their future.

CHAPTER NINETEEN

The waning moon sank into clouded night. Since sunset the previous evening fitfully persistent rain had spattered Aller-stead from the indigo cavern of the sky. Now and then it had eased, admitting moonlight in crazy webwork patterns among the clouds before emphatically reestablishing its dank tyranny over the isles and marshes of Somerset. Toward dawn, its force spent, it had died away. For a while water gurgled in the drainage gulleys of the stead; thatched roofs shed plashing droplets; the moist air smelled of damp straw, of mud, of plants, of animals, of people. Stillness returned as light crept through the clouds. Gradually the gray-blue, steel-blue, inverted landscape of the sky broke into clumped, sooty smudges, ripped apart, first here then there, in vivid turquoise gashes of open air. By four o'clock friend could be distinguished from foe at a hundred paces; by five the effulgent yellow disc of the sun itself had cleared the hills, dispelling the last loitering traces of the night.

A moorhen cried out harshly, was echoed by the hillside. A nearby sparrow paused in its mindless chirping. Sarnvig raised his eyes and moodily surveyed the brightening marsh.

"It's like to be a hot day," he said to Nilssen and Eorhic. "Pity to waste it."

They were alone on the north shore of the River Parrett on the last of the firm ground before the peat bogs. Directly opposite them in midstream was the island designated for the duel. To reach it dry-shod they had hired the services of a local fowler and his skin boat. Now they only awaited the peasant's return from the island. Already he was approaching, making laborious progress with his single paddle.

"Be guided by me," Sarnvig said, too proud to plead with them openly, "Alfred would rejoice if your feud were to be abandoned, even so late as this." Significant glances at Nilssen and Eorhic won him no response. The fowler came on slowly; his paddle flashed, dripped water, dipped, stirred the surface flecked with duck-weed, rose streaming. The boat waggled its fat hull as he stroked alternately to port and starboard.

Sarnvig rubbed his eyes with the backs of his hands. Seemingly despite himself, he yawned. His youth could have been no match for the long hours he had invested in arrangements for the duel. At supper in the virtually empty mead-hall he had been drinking heavily. Few words had been said; ale had filled the social void. Afterward, the rehearsal of the ritual had been perfunctory. Later still, when most of the stead folk had been asleep, he had remained awake, patrolling the rainy walkways amongst the buildings, talking to himself in an angry undertone. Nilssen had lain on his pallet, listening to the splashing of the eorl's boots in the muddy alley outside his room. There was no mistaking Sarnvig's opinion on who would win, but his consequent concern mystified Nilssen.

"So be it," said Sarnvig, clapping his hands once. "It is in God's care now."

The boat bumped the bank. Its frail hull surged as the fowler climbed out. It bobbed, jostling the river weeds while the man tethered it by a leather leash to one of the numerous willows.

Haughtily Sarnvig demanded, "Are all your traps cleared?"

Breaking out into a grin resplendent with ruined

teeth, the peasant imitated his boat, bobbing his head obsequiously.

"Safe now, masters," he croaked. "No snares." A gust of foul breath from him attested to the severity of his dental decay. "Masters come in my boat now, *hoi*?" He extended a bare, muddy foot to steady the craft, clamping its gunwale deftly between big and little toes.

Sarnvig addressed the two duelists. "Let this be done according to the customs," he warned them. "Neither of you will cut his peace strings until I raise my sword, or his life is forfeit. We shall draw straw lots. The longer may decide which end of the eyot he starts from; the shorter takes the other end. You will be ferried over. Once my signal has been given, the hunt continues until one of you is dead. Only then may you return to the mainland. Is all plain?"

They had been schooled impeccably, so the speech was a formality. The rules were strict. They were also simple: once begun, the duel must run to a fatal conclusion.

The island was a one-hundred-yard spit of peaty ground about thirty yards across at the middle, its widest point. Downstream it tapered to extensive reed beds and boggy ground. The upstream end was comparatively dry and supported a thicket of willows that fringed each flank of the island. Through this leafy wall could be seen light scrub which would be easy to penetrate but also afforded good stalking cover. At the island's center a U-shaped copse of mature birches mixed with alder presented its open side to the nearer arm of the Parrett. Visible within it were dense carpets of ivy and ground elder. Elsewhere, away from the shadows of the larger trees, flowering brambles sprawled amongst lofty thistles and cow-parsley.

Nilssen considered which end he would opt for, given the choice. Neither attracted him. Downstream would be treacherous footing and alive with blood-

sucking insects; upstream was too exposed. There was
no disputing Eorhic's commanding lead in legitimate
swordplay. His defeat would only be managed with
the aid of foul tactics, to which the island was poorly
suited.

Perhaps, for the sake of randomizing the setting, the
reeds and mud would be preferable, marginally.

But Eorhic won the draw.

He chewed the tip of his straw, making up his mind.
A sly smile warned that he was aware of his nominal
superiority. When he said finally, "Upstream—fast
going there," it seemed probable that he hoped to trap
Nilssen in the mud or between it and the trees by
running along the island. The omens were not auspicious.

Eorhic was ferried across first so that Sarnvig might
keep him in view until Nilssen was in position. He
embarked with no words of farewell. When the fowler
began chattering nervously, a curt threat of a ducking
silenced him; and thereafter the only sounds from the
boat were the inrush of water behind the paddle
strokes and the peasant's wheezy breathing.

Sarnvig too stayed quiet. Despite his earnest show
of impartiality the young eorl's sympathies had
seemed to Nilssen to lean away from Eorhic. But
honor demanded that custom outweigh personal opinion, so that when Nilssen's turn to board the boat
came, there was an awkward moment. In assisting him
Sarnvig's grip on his arm tightened significantly.

"Saracen," he whispered, "go with your god."

His expressionless face provided no coda to this
encouragement. The fowler gave no sign of having
overheard this breach of duel etiquette, so Nilssen
confined himself to a surreptitious nod. He watched
the eorl as the boat swung out into midstream, noticing that the ranks of reeds beyond him seemed to
mimic his upright stance. They too were dark, though
the rising sun had spread a froth of pale green across

their waving tops; their stems shone with a hard burnish, as did his leather tunic; they cast back shards of the sun, as did his buckles and brooches. Man and marsh merged into the foot of the hill.

His gaze wandered upward, following the ascending mists of dawn up the wooded slopes to the vill where Yaer and Morwena waited for him. The haze bleached color and detail from the distant roofs, and the smoke plume from the mead-hall's fire was barely discernible. He felt a heart-thrust of panic, realizing that he had gambled such friends against the hope of worthless revenge.

"Here be, master," advised the fowler, his rough peasant voice blundering into Nilssen's thoughts accompanied by a blast of his halitosis. "Best you go wary. Bad mud here."

Up to his hips in brown peaty water aswirl with rising silt, his boots clutched at by mud that responded to his plunging paces with shoals of gas bubbles, he waded to firmer ground. The top few inches of water were cold from the night's rain; that lower down was warm and made the insides of his boots feel slimy as it sluiced between his toes. He was beset by the gagging stench of methane and hydrogen sulphide. More biting insects than seemed the due of any marsh hummed about his head, diving at him incessantly while he was within the dense reed beds that harbored them.

Once on dry land he thankfully discovered himself free of the insects' closest attentions, only to find that he was now under surveillance by Sarnvig, who awaited his signal of readiness.

By agreement he was permitted a period of grace for prayers and preparation, which he devoted largely to an examination of his surroundings. Surprises were few: the midway belt of trees across the island was thick enough to obscure the rising sun; the bramble brakes were wild and trackless, suggesting that few folk ever came visiting. Another sign of the islet's isolation from humanity was a napkin-size plot of verdant turf near the water, a mark of otters in the area . . .

He realized he was sacrificing time to trivia.

His left hand almost raised itself involuntarily to wave to Sarnvig.

Escape is a state of mind . . .

He spun on one foot, searching out the source of the voice. The river was empty, the reeds still. He was alone.

And pursuit? Clapping his hands over his ears, he heard the voice speak clearly; but this time it was soundless, merely a clarity of sense without substance. An awareness. The voice of his obsession.

"This is where the chase ends," he said aloud.

Nothing ends . . .

The leaves of a lone aspen shimmered. Silver winked at him from amongst the greenery before the gust which had stirred the tree subsided. Air that had turned chill regained its warmth. A red-and-black butterfly came dodging through sun and shadow, flying a drunken course between trees and islands of undergrowth, then settled out of sight.

Pan lives. No wonder this age had time for gods.

Sigewulf's scabbarded sword banged against his thigh as he moved. Reminded of his business, he looked down at the wet leather encasing the steel and thought of the Welshman whose bones shared a grave on Bishopstrow Down with those of other men who had known what they fought for. His eyes went to Aller-stead on its hill. They came to rest on Sarnvig and the fowler.

His left hand rose. Stretched aloft, its fist punched at the sky and fell. Committed, he waited, finally prey to the eviscerating fear he had denied himself all along.

The tense idleness was almost worse than he imagined the fighting would prove. He recalled Eorhic's nervous irritation over the delay prior to battle at Edington. And the man's account of past mêlées. The fear would be shared; no matter how cool Eorhic pretended to be, he could not repress the Pavlovian anxiety this context would engender.

Sarnvig was being tardy. Nilssen raised himself on tiptoe to look over the reeds which hemmed him in. The fowler was talking to the eorl, gesturing to his boat; the eorl shook his head, waved the peasant back, finally shouted at him. The shout sounded faint, though the two men were barely fifty yards off. The eorl's right hand clasped his sword's hilt. Polished metal gleamed as it slid from the sheath. In blinking, Nilssen missed its skyward arc. His heart thudded out a count of its own: *one-two-three-four . . .*

Flashing down, the sword slashed the turf at Sarnvig's feet.

The gaudy butterfly reappeared between Nilssen and the screen of trees, jaunting amongst the white bramble blossoms. Intent on his own life, he now paid it no heed. Eorhic would not be bothering with nature notes; Eorhic would be hastening through the undergrowth, hacking aside brambles, flowers and all, anticipating an early lunch.

Miraculously the onset of action pushed all fear to the back of his mind, though his plan of counterattack was vague and relied on unorthodoxy. Unstrapping his scabbard and harness, he freed the sword by slashing at the peace strings around the hilt with his dagger. For a moment he held the ornate but useless harness in his hand, reluctant to discard such remarkable leatherwork. Then he pitched it into the river beyond the reeds. Eorhic must gain no clues to what clothing or equipment he had retained, so as to multiply his difficulties in the hunt. Next he rid himself of his City-made djellaba, the cloak which had been with him since the twenty-seventh century. Dropping it on the ground, he destroyed its inbuilt stabilizer by grinding the collar seam beneath his heel. A crawling itch spreading up his leg warned him to withdraw as the smashed control box relaxed its hold over the cloak's atoms. While the last scraps of cloth and the delicate stabilizer mesh faded away, he completed the rearrangement of his garments.

As part of his preparations he had procured a dark green shirt from one of the huntsman-guides at Aller. Tucking this and his undershirt well into his trousers, he tightened his timeshift belt an extra notch. Then, sword in hand, he again stepped into the cold, malodorous river.

Retracing the path he had trampled out on landing, he came to open water and halted in full view of the mainland. Now he would learn how liberally Sarnvig was willing to interpret the rule barring the duelists from leaving the island. No hue and cry was raised. When the fowler began to point and babble, Sarnvig subdued him with a blow from his fist that hurled the peasant into the water.

Gratefully Nilssen waded upstream, pushing cautiously through the reeds. Toward autumn the shoots which now were young and green would stand stiffly proud of the lowered water level; for the moment they allowed him free yet concealed headway. Though they rustled against each other and the water gurgled past his waist, he was confident that no one on the islet would guess he was there.

By the same argument he was ignorant of Eorhic's whereabouts. His enemy ought to be nearing the downstream thicket, would be stealing up on his intended victim, would at any instant discover the disturbed way through the reeds.

There was a small splash. A yard away. Perhaps two yards. Caught in midstride, he eased his free foot into the mud and listened, feeling his pulse surging in his temples. The sword was a dead weight in his right hand, but he held it steady, horizontally across his chest, in readiness for an immediate side-cut.

Another splash, a stealthy one. His arms were trembling. Soon, he suspected, his entire body would be shivering. He ached to move and break the deadlocked hush.

A duck paddled from behind a clump of water plantain. For several seconds it continued scooping up beakfuls of water, swallowing them with rapid backward flips of its glossy brown head. Then it saw him. There was the briefest exchange of stares while the stunned duck gathered its wits, before it gave vent to a torrent of quacking and flapped wildly away through the reeds.

Nilssen cursed the duck under his breath. Sinking down into the water to hide, he crouched until no more than his nose and eyes broke the surface. Cold as the rain-freshened river had seemed, it suddenly felt warm, now that he had to conceal himself in its murky flow. Though glad to be out of the semistagnant backwater, he wished he could have been less exposed. His ears, covered and filled with water, were deaf to Eorhic's movements. The silence pressed in on him as if it and not the river lapped at his face, pushed at him, streamed out his clothes in gentle eddies. Flies buzzed about his face in a frenzied show of soundless motion. An iridescent, blue-green dragonfly flickered by, considered his nose as a resting place, instead opted briefly for a reed stem, and was off once more, lost against the blue sky.

Eorhic would come running at the duck's alarm call, so Nilssen examined what he could see of the islet's shore. He had crept about halfway to the upstream end; to left and right the land receded toward narrows. About five yards in front of his chin the fronded wall of reeds was overtopped by two live willows whose sprays of bushy branches cast deep shadows in which, tipped over as if imminently liable to fall into the river, was the gray, ivy-shrouded corpse of an older willow. Jutting into the sunshine like the figurehead of a rotting ship stranded in the marshes, this afforded a perch for a trio of squabbling sparrows. The birds, he decided, would be his Eorhic-alarm.

Suddenly the sparrows took fright. Two flitted towards the interior of the island, while the third bore off upstream the tidbit for which they had been contending. A man emerged from between the live willows and stepped up onto the sloping deadwood for a better view of the riverside. It was Eorhic. His face was inert, as though all emotion had drained into his sword hand, which continually twitched, responsive to his poise.

He too had stripped off his superfluous clothing. Naked to the waist, he disclosed head, neck, and hands tanned a midbrown; all else was sickly white, spotted by fleabites, fresh and old. His lower torso was streaked with the horizontal scratches a man might receive by rushing carelessly through brambles. Wet slime caked his boots and lower leggings; muddy strands of plant stems adhered to the flats of his blade, suggesting that he had prodded the waterline vegetation with it. Evidently he had crossed the island far faster than anticipated. Furthermore, his hunter's imagination had not confined itself to the land but had turned outward to the river. Surprise, Nilssen thought sourly, was strategically overrated.

Now Eorhic balanced on the dead willow, angled forward, scrutinizing the reed beds. At intervals he would raise his left hand to brush aside his hair whose fringes were already damp with perspiration. Otherwise only his eyes and neck muscles moved randomly as he swung his head in a slow traverse that covered the whole river prospect. That done, he turned to look inland. This preoccupied him for no longer than a minute; experienced as he was, he could trust his hearing to guard that flank. Besides, he still appeared to suspect the river. Again Nilssen wished a horrible fate upon the duck.

For a full five minutes Eorhic stood, squinting slightly against the glare of the pearly haze which hung over the river, scratching himself at intervals, sniffing the air, cocking his head attentively at sounds inaudible to Nilssen. Never did he actually look directly down at his quarry, though his eyes often came near the handsbreadth gap in the reed wall that made the two men mutually visible. It almost seemed he pretended not to see for the sake of a game.

The strain of uncertainty was fraying Nilssen's nerve. With his head tilted back, his throat felt nakedly exposed despite the water covering it. If he held still, he might not be noticed. If he moved aside, the movement or its ripples might attract Eorhic's attention. The compulsion to act grew intolerably strong. He was on the verge of giving himself away, not because he wanted to but because he had to.

His entire body tingled. A sharp, prickling sensation brushed across him, departing before he remembered what it implied. Years had dulled his recollections of the Collapse; but there could never be any mistaking the signature emission of a Change for anything else. Nor could its implications be overlooked: the world had been rearranged at a critical moment and history had been forced back onto its proper course.

Eorhic's reaction was to jerk and give a startled outcry that penetrated the water. He too had recognized the nature of the transient tactual pulse, and the violence of his response indicated that he had been close to its epicenter. Bending double, he massaged his left foot vigorously. Then he stood upright and absolutely still for a second before leaning forwards to resume his search. His body was taut with the hunter's fervor that mobilizes every muscle.

But if he had correctly interpreted the Change as a

warning of Nilssen's nearness, he had also misjudged
its purpose, for it had been worked against him. As he
swung around, transferring his weight from his right
foot to his left, the dead log splintered. His left foot
dropped through the ivy shroud, displacing a gray fog
of rotted wood. Though dead, the timber had formerly
been sound, mere seconds earlier; as he was pitched off
the log into the muddy shallows, his face was con-
torted by outraged shock.

Scrambling out of the water before Nilssen could
rouse himself to take advantage of the miracle, Eorhic
dripped mud and weedy slime. He shook his fist at
the river, saying something that came over as an angry
mumble, and made off into the trees.

Nilssen allowed a few minutes to pass, lest the departure be a ruse. Then he stood up with water
streaming from his ears. They popped, admitting the
sounds of the marshes. As he stumbled to the bank and
climbed out, his clothes were already steaming in the
sun's heat. The dead willow log lay broken, dipping
into the river now; but otherwise it was unremarkable.
Rot had plainly eaten out its heart over several seasons: Changes invariably falsified the past to perfection.

The onset of virtually supernatural intervention
did not persuade Nilssen to relax his guard; rather, it
increased his wariness. As he crept into the dappled
shadows in Eorhic's wake, he was ready for almost any
development, save that which came to pass.

The trail took him through many turnings, one of
which unexpectedly gave onto the clearing amongst
the silver birches. So preoccupied was he in searching
for his enemy in hiding that he completely missed
him in the open. Eorhic was comfortably seated on a
bed of ivy with his back against one of the far trees.
The four yards of uncluttered ground dividing the two
men were no obstacle, yet all he did was to look up,

showing neither surprise nor pleasure at their encounter. Though his sword lay within easy reach, his
empty hands did not stir from his lap. Relaxed, he
appeared confident of his position.

"It would have been a cinch to skewer you," he remarked in Modern English. "You make more noise
than a troop of cavalry."

"Would it have been so simple?" Nilssen asked.

"Ah." Eorhic scratched at a fleabite. "You *have* had a
phenomenal run of lucky breaks, I admit. That's why
I'm sitting here and you're standing there and neither
of us is raring to strike the first blow. The reason's no
great mystery, is it?" The pause he allowed for an
answer was rhetorically brief. "You're bloody useless
as a swordsman, Nilssen. Big words and bog-wallowing
is your limit. But I know damn well that if I tried
seriously to wipe you out, something pretty dire would
hit me: that Change was a warning. So I'm throwing
in the towel. I can't touch you; I can't outmaneuver
you; I can't trump you. All that's left is to call you."
With his right hand he tossed his weapon over to
Nilssen, at whose feet it half-buried itself in the ivy
leaves. "Take me back. I surrender."

As he retrieved the heavy sword, Nilssen found the
anticlimax had robbed his fingers of their strength.
His entire arm shook. Dangling a sword from each
hand, he asked, "And what will Sarnvig say?"

"Not a word," replied Eorhic. "We'll skip out from
here . . . you can, can't you?"

"Friends of mine are waiting at Aller."

"Would you rather be branded as craven?" Half
rising to his feet, Eorhic relapsed into a squat with his
back pressed to the tree. "God in heaven, man, don't
be a damned fool!" He swallowed. "Leave Yaer and
that woman; they'll take no harm."

"Because you say so? Of course, your word is your
bond."

368 ANDREW M. STEPHENSON

Eorhic's right hand, which presently touched the
ivy, dug its nails into the soft soil. Belying his displeasure, he answered softly:

"If you can't trust me, then trust Sarnvig. What
would he do?"

"All right," Nilssen conceded. "All right." The desire to account personally for Eorhic was still powerful
in him; but out of curiosity, the better to gauge his
enemy, he asked, "What variety of belt have you?"

"The one I brought with me." Eorhic tapped his
waistline; metal clinked. "Been through the wars, of
course. But it started with a new power pack and
hasn't been used since . . ."

"Since when?"

Reluctantly he said, "About seven years ago."

"It's important," Nilssen insisted. "Tell me your
exact dates of origin and insertion into this era."

Eorhic obviously was struggling with instinctive
secrecy. "Okay," he said at last, "the day after the
Battle of Reading: January the fifth, year 871 . . ."

"And your origin?"

"2580 . . . Thursday . . . Thursday the twenty-third
of November, 2580."

Drained by the effort of revelation, he seemed to
shrink, folding still closer upon himself.

"It's no good," said Nilssen, and Eorhic's face came
up, staring. "Your belt will be one of the early sort.
It'll echo you back to a time roughly seven years after
you left the City, or to about November 2587. Far too
early. We've no record of your return—"

"Nor of my departure."

"Security improved very fast. By 2587 nothing could
come or go without tripping the alarms. Anywhere on
Earth. You must have escaped by a whisker's thickness."

"A cargo gate," said Eorhic. "The authorities forgot
to watch those."

An awful possibility occurred to Nilssen, one which

made nonsense of months of foolish optimism and misplaced trust. Someone in the City—someone other than Laheer—was willing to help the CNI. Their enemy was still in hiding. "A cargo gate?" he repeated. "May I see your belt?"

Tugging up a handful of cloth from beneath his swordbelt, Eorhic peeled it back, exposing the brassy color of worn bronze.

"A bit more," prompted Nilssen. Two notches filled with blue plastic plugs appeared and he relaxed. He did not quite smile. "I've seen enough," he added. "I'm sorry, that's just so much deadweight now. Indeed I doubt if it did any real work on your outward journey—that's what we call a Mark One: a pun, besides a name for the unit. Cargo gates are like cranes; they latch onto a marker and manipulate their loads remotely: so that unit marks one. . . . A good joke?"

Eorhic stared.

Nilssen went on, "Whoever sent you out was an amateur. Or they were making sure you'd never come back." *But—accidentally or on purpose—they made you conditionally stable in this world. Cargo gates do that. Somewhere in the City will be a heap of earth that represents your mass, Eric Halvey. Which makes you infinitely more dangerous to me.*

The man's nostrils flared and his lips whitened for a moment. "Trash," he said. "That's all the bitch ever was: trash. And would have birthed trash, just as she married it, except he was lost . . . Thanks to the Collapse. She couldn't see it, though: blamed me. Glad to see me go, I'll bet, with her knife in my back."

"Who?"

"I'll tell soon enough. Everyone will hear: when they're all scared sick, Nilssen, I'll name them. Your marvelous City has rats in its cellars. Helping you to catch them will be my homecoming present to us both."

"When we get you there," said Nilssen. Eorhic had

expressed a vicious anticipatory pleasure in revenging himself on whoever had palmed off useless equipment on him. A woman? Few competent gate operators were of the right age. All were Nilssen's friends to some degree; people whose histories it might be wisest to leave fallow, given this tardy demonstration of true, if miscalculated, loyalty. Eorhic had nothing to give but unhappiness. Forever careless of human feeling, casual with life, property, and moral rights, the leopard's spots were fixed. Eorhic would always be a predator.

"Then we may have a problem," said Eorhic, rising to full height without shifting his feet away from the tree. "Would your belt carry us both?"

Bluntly Nilssen said, "I don't think so."

"Ah," said Eorhic pensively. "You sound unwilling to try."

"That's right."

"Why would that be?"

"Because I've given up trying for you. Because I no longer find it convenient to take you home with me. Because there's a limit, and you've exceeded it. We'll have to finish this affair as we agreed."

"Then give me back my sword," said Eorhic, extending an open hand for it.

"Not convenient. This duel goes by your rules." And he threw Eorhic's inferior sword into a clump of brambles while retaining Sigewulf's masterpiece of cutlery and waving it mockingly.

Apart from a fleeting frown Eorhic appeared unperturbed.

"At the risk of quoting out of context," he said, "I will quote to you the opinion of Stephen Vincent Benét: *'We do not fight for the real but for shadows we make. A flag is a piece of cloth and a word is a sound, but we make them something, neither cloth nor a sound, totems of love and hate, black sorcery-stones. . . .'* What flag do you fight for, Nilssen? What is the sum of your words? I am going to make you a bet: that your will is weaker than mine; that you've lost your footing on those stones. Will you gamble with me?"

"No," said Nilssen, "I'm going to finish you."

"There can be no higher stake than life. Mine will be the same."

Without warning Eorhic doubled up and bent his knees so that his buttocks struck the tree trunk and threw him forward into a perfect dive. His legs straightened, propelling him across the narrow interval dividing them. Colliding with Nilssen, he grappled him about the waist and bore him to the ground. Sigewulf's sword fell far from reach as Nilssen flung his arms back to break his fall. Before he could take a breath, he found himself embroiled in a hand-to-hand struggle.

By turns each man gained the advantage as they rolled about the ivied turf. Eorhic had abandoned all civilized manners, possessed by grunting, manic ferocity that appalled Nilssen by its suddenness. Neither kicks nor punches fazed the man as he bit and scratched. Nilssen saw that only a knockout blow would save him; but in falling he had winded himself; from that poor start he was barely beginning to recover, hindered by Eorhic's assaults. Furthermore, his will was sapped by the dread of what would ensue should his belt be taken: the disintegration of his living tissues as his atoms fled futureward in a chaotic stream—

His right fist was suddenly unencumbered. Driving it into Eorhic's jaw, he heard a crack and saw the man's head fly back. Dazed, Eorhic relaxed. But Nilssen too had been hurt: in attempting to push the other off him, he felt his right hand go limp as shooting pains filled it.

His left arm was pinned by Eorhic's knee, so he used his whole body as lever, setting the other swaying. But

Eorhic quickly shook off his befuddlement and returned the punch repeatedly with both fists until the blows ceased to add to Nilssen's pain.

The pounding stopped. A weight lifted from Nilssen's chest and he sensed hands pawing at him, tugging at his belt.

That, he dimly recalled, was wrong: they weren't allowed to do that—

Do what?

Take the belt—

No!

No one listened. Because he hadn't spoken.

"No," he croaked. "Don't take it . . . I've got to wear it . . ."

As he opened his eyes, he found Eorhic leaning over him.

"You don't need it," said Eorhic. "I do." He continued to fumble with the intricate clasp that held the belt closed. There were panels that had to be pressed and sliding catches designed to baffle meddlers. He began to swear, then to weep with frustration.

"Get away from it," Nilssen said, recovering rapidly, aided by panic.

Suddenly there was no more time for argument, for Eorhic's wandering fingers found and filled the trigger holes in the proper sequence. The bright day blinked; the sun lurched across the sky into premature dusk; shadows flicked across the island.

Eorhic still kneeled at Nilssen's side; but he swayed and groaned, seemingly no longer interested in the belt. Raising shaky hands to cradle his forehead, he massaged his eyes. His lips drew back in a snarl; his hands clamped themselves over his ears; then a shriek of consummate agony belled out from his upturned face. His eyes were wild, wide, and bloodshot. Bestial howls broke from him. Standing, he walked stiff-legged away from Nilssen, clutching his head, screaming again and again, forcing every lungful of air into a vocalization of pain.

Nilssen got up, bewildered and shocked. He felt no different. Past experience showed that a timeshift belt transported the whole of a solid body or none of it; so Eorhic ought not to have been injured by the abortive shift. The belt had tried to move both men, had been overloaded, had cut off. No blame attached there, surely; but if not there, then where?

As a precaution he recovered his sword. He felt foolish holding it, however, for Eorhic obviously was no threat and was unlikely to become one soon, though his cries were slowly weakening as he tired himself with screaming.

Nilssen tried to estimate the extent of the shift and its direction. The sun stood at its late afternoon position. The season was still summer. But pastward or futureward?

He ran to the dead willow. From it he looked across the river and at once saw Sarnvig in the fowler's boat being rowed hastily toward the island.

So, the same day, in the future. Well and good.

Mercifully Eorhic had stopped screaming and his expression had even relaxed somewhat, although he glistened with sweat and shook as he patted himself all over like one searching nonexistent pockets.

"Did I make a lot of noise?" he asked hoarsely.

Nilssen nodded. "What happened?"

Eorhic blinked, then coughed. "I was hot all over. Burning. And shocks, like jolts of electricity, right down inside me, deep—oh, my God, so deep. . . . And sounds—all the sounds possible, all rolling and rumbling and screeching in my head . . ." Coughing again, he wiped his mouth. A smear of blood stained his hand, whose skin was aswarm with proliferating red blotches. Eorhic stared at Nilssen; his eyes were misty, their corneas turning white, blind-white. "No," he whispered. "No. How could you?" More extensive coughing brought up copious gobbets of blood mixed with gelatinous particles. The last words he spoke were blurred by a chesty bubbling; and as he spoke them, his gaping mouth widened, splitting up the left cheek in a parody of a grin.

"If I had known . . ." he managed to splutter before he seemed to comprehend that words were worthless to him, that his life had run out, down to the last dregs he had never thought to taste. With hairs raining from his head, he fell to his knees before Nilssen, his rotting neck inviting execution in a wordless plea.

Sigewulf's sword had beheaded many men. It did so again with hardly a whisper. Before the fowler's boat bumped the bank and Sarnvig came ashore, the lingering shreds of Eorhic of Æsces-dun, born Eric Halvey, late Lord Lieutenant of Middlesex, Commissar General of National Integrity in a world far away across the years, had faded into the future, launched thither by a freakish disturbance of the balance that had held him in the past.

They found Nilssen at what they thought his prayers. The evening had grown dark, so they missed the significance of his careful wiping of his mouth. Sarnvig seemed to attribute his taciturnity to the aftershock of dueling. They suspected no vile miracles. Nilssen was careful not to hint at what he had lately seen of a man falling apart. He let them think that the body had been claimed by the river, which might someday surrender it up for burial. Packed into the small boat, sunk almost to its gunwales in the sleek flow of the Parrett, they returned to the mainland, their thoughts preserved in privacy.

CHAPTER TWENTY

They saddled their two horses at dawn while mists still curled about the marshy reaches below Aller.

"Our work is done," said Yaer. "Cheer up."

"Mine is barely started," said Nilssen, oppressed by the dank somnolence of the twilit stead and by his thoughts that spilled over from the past day's horrors. "The certainties are behind us; ahead lie mysteries."

"That's stupid talk," said Yaer. "Yesterday you disposed of the CNI. Alfred and the Danes are free to follow their heads. Morwena—"

"She is the problem."

Involved with tightening a cord about a bundle of furs, Morwena completed her task before tucking the load under one arm and signing:

Why am I a problem? Is it that I wish to come with you? No difficulty there.

Nilssen accepted the bundle from her and tied it to his horse's saddle. Hiding his face from her as he spoke, he said, "Khaled and I are homeward bound, Morwena—"

Her hand touched his arm and he turned.

I also.

"That is impossible. Ours is a drear and deadly land, and not for one second would I hazard you there." Once more he seemed to witness the scouring of Eorhic's living flesh from his skull by entropic reversion; by some diabolical trick of the mind Eorhic's face was transmuted into Morwena's, and Nilssen shuddered spontaneously. His horse shied from him, whinnying, so that Yaer had to restrain and calm it.

What troubles you, my love?

"That I must go away, far away, forever."

Must that be so? The willing heart can triumph over much—

Taking her hands in his, Nilssen stilled her flickering fingers.

"This was willed when the world was caused to be; and those are no empty words. Trust me. It is so." He released her and, heavyhearted, completed the loading of the horses with the few goods and supplies that were theirs to take. Yaer voiced no opinions. Though his command of sign language was poor, he appeared to have read all he needed to know.

When they were ready for the road, they led the horses from the stead without ceremony or backward glance, seen out only by a sleepy guard and a gravid sow rooting in the rubbish tip.

Where are we going?

An hour of walking along the eastward road had reduced Aller to a smudge on its hill marked by small trails of smoke. Thus far Morwena had questioned neither the cause of their departure nor the journey ahead. Her faith in him, her spontaneous devotion, unsettled Nilssen. She was no mental defective. Those in the camp at Athelney who had learned the limits of her disability generally gave her her due, for Saxon society subscribed to few superstitions about female inferiority. Only in the world at large would she have been at a disadvantage. That she should voluntarily forsake the refuge of Alfred's court, having submerged her identity formerly in Sigewulf's life-style and now in his, left Nilssen dissatisfied. But knowing that his persuasiveness would necessarily prove inadequate to sway her, he had argued only briefly against her at Aller. Steeling himself for the moment when he must seem to abandon her and Yaer at the wayside, he had become increasingly confused until, in a moment of lucid honesty, he understood why. She and Eva were too much alike. She had surrendered individuality, but he dared not respond and render himself vulnerable again. And through understanding he found an answer to her question.

"There is a village a hundred miles from here," he said, "where you must stay for about two years while I attend to . . . certain business elsewhere. It is called Henglafingasham. The high-reeve there, Henglaf, is a rough man but can keep a bargain . . . if well paid, I must suppose—"

"Ahoy! . . . Hoy there!"

The shout came to them faintly from far back along their path. Yaer steadied the horses, gathering their reins in one fist. He looked to Nilssen.

"Bandits?"

"It sounded like Sarnvig," said Nilssen. "But how? He went to Wedmore last night after the duel to report the outcome."

Ascending a grassy hummock adjacent to the path, he spied out the land. About two hundred yards off a big man on a full-bodied black warhorse was galloping in hot pursuit, waving an arm as he came. As Nilssen had thought, it was Sarnvig.

Seeing Nilssen, the eorl called again, *"Hoy! Wait!"* Within half a minute he had caught up with them. Dismounting, he allowed his horse to take a short drink from a pool, then pulled it away, all the while himself breathing heavily from the chase.

"Christ keep me," he gasped, "that was a wild ride!" He refilled his lungs with a deep draught of air. "Clear to Wedmore and back in one night; and an audience with Alfred besides! Then to learn at Aller that you'd gone. . . . But here I am, so none's the worse."

Yaer said politely, "We had not thought to see you again, Sarnvig. A pleasure, of course."

"Don't give me that gilded horseshit," retorted

Sarnvig. "Ask me directly: what devil's errand am I about? Hey?" A grin split his scowl when he observed Yaer's discomfiture. "We shall soon redress your fancy ways with words, Khaled." A nod towards Morwena. "She's what brought me."

Morwena's brow crinkled in a frown. She signed to Nilssen, *It seems the world and his wife wishes to hold my hand.*

"What's that?" demanded Sarnvig, caught off balance by not being privy to her remark.

"Like us," said Nilssen, "she wonders at your concern."

Sarnvig blew out his lips, then chewed at them. "It's this way," he explained soberly. "Many of Alfred's companions owe Sigewulf a debt of honor. Often when the shield-wall broke in battle, it was he who rallied our men. A host of Saxons live because of him; not a few would be glad to render him some like service, were he not beyond mortal reward. Their next best recourse is to aid those dear to him."

"All praise to you for your good intentions," Nilssen answered him. "But your help is not needed."

"Let him finish," said Yaer. "Sarnvig, that's not the true cause that fetched you after us, is it?"

Sarnvig made a great show of seeing to his horse, adjusting its harness, stroking its neck. Then he glanced shyly at Yaer, saying, "There are rumors at court—as ever there are when outlanders leave us—that you are bound upon a quest. Mayhap to the frozen lands of the Ruotsi, or perchance to rob some dragon of its hoard. Folk say that beyond Christendom in those places wherein God has not walked there yet live creatures unremarked in any bestiary of the ancients. The wealth of ruined nations lies open to the man who dares take it. You were known to Eorhic; and he spoke of awesome wonders when in his cups, so that some would have slain him for witchery had Alfred's favor not protected him. And now, Ibrahim, that sword you bear is accounted potent magic in the hand of the adventure-prone. Eorhic's death lost nothing in the telling; even as I speak the bards embroider the story of how Sigewulf's sword brought you the same victories it won for him. Lies, of course, for a sword is mere metal. It is the man who conquers. But no blade released that scream of Eorhic's when his wyrd overtook him; and I felt the omen when he fell into the water. Alfred has granted me leave of absence, to visit my kinfolk as he fancies, so I am free to catch fortune's wind. Whatever your destiny, Saracens, I would fain be of your company."

"Sarnvig, you are ever generous," said Nilssen, anxious to shake off the eorl's attentions, "but we court no dangers. Our journey will be uneventful, our destination so ordinary even its name would lull you to sleep."

"Do not jest with me," Sarnvig begged with evident acute disappointment. "If kindness bars you from saying I would burden you, why, I rebuff the notion unasked. I am all a warrior ought to be. Tenscore fearsome enemies have I made as Adam's sire; twice ten score have fled my fearsome aspect at the places of battle. No adversity can enthrall my will. In all things manly I excel. Oh, let me come with you!"

Yaer coughed and said in Arabic:

"Something tells me he's burned his boats with Alfred. It's us or exile."

"Why should he do that?"

"Look at his eager face. Recall that guff about dragons. What happens to someone raised on escapist tales about heroes and their adventures who falls into what he thinks is his favorite plot? This man—this oaf —takes normal warfare in his stride. But we smell of something far more exciting. He wants to get involved."

"Is that our fault?" asked Nilssen. "If we can't take the girl, we certainly can't take him."

"We could as far as the village. I think he'd be most useful."

"There's no adventure in that."

"It's all in the mind. Properly handled, someone like him could be a godsend."

"And you'd do the handling?"

"Of course. Because you'll have to go back to the City, tie up those loose ends, and come back for us."

Nilssen considered Yaer's forthright suggestion. *I never said a word about the sick guardian. Still, he seems to suspect—*

Making up his mind, he said in Old English, "Yes, you're right. The dangerous part must be done properly, so Sarnvig is the natural man to take with us."

"I am chosen?" asked the Saxon, trembling with expectation.

"If you can accept both good and bad in the quest," Nilssen said with a straight face. *Forgive me, Sarnvig, for what I'm doing to you.*

"Merely give the command."

"For two years you must be content to live as a common villager, biding your time until the stars are favorable."

For a second Sarnvig hesitated. Then: "So be it," he said. "But later . . ?"

"Later there will be such deeds done as to make your fame live until the day of Resurrection," Nilssen assured him.

So Sarnvig joined them in the hope of glory. For an hour or more they led the horses through the sunny byways of the marshes, aiming for the green-gray ridge of the Selwood-shrouded hills. Little was said. Sarnvig at the rear was fired with ambition and sang ballads in an undertone, but the others were less cheerful. Morwena walked beside Nilssen. Yaer went ahead, stolidly pacing through the dewy grass, trailing crushed stems underfoot and his plodding pack horse at the end of its reins.

At noon they halted for food within a couple of miles of the forest. It was then that Yaer said calmly, looking at Nilssen, "Ibrahim, isn't it about time you were leaving us?"

At once Morwena tensed and laid down her food. Sarnvig merely paused in his chewing, glancing at Nilssen as he got to his feet.

"I had hoped to delay this parting," Nilssen said. "Sarnvig?"

The eorl swallowed. "Aye?"

"Will you be the guardian of this band?"

Hastily the Saxon wiped crumbs from his beard and stood up. "Gladly," he said. "But where are you going? And why? And will you not require my aid?"

"So many questions!" Nilssen said, laughing. "No, this journey is for one man alone. However, before I go there is one small favor I would ask—" As Sarnvig watched with widening eyes, he unstrapped his sword in its new scabbard and held it out to him. "Sigewulf intended that this sword should earn its bearer great honor. By rights it now passes to you. Take it, please, and use it as he would."

Sarnvig allowed Nilssen to place the sword in his hands. "This is a gift beyond gratitude," he managed to say before being rendered speechless by emotion.

Nilssen bit the tip of his tongue. There were tears in Sarnvig's eyes. Yaer began to tie knots in a piece of grass. Only Morwena seemed not to be at a loss, for she prised the sword from Sarnvig's hands and strapped it around his waist.

The big man blinked, unashamed of his tears as later men would not have been. Drawing the sword, he admired it minutely. "It is our custom," he said, "that when a warrior takes service with a chieftain he exchanges tokens of fealty. I deem this sword one such; will you treat with me?" He sheathed the sword and pushed back his left sleeve, revealing a woolen undershirt banded from elbow to shoulder with thin gold rings. From this personal treasure hoard he carefully removed one ring by sliding it down his arm.

Accepting it, Nilssen said, "We are in each other's debt." To Yaer he said in Arabic, "I'll walk a short way off. See they don't follow me. If it's safe in the City, you can expect me around springtime two years from now. Sure you'll be all right?"

"We've been over that ground," Yaer answered; a trifle impatiently, Nilssen thought. "Sarnvig makes it that much easier. Go while you can."

"Oh," said Nilssen, "and make sure Morwena thinks of Sarnvig as her guardian. . . . You are just a friend."

"Why?" asked Yaer with a suspicious expression.

"For your own good do it without asking questions."

"Have you been less than frank with me?"

"No less than you," Nilssen said, then realized he had inadvertently scored a hit, for Yaer yielded to him with a look of displeasure and a terse, "I'll take your word on it."

Tempted to pursue the mystery, Nilssen decided that Yaer would hardly give himself away in the time remaining. If Yaer had a plan, there was no interfering with it to be done now.

"Good luck then," Nilssen said.

With apparent sincerity Yaer answered, "And to you. . . . One thing, Jerlan, one special request. Give Laheer my . . . forgiveness." Turning away, he seemed lost in a study of the forested slopes of the Selwood.

"I will," Nilssen answered him after a moment. Speaking again in Old English, he said to Morwena, "I must talk to you alone."

They went apart from the others so as not to be overheard. A willow beside a clear stream afforded welcome shade from the sun.

"There is uncertainty ahead for us both," he told her. "You must go with Sarnvig, your new guardian, and with Khaled, who is our friend. Trust them both. Have patience. In time I will return: this I swear." How to phrase the absurd credibly?

Morwena spoke before he could:

You are a man of wyrd. You and your friend. Ever since you spoke my name when no man living could have known it, my folk all being dead, I have seen marks of strangeness in you both. If wyrd calls you, go. Return when and how you may. There is no need to swear; I know you will it, and that you shall if wyrd permits.

She kissed him lightly on his cheek, then on his lips.

"Why do you leave your life in my hands?" he asked on impulse. "We are strangers, cast out of Wessex by the king's ordinance, heretics according to the Church—"

You are who you are, she replied.

"And who is he?" he asked. "Morwena, even my name is a falsehood. It is not Ibrahim, nor am I a Saracen; neither is Khaled what he claims."

Do you imagine that escaped my notice? Her voiceless laugh blunted her question by blending with it. *Names are strange. Voiced folk count it wrong to err in the sound you make when naming each other, forgetting that its truth lies not in its sound but in the one whom it signifies. I loved Sigewulf because, for all that he had no name for me, he knew who I was. I am myself. As you are yourself, whatever the sound you go by.*

"Nevertheless, my proper name is Jerlan Nilssen. You must memorize it, along with certain other facts, some of them lacking in plain sense."

Tell me once. I will remember.

"There will come a night, the second winter hence, after a day of frequent snows, when the men are drinking in the village hall. You will be in your hut. Shouts will come from the hall. When you hear them, wait by your door for me."

Will we then leave that place?

"No." His voice caught in his throat.

Why do you halt? Are there evil tidings?

"On that night I will not know you—" *How so?—* "—Not through any wish of mine—" *—Will you deny me so readily?* "Never! I would never deny you. But, this once, my memory will be at fault . . ."

The explanation sounded lame, even to him.

This is madness, she signed. *No man can predict all you have described unless it be planned.*

"Will you take my word on it?" he asked in desperation.

Briefly her dark eyes studied his, then took in the whole of his face. Apparently she saw something that convinced her, for she relaxed.

I will hear you out, she said.

As concisely as he could, he summarized their next meeting. The sensation of approaching the event from a radically different angle was extremely peculiar, although he knew exactly how much to tell her, secure in the complementary knowledge that she would carry out her part perfectly. In the end he had to avoid her gaze, which troubled him by its calm acceptance of all he was saying. Surely she now thought him insane.

But when he was finished, she merely kissed him again and said, *It will be an eldritch tryst indeed, my love, if the half of it comes to pass. Yet it is a comfort. Go now, as I go to our friends. Hasten your departure, that your work may be the sooner done.*

She left him by the tree. He watched her slim figure until the high ground hid her from him. Then, with his heart pounding and a cold weakness in his legs at the thought of what might await him in the future, he touched his belt in the proper places.

The pearly, sunbright haze of the marshes was extinguished, as if a shutter had crashed down.

CHAPTER TWENTY-ONE

Unyielding slabs of staging materialized beneath his feet. Glaring lights stabbed at him from all sides. Armed people in menacing poses to left and right bracketed him; ahead, resolved into triple septuplets of close-packed crosses, the flier's flare guns confronted him. Overhead and all around the Fregar dome's colors crawled and flickered.

He took a slow breath of moist air. Otherwise he stayed absolutely still, aware of the hair-trigger scrutiny he was under. Then an amplified voice addressed him from loudspeakers mounted above the platform:

"Identify yourself."

"Jerlan Nilssen, masquerading as Ibrahim ibn-Haroun."

"Are you alone?"

Looking down to his left where Yaer would have stood, he saw an empty space. "I am now," he answered. "Psychologist Yaer, disguised as Khaled, has remained in the ninth century . . . according to plan." `

"Hold your arms straight out sideways." He quickly obeyed. *"Step forward for positive identification."*

At the edge of the platform a single medical technician subjected him to some short tests which would have detected any impostors returned by the CNI. Finally the technician stood back and said clearly:

"This is not Nilssen. It can't possibly be."

Stunned, Nilssen gaped at him. Cold all over, he waited for the flare guns to sweep him away.

The loudspeakers rumbled and the hidden overseer said, "Then move out of the field of fire . . ." He remembered the drawn-out moments before Leofric's sword struck at him in the woods on Windhurst Hill. He remembered the bitter taste of futility. But at that time he had had only his life to lose; and he thought of Morwena, waiting for a certain midsummer's day in vain. How unfair life seemed: one small but deadly error had frustrated his hopes. . . . He closed his eyes to shut out the sight of the encircling guns. Then the overseer spoke again: "Welcome home, Commissar. Sorry about the last shock test."

People were surging toward him, their mouths working silently as they and the lights blurred together. Then his left cheek was slapped; and after it his right.

"*Jerlan?*"

He blinked. The people had vanished. A familiar, chocolate-brown face welcomed him with a broad smile.

"Hector," Nilssen muttered. "Thank God."

Kwambe pulled up a blanket around Nilssen's chest. "Keep warm for a few minutes longer," he said. "The doctor says you'll need feeding up and special care. Our little surprise must have been too much for you."

"The last straw," agreed Nilssen. He saw that he had been carried into the cabin of the armed flier and now sat in one of the padded armchairs that served double duty as an acceleration couch. It felt indecently comfortable after the wooden benches of the ninth century.

"Coffee?" asked Kwambe.

"Thanks."

Having poured and delivered the beverage, Kwambe dumped himself on a foldout chair opposite and rested his elbows on his knees. Nilssen cradled the plastic mug between his palms. Steam writhed up in misty snakes from its surface, reminding him of the marshes around Athelney. That much was familiar. That and the clothes he wore. All else had become strange to him. One sip from the mug warned him he had a world of experiences to relearn: the look and feel of plastics; metals employed copiously as building materials; dependable artificial lights that neither smoked nor ran hot; foods of predictable taste and quality; the sciences of medicine, of matter, of life itself; comfort on command.

And sounds. The cabin ventilator hummed; its airflow indicator blinked at him as it spun lazily, red-white-red-white . . . Below it on the bulkhead a mechanical chronometer ticked synchronously with the courtly slow-step of its second hand. And beyond the closed cockpit door a radio receiver blatted intermittently, exchanging with the operator information that would have been trash on a Saxon's scale of values.

"Simple things," he remarked. "They make all the difference in the world."

Kwambe appeared to guess his meaning. "Sure." Absentmindedly he rubbed his right palm across the back of his left hand. "I remember when I was building one bridge in Uganda, we were camped near a village that had never been visited by machines like ours. The locals were impressed. But not so much by the robot 'dozers, crawlers, or cranes. Those things were just too huge—I took a photo of one power scoop with a hundred and nine full-grown men standing in its bucket. What the locals liked were the little details. What stuff was it? they'd ask, touching the chromophoric alloy of a splash guard, trying to feel those crazy patterns. . . . Sure, Jerlan, I know."

Nilssen took another sip of his coffee: reverently, for the act seemed like one of communion with the Modern Age, a reaffirmation of membership. "I'll have to break myself of a lot of habits," he said. "Going to bed with a sword by me for one."

Kwambe repeated his odd hand-rubbing. Nervously he asked:

"What happened, Jerlan?"

How surprising it was to be called by that name in Modern English. . . .

"Jerlan?"

Nilssen bestirred himself to answer. Fortified with the rest of the coffee, he said, "We won."

"Good," Kwambe whispered, making the utterance bear a disproportionate weight of significance by the way he collapsed back into the ribbed upholstery of his seat. "When you said to me in here a quarter of an hour ago that we had rotten apples in our barrel, I had to think to be convinced. But when you came back without Yaer, I was so afraid I hardly dared to ask. It was a bad medicine trip for me, no joke."

"It wasn't so easy for us either," Nilssen said.

"So where *is* Yaer?"

"Relatively? Or absolutely? If you mean, where is he now, his atoms are out there somewhere, blowing around with the dust. If you mean, where did he go, then he's safe in the ninth century, preparing himself for an unspectacular disappearing act."

Kwambe started up, then subsided into his seat with a faint squeak of plastic cloth.

"Yaer is finished with us, Hector. He rigged his ticket to the past so he'd have an escape route into a world with people, and domeless skies, and plants growing wild and, perhaps, a prospect wider than how fast the reconstruction plan can be fulfilled. If he were coming back, he'd have been beside me on that platform. But don't suppose that we've been betrayed; Yaer won't rock the boat for us if he can help it. A quiet life is what he wants. What Eric Halvey of the CNI wanted too, except that he lacked Yaer's cleverness and modesty. And do you know what, Hector? I think Yaer is right. I wish him all the luck in the world. In all the worlds there are, or may be."

Kwambe's expression had rapidly changed from puzzlement into outright alarm.

"That could be called treason, Jerlan. You should have thought twice before conniving in his defection."

Nilssen set his empty mug on a convenient shelf. Kwambe's hand hovered close to the intercom; one touch of the alarm would alert the whole field station.

"I could never have stopped Yaer," Nilssen said rapidly. "At the last moment I suspected. It was too late when I finally had proof."

"Still, this ought to be investigated," said Kwambe.

"With a mindscan? Dispense with the party line for once! Laheer's way of bulling through problems isn't the only one. You know me. Must all your decisions bear the official seal of approval? Besides, there've been serious discoveries about Laheer that put him in a very peculiar light. There are loose ends everywhere I turn in this project. Consider the outstanding question of who stole Rhy's trick sword, for instance. Why was the thief not photographed at close range? Who is being hidden? And someone here helped the CNI to reach Alfred's Britain—a woman, if Halvey is to be believed. Which woman, though? Hector, Yaer is the least of our problems. He can be trusted. Furthermore, I know where he's headed and roughly when he'll get there, so if we must, we can pick him up. That might explain why his belt hasn't returned with me."

The balance of Kwambe's uncertainty seemed to tip in his favor.

"If you had a free hand, what would you do?"

Nilssen risked a joke to test him. "I'd take a hot shower."

Kwambe made a noncommittal noise. "Be my guest. You smell like you fell in a swamp."

"A river."

"All right." He frowned. "But afterward?"

"Afterward—" Nilssen stood and began to remove his belt preparatory to stripping off his malodorous outer garments; but he stopped and let the buckle re-engage with a click. "Hector, I haven't a single idea. How does one man overthrow an entrenched autocratic government?"

"Don't ask me," said Kwambe. "I've been trying for years." He rubbed his hands together. "But we can't afford a bloody revolution. And I wouldn't want one anyhow, for personal reasons."

"Why did you never vote against him?"

"Because I enjoy my job, Jerlan. I'm not saying Laheer is so bad, but one of his foibles is ruthlessness when crossed."

"Yaer said something like that."

"Did he now." Kwambe recovered Nilssen's empty mug from the shelf and rammed it into a locker. "I long ago thought you'd make a good substitute for Laheer. If you care to cross swords with him, you can. But officially whatever you do after that shower is on your own head."

"You're letting me go?"

"Why not? You aren't my prisoner."

"Wasn't I?"

Kwambe made for the cockpit door. "Go clean yourself before I change my mind and have you quarantined."

As Kwambe pressed down the door handle, Nilssen disengaged his belt buckle, letting the two halves fall apart. A familiar impression of disembodiment wrapped its numbness about his senses. The cabin darkened and objective time slowed for him. The ventilator's airflow meter winked like a lethargic, bloodshot eye. The chronometer clunked dully. The white lights on the ceiling reddened, and seconds crawled by before Kwambe's hand reached the downward limit of the door handle's travel.

With a convulsive jerk Nilssen grabbed at the ends of the belt which were drifting away from him. As he snapped the buckle together, the red lights flared white and Kwambe's movements lost their treacly slowness.

"Hector!" Nilssen gasped.

Kwambe spun on his heel and dropped into a crouch, his fists raised. When Nilssen made no move, he straightened. "What's wrong?" he asked.

"Get me to Rhys," Nilssen said urgently. "Turlough Rhys, Area Five."

"The shower—"

"I can't take this belt off, Hector!" He shivered. "I mean, if I do . . ."

Rhys adopted a more phlegmatic attitude, expressing more interest in Alfred and the Danes than in Nilssen's predicament. As he examined the belt *in situ* with a battery of instruments, he insisted on a full account, to which Kwambe also listened. The flight north had been fifty minutes of strained silence between him and Nilssen, neither man feeling inclined to make small talk, into which category historical reminiscence seemed naturally to fall.

Nilssen had to remind himself that Rhys was not being callous. By his calendar, two days earlier they had shared conversation at Laheer's dinner gathering. By his standards this was a technical consultation.

However, Rhys quickly demonstrated that his mind was primarily attuned to his task, for within a few minutes he interrupted the narrative with an abrupt, "You can save the details for later, Commissar."

Putting away one set of instruments, he pulled another set from a cupboard and began to pack them into a padded suitcase.

"I wasn't sure," he said. "Could have been a software fault. Not likely; but sometimes even triple redundancy can fail. The routine for powering-down the belt stabilizer is only called on when you disconnect the buckle, so best to play safe. But it's not that."

"What is it then?" asked Nilssen, restraining himself from shouting only with difficulty.

"There is something wrong with you," said Rhys, closing the case. "To be precise, the stuff you're made of. Commissar Kwambe will remember it as a familiar problem of the old days."

Kwambe seemed to search his memory and form an association, for his face cleared. "Aha," he said.

"Commissar Nilssen," the scientist said, lugging the case toward the laboratory door, "the months you spent eating, drinking, and breathing ninth century matter has led to partial replacement of your body's atoms with ones which don't belong in the City. You are caught between two stools. . . . Are you coming, either of you?" Leaning on the door, he held it open for them.

"Where to?" asked Nilssen.

"To get you fixed up, of course. Come along."

He preceded them along the corridor that led to the hangar where their flier was parked.

"By the way," he said as they neared the first of the paired glass exit doors, "just as you were landing, I received an order from Chief Commissar Laheer to detain Commissar Nilssen on arrival."

Kwambe's steps faltered. The door slid aside for him and he went through, turning to face Rhys. "We heard nothing on the flier's radio."

"The mountains around here," said Rhys with a small shrug, "they block out practically all radio traffic from the City. That's why our aerials are up on Ben Stack."

"Then you ought to have complied with the order!" Kwambe was indignant. "There will be questions in council about this infraction of the rules, Doctor Rhys."

"I rather thought there might," said Rhys, touching a wall panel. It flew open. His forefinger stabbed a red button behind it.

At once the doors slammed shut, cutting off Kwambe's startled outburst which continued as a dumb-show beyond the glass.

Rhys touched a second button and the space between the two sets of doors turned misty.

"We are prepared for most emergencies here," Rhys said calmly. "Civil insurrection amongst others. The gas will subdue him for about six hours, long enough, I hope, for you to complete your business with Laheer, Commissar?"

Kwambe's frenzied hammering on the glass with his fists lost headway. Gradually he slumped to the floor, his limbs slack and his expression vacant. Rhys bent over to examine him through the glass.

"Well?" he said without looking around.

"You're taking a stupid risk," said Nilssen. "I argued Kwambe over to my side once; I could have done it again."

"Could you?" Rhys laughed sardonically. "I tell you, boy, that one's Laheer's poodle. Takes him for walks, he does. Laheer says 'boo' to him, he jumps."

So Kwambe's bid for power had been less whole-hearted than he had pretended, Nilssen thought; a weak man, resentful of his weakness.

"But he could be useful."

"If you win. But first catch your hare."

"I haven't a trap large enough."

"I have, though." Rhys went to the control buttons and cleared the gas from the airlock, then opened the door nearest them. "Help me shift this lump into my rooms," he said, and between them they carried Kwambe down the corridor to the lift and up into the residential levels of the laboratory complex. No one discovered them at work.

"What about this jam I'm in?" asked Nilssen when they had tied Kwambe securely and settled him in Rhys's bedroom.

"Two birds with one stone," answered Rhys. "One

pass through a cargo gate will fix you, no bother. But we'll have to use Dispatch, in the City."

Dispatch was the most active part of the entire Police operation, the place where agents came and went almost twenty-four hours a day; for that was where the permanent gates were installed. Nilssen put his hands over his face, then slid them down and stared at Rhys.

"No, boy," said Rhys, "I'm not daft."

"Convince me."

"Datum: that's where the targeting and tracking computers are, as also the controls. Even belts like that one you're wearing have to be taken there for programming. Datum: unless I've miscalculated, there's a certain item of cargo you'd like to import from early 880, a young lady . . . ?"

Nilssen said nothing; his own thoughts were still none too clear on that subject.

"Datum . . ." and Rhys clenched his fists ". . . Laheer won't dare to stop you."

"After trying once already?" Nilssen pointed to Kwambe on the bed.

"The difference, boy, is that I'll be backing you. Oh, I know Laheer's a big wind in the City and blows hard when it suits him; but you name me one world-conqueror who ever ruled without helpers. Can't be done. Stands to reason."

"And what kind of competition are you?"

Going to the window, Rhys looked out of it, through the Fregar dome covering Area Five, to the barren mountains. Irresistibly Nilssen recalled Laheer's similar stance and his premonitions about Rhys's ambitions. "I have the power," said the scientist. "And I choose to support you."

"I'm not sure of your reliablity," Nilssen replied. "So you support me now; what about a year hence?"

"Guarantees?" said Rhys. "Is that what you want?"

"Yaer used me. Why shouldn't you?"

"Exactly: why should I not? Doesn't everyone have a price?"

"Then tell me yours."

Turning his back on the window and its panoramic outlook, Rhys said, "I want the right to continue working here, Commissar. The gun I plan to hold to Laheer's head has a short effective life; very soon my talents will be overtaken by those of younger men and women already based in Area Five. And there's your guarantee: when I begin to fail, I shall be transferred, away from this work, away from everything that seems to me to be important. This is vital work, no doubt of it. No room for deadheads, they'll say; but who are they to judge me? So I want immunity from the Commissariat of Labor."

"You'd ask me to break the law?"

"How much is one liberal interpretation of it worth? I can give you fair payment. Just give me your promise."

"Bribery, Doctor Rhys? Before I've taken office?"

"Call it a small arrangement."

"Leading to bigger arrangements? Administrative decay has a habit of creeping downward from the top. The City is all we have; let's keep it healthy while we can."

"So you'd leave her in the lurch?"

"I have the rest of my life for that," said Nilssen coldly. "One day I'll go back. But on my own terms. Unless we maintain our standards, we betray ourselves; that much I learned from an illiterate Saxon king who thought nothing of bloodshed but would have died to defend the law as he understood it. Doctor Rhys, if you want to bargain with me, don't offer tainted goods."

Opening the outer door, Nilssen left Rhys alone with the unconscious Kwambe. He had reached the lift when the scientist caught up with him.

"I'll do it anyhow," Rhys said resentfully. "But

when you're top dog, Commissar, don't you forget this favor."

Within himself Nilssen smiled with smug contentment.

A sandstorm was blowing. It engulfed the City and its outlying domes, so that from the air the seven hemispheres resembled water-worn stones in a fast-flowing, brown river. For all the height that raised the flier landing platform proud of the ground-hugging grit, even its radar antennae were blurred by whirling dust; and the markings on the wide circular platform itself were well-nigh invisible beneath a mobile blanket of fine sand. When their hijacked flier descended for an attempt at landing, it seemed improbable that the autopilot could locate a solid surface and not pitch them into the heart of the storm.

A bump signaled impact, and they heard the flier's engine switch off. Simultaneously the wind noise ceased. Light from outside took on a multihued cast as a Fregar dome was developed over them. A sinking sensation showed they had arrived safely and accurately on an elevator.

They did not halt at the commercial level where normal activity prevailed, dropping instead to the level reserved for special or dangerous cargos. Here the lights burned brightly, illuminating depopulated, uncluttered hangars. Freshly sanded oil stains on the floor revealed recent occupation, but the service bays had been carefully cleared and all machinery covers were in place.

Once flush with the floor the elevator engaged with the travelator and offloaded the flier. That done, it returned to the surface.

They peered out through the windows.

"We came to see Laheer," Nilssen said. "This is just intimidation."

"More like a trap," murmured Rhys. "Someone expects trouble. They must have found Kwambe and his crew."

"So they'll know we didn't harm them. Tell me, what will you require from Dispatch?"

In the flier's starboard wall was set an electrical connector whose snout was capped by a black plastic lid. Rhys placed a hand on this, saying:

"A timeshift controller to plug in here. And a collapsible cargo gate keyed to any of those in Dispatch Concourse F."

"Any special type numbers?"

"There should be a controller for this particular flier in store. Failing that, any Mark Four will do, though it'll take an hour to align. The gate, well . . ." Shaking his head, he said, "It's no good, Commissar. You've got to let me do the choosing or they could palm us off with any old rubbish. How can we tell who's on Laheer's side?"

"I'd rather have you under cover."

"If the two of us can't force Laheer to resign, we won't be visiting Dispatch," Rhys said flatly. "Once he has, we only have sneak-saboteurs to watch for. And I think Laheer is realist enough to surrender gracefully when he sees I'm with you, not him."

"He must have seen already; he has cameras everywhere."

"Then we're safe." Rhys grasped the hatch handle. "On every occasion that you've used a timeshift belt, your life has been in my hands. Why won't you believe in me now?"

"Because Yaer left a note advising Laheer that some old bones he thought buried years ago were about to be unearthed and paraded around in public. I don't think a double accident would be beyond him, out in the City where safety standards are relatively lax."

"Nonsense," declared Rhys. "I know the Chief."

"If you come, we stay close and move fast. And don't complain to me if something happens."

Rhys thought over the proposition. "I promise not to," he said genially, "if it makes you any happier."

They left the hangar without incident. Monitor cameras swung to track them as they entered the subway connecting the airport to the City. Never before had he been so acutely aware of them, or of other people, whom they now began to encounter and whose unwelcome attention was drawn magnetically to his outlandish Arabic-Saxon costume.

The beltway felt endless and lethargically slow. The tunnel stank of oils and ozone; and it reverberated with the rumble of the moving ways that glided in both directions. Cameras never left them unwatched.

It became apparent that Rhys had not been unaffected by Nilssen's apprehensions, for he asked:

"How obvious could Laheer afford to be?"

"A quarter of the City's adult population has grown up under his regime with his ideas drilled into their heads. He could explain away almost any action of his as being for the good of the state. His flock of hand-picked yes-men would back him to the hilt; look how fast Kwambe knuckled under—remember your own description of him?"

"But not you."

"I'm not alone. There are those who only need the proper stimulus to awaken their independence."

"What woke you?"

"A breath of fresh air, you might say. And a very special rebel."

There was a lull while the beltway pitched and rolled beneath their feet, bearing them along the tunnel.

Rhys said, "Do you think it's sensible to waken the others, though?"

"Why not?"

"I mean, a sleeping man uses up less air, doesn't he? You said yourself: the City is all we have. How many Chiefs can we afford to have; and how many Indians?

There's only so much independence to go around."

Faces passed them going the other way; faces briefly animated by a placid curiosity that repelled Nilssen all of a sudden. "Are you saying that it's not Laheer's fault?" he asked Rhys. "That *this* was inevitable? That we have to let it be?"

"If the City is to live, we must. We are part of an evolutionary process that requires someone like Laheer to take firm charge. We can disapprove, Commissar, but we are helpless. That is the power I hold and which I can share, by showing you how powerless we are. We inhabit a city-state of strictly limited boundaries in which political expediency is carried to extremes for the sake of survival. There can only be one master here. So far, Laheer has ruled. Now, Commissar, you have challenged him. Your assumption is that he will take all measures to suppress you; but my prediction is that good sense will prevail."

"You are too logical," said Nilssen. "Human nature is selfish. If I'm a challenge, then there must be revolution, because an autocracy—of whatever degree—necessarily denies the right of government to any upstart power. Yours included, Doctor Rhys. Laheer will throw all he can at me—and you."

Rhys appeared flustered, as though his confidence had ebbed.

"For how long can we avoid him? Just the two of us?"

"For as long as we can stay out of his reach or that of his troubleshooters. Our objective must be to catch him alone; and at moments like these, when crises threaten, he always retreats to his office."

"But that's in the Citadel!"

"You're giving up too easily," Nilssen said angrily. "Don't call it that; all it is, when you come down to it, is a perfectly ordinary block of offices that happen to occupy a whole damage control sector. Every sector has blast walls around it. Maybe Laheer installed a few extra obstacles, but they're far from being in-surmountable. You have to know how they work, that's all." He looked away from Rhys along the tunnel. "This is a three-minute journey, quite long enough for Laheer to have arranged a reception at the station he'd expect us to use, so we'll leave early, at Perimeter."

The tunnel widened, as did the beltway. Briskly they stepped off into a side tunnel where an escalator bore them rapidly up toward ground level. Thirty seconds after leaving the beltway they felt a puff of air from below and heard a screech of rupturing metal. Ambient sounds changed slightly.

"The beltway's stopped," said Rhys.

"I heard," said Nilssen. "Take the second right."

At the head of the escalator a camera tracked their progress into an express lift. A sanitary inspector in spotless uniform eyed them dubiously and wrinkled his nose at Nilssen but made room as they dictated a destination to the attendant computer. At the next stop up he left them, and they continued with a trepidation that mounted as fast as the lift.

"Theoretically this mechanism is tamper-proof," Nilssen said, counting off the levels. "But at Level Sixteen it comes under the control of the Administration sector computer; then anything can happen."

As the indicator showed Level Fourteen, he punched the HALT button; obediently the lift slowed and let them out at Level Fifteen.

Another camera caught sight of them as they turned the corner into a deserted corridor enfiladed with identical doors surmounted by stenciled numbers. Far down the line near the point where perspective made seeing difficult, a small splash of color, a red vertical strip, disrupted the monotony of the pattern.

"Quiet place," remarked Rhys.

"That's nothing to do with us," said Nilssen. "These are reserve quarters for Admin. staff in case they have to live near their work. So far—" Memories so abstracted from his present and recent existence that they might have belonged to another person surfaced in his consciousness. "So far," he repeated himself, stumbling momentarily over his recollections, "they've remained unused . . . except unofficially. You'd be amazed how often the linen gets changed in some of the bedrooms."

Rhys smiled wanly. "A good spot for an ambush."

"If Laheer can take advantage."

"He doesn't give up. You saw that camera back there."

Nilssen almost did not hear him, so engrossed was he in recalling the layout of the building around them. Architect's plans had crossed his desk almost daily; but his function had hardly been more than that of a human rubber stamp, so his accretion of knowledge had been skimpy.

"There are two meters of reinforced concrete and a layer of structural deformation compensators between us and Admin.," he said at last. "But I think that red panel ahead is an escape exit which automatically unlocks in the event of fire."

"I don't carry matches," said Rhys.

"We don't need a real fire. The computers in charge of the extinguishers are very credulous. With luck and an oversight by Laheer my voice will still carry some authority in those quarters—but we'll have to be careful."

"You mean, we might get arrested for turning in a false alarm?" Rhys shook his head in wonder. "A fine moment to worry, boy."

"I meant," said Nilssen evenly, "that it won't unlock *above* a fire, to stop updrafts." Finding a telephone by the exit, he took the handset from its cubbyhole and waited for the computer to attend him.

"SECTOR WEST ONE FIFTEEN," it said.

"Sonogram identification," he said. "Jerlan Nilssen."

402 ANDREW M. STEPHENSON

The computer was slow to affirm his identity but did so eventually.

"There is a fire on Level Sixteen," he told it, "underneath Chief Commissar Laheer's office. Sensors there have been made inoperative or faulty. Institute remedial measures at once. Full damage control."

"GIVE EXTINGUISHER NUMBERS."

He read off as many of those on the overhead spray nozzles as he could see and guessed at a few more for good measure, altering the prefix to that of the floor above.

"CONFIRM IF NOW OPERATIVE."

"All working," Nilssen said, though not a drop had emerged from those on their floor. "Please unlock escape exit."

"HATCH RELEASED."

"Nilssen clearing. Out."

Hooking the handset onto its rest, he said to Rhys, "Try it."

The red panel opened for them. The spiral stairs beyond were bone-dry; but when they pushed open the door at their head, a torrent of water poured through.

"I don't believe it," said Rhys.

The corridor was awash already. Spraying at full pressure without competition from other parts of the fire fighting system, the overhead nozzles were dumping thousands of liters a minute into the cramped space. Such a fog of water droplets filled the air that it was difficult to see more than a few meters in either direction.

"Someone will cut the flow soon!" Having to shout to be heard above the hissing and drumming of water, Nilssen pushed Rhys toward their left. "While this lasts, let's make the most of it. If we can't see far, neither can the cameras."

They waded past an open office wherein two clerks were sheltering under their desks, bellowing into telephones. A few paces further a low-slung domestic robot immersed eye-deep in water bumped along the wall as it tried to escape the flood.

There was a sharp explosion behind them; a shaft of heat slapped the wall near Nilssen, stripping away a stretch of waterlogged plaster amid a cloud of steam.

"Laheer's friends," said Rhys.

"Must you state the obvious?" asked Nilssen irritably. "Up these stairs."

Rhys mounted the carpeted stairs rapidly, but Nilssen paused to look back the way they had come. Curtains of water still hid their pursuers.

Another shaft of heat skimmed the ceiling, rupturing the sprinkler supply pipes as it dislodged masonry and metalwork. Sparks crackled amongst wiring and started a genuine fire that was doused immediately by the redoubled flood; at once all the overhead lights along the corridor went out. A nebulous watery glow shone through the downpour from open offices.

"*Lamps!*" called an authoritative voice from no more than three or four meters away. "I said—" There was a pained outcry. "Blasted robot," the same voice howled. "Get the damned thing out of the road."

Nilssen turned and dodged up the stairs, away from the confusion and into the light and warmth of Level Seventeen where Laheer had his office.

Rhys was leaning against a wall, recovering his breath. Water streamed from his clothes, forming puddles on the expensive carpet and ruining the floral wallpaper. "There may be more inside," he panted, nodding towards the entrance to Laheer's outer reception room.

"There may," Nilssen agreed. "But we know for certain where one lot are."

Someone said at the foot of the stairs, "This carpet's wet."

"Then get up after them!" ordered the authoritative voice.

"Inside," whispered Nilssen.

Rhys tried the handle. "Locked," he said in a despairing tone. Trying several other doors, he failed to find any that would yield to him. "How obvious . . . Well, Commissar, I suppose you can make another phone call?"

Settling himself on the top step, Nilssen sighed. "No," he said. "That's it."

A soldier in wet thermal armor bounded around the turn of the stairwell, saw him, and leveled his flare gun. Nilssen looked at him disinterestedly and at the second soldier who came up behind him.

The second wore Leader's stripes and appeared to have some idea of what to make of the encounter, for he pushed aside the first one's gun and mounted the stairs purposefully.

"Commissar Jerlan Nilssen?" he inquired.

Nilssen waved down the stairs, muttering, "He went that way."

Unruffled, the Leader continued:

"And you would be Doctor Turlough Rhys of Area Five?"

"No!" screamed Rhys. "I've done nothing wrong—"

Embarrassed, Nilssen tried not to hear the man's useless protestations. There was to be no reprieve; he knew the type of men with whom they were dealing: latter-day analogues of Wulfstan and Leofric, better-armed but no more civilized. Rather than waste his last seconds in watching their preparations for the kill, he admired the elaborate wallpaper and its vibrant colors. Dying, he remembered well, was so easy.

He traced the fronds of intertwined vines and roses that adorned the paper as high as the ceiling, where they spread themselves in a splendid floral and fruitful mass around the light fixtures. Aligned with the top step, directly above his head, was a slot within which nestled the edge of a thick slab of metal.

Reflecting on this, he took a second look.

They had, he realized, run up the stairs between levels even though there was a fire alert in force. By rights free access ought not to have been possible; yet . . .

It dawned on him that he was sitting directly underneath a gravity-operated blast barrier. Through some trivial fault the three hundred kilos of steel alloy had failed to drop when ordered to do so by the computer. Now it merely hesitated; perhaps the slightest jolt would bring it down.

Without personal recrimination for overlooking this obstacle in the first place he got up casually. "Well," he said, terminating Rhys's pleas, "my congratulations on a good chase."

The Leader studied him suspiciously from five steps down. "That won't help you," he said. "We have orders."

"I know." Nilssen took a pace backward as though only avoiding the steep pitch of the stairwell. "I just thought you could do with some appreciation."

Suspicion reinforced, the Leader advanced to the top step and pushed the cruciform barrel of his gun into Nilssen's stomach. "I can do without your jokes," he said.

In a conversational tone Nilssen asked him, "Did you know that if you were to pull that trigger right now, you'd probably be committing suicide?" The man's arrogance mellowed into partially convinced alarm. "The human body," Nilssen went on, "contains an awful lot of water, like downstairs. Firing that gun would vaporize most of my internal fluids in a flash. I'd hardly feel a thing; but you'd probably suffer third-degree burns or worse. Think about it."

For a crucial instant the man's trigger finger eased its tension. Nilssen seized the gun. Wresting it away, he clubbed him under the chin with the butt. The soldier fell back, colliding with his subordinate, so that they both tumbled down the stairs.

Reversing the gun, Nilssen aimed it at the ceiling and lightly squeezed the trigger. His face dried instantly; had he not shut his eyes, the flash might have blinded him. With a shrill squeal the blast barrier freed itself, shaken by the shock, and descended ponderously. Fragments of powdery plaster and cement fell past it. As it thudded into the carpet, pushing through into its mating recess in the floor, the thick metal resounded to a blow from the far side and glowed red near its lower edge.

Nilssen regarded Rhys sadly. "So much for logic and human decency," he said. "And so much for power."

Rhys was in no state to offer comment, for he was still whimpering from his ordeal.

"There was a lock to be dealt with," Nilssen added thoughtfully.

Laheer's office suite was simply entered. As the charred and shattered outer door swung wide for him, Nilssen took hold of Rhys and propelled him ahead into the darkness.

CHAPTER TWENTY-TWO

Darkened, the emptiness of the outer reception room was unwelcoming, its stillness as unresponsive as a stagnant pond. Nilssen rapped on the inner door, rather than simply open it, so that the natural sound and the bruising of his knuckles by the dense outworld wood might help establish his presence there. Already he felt too much the intruder in Laheer's domain.

A quiet voice answered. Laheer was inviting him to enter as though there had been no changes wrought between them.

"Open it," Nilssen said to Rhys, who obeyed stiffly. "Walk in."

Dim light fell across Rhys and his shadow stretched to the wall.

"Ah," said Laheer from within the room, "Doctor Rhys. Is Jerlan with you? I assume he must be."

"I'm here," said Nilssen without showing himself.

A low chuckle greeted his wary reply. "Jerlan, you must take some risks for yourself, you know."

"It's all right," said Rhys over his shoulder.

Stooping, Nilssen thrust his face into the light. Reassured by what he saw, he entered.

Laheer sat alone in his shuttered sanctuary, reclining in a tubular alloy armchair with his back to the door. To his right was the low table, on it a full glass and an unopened bottle whose label was averted. The television receiver had been hung in a corner out of the way; it was now switched off. At his feet was the incomplete model of the City, from which came all the light in the room. Laheer seemed rapt with contemplation of the sparkling domes, sunk forward in his chair with his bony hands drooping over the ends of its rests.

"Why not allow Doctor Rhys to leave us?" he suggested.

Rhys turned a worried face to Nilssen.

"We've had the battle," said Nilssen. "Now we have to talk. Please, would you wait for me outside?"

The door closed and Nilssen walked forward to where he could see Laheer in right profile. He held the flare gun cradled in his arms. The room was vague with shadows, but they saw each other plainly; yet Laheer seemed not to be discomfited by his downfall. Without shifting the rest of his body he raised his right hand. It dipped; the skeletal forefinger aligned itself on a chair beyond the low table.

Nilssen sat.

The gun was distressingly heavy in his lap. Unable to forget it, he could not forget its purpose either. But all Laheer would say was, "They said you'd come home safely, Jerlan. Why so slow to visit me?"

"Some trouble," he answered.

"Necessitating a visit to Area Five?"

The old bastard was being obtuse, he warned himself. "If you know, why ask?" Never allow others to command any interview, that was Laheer's rule; keep them running, hit them repeatedly at the point of balance.

"To be sure of my facts," murmured Laheer.

So softly said, so piquantly reproving.

"I came here for a reason, not to gossip."

"And my wish is to talk, Jerlan. You would be surprised how well that will satisfy us both, if you give it a chance."

"Then of course I will listen."

Laheer tipped his head on one side. "Are you
making fun of me, Jerlan? Your customary, ah, *defer-
ence* is absent. Would this be a consequence of your
expedition?"

*Why didn't I ever notice how alike he and Yaer
were?* "Must we be so civilized? I'm trying to find the
best way of telling you something . . . sir." The gun
was so desperately heavy; there were five kilos of lead
in the power pack alone—

"And I'm not helping?" Laheer laughed heartily,
the muscles on his neck prominent like parasitic
creepers on a dying tree. "Then as a jewel of advice
from an old man to a young one, allow me to suggest
that you put it in the best way there is: simply and
directly."

*Not so simple. Old man, you trade upon your heart-
lessness. We who care, care even for you, even now.*

"Yaer told me who you are," he said. "And who he
is." He repositioned the gun in his lap. "Obviously
you already know that."

And Laheer responded; not with anger or with
bluster, but held as true to himself as ever in that he
absorbed this confirmation with no more than a
slight display of disappointment.

"Jerlan," he said, "if we are to make anything of
you, we must cure your diffidence. Come now, you
were not afraid to take me on when there was deadly
danger. I told you to put it simply and directly. Again,
please."

Irritated, Nilssen said, "How direct must we be?
Yaer accused you of being with the CNI in the old
days; he knows because he's your son and remembers
how it was in your home. Is that simple enough?"

"Perfect."

"And?"

"Were you expecting more?"

"A word or two in self-justification at least."

"A confession, perhaps? A tearful outpouring of my

evil past, immediately prior to a fumbled suicide, foiled by you so I can stand trial for my crimes?" Picking up the glass between his thumb and forefinger, Laheer elevated it so that the lights of the model swarmed in the cut crystal. "This, for example, would be poisoned, prepared by me in anticipation of your victory."

"I don't see how you can treat it so lightly," Nilssen said. "The slightest rumor of this accusation, coupled with your actions today, would certainly bring you to the gallows."

"Do you suppose I am unaware of that?" answered Laheer, intent upon the distorted image of the model refracted up through the base of his glass. "We gave them good reason to hate us."

"Is that an admission?"

"A wicked word," said Laheer. "So slimy with implied proof of heinous guilt when you say it like that. Yes, I was in the CNI. And since I never resigned, technically I still am. And I am Yaer's father, for all the good that ever did me. Name me anyone well-placed in the City, Jerlan, and I could tell you what they were in the old days. We were all in the CNI. Every one of us who's old enough. Every last one."

The tableau broke. With an abrupt movement Laheer tossed back the contents of his glass. When it was drained, he replaced it on the table, so gently it no more than kissed the surface as it made contact.

"Do you choose to believe me?" the old man asked.

Sweating, Nilssen shook his head. "I can't afford to. That would mean throwing out all we've stood for."

"One day," said Laheer, "you will learn that to be truly pure you must know what it is to be truly foul. But I think, for the moment, you would agree that we ought to keep it secret?"

"That would be almost as bad."

"A lie to the people?"

"Yes! And a cruel lie at that: a derision of the ones who were lost."

"Is there to be no pardon, ever?" asked Laheer. "Be honest with me, Jerlan. Suddenly I need to know."

"Yaer—"

"Don't say that name in here. My son used it to taunt me long after I tried to rid myself of it. And this morning it was on the letter. He likes the last word, always; when he was a child he loved his puppets."

The gray eyes blinked at Nilssen. They were shinier than they had been.

"Yaer sends his forgiveness," Nilssen said. "I think he meant it."

Laheer's voice shook as he answered, "That con man . . . When he sees me—" Checking himself, he said, "When he returns, he'll scorn you for being his patsy."

"Yaer has changed. Changed so you'd take him for another person. Believe me, sir."

A timid smile plucked at Laheer's mouth. "If only I could; but there's no time." More aggressively he said, "Jerlan, my statements about the CNI were true. But bear with me and you'll understand why there's no profit in stirring up another Purge; you may even gain an insight into my motives in attacking you today. To start with, what did you find at Alfred's court?"

"Are you about to tell or asking?"

"*Answer me!*"

Through habit Nilssen complied with the instruction.

"We found one of your friends—Eric Halvey."

Laheer released a happy sigh. "Thank God. That accounts for them all. And what did you do to him?"

"He died," said Nilssen, not wishing to dwell on the subject.

"Good. Halvey was the one person to pose us any real threat. Now, Jerlan, I have a truth to bequeath you. You may reject it; quite likely you will eventually hate me for it. But if fundamentals are what we are clarifying now, I need your promise of a close hearing."

"Wait a minute," said Nilssen. "Halvey's death doesn't bother you? He was your boss in the CNI."

Patiently Laheer asked, "Am I supposed to mourn someone like that? You met him; I infer that you also killed him. Yet I see no tears in your eyes. Our shared membership of the CNI is poor evidence of mutual compatibility. Your myopic character assessments depress me profoundly. Are we all to be tarred with the same brush?"

"If it suits. What made you join?"

"I was drafted. Drafted from Social Services, Housing Department. They found I could get things finished to deadlines. Likewise Hector Kwambe: he was bought-in to manage the construction crews which built the City. Maia Kim was a job motivation expert. And so forth. Legally we were CNI; yet we had no part in Operation Damocles, which was Halvey's concern from start to finish."

"But you weren't slow to take power here," said Nilssen.

"It struck me as a natural progression. From one housing development to another." Moistening the tips of his left thumb and second finger with his tongue, Laheer rubbed them together, blew on them gently, pursed his lips. "Recriminations will have to wait," he said. "My suggestion that my drink was poisoned, Jerlan, was a ruse to distract you from guessing that it might be. Already the feeling is dying in my hands." With a struggle he pushed himself straighter in his chair. "Don't gape at me that way, man. I almost wish you'd sent a message, so I wouldn't have to see that doleful face you're putting on. And sit down, relax;

it's too late for desperate rescues. Georgiana Hartmann wouldn't come anyhow. I asked her not to."

"She let you . . ?"

"Did she, didn't she—for God's sake, Jerlan, must
you waste my life with this piffling querulousness?"

The old man had won again. Nilssen felt ashamed:
of being outwitted; and of not having the courage to
pick up the telephone.

"Listen," said Laheer. "I've served the City for a
quarter of a century. In death I can serve it further:
firstly as a scapegoat for Hector, Maia, and the others;
secondly by vacating this seat for you. It ought to have
been yours years ago; now I think you've proved you
can fill it better than I. The others on the Council
have long agreed with me that the City needs a
leader who isn't always looking back to the Old World.
You have your memories; but you belong in the
present more than we do." Tentatively Laheer slapped
a knee with one hand. "Damn, I can't feel with
either." Talking faster, he went on, "There's very
little left unsaid, but all of it matters. On my desk
you'll find a roll of brown cloth about a meter long
which I want you to give to Rhys. That is the sword
which was stolen. Maia Kim went for it last night.
It was she who ambushed you, who dragged you to
safety, whom you followed through the woods." Laheer smiled. "She said she was never so scared in her
life. Be sure to thank her."

"But," said Nilssen, glancing across the office at the
desk where, in the gloom, he could just discern the
package. "But what use is it to Rhys now?"

"Am I the one to ask?" replied Laheer. "Restrain
your impetuousness. I won't detain you much longer."
He tried to waft a hand in the direction of the City
model, but his arm moved clumsily, and the hand
flopped limply at the wrist. Giving a small snarl of
frustration, the old man lowered his arm onto the
rest again. "Had I been able, I would have said what

remains so much more gracefully. But, of course, our affairs are eternally untidy, hairy with the stray ends of unfinished living. When you take over you'll discover how many."

"Sir," said Nilssen, "I'm not taking over."

Laheer's fierce eyes bored into Nilssen. "What's that you say?" he demanded. "Explain yourself!"

"I'm saying I don't want your rotten job!" Nilssen snapped. "All along you've taken it on faith that I came here to take over. Well, I didn't. Someone else—"

"No one else!" roared Laheer. "By God, Jerlan, you've made an ass of yourself on occasion, but now you've broken all records." Shortness of breath interrupted his tirade; he fought for more with lungs that scarcely responded to his labors. When he next spoke, it was in a whisper. Only his head and neck seemed fully alive. "Only one thing could steal you from us, Jerlan Nilssen, when we need you most. Is it a woman, Jerlan?"

Nilssen's face answered for him. Laheer forced his head away.

"The horseshoe nail," he said.

"Isn't my life my own?" asked Nilssen.

At that Laheer began to laugh, hacking and wheezing as his semiparalyzed torso heaved with mirth.

"Tell me," he asked weakly, "tell me what she's like."

"Like?" Nilssen cast about for comparisons. "If she's like anyone—"

"Eva, perhaps?"

"How did you know?"

Rather than explain, Laheer asked a question of his own:

"Jerlan, who was Eva Nilssen?"

"You remember damn well who she was!"

"But do you?"

"Is this what the poison does?" he asked, intending

to hurt but discovering that his anger left him with the words. The old man's mind was fading, that was all. "Sir," he said calmly, "Eva was my wife. And my friend."

Laheer's head wagged from side to side, so slowly the motion resembled a further phase of his decline. "No," he said, "she was never your wife."

Nilssen shut his eyes. A kindly poison; but in the last moments so cruel, to steal a great mind before death could silence its ravings.

"And you," Laheer continued in the same tone, "are not Jerlan Nilssen."

His eyes blinked open. Laheer was neither smiling nor frowning.

"Your real name is Gwillem Yorg Crewkerne. You are thirty-three years old. Not forty-seven. You joined us on Tuesday the seventh of January, 2606, around fourteen months ago, not Wednesday the nineteenth of July, 2580, as you believe. The man whose memories you carry as your own died of incurable leukemia two months after you arrived, as the consequence of a disastrous expedition to the ninth century. Georgiana Hartmann performed a mindscan and imprint, combined with comprehensive cosmetic surgery to recreate the whole man. You are Jerlan Nilssen, yet you are not. You cherish the memory of another man's wife; and in loving this Saxon woman you are merely responding to the lure of high ideals that we set for you. Our intention was that you should never find anyone you could love more than your duty to the City. She must be very special indeed. There you have two truths in one. And this is who you really are."

His unwavering gaze at last relented, releasing Nilssen's mind for its long dive into doubt.

Which of us took the poison?

He could not move. The gun in his lap weighed nothing.

Crewkerne. His own name? He remembered it because Kwambe had talked of him at the dinner party.
But could a man forget his own name and push it
aside into obscurity at the touch of a switch?

No, he insisted.

. . . No more than a machine could cram him with
a language overnight.

Gradually he experienced the onset of terror. *Am I
real? Am I a whole person or a patchwork? If two in
one, why not many more—my name is Legion, for I
am many . . .* The whirlpool's racing coils carried him
deeper: *if a man's body can fall apart, why not his
mind*—the upended funnel had no bottom, no top, no
purpose but to drag him, a toy carved by Yaer, down
with it: . . . *when he was a child he loved his puppets.*
Project Yardstick? He had been Yaer's project from
the start.

"Does it surprise you," said Laheer, "that I find it
hard to stay alive? It hardly matters that Crewkerne
volunteered. We exploited you. And I . . . sanctioned
my son's experiment."

Intuitively he believed Laheer. So many mental
lapses that he had dismissed without a second thought
were explained. As were chance remarks by Yaer and
even by Rhys.

"Where does that leave me?" he asked. "Who am I
in the end?"

Laheer answered, "Whoever you are, the honest answer must vary from minute to minute. You are Ibrahim ibn-Haroun; and you are Jerlan Nilssen; and you
are Gwillem Crewkerne. All of those. And more. Don't
divide yourself, because the names don't matter a jot."

"She said that."

"This woman?" Laheer paused. "Jerlan, I was
wrong. Disregard your duty to the City; it was a duty
wished on you. You're free to leave. Of course you are;
that must always be fundamental to a citizen's rights.
Otherwise we might as well breed machines as hu-

mans. But notwithstanding that freedom I hope you will stay."

"Before I came back, I had found my right course. Now you tell me I'm a fake. How can I decide?"

"Because the process was so successful. Because if Crewkerne and Nilssen had not been alike, the imprint would have been thrown off. No more time for deception. You would both have loved Eva; and you would both have given up your lives here for this other woman. Be your own conscience."

His anxiety drained from him. The whirlpool slowed, flattened out. Becalmed, it became a shallow sea. Wading ashore, he found his crisis was over. "I am Jerlan Nilssen," he said. "One name is as good as another."

Laheer did not speak, but his eyelids flickered.

Nilssen stayed a further five minutes to keep him company. When the last breath had rattled from the old man's throat, he went over and folded the drooping hands together. Noticing that the left armrest housed a music playback socket, he checked and found a pinsette there; the readout confined itself to two words:

Parsifal—Wagner.

He looked at Laheer again, beginning to understand the old man.

Then he left, taking the rag-wrapped sword. The lights of the City model still burned beneath their luminous domes as he shut the door, softly.

"Jerlan?"

Maia Kim stood by the shattered outer door with Rhys beside her. They both looked anxious, yet afraid to intrude.

Quietly Nilssen answered her, "That's right."

"And Laheer?" asked Kim.

"The king is dead," said Nilssen. "Long live the king." Laughing cynically, he glanced at Rhys. "We need a volunteer for Chief, Doctor. Are you game?"

Rhys walked from the room out into the hallway.

"What about you, Maia?"

Kim shook her head silently.

"Incidentally," Nilssen went on, "thanks for knocking me senseless so expertly. Why did you go to all that bother?"

"Laheer told me you'd left us and wouldn't be back. Someone had to tidy up that job. I seemed to be qualified—best to keep it in the family."

"Ah, yes, the CNI. I remember, Yaer said—"

Again she shook her head. "No, Jerlan, I meant my own family. Before I married, much against my brother Eric's prejudices, my surname was Halvey. Maia Halvey, that was me. And for the sake of that connection, years ago I made the mistake of giving aid and comfort to an enemy. That had to be paid for."

"So you were the woman who smuggled him to the ninth century?"

Her nod confirmed this. He regarded the brown, ragged parcel in his hands.

"All for this," he remarked ruefully. "His scheme was ruined by a single sword."

"That, or some other excuse to visit Alfred's camp," she answered softly. "Yaer prised my secret out of me, a long while back. There's not much he doesn't see, or guess at."

"Then Yaer must have known who our man was from the start," said Nilssen. "What was his game? What did he hope to gain by his subterfuges?"

"For more than three years he was waiting. Yaer is good at that: waiting for opportunities to come to him. When Rhys decoded Frobisher's seventh equation, Yaer was ready to put Project Yardstick into effect."

"And he told no one about your brother?"

"He can be very secretive."

Nilssen reflected on the upheavals that had followed him since the project began. If one tenth part had been intended by Yaer, the man's secrecy was understandable.

Kim said, "So now you will stand for election, in Laheer's place?"

"No," he said, "or at least, not yet. Not until I have a question answered. And for that I must go back again."

"I understand," said Kim. "Good luck."

"Thanks," he said, his throat tight. "To you and to Georgiana Hartmann. And, Maia: perhaps, also, good-bye."

CHAPTER TWENTY-THREE

It happened that, as the winter bridging the years 880 and 881 drew on toward its close, a man came to the gates of the village of Henglaf's Folk. He was strangely dressed: a man of the Saracens, as he declared himself. His garb was of no one nation; and in his right hand he carried a short staff unlike any seen in Britain before. His speech, too, was of indeterminate origin. At once the guards were wary and would allow him no closer than thirty paces, for the village had been given cause to distrust strangers already that year.

"What do you wish with us?" cried one guard, aggressively showing his bow with an arrow nocked in readiness.

"The woman Morwena," Nilssen answered.

The guards conferred.

"None by that name here," they told him.

"She is mute and had two companions when last seen. A big man, a warrior; and a small one, a Saracen like me."

There was another discussion on the ramparts.

"No Saracens have been by this way. But a mute woman did come, and with such a guardian as you describe. That was in the summer that Alfred checked the Danes."

"Then may I speak with them?"

Obviously troubled, the Saxon answered, "The man is dead, stranger. This fourteen-night. For want of fair weather his interment was delayed. As we speak they bury him."

So Sarnvig had, after all, paid the price of glory and of friendship.

"Where away?" asked Nilssen. "The grave-place! Quickly, where is it?"

The guard extended a hand to mark the road. Thanking him hastily, Nilssen ran from the village along the slushy way between the snow-capped trees that overhung it. The cold air he gulped burned in his throat and his feet were nearly numb; but he went with no heed for discomfort. When he stopped off at the hidden flier to tell Rhys the news, he would stay only as long as the sentences took to tumble from his lips before running out into the snow again.

Rhys pursued him from the trees and down the road. Nilssen leading in his flapping robes whose newly laundered colors shone in the wintry landscape, and Rhys close behind in his anachronistic green, heat-retaining flying suit; together they made a weird procession.

They met the cortège as it was leaving the grave-yard. Sarnvig's grave stood out prominently, an oblong heap of snowless turned earth, crisply dark amongst the whitened mounds. Feet had trailed muddy tracks to and from it.

Henglaf led the group. Behind him came seven villagers armed with swords. These in turn preceded a tonsured priest who shivered in a brown robe and thin gray cloak. At the rear, their heads bent low and hidden within closely wound scarves, came three women, huddled together for warmth and moral support.

Without waiting for Henglaf's recognition of their presence Nilssen shouted:

"*Morwena!*"

One of the women raised her head. He saw her eyes

widen. Then she peeled away her scarf and he saw her face, exactly as he remembered it.

"You are too late, my friends," said Henglaf.

"No," said Nilssen, "this is the proper hour. I have come for Morwena of Gwerfa Iwrch."

"There is no one—" Henglaf began. Morwena ran past him at that moment and his denial died. The whole group, and Rhys besides, watched as she and Nilssen embraced. For almost a minute they held each other tightly. Then Henglaf ventured:

"You are of her kin?"

"I hope to be," said Nilssen, watching her face.

She answered him with the nod that was all he required.

"Then this is a timely coming," said Henglaf. Closer now, he peered at Nilssen. "Are we not acquainted?" he asked. "I seem to recollect your voice, though not the circumstances of our meeting."

"A chance resemblance," said Nilssen. "Our homeland is very distant."

"That may be," concurred Henglaf. "This has been such a season of mishaps my wits are to the four winds. Your pardon. But now you are come, will you sup with me tonight ere you depart?"

Nilssen sensed the invitation was a formality: the high-reeve fulfilling his social obligations. By the way Morwena pressed closer into the curve of his arm, he knew she had no desire to stay. For his own part he wanted no prolongation of contact with the village or its people.

So he said, "I thank you; but our road lies homeward, and we have been too long upon it already. Our camp is nearby. With your indulgence . . . ?"

Henglaf scarcely bothered to conceal his relief. "Then we leave you. God speed you, friends."

Alone, they paused by the grave.

"And what of Khaled?" Nilssen asked Morwena.

The morning after you left, he too had gone, she signed.

"No word of explanation?"

Perhaps. I have puzzled it often. As we composed ourselves to sleep that night beneath the Selwood's trees, he said, as though he pondered some secret that gave him pain: 'Escape is a state of mind.' And he looked at me. Not as a man might to a woman. Nor as a friend might to another. But as one whose eye is lost to unfathomed depths. Though you and he were close, I will confess I never sat easy in his presence. It was as well he went, I fear.

Nilssen was not surprised to hear of Yaer's premature departure in search of pastures new. The psychologist was liable to be more than a match for everyone he encountered on his travels unless his glib tongue got him trodden on out of sheer irritation. Which, Nilssen thought with some pleasure, was highly likely.

The flier lifted from the copse in which it had lain concealed and drifted south, settling by the recently disturbed tumulus on Windhurst Hill. Opening the hatch, Rhys hefted the special sword.

"It'll take me ten minutes to bury this," he said to Nilssen, "and another five to set up the collapsible cargo gate. That is, if you still want it set up. Will you be coming back to the City with me?"

"Can I tell you in ten minutes?"

Rhys went away, a spade in one hand, the sword in the other, whistling happily as he waded through the snow on his snowshoes. His difficulties were minimal now. Having recovered the sword from the tumulus after the original experiment while keeping the fact a secret from Nilssen in obedience to the message he was about to scratch on its blade, he knew exactly what he must do. One hole would complete a tidy loop of cause and effect.

Nilssen envied him.

"Morwena," he said. "You and I, we have a choice to make. Actually, we have several; but they reduce to two alternatives. When you saw this . . . boat . . . of ours, you asked many questions. If we choose to return to my home, you may never cease asking after the un-natural wonders we keep about us there. And I em-phasize that they are un-natural. Some are so far removed from God's creations that you may learn to fear them, as we do. So what may seem a paradise is no more perfect than this land to which you were born.

"Our alternative is to stay here, amongst people who are strangers to us both. If you so choose, I will too."

Come with me, she said, conducting him to the open hatch of the flier. She sat, her legs dangling above the snow, and waited until he too had seated himself. She gestured toward the hills and valleys, to the snowy forests, and to the horizons misty with a hint of the impending spring thaw. *This is beautiful,* she said. *It steals my heart, and my eyes drink it when I am sad. See, the sun goes down, the stars shine, the birds seek their shelters. There is peace. Do you feel it too?*

"Ever since the day I came."

And yet I also mind how it was at Gwerfa Iwrch.

"How was it, then?"

Her hair fell across her face as she looked down at her lap. Brushing it aside, he turned her head his way and repeated the question gently.

Her signs came stiffly and unwillingly:

My memory is of the red cock crowing from our thatched roofs and the smoke of it billowing up to heaven. I see my mother and sister raped and spitted by the swords of beasts. I see my father and brothers tied to the ground with fires lit upon their naked bellies . . . Her speed blurred the signs, so that Nilssen could scarcely interpret them fast enough. Then she slowed. *I see also the far slopes, where the moun-tains meet the meadows and the forest becomes fields: there the deer stand, wondering at the tumult.* Tossing her head, she settled her hair well away from her face. *The air is still; the smoke gathers in our valley as the mist does yonder. I am eight summers old, so the king's soldiers are not unkind to me. One even carries me on his shoulders as we abandon that place of death.*

"You need say no more," he urged, sharing her distress though not her bitterness.

It is all said, my love. She searched his face. *Are your people any worse than that?*

"They are different," he replied. "That is all."

Then I would see that difference for myself, she said. *But if the question hangs in the balance, let God decide.* Rummaging in a concealed pocket of her flowing dress, she produced a small silver coin which she pressed into his hand. *So. Throw the coin, and as it shall fall, so shall we do.*

"It's too important—" he said.

But if it's all one, hither or thither, yea or nay, how can you protest?

Chucking the coin into the air a few times, he observed how it turned. The throw might be as fair a test as any. The choice was so riddled with ifs and buts anyhow—

"No!" he yelled, hurling the coin away from him. It spun through the air, winking silver-red against the darkening blue of the starry sky, and fell beyond the crest of the tumulus. With both arms he held her. "This is our decision. *We* will say how and where we live. For once the universe can go—"

She broke free. *Speak so I may understand you!*

He had relapsed into Modern English. More quietly he said,

"Morwena, we were given what free will we have to guide our lives when wyrd allows. This is such a moment."

Then the moment is yours, she replied. *I have no home to lose.*

He thought about the City afresh, stirred by the wistfulness in her words. If he belonged anywhere, it was in the City, for all its faults. The City had made him; he could remake the City.

"In that case," he said, "welcome to my home."

Rhys rounded the tumulus as Nilssen was speaking. "Some daft beggar," he said pointedly, "has been tossing his cash about. Damn near brained me too." He dropped the silver coin into Morwena's lap. "For you, as he doesn't know how to take care of it."

She stared blankly at him, not comprehending his English.

"Have you two decided?" Rhys asked Nilssen.

"She comes."

"Then help me rig the gate."

They worked to assemble the parts, using artificial light, for the night was almost complete. When every bolt was tight and Rhys was satisfied, Nilssen took a last look at the hillside and the bare trees.

"I can't help but feel uneasy," he remarked to Rhys.

"The flier will warn us of people or big animals."

"Not that. The place itself seems to be watching."

"Ghosts?"

"No." He knew who Rhys meant. "I didn't get here until the spring."

"Imagination then."

"It's a strong feeling . . . Do you suppose the universe ever *cares* about our activities?"

The sense of being under scrutiny grew with every passing second.

Rhys only laughed.

Going to Morwena, Nilssen said:

"May I borrow that coin again?"

She gave it to him and he tossed it onto the flier's cabin floor.

"Amazing," said Rhys. "Never thought to see that twice in one day."

Distracted from the sight of the coin perfectly balanced on one edge, Nilssen glanced at him. "What did you say?"

"When you pitched it at me earlier, it landed in a bush. Got jammed between two twigs. Uncanny it was: no way to tell whether it meant heads or tails. I tell you, boy, you must have the knack."

Nilssen looked at Rhys, the scientist fiddling with his equipment to align it according to known laws. Then he looked at Morwena. Finally he favored the sky with a thoughtful scrutiny.

"Thanks," he said to the darkness up above him. "Thanks for everything. Now will you kindly get the hell out of my life?"

Only a meteor, trailing fire across the stars, seemed to answer him.

EPILOGUE: *se scop*

The snows of hardest winter were falling from the trees as the sun grew warmer. Hunters had reported deer moving from the south and foxes no longer called their love in the forests. The nights were still cold, but the chill was scarce as severe as it had been the night the ghost had come calling for his wergild. To-morrow, the bard told himself, he would move on if the weather held fair. This village was too troubled by recent events to be safe for a stranger, even one such as he.

But then the revelers began to pound the tables and chant their desire for entertainment and he had perforce to yield to their wishes, though he was weary of many nights of late singing.

"My lord?" he said, bowing to Henglaf as usual.

Henglaf did not reply at once but looked uneasily at those who sat to either side of him. One made a face as if to suggest he proceed with some agreed plan. He faced the bard.

"Master minstrel, soon you will be leaving us, I think?"

"Indeed, High-Reeve Henglaf, I had thought to."

"Hmm . . . And doubtless you had also thought to sing on other nights of what passed here not long ago?"

The bard hesitated. Honesty or tact? He chose honesty; no one would believe the obvious lie. "Aye, my lord."

"Then sing of it now."

Surprised by this, the bard did not immediately answer. Angrily Henglaf stood and pointed one thick finger at him. "I command you to sing of it now! Do you defy me? Would you rather play the ale-minstrel to those gibbet-fowl I set to roost in the woods?"

"No, my lord, I will sing!" The bard set his cloak and prepared to strike the first notes from his harp. Henglaf interrupted him.

"Be sure you tell it well. I would have no man think that Henglaf, son of Welnoth, does not keep good customs."

The bard nodded, swallowed to clear the lump in his throat, and began:

"Hear me now!" He coughed. Henglaf scowled. Though he hated to do so, the bard felt that the story had better be rushed, at least at the beginning; he was not too sure that Henglaf would sit still for the usual genealogical tables.

"Many will have heard of the glorious deeds of Alfred, King and Guardian of the treasures of Wessex; and of how he drove the shield-bearers of the beast-prowed ships back from these hills and vales." A minutest rearrangement of the truth, to be sure; but good politics. Henglaf was pro-Alfred. "Hear now of the still more glorious deeds of Henglaf, son of Welnoth, son of Henglaf of the Iron Arm; hearken to the exploit by which he has won his fame forever." Henglaf began to smile broadly. The bard got his second wind and pressed on, sure of his ground now.

He sang of how the drinking and feasting had gone on long and loudly in the stout mead-hall of the Henglafingas, of the warriors who lined the tables and the deeds they each had done. He pandered to their individual vanities, carefully contriving to build a sense of security and of well-being, so that when he came to the moment when the ghastly shape had walked into the festivities, they all fell deathly quiet, several showing signs of nervousness as they recalled

that night. By his skills he played upon his audience
like the harp he plucked and stroked; and as the time
passed, he knew this tale would make him famous
from the western isles to the Danelaw. This was the
stuff of legend; this would be his lof-daedum that
would inspire respect from other bards even after he
was dead. Happily he sang and told the tale as he knew
his listeners would wish to hear it told.

". . . See, their crime has rebounded upon them. No
folk-moot need adjudge the guilt of Wulfstan and
Leofric: the wronged man's soul, unable to rest, seeks
the wretches out. He points the finger of accusation;
they cannot stand against such an oath-bringer and
confess their wickedness. Their lord, the High-Reeve
Henglaf, heavyhearted, pronounces sentence upon
those he thought his loyal gesithas, sharers of his mead-
hall's joys. *'Are we Northumbrians,'* he asks, *'to slay
our own folk? No; but neither are we the murderers
of innocent travelers. This man they slew has no lord
we know of to claim his wergild. Thus heriot must be
given to him alone, even in death: our own treasure
will gild his graveside; our own tears will mourn his
passing, though we know not his rank or value and
must for honor's sake pay the twelvefold price lest we
slight his memory and he come again demanding
vengeance.'* Thus are the customs kept, though brave
men weep to see how wyrd punishes those who seek to
break them. For this bootless crime the murderers
hanged at dawn: the gallows-tree received their bodies;
their souls flew high to face their Lord, the World-
King, and His justice."

His tale finished, the bard waited. At last Henglaf
nodded and smiled. He handed the bard a whole gold
arm-ring, saying for everyone to hear, "Well told,
master minstrel. That was indeed the way of it, as all
men will testify who were there that day."